The Conquest of Liberty

Book One
Moors, Monarchs & Monks

Kent Merrell

The Conquest of Liberty

Book One: Moors, Monarchs and Monks

jremingtonpress.com

kentmerrellauthor.com

Mankind's march toward liberty spans millennia. Just as we struggle for life, liberty, and to pursue happiness, there is and will always be others contending to strip them away. My passion for telling stories from the perspective of others may stem from my four and a half decades visualizing the needs and desires of my client's customers. I attempt to, as Mary Lathrop's poem says, *"Walk a mile in his moccasins."* This practice fuels my love to retell history from the perspective of both fictional and historical characters. In this book, the first of several, I share how the struggle for liberty collides with the crusade for domination and control. I introduce you to some of my favorite characters both real and imagined who are entrenched in that eternal struggle. May you love them as I do. I hope one day to meet a select few of them.

ISBN: 979-8-9903523-0-8 (Paperback)
ISBN: 979-8-9903523-1-5 (Hardback)
ISBN: 979-8-9903523-2-2 (ebook)

First Edition 2024

Dive even deeper into their fascinating lives of the many
historical characters in The Conquest of Liberty.

Sign-up now to receive regular "Historical or Fictional"
biographical character videos.

Enjoy these videos, as well as Kent's blog posts
and articles when you follow Kent at:

https://kentmerrellauthor.com/

IV

Maps of the New and Old World

Meet the historical characters in The Conquest of Liberty.

The thrill of meeting true historical characters and inviting them into a fictional story creates an exciting and challenging opportunity. It demands maintaining enough plausible reality in both time and space so as not to suspend all credibility. Each of these many historical characters are represented as accurately as possible. Please consider the sources of information are five hundred years old, and they are written by humans with personal insights and motives. Many times, respected sources disagree with each other. In those cases an author gets to choose how a character is presented. Forgiveness in these cases is appreciated. But the historical events are as accurate in time and place as possible. With one caveat— sometimes the years needed to be squeezed or expanded a touch.

Please enjoy your journey through history with these historical characters.

Alonso de Ojeda – Appointed Governor of San Sebastian

Alonso Sanchez de Cepeda – Wealthy wool merchant in Ávila Spain

Armando Gonzalo – Friend of Vasco Nuñez de Balboa

Bartolomé de las Casas – Conquistador/Dominican Priest

Beelzebub – Humphrey Kynaston's horse

Cacica – Careta princess, Balboa's wife

Charles V – Holy Roman Emperor

Chima – Chicque (Chief) of Careta tribe

Christopher Columbus – General of the Seas

Diego Columbus – Governor of Indies –Eldest son of Christopher Columbus

Diego de Almagro – Partner of Pizarro and Luque

Diego de Nicuesa – Appointed Governor of Nombre de Dios

Diego Rodrígques de Lucero – Harsh and unjust inquisitor

Don Pedro de Los Rios – Appointed Governor of Panama

Ferdinand II – King of Aragon

Francisco de Bobadilla – Appointed Judge, Retched Governor of Hispaniola

Francisco Hernando Cisneros – Cardinal, Archbishop & Regent of Spain

Frederick the Wise – Elector of Saxony, Martin Luther's protector

Gaspar de Espinosa – Mayor of Darién

Germaine of Foix – Second wife of Ferdinand II of Aragon

Gonzalo Pizarro – Francisco Pizarro's father

Hernando de Luque – Friar, partner of Pizarro & Almagro

Hernando de Talavera – Archbishop of Granada

Humphrey Kynaston – English outlaw, highwayman, mercenary

Isabella I – Queen of Castile & León

Johann Eck – Grand Inquisitor and Martin Luther's principal adversary

Johann Tetzel – Grand Inquisitor & Commissioner for indulgences

Khayr al-Din – Ottoman corsair known as Hayreddin Barbarossa

Lioncillo - Balboa's war dog - likely a Spanish Mastiff

Martín Fernández de Enciso – Partner to Alonso Ojeda

Martin Luther – Seminal figure of the Protestant Reformation

Michelangelo – Famed sculptor and painter

Pablo – Balboa's Mayordomo

Pedro de Ruiz (Navarro) – Brilliant Spanish Military General

Pope Julius II - Catholic Pope - From 1503 to 1513

Rodrigo de Bastidas – Successful Explorer & Conquistador

Sayyida al-Hurra – Corsair, Queen of Tétouan

Teresa of Ávila – Saint, Carmelite nun, daughter of Alonso Sánchez

Tomás de Torquemada - Castilian Dominican friar and first Grand Inquisitor

Vasco Nuñez de Balboa – Conquistador, Explorer, Founder

Learn a bit about the historical characters.

Watch short historical videos that separate fact from fiction.

BAY OF
BISCAY
Leon
Navarre
Kingdom
of Castile
Kingdom
of Aragon
Kingdom
of
Portugal
Granada
MEDITERRANEAN SEA
ALGERIA

Introduction

Permit me to set the Geo-political stage
in the early 1500s.

The Iberian Peninsula was known as five independent kingdoms: Portugal, Castile and Leon, Navarre, Granada (Muslim) and the Crown of Aragon. In the year 1492, after the fall of Granada, which was the last of the Moorish strongholds, and with the union of the monarchs, Isabella I of Castile and Ferdinand II of Aragon, the whole peninsula apart from Portugal, converged into a single political entity. With the union of the kingdoms of Castile and Aragon, the term Spain began to refer to the kingdom that emerged from this union.

The final unification of Spain as we know it today still took decades, even centuries. Conquests, revolutions, unifications, and subjugations took years to bring lands, nobles, kings, religions, languages, and races together. For simplicity, in The Conquest of Liberty, we will refer to the Iberian Peninsula as Spain yet we will often be specific with its various kingdoms at the time.

From early Phoenician, Greek, and even Roman writings centuries earlier, Hispania with its various spellings became a name used to describe the peninsula. When the Visigoths arrived eight centuries earlier, they referred to the area as Hispania Visigoda.

Thus, during the late 1400s and the early 1500s, the geo-political landscape included diverse peoples identifying with their own cultural heritages, languages, and religions. Throughout Europe, Northern Africa, and the Middle East as we now know it, the same struggle for unification, independence, and liberty has played out for centuries, and continues even today.

Prologue

1499 Cathedral of the Incarnation,
Granada, Spain

Isabella's stern countenance softened. A tiny smile crept across her face. Her attendants showed great deference as she entered the cathedral. All bowed but one. As Queen of Castile, only one man was permitted to stand in her presence without her permission. Archbishop Hernando de Talavera stood respectively and returned her smile. A slight nod was all she received. That is all she expected. When they first met, his insistence that he kneel only for the Eternal King demonstrated his loyalty to God. She had not met any other with that conviction or courage. For that reason, he served as her personal confessor those many years and why he was now the first Archbishop of Granada. And today, she came to him, rather than summon him to her court.

Her footsteps echoed throughout the church. The Cathedral of the Incarnation was a magnificent edifice. It was built centuries earlier by the Emirate of Granada, and enlarged during the Nasrid dynasty. For two hundred years, it served as the central mosque in Granada. It became one of the largest mosques in the Islamic world during the 1300s. Eight years ago in 1492, after the conquest of Granada by the Catholic monarchs, Ferdinand II and Isabella I, the mosque began its conversion into the cathedral that now served as the principal Catholic Church in Granada.

"My dear Hernando, what is this I hear about you?" Isabella asked.

His smile broadened, he reached out his hand, and ushered the queen to a large red velvet throne-like chair. "Well, what you might hear depends on who you choose to listen to," he said. She nodded.

"I suppose you compare my meager conversions of Arab Moors to the mass six thousand baptisms, of which your Cardinal Cisneros brags," he said. The archbishop wanted so badly to denounce the efficacy of the group baptism where more than six thousand Moors, fearful of losing their homes, knelt at the command of Cardinal Cisneros who then splattered holy water into the air landing randomly on some of the gathered Arabs. Talavera held his tongue.

"Hernando, you are my most faithful servant. It distresses me to receive reports from your detractors that doubt your sincerity."

"Detractors? Sincerity?" he asked. "You know Cisneros and I differ in many ways. Or is it Torquemada? With Torquemada we differ in every way. Conversos unconverted are trouble. You know that. That which is done in fear or by force rather than by one's own will is not lasting. In order to endure, it must be done with love and charity," he said.

"Hernando, Hernando." She put her hand on his arm, "Come with me." Isabella stood. The crowd, so interested in hearing this interchange, came to attention as if they had been oblivious to the gentle reprimand given by their queen to her archbishop. She motioned for all to remain back. She led her archbishop from the chapel. They quietly walked to the Courtyard of the Oranges, which featured an elaborate central fountain surrounded by rows of orange trees. The trees were in blossom, which added to the sweetness of the opportunity for Talavera to once again converse privately with his queen. It was not to be. The serenity evaporated when the pounding of boots and the squealing of young boys burst into the courtyard. Cardinal Cisneros, followed by six of his personal guards, dragged two young boys toward Isabella and Talavera and threw the boys to the ground.

"This is what your permissive policies create," Cisneros said to Talavera. It was not that the cardinal ignored the fact he was in the presence of the queen; it was he felt the importance of his demonstration was more serious than respect for Isabella. Cisneros signaled to a guard who pulled a whip and cracked it over the back of one of the boys. The second boy's back was saved when Talavera snatched the whip from the guard and threw it to the ground.

Nothing was said. The archbishop and the cardinal stared at each other for several seconds. Finally, Talavera turned to the boy who received the lash. "Miguel, what is this?" Talavera said.

Miguel stood. For a boy barely ten years old, he stood taller than the other boy and nearly as tall as Talavera. His tousled blond hair and fair complexion testified of his Basque heritage. His innocence, which might have been credible hours earlier, was betrayed by the mud on his tunic and smudges of dirt and blood on his cheek.

Miguel lowered his head in respect to Talavera. When his eyes noticed the hem of the brilliant blue gown, they shot up to the queen, opened wide, and he dropped to his knees.

"Rise," Isabella said. "I am curious. Please answer the archbishop."

Miguel's eyes raised to the queen, but his head remained bowed. "We took bread to the families on San Cristobal Hill." Miguel was talking to the ground as if not daring to face either the queen or Talavera.

"Albayzin neighborhood?" Cisneros demanded.

That shook Miguel. He jumped. Miguel nodded.

"Moors? You are feeding the Moors? Is that how you convert the pigs?" Cisneros' coarse insult brought Miguel's humble head sharply around and he glared into Cisneros' eyes.

"Cardinal, you have offended our young friend," Isabella said. She chuckled, then said to Miguel, "Forgive my cardinal, he seems to offer neither of us respect this morning."

Miguel turned back to the queen. The red on his face matched the blood on his cheek.

"Miguel, apologize to the cardinal. You know you must show respect," Talavera said.

Miguel started to answer, "But…" Talavera raised a hand and Miguel held his tongue. Miguel did not apologize.

The other boy stood motionless. He was a local Moorish Morisco converted to Christ. His tunic and thick black hair were no less dirtied by the skirmish than Miguel's. The boy never looked up as he dared to speak. "They called my family pigs and said Miguel was a pig farmer and knocked the bread into the dirt and said we should wallow there if we wanted to eat."

Isabella smiled at the innocent tussle between young boys and how it brought her cardinal to the judgement seat. "You interrupt us for this?" Isabella said to Cisneros.

Cisneros' face glowed red at the queen's rebuke, but not from embarrassment. His demonstration to challenge Talavera's lenient policies failed. Anger pushed all humiliation aside.

Isabella turned to Miguel. "I'm curious to know who got the worst of it?"

The boy and Miguel both smiled. It was enough. Talavera scooted the boys away. "Miguel," he said, "I need you cleaned up by tonight's mass." He reached down, picked up the whip, and handed it back to Cisneros' guard.

PART
ONE

BRITAN
BAY OF
BISCAY
FRANCE
SPAIN
Granada
MEDITERRANEAN
SEA
MOROCCO
ALGERIA

Chapter One

Ten years later
1509 - Cathedral of Incarnation,
Granada, Spain

Miguel put his powerful hand on the gilded hilt of his sword ready to pull it free. Soldiers burst open the chapel doors. Archbishop Hernando Talavera, with his deep confidence in God, rested his hand on Miguel's arm, preventing the sword from leaving its sheath.

"If they arrest you, they must take me!" Miguel demanded.

The archbishop looked up into Miguel's defiant eyes, "Isabella is dead. I have no other protector. They will arrest me and if you are here, they will take you. And, you, my faithful friend, they will torture until you confess, and then you will die by fire. You are all I have left. If you care for me, go. Go! May Pope Julius receive you and extend mercy."

Talavera squeezed Miguel's arm, pushing him toward the south transept of the cathedral.

"Go. Appeal to Julius!"

Miguel hesitated only a moment. Looking down into Talavera's beloved deep-set eyes, he obeyed. He turned and rushed from Talavera's side and dashed across the nave and into the south transept chapel.

Outside the cathedral, crowds gathered. Soldiers, fully armed and on horseback, kept the mostly Muslim Granadians back. There had been far too many uprisings for Cardinal Cisneros to risk a riot. Not now. Not while his personal guards were arresting the sole hindrance to his solemn promise made to the queen before her death. He swore to her to convert every soul or expunge them from Granadian soil. He knew the possible danger of an uprising was extreme since Talavera was the sole source of hope for liberty the Muslims clung to.

Escaping through the private exit, Miguel mingled among the crowd and watched as Cardinal Cisneros' officers dragged Talavera outside and paraded him to the center of the large cobblestone plaza. Other officers had already arrested and imprisoned Talavera's friends, family, and fellow clergy—all accused of heresy.

How could Talavera possibly convince him to flee? Miguel anguished.

Miguel thought he knew how Peter felt watching the Christ taken from the garden by the temple guard. So badly he wanted to pull his sword, as did Peter.

Talavera held his head high, unashamed of his dedication to the truths he taught and fought for. Archbishop Talavera intentionally wore the tall white cardinal mirk and his long red cassock with wide sleeves contrasting with his signature white mozzetta, the fur-lined cape, his cappa magna, the velvet fur-lined hooded cape along with his large gold ring. No man looked nor acted more regal and so majestic. There was no question in Miguel's mind why Queen Isabella chose Talavera to be her confessor those many years. Several years ago, Talavera was again her perfect choice when she appointed him Archbishop of Granada, after she finally conquered the city. When Talavera chose Miguel to serve as an emissary for the Moors of Granada, Miguel could not have felt more honored.

To Miguel, the stark contrast between the respect and honor the Moors showed his friend and mentor, Archbishop Talavera, and the disdain they showed the archbishop's accuser, Cardinal Francisco Jimenez Cisneros, could not be more pronounced this very minute. Cisneros stood tall in his saddle atop a strong, white Andalusian. To Miguel, the horse seemed to radiate the same arrogance as its rider. Snorting, clawing at the ground with its front hoof, anxious for action.

Cisneros' bright red cassock with black trim fell across the horse's bright white flank. The strong contrast in color and stature broadcast to the crowd; 'do not challenge me.' Miguel watched Cisneros' dark eyes scan the crowd. He was a tall man accented with sunken cheeks and a large narrow nose. Miguel never saw him without a cap, but he imagined his traditional monk tonsure hair style was immaculately trimmed as an example to be followed by other monks.

What is Cisneros looking for? Miguel wondered, victims, threats? Miguel turned back to watch the officers unnecessarily pushing and prodding Talavera toward the center of the plaza. Talavera was not a large man but stood so regally, he appeared to stand heads above all others. Talavera seemed to be focusing on individual faces in the crowd. Miguel's hand on the hilt of the sword itched to free the steel and put it to the work of true justice. When Talavera caught Miguel's eye, he casually raised his hand to once again hold Miguel at bay.

Cisneros, who was closely watching Talavera at that very instant, glanced to see who he so subtly communicated with. He followed Talavera's eyes.

"There! Take him!" Cisneros' command reverberated across the plaza. Soldiers' eyes turned to Cisneros and, following the direction of his outstretched arm, quickly recognized the 'him' Cisneros meant.

Miguel stood several inches taller than the native Granadians, most of whom descended from the Muslim Moors of North Africa just across the Strait of Gibraltar. Though his clothing was a blend of colorful Moorish layers, his height and lighter skin added to his difficulty of blending into the crowd.

He dropped to his knees, scooted to a crouch, and tried to shuffle out of sight. Horsemen pushed into the crowd. The sounds of horse on stone and screams as they plowed onlookers out of the way convinced Miguel he could not hide. He stood and ran at full speed. Many from the crowd recognized Miguel as one of the few friends of Talavera and of the Moors. They parted for him and then crowded the horses, giving Miguel an advantage. Miguel left the plaza but knew within only a few moments the horsemen would be clear of the crowd. He could never outrun them. He decided he needed a higher escape and went skyward.

A small wall surrounding a fountain pouring crystal clear water into a pool gave Miguel the step to leap to the eaves of the building. He swung himself up. Before clearing the edge, an arrow dove deep into his leg. The shock paralyzed his progress more than the pain. Once over the edge and onto the flat roof, he dropped to his side and tried to remove the arrow. His leg would not support his full weight. He grabbed the arrow free, leaving a trail of blood as he limped across the roof. He had to clear the other side before the soldiers reached and surrounded the building.

Pain slowed his progress. If only he could jump from this flat roof to the next, he thought. His leg grew limp. It would never hold. Stairs along the side of the building provided access to the roof. What was this building? Then he smelled the rancid remains of discarded flesh. A butcher shop! He stopped. Could he hide? He tore a sleeve from his shirt and tied it around his bleeding leg. A faint smell wafted across the rooftop. Pork. This was a

Christian business. His heart sank. If it were a Muslim tienda, he might talk the owners into helping him. But not the Christians. They feared being labeled as heretics for aiding a heretic. He reached the edge of the roof and tried to listen for the pounding of horses. Soldiers yelled to one another, giving commands to secure the building. The sound of clanging swords and boots on the stairs reached the rooftop only seconds before four of Cisneros' soldiers surrounded a kneeling Miguel.

In an act of submission, Miguel raised a hand to hold the men at bay as he appeared to remove his sword and climb to his feet. Confident they had Miguel subdued, they relaxed slightly. Taking advantage of their ease, Miguel quickly pulled his sword, then slammed it against the first soldier's sword, which gave Miguel the edge. Miguel drew it so quickly a second guard stood motionless. Empowered, Miguel spun with both hands on his sword and knocked another sword free, sending it flying across the rooftop. It was now two swords against one. That would only last seconds. Stupor ended and the two unarmed soldiers quickly retrieved their swords and, as Miguel parlayed with two soldiers, they surrounded him again, swords well in hand. He couldn't flee, the pain in his leg wouldn't permit it. With each movement, he depended on that leg. But with each shift of his weight, it screamed for relief. It surprised him how much energy it required to hold the pain at bay as he demanded his leg to support his movements. He was certain he could best two of these men, but not four. A sudden thrust pierced his shoulder, which loosened his grip, and Miguel's sword fell to the ground. A sharp crack on the back of his head and all went black.

Chapter Two

1509 - Granada, Spain

In the darkness, Miguel's eyes blinked open. Putrid air filled his lungs when he sucked in to steel himself against the throbbing pain. One hand rested on the cold, damp floor. With the other, he tried to rub the source of pain on the back of his head. Sharp pain from his shoulder joined the pounding in his head. When he tried to stand, he remembered the arrow which crippled his escape from the plaza. He made it to his knees and breathed slowly, letting the pain calm. He felt the rough bandage wrapped around his shoulder. His shirt was gone. The quick bandage he used to stop the bleeding leg was still there. He rubbed his hand over the hard, caked blood he knew was his.

He hoped they treated the archbishop better than this. Would they both be in this same dank prison? Slowly, he stood and tried to get his bearings in the darkness. His eyes refocused, adjusting to the light sucked under the door. Miguel recognized where he was. This was the prison built to hold Moors refusing to convert. From here, they would be expelled from the country. Or worse—expelled from life.

Time passed. How much he could not tell. Silence was only broken by the occasional creaking of a prison door and the clomping of boots on stone. How long until his door would open? The light under the door eventually faded. Total darkness lasted hours. Miguel guessed it must be night, or at least a time when guards no longer needed the light. Walking throughout the small room, he discovered there was no bed or chair. Just cold, hard, moist floor and stone walls.

He carefully sat down, back against the wall opposite the door. Heavy, hard footsteps disrupted the silence, and Miguel's growing dread. It creeped open. Lit by a tall narrow lantern held high by a guard, Miguel recognized his visitor.

"Drag the heretic out here." The command was sharp. Two guards scooted past the man, yanked Miguel to his feet, and pulled him into the hall.

A large steel ring cemented into a wall hung at eye level. The two guards quickly tied Miguel's hands and secured him to the ring.

"Teach him he cannot worship with swine and be worthy of the grace of Christ."

Cisneros in his black cassock stormed away.

Miguel crumbled when the first lash ripped the flesh off his back. Again and again, the lash tore into him. He hung powerless from the steel ring. Untied, he crumbled into a heap on the stone floor. Two soldiers dragged him back into the cell.

Miguel lost sense of time. There had been no food or water since he regained consciousness. Thirst blinded all other senses. The pain of the lashes would have crippled him at any other moment. Head-strong and independently athletic, he always felt confident in his physical capabilities. One of the many reasons Archbishop Talavera recruited Miguel into his close circle of monks was for his keen eye, physical presence, and astute mind. Miguel never considered himself worthy to don the robes of the ecclesiastics, and thus he never made the vows to serve only Christ. Talavera never insisted, and the two men accepted the unspoken understanding that Miguel would serve as the most pious of priests, valiant of soldiers, or even rowdy of peasants, if that is what building the Kingdom of God on Earth required.

Today, Miguel served God as the lowliest of all. The least of these. Persecuted for righteousness' sake. Could it be true, mine is the kingdom of heaven? Can I possibly rejoice or be exceedingly glad? His mind turned from his thirst. Has the archbishop received the stripes I've received? And from the very representatives of Christ? The archbishop would certainly receive that promised reward in heaven.

The thirst returned, clouding his thoughts, serving as an antidote to dampen his rising hate. No, I do not think I can pray for those who so despitefully treated the Archbishop Talavera, for truly he was as the prophets of old.

The door screeched open suddenly. The burning flame of a small torch struggled with all its might to chase the gloom from the dark, dank cell. It failed to chase the darkness from Miguel's mind.

Miguel could not stand, too weak from hunger, thirst, and what he guessed might be a loss of blood. His eyes struggled to envision the fate that now awaited him. A single young man stood in the doorway, lit by the dancing flame held in one hand. With a pail in the other, he knelt and offered it to Miguel. Miguel's hands shook as he balanced himself on his knees and reached to take the pail, hoping it might stave off the crippling thirst.

His eyes met those of the visitor. The face looked familiar, but the face of a horse would seem familiar to the eyes that had not fully focused on anything for how long, days, weeks?

"Thank you." The dry, raspy whisper barely uttered the words. He brought the pail to his lips and let the cool water trickle over his parched mouth and down his barren throat. He paused, letting his system accept this salvation, then swallow after swallow, each one longer and deeper than the last, soon emptied the pail. Eyes closed, still holding it firmly with both hands, he thanked his God in Heaven for the angel and the simple gift of water.

"Your trial draws near. I am to get you fit enough to stand and denounce the heretic Talavera."

Miguel slowly opened his eyes and raised them to meet the visitor's. He was young, maybe Miguel's junior by a few years. The accent was Moorish.

"I will not," Miguel said.

The visitor reached down, took the pail from Miguel's hands, and turned toward the door. "We will see," he said.

Miguel could not resist or do anything but hunger for more water and yearn for the light that followed the man out. Before the light fully escaped, he saw the visitor set a fresh pail inside the door then pull it closed. Its creaking echoed through the cell. Keys clanked, sealing Miguel again in the darkness.

Slowly, on hands and knees, Miguel crawled across the cold stone floor to the door. He felt for the pail, and finding it, sat down warily as not to overturn it in his blindness. Carefully, he took it in his hands and drew it to his lips. He knew that smell. Subtle, but fresh. His lips wanted to smile as they welcomed the cool, fresh milk into his mouth. He cherished every swallow. I am being fattened for the slaughter, he thought. "I will not," he muttered to himself.

Time passed. The pails of water and milk relaxed his trembling body, and he dozed off. Sometime later, clanking keys dragged him from his sleep. The large door pushed open, but Miguel couldn't move fast enough.

It pushed into him sharply, hitting his wounded leg, sending a sharp pain through it. He scooted away. The same young Moorish visitor stood in the doorway. Miguel's eyes focused better this time. The flickering light from the torch reflected off the bright white teeth behind the smile.

Miguel wanted to say thank you. He wanted to appreciate the visitor for his help. All he could say was, "I will not denounce the archbishop."

The visitor's smile never faded. "He said you would say that." The visitor reached out a hand to help Miguel to his feet.

"Who are you?" Miguel asked, blinking his eyes, trying to focus on the young man's face.

"Nobody. But if I had friends, they would call me Jalaf." He put his arm out for Miguel to steady himself and pulled him out of the cell. The last time he left the cell, he lost much of the flesh off his back. Yet the gentleness of Jalaf told him this was not like the last time. They walked slowly past other cells locked tight, keeping what or who securely behind them.

"Where are we going?" Miguel's eyes were adjusting with each step they took closer to the light tumbling down a stairway.

"To get you well," Jalaf said. "This is an important trial."

"I will die before I will betray my friend," Miguel said.

"He said you would say that, too."

"You spoke with Talavera? Where is he?" Miguel's strength increased with his passion.

Jalaf looked deeply into Miguel's blue eyes. "You love him," Jalaf said.

The nod confirmed Jalaf's comment. "You would give your life for him?" Another nod. "You won't," Jalaf said, turning away and guiding Miguel through a door and up another set of stairs that led into a light-filled hallway. They were now above ground level. Both the light and clear air seemed to refresh as much as the water and milk.

Guards stood at each door they passed. Miguel thought it odd. He was a prisoner, yet his escort, a Moorish boy, was no soldier. They must have soldiers posted elsewhere or he would be at too much a risk of escape. Jalaf escorted Miguel into a room with small openings that overlooked a plaza in front of a mosque destroyed in the battles of Granada. The mosque waited helplessly to be rebuilt. The tower laid in pieces, obviously destroyed by cannon fire, and its full left side bore witness to a major assault, again by cannon. Black charred walls testified of a fire that finished the siege.

Miguel had never been in this fortress during his time in Granada serving Archbishop Talavera.

On the plaza stood five empty stakes ready to redeem men's souls, as the inquisitors claimed. "One of those for me?" Miguel asked.

"No. Your day is tomorrow."

The room was much like the dungeon cell where Miguel had spent the past countless days. Stone floor, walls, and ceiling. No furnishings. Only a pot in the corner. The difference was light. The large door sounded the same when it closed behind Jalaf, the clinking of keys as well. But what light did for his spirit was healing.

What seemed like hours later, the door creaked open, but this time, a short, muscled man wearing only the pants of a peasant Moor, accompanied Jalaf. A tight, wide belt at his waist contrasted against his bronze chest. Uncommon among the local Moors, the man was bare chested, yet he wore the woolen ghifara cap on his head rather than the typical colorful turban. This man was here on business. He dropped a bundle of cloth next to Miguel, and without a word turned him around with strong, sinewy hands. From the bucket of water he set down with his other hand, the man quickly washed clean Miguel's torn flesh. The pain returned with such vengeance Miguel dug deep to remain standing. The pain slowly subsided as the man rubbed a greasy balm into the freshly cleaned wounds. He turned Miguel back around, pointed to the bucket, the rags sitting next to it, and pulled a clean gandura, the straight sleeveless tunic, from the bundle of fabric and laid it on the floor. He laid a burnous over the tunic next to it.

Looking directly up into Miguel's eyes, he said, "Bathe, dress." He excused himself, taking Jalaf with him. The door pulled closed and locked.

They dress me like a Morisco. Is this a strategy to frighten me to denounce Talavera? He wondered. "You forgot the turban," he whispered.

Miguel washed quickly. He almost felt human again. A hungry human. Now clean, his nose recognized a new scent—fire. Fire which gently delivered the news, the cardinal put the pyres in the plaza to use. He hated to chase curiosity and fought to resist the urge to rush to the small opening in the outer wall. He realized this was part of a grand show. His preparation required this new Moorish dress, his witnessing first-hand the fate that awaited if he refused to denounce Talavera, the former counselor and confessor to Queen Isabella. With her death, the new counselor and confessor, Cardinal Cisneros, became regent of all of Castile and now aimed to destroy the very people Christ came to earth to save.

The room soon filled with smoke and ashes from the burning flesh below. Looking through the small openings, Miguel heard the anguish, the cheers, and saw the tears of onlookers. Yes, Jalaf is right, he thought. Tomorrow is my day.

He turned away from the horrible sight. Miguel looked toward heaven and at the moment he prepared to question God, he noticed a small earthen bowl tucked against the stone wall next to the door. He walked to it. Only a gentle thank you escaped his lips. He pulled one of several mollets, his favorite Spanish bread. He tore through its crisp golden crust. The soft spongy inside practically melted in his mouth. All he needed was fresh olive oil sprinkled on top. Then he saw it, a small vial of oil. Along with the bread was a local cheese and smoked fish. He ate and as he did, so the smoke lessened.

The noises from outside faded, as did the light. Jalaf never returned, nor did the physician.

Chapter Three

1509 - Granada, Spain

Hours passed since the first morning light gently crept through the small openings in Miguel's cell. The light strove with all its might to provide hope. Miguel rose and went to the windows expecting to see the aftermath of the gruesome events of yesterday's spectacle. The strong metal stakes stood bare, prepared ready for today's show of their redemptive power.

Miguel wondered which of the pyres would be his. The clanking of keys and the whine of the opening door interrupted his thoughts. Who would greet him this time? More preparation from Jalaf, or the religious escort from Cisneros? To Miguel, in the light and feeling rested, Jalaf's smile, which on any other day would challenge the morning sunlight as the provider of hope, reminded Miguel this would be his last day on earth.

Accompanying his smile, Jalaf brought another pail of water, a cask of wine, and a basket filled with what looked like a feast. The warm bread broadcast its freshness as Miguel lifted it from the basket.

"They want you to be prompt with your denunciation this afternoon. You will be the first of several witnesses. They will then expect you to recant your own writings against the alleged injustices of the Church's inquisitors." Jalaf's announcement stung deep.

Miguel's heart pounded, mouth stopped in mid-bite. How did they get my writings? The betrayal cut deeper than the lashes. Only two men knew of the records Miguel kept for the archbishop. For one, he knew Talavera would never give them up. It would be a guaranteed death sentence for him. And for the second, the Bishop of Málaga a trusted friend, how could he ever betray them? Miguel's appetite vanished. He put the torn loaf back into the basket, set it down, and walked to the window. He ignored the pain from his healing wounds.

"Will the bishop be on trial?" Miguel asked, not turning to face Jalaf.

"He testified yesterday and will need no penance," Jalaf said.

Miguel stood silent, looking past Jalaf and out through the small openings in the wall. He said, "The Pope alone has the power over Cisneros to free Talavera. But if Cisneros has my writings, he needs no permission from the Pope to destroy the archbishop. Talavera will join me today in the plaza."

"Or not," Jalaf said.

Miguel turned quickly. "Or not?" Calm left Miguel's tone.

Jalaf picked up the basket, pulled the partially eaten bread from it and took a bite. He walked over to the window, if you could call it a window. The room had two such openings, both too small for a man to climb through but large enough to see clearly to the plaza, and beyond the plaza past the ruins of a partially demolished mosque. The splendor of the massive hills in the distance, purple layers, one in front of the next till they merged into the morning light, contrasted sharply with the immediate scene of impending executions ironically held in the plaza bounded by the destroyed mosque. The scene in the plaza was a statement Cardinal Cisneros made to the citizens of Granada that they cannot stand against him or the Church.

"Or not," Jalaf said. "Cisneros needs your testimony. Without you, Cisneros will be afraid to execute your friend. Talavera was a former confessor and counselor to the queen." Jalaf's smile never faded.

Miguel squinted at Jalaf. "King Ferdinand fears the Church, he will not protect Talavera."

Joy danced in Jalaf's eyes. It danced to the rhythm of his voice. This Morisco held more behind those eyes than the words revealed. Miguel looked deeply trying to decipher what great sermon was packaged in those two words, 'or not.'

Jalaf pointed toward a small building to the left of the plaza. "The finest horseman in Granada." He took another bite of Miguel's bread.

Miguel looked from the building to Jalaf, squinted at him again, trying to follow his thinking. Jalaf pointed toward another building. "Our finest tailor." He handed the basket to Miguel.

"Today is your day." Jalaf spun, set the pail of water down, and left the cell. He pulled the door closed. Miguel expected the sound of its slamming shut and the rattle of keys locking it. He did not hear either one. He pulled the bread back out of the basket and with a mouth full limped curiously to the door, which stood slightly ajar. He looked back toward the windows, set the basket down and pulled gently on the door, expecting to hear the familiar whine that had announced previous visitors. It eased open. There was no guard. None in front of any of the cells. Where were the prisoners guarded days earlier? Yesterday's victims?

Miguel went quickly back to the window and memorized the two buildings Jalaf pointed out. He should have paid more attention to such an odd discussion. A tailor and a livery? He ate quickly, drank, and splashed his face with the remaining water. The bundle of cloth left behind by the physician served well as a pillow during the night. He pulled it loose and recognized it was not just a pile of rags, but a colorful aljuba, a fine long linen robe, commonly worn by both Moorish men and women. He pulled it over his tunic. He went back to the window and tried to perfect his bearings on the two buildings. Jalaf's intent was now clear enough. Miguel quietly stole from the cell and silently ran painfully down the cold, empty hall.

He left the fortress and tried to blend in with the morning merchants.

He followed several women heading toward the building he hoped was the one Jalaf indicated housed a fine tailor. Fine linens, silks, cotton, and wool hung in the wide open door, ready for a day of trade. In Miguel's time in Granada, he'd grown to love the Moorish clothing. Beautiful fabrics of every kind and color. The Moors of Granada were esteemed for their fine silks and linens. The soft cotton they used for undergarment was also cherished. These fine tailors turned out such beautiful work. He felt the Christians many times envied the lively attire.

Miguel took a moment to compare the shaya he wore, which was a shorter robe with tighter sleeves, to the hooded cloak displayed on a large, padded dummy.

"You prefer the albornoz to the shaya?" It was a soft, gentle female voice hidden behind a veil. The woman stepped up to Miguel, reached out, and pulled the larger hooded cloak open displaying beautiful golden threads used in the stitching.

"A friend mentioned your fine work," Miguel said. He reached out and caressed the silk between his fingers, appreciating its genuine quality. Jalaf was right. These people here are fine tailors.

"Are you the heretic?"

Miguel's slight nod affirmed her assumption. She loosened the veil, a move welcomed by Miguel. Her beautiful face and cheeks matched the soft brown eyes. Her perfume enlivened his senses. He was often taken by the beauty of the Moorish women. They walked and communicated with confident, expressive eyes. Silky long dark hair fell over richly embroidered fabrics, veils, and intricate jewelry. All this added to their graceful posture. Talavera reminded him frequently that he never took the vows of celibacy as other men of the cloth. He also insisted the time was coming when Miguel needed to find himself a wife and have a family. Miguel resisted. However, if that time came, he knew she would need to be a woman of faith. Was this Moorish woman one of faith?

In his heart, Miguel's perception of what made a woman of faith changed as he taught the Moors about Christ. Few were receptive to the invitation to follow Jehovah, the God of the Christians, but they respected the new Archbishop Talavera and the priests with him who learned Arabic. They appreciated the effort to be conversed with and taught in their native language. The mutual respect that grew between these people was abhorrent to Cisneros and his kind. How could Cisneros and the Catholic monarchs be so blind?

The woman helped Miguel out of the colorful aljuba, a fine long linen robe, and handed him a fresh gandura, a long sleeveless tunic over which she added a burnous which was fuller and had long sleeves. With each piece she added, the more Miguel became a Morisco. To finish the disguise, she offered the blousy pant common to Moorish men and held tight around his waist with a beautifully studded belt.

"What do they call you that I may thank you properly?" he asked. Then he added, "You must know I cannot pay you."

She gave a smile that quickened his heartbeat. His eyes could not leave hers.

"Sukayna," she said, tucking the last edge of the turban behind his head, "This gift is presented to you for what you have done for my people."

"Sukayna. The Basque Princess?" His smile outdid hers when he said it. "My people up north talk of a legend that the finest one of our young women was chosen by the gods for her fair beauty. She was called Durra Sukayna." He slowly nodded his head. "Yes, Sukayna, your parents named you well."

Chapter Four

1509 - Nasrid Palace, Alhambra, Granada, Spain

Cardinal Cisneros bowed as he entered the Nasrid palace and approached the king who sat with his hand on the queen's. Queen Germaine, Ferdinand's new wife, was young and beautiful. The cardinal suppressed his smile, remembering the words written by the Italian historian Pedro Martin de Angleria.

"Our king, if he does not rid himself of his appetites, will soon give his soul to the creator and his body to the earth. For even this beautiful young wife is not enough for him. At least in his desire."

The cardinal certainly understood the talk about the fifty-four-year-old king marrying the young eighteen-year-old niece of France's King Louis XII. It was a cunning political marriage, with King Louis ceding the Kingdom of Naples and the Kingdom of Jerusalem to his niece as part of the arrangement. And she was young and beautiful.

With Queen Isabella's death, the cardinal lost some of his leverage in court, having been her confessor and counselor for several years. Yet with some careful positioning, Cardinal Cisneros felt confident he could navigate the rocky roads ahead as royal succession became treacherous.

Today, the cardinal desperately needed Ferdinand's blessing with the foreign conquests in North Africa. He preferred to deal directly with Ferdinand because Cisneros remained unsure of the influence the young queen held on him. Yet, the king set the agenda before Cisneros presented his petition.

"Cardinal," Ferdinand began, "explain to my queen the necessity of the arrest of Isabella's former confessor and our Archbishop of Granada. Archbishop Talavera has always been a loyal and devoted servant to me and the Church."

Cisneros had discussed this at length with the king. Why was he insisting they rehash it again?

"Your highness," Cisneros bowed, addressing the queen, "our archbishop, a beloved brother, has so descended to the deceptions of the Moors and the Jews, he stands accused of worshiping in their synagogues, and defying His Excellency our Pope Julius II, and refusing to enforce the very decrees of your husband, our king."

Germaine heard all of this from Ferdinand before, but her questions hadn't been satisfactorily answered. She met and conversed with Archbishop Talavera briefly during her visits to Granada, and each time she sensed no rebellion or heresy. Although very young, Germain was an astute learner in the way of kings and kingdoms. Her beauty gave ample reason to be held close to the powerful people in the courts. Few recognized that behind her innocent beauty was a sharp, perceptive mind.

"And a trial is to be held here in the Alhambra tomorrow?" she asked.

Cisneros knew she feigned her innocence. What he did not know was how she might influence her husband and the court. Though the king had great power, even he had to carefully manage the relationship between his kingdom and the Church. An archbishop accused of heresy was a difficult challenge.

"We are not so anxious, my queen," Cisneros said. "However, we are receiving reports and gathering testimony and will soon hold a righteous tribunal."

Cisneros had one last witness to deal with. With Talavera safely in prison, he felt confident he would soon be free of the archbishop. His guards had Talavera's Basque protector Miguel Ziortsa de Bolibar safely locked up and soon he hoped to have him ready to testify against the archbishop. Although other bishops and clergy stood with Cisneros in their condemnation of the archbishop, it was Miguel who kept the writings of Talavera which included the archbishop's declarations against many of the customs and teachings of the Church. Under threat of Cisneros' wrath, the Bishop of Málaga revealed some of those writings, and indicated other writings existed that were much more damning. As soon as Cisneros could turn Miguel against Talavera and recover the evidence, he would hold the trial. Miguel received one set of lashing. They then moved him from the prison to where he watched the burnings of the previous night. Another beating and this willful heretic would sing against Talavera; and then Talavera, the heretic archbishop, would serve as an example that no man can stand against the

Church and escape the wrath of God.

"Yet, you believe our inquisitor Lucero's accusations?" Her question landed like an accusation.

He wondered why she cared so much. She was as eager to rid Granada of the Moors and Jews as Isabella was. Is she testing me, he wondered, and why does the king give her such freedom? After all, when Isabella died, her daughter Joanna stood in line to be queen. I was the one who helped to remove Isabella's daughter, Joanna of Castile, the rightful queen. I made it possible for Ferdinand to retain control of Castile, a move giving Germaine her royal rights. And Germaine knew Talavera was sympathetic to Joanna. She should not question me.

Cisneros remained calm. "Lucero's methods needed tempering, but his work is thorough," he said.

Ferdinand finally gave Cisneros a reprieve. As if he were training his new young wife to become a strong monarch, as was Isabella, he brought her inquisitorial practice session to an end.

"But you did not come to us on a matter of the heretic, did you?" King Ferdinand asked.

Cisneros bowed, welcoming the change of subject.

"General Pedro de Ruiz is insisting the time is now to quell the attacks on Mers-el-Kébir. He has added much to your coffers from the successful raids on local villages, yet he fears the Zayyanids may be successful raising another army." Cisneros remained submissive yet firm in his request for support in his conquest of North Africa.

"How long will it take to outfit the forces you request?" Ferdinand asked.

"Weeks only."

"See to it," the king answered. Cisneros knew the financial arrangements. Except for financing the Columbus expedition over a dozen years earlier, Ferdinand and Isabella approved many expeditions with the understanding that those leading them were responsible for their funding. Investors received their reward from the conquest, often taking half of the plunder or more. With General Ruiz's plunder in North Africa, the conquest was already profitable for Cisneros. He planned to finance the conquest of the neighboring Algerian city of Oran with tithing money. He knew the plunder and potential sale of captives will certainly return a handsome profit to himself personally as well as to the king.

He bowed and meekly retreated from the audience with King Ferdinand and Queen Germain. Within days, he would be free of the threat of Cardinal Talavera's followers. The monarch and his new wife will return to Toledo, and then he planned to lead the attack on Oran. His smile betrayed his attempt at submissiveness to the crown. Cisneros was 'the crown.' He owned the Church. He owned this palace, the great Alhambra. Soon, he would own North Africa.

Pride of this conquest, the magnificent palace and fortress, rolled through him each time he was here. The Moors were superb architects, he admitted. He had not seen many other Islamic cities, but assumed they couldn't feature finer architecture than this. He was excited to conquer more.

The Alhambra complex amazed Cisneros with its intricate geometric patterns and ornate tile-work. He stopped as he always did when he entered the Court of the Lions. Crystal clear water flowed from its central basin into smaller channels that led into four smaller basins. Twelve intricately carved lions, each in a unique position, surrounded the central basin. It amazed him how the positioning of the lions gave the impression they were in motion. Even now, having examined each lion, he was not convinced there wasn't some otherworldly spirit attending this fountain and its pride of lions.

The tiniest regret tinged his heart as he worried if the Moriscos, the baptized Moors, could keep up these beautiful gardens and maintain the heart of this complex. He knew just as the Great Mosque of Granada remained magnificent following its Christian conversion, this complex with its magnificent gardens seemed to resist, just as so many of the Islamic Moors persisted in their resistance. He held more respect for the architecture of this grand monument than the beliefs of the swine who created it.

Cisneros reached the grand porch and again paused in awe of the stunning, picturesque views. Beyond the red-tiled roofs, the labyrinthine streets of the Albayzin Moorish quarter and the lush gardens with their intricate fountains and vibrant flowers stood the majestic Sierra Nevada mountains capped with snow. Even among everything he despised about the heathens who, for eight hundred years, occupied this land, he could not fault what they created here.

From the king, he got what he sought, the blessing of his king to arm and prepare an army to conquer the second, yet most important, port city in Algeria. From there, his conquest across North Africa would be assured. In the streets, there was no sign of revolt following the very public arrest of the only remaining person blocking his cleansing of Granada.

He walked casually through the marketplace. He felt almost lighthearted as he met the bustling scene of merchants and shoppers haggling over the goods of the day. The air was thick with the scent of spices and fresh produce. The sound of vendors shouting their wares filled the air.

He passed the colorful array of tents and stalls, each one with its own personality. The wafting aroma of fresh baked bread quickly disappeared as he passed the fishmonger, his stall gleaming with fish caught overnight on the nearby coast.

He approached his favorite collection of tents. Vendors displayed exotic spices, their vibrant colors and fragrances mingling together, making an intoxicating atmosphere. He continued weaving his way through the throngs of unimportant people who were oblivious of his grander mission to bring the world to Christ. His mission. He became so caught up in the glory of the impending conquest he knocked into a man bargaining for a handcrafted pot. The pot slipped, shattering when it hit the cobblestone. The shop keeper's quick temper faded immediately when the man turned and realized it was the cardinal himself, the very one who had demanded the arrest of one of the city's few favored Christians.

Cisneros, with no acknowledgment of the broken pot, turned and continued on his way. He finally reached the cathedral where, just days earlier, he and his royal guard arrested Archbishop Talavera for his accused heresy. Now known as the Cathedral of Incarnation, the majestic cathedral was once the Great Mosque of Granada, originally built in the mid-1200s. For centuries, it served as one of the largest mosques in the Islamic world.

When the Catholic monarchs Ferdinand and Isabella conquered Granada fifteen years earlier, they converted it into its current state. Secretly, he regretted the loss of much of its original Islamic architectural features. Its new popular Gothic and Renaissance styles lacked the romance that impressed the cardinal.

The tall, finely carved, solid walnut doors of the cathedral hung open. Where were his sentinels?

He stepped inside where usually he would breathe in the grandeur of the ornate interior with its soaring vaulted ceilings and elaborate altarpieces, but now he sensed a coolness. He stood at the entrance of the main chapel and saw three bishops in animated conversation. Disagreements amongst the clergy were not uncommon, but their words tumbling over each other crafted a message full of accusation, fear, retribution, and embarrassment. His earlier jubilation deflated, and with uneasiness Cisneros crossed the chapel.

The senior bishop silenced the other two with a wave of the hand when he saw Cisneros approach.

"Your Eminence," he began, knowing Cisneros appreciated the lofty honor accorded only to the Pope, "by some cunning of Satan himself, your prisoner was delivered from justice. He escaped." The bishop made a slight step back as the news filled the cardinal with rage.

He said no words. Red faced with anger, Cisneros turned and with the echoes of his pounding boots reverberating through the chapel, he charged out across the plaza where stood four empty stakes ready for the night's cleansing fires. In but a few bounding leaps, he ascended the stairs and into the long hallway where, surprisingly, none of his royal guards stood as sentry. The door to the very room where he had Miguel taken to witness the fate of Talavera's other supporters was unlocked. It slammed open when the force of Cisneros' full body hit it in full stride.

An empty basket, bloodied rags, and an empty pail laid strewn on the floor. The bishops, who would certainly prefer to avoid this moment, remained outside the makeshift prison door. The fury in Cisneros' face did not need the words to demand an explanation.

"When they brought water, they found no guard, the door open, and the prisoner gone. When asked if you commanded him moved, I was certain you had not, so I instructed them to tell your royal guard to search the city," the senior bishop said.

"He will not be in the city!" barked Cisneros. "He will be gone to the Pope as quickly as possible. Call my guards to my stables. We cannot let him escape. He will likely attempt to sail from Almeria."

Within minutes, two columns of six royal guards charged out of Granada toward the coastal city of Almeria, led by Cisneros himself, on his tall, powerful white Andalusian mare, the pride of his personal stables. As he rode, pride in his quick response joined his self-satisfaction knowing he would accomplish two important missions this day—prevent Miguel from sailing on the Isabella, which was most likely his aim given that the Isabella was sailing to Rome, and while in Almeria he could begin preparations for the siege of Oran, which he would launch from Almeria, the beautiful former Moorish port city.

Chapter Five

1509 - Granada, Spain

Loud horns blew across the plaza, echoing against the buildings. Soldiers charged through the alleys, followed by monks, all on the run. Sukayna stepped to the front of the shop and watched the crowds gather and scatter. Soldiers ran in every direction. Sukayna stepped back inside, tidied Miguel's shaya, and placed an alquice over the turban, positioning it to hang down over his shoulders. She turned him around, admiring her work.

"We have not time to fit you properly, but please take these." She handed him a pair of fine goatskin boots. "They may fit."

Miguel motioned with his eyes toward the commotion in the plaza.

"They discovered you escaped. They will not find you now." She stood, admiring her work again. "Come with me." She wound through the back of the shop and quickly crossed an alley, cut through another building, and passed from alley to alley until she led him into a fine stable where stood magnificent Arabian ponies.

"This is Ubayd." Miguel bowed respectfully. "Ubayd, this is Jalaf's friend. They know he escaped. You know what to do." Ubayd held the reins out to Miguel, who with no hesitation except to take one more look into Sukayna's eyes, mounted the shiny black stallion. "How do I repay—" Miguel's question was cut short as Sukayna held up a hand. "Jalaf has paid us already. Without you and your archbishop, the Christians will finish the destruction of our people. Go to your Pope. Free us from the Christians." She bowed her head. Ubayd led Miguel out and through a labyrinth of alleys. When they were past the city walls, he gave his horse its head and the two men flew up through the hills and across the verdant green fields.

They dropped into a deep ravine, thickly overgrown with brush and poplar trees. With the smile of a fox that just emptied a henhouse, there stood Jalaf, arm resting on the saddle of an equally high bred mare, saddled and packed for a long journey. "Welcome, my friend. I see you found Sukayna. Did I disappoint in my praise?"

Miguel looked from Ubayd to Jalaf and back. Ubayd, still mounted, nodded, turned his horse, and charged back up the hill.

"Big talker?" Jalaf said, motioning toward Ubayd disappearing over the ridge.

Miguel shook his head.

"He is like that. Does not seem to think you Christians should force us to convert."

"And you?" Miguel said.

"I do not think it. I know it," Jalaf said as he practically jumped onto his horse. He led his horse down a narrow trail winding through the thick vegetation. Once clear, both horses broke into a full run across wide open fields toward the rugged Sierra Nevada mountains that nestled the harbor of Almeria on their southern slopes. Jalaf slowed as they rose over a small hill. Miguel pulled up alongside. The two horses appreciated the slower pace. Warm, moist air rose from the valley behind them. Miguel felt like it would be nice to remove a layer or two of Sukayna's masterpiece. He did not, concluding it was safer to maintain the disguise. Deep breaths filled his lungs. It tasted of freedom. Yet his mind pondered on Talavera's fate. What would Cisneros do now that he lost his key witness? How had Jalaf helped him escape? Why not Talavera instead? Maybe Talavera did escape.

"You rescued me?" Miguel asked. "Why not Talavera?"

"Your Archbishop is under personal guard. He will only be freed by your Pope."

"Who are you?" Miguel asked. Miguel struggled to put the arrest, the beating, betrayal, and escape into a timeline. Was it three days, maybe four? Or weeks? Jalaf was kind and confident each time they interacted. Why? He waited for an answer.

"Your archbishop taught my family. He was kind. He told us about your Jesus and of His love. How Jesus died for us. My father asked how Christians who follow a loving God can conquer other lands, force the people to believe in their God and if they refuse, drive them from their homes and even take their very lives."

Jalaf's declaration was not new to Miguel. Yet no bitterness ever revealed itself. Jalaf continued his cheerful tone.

"Your Cisneros, your cardinal, arrested my family when he learned my father refused baptism. My father told me to convert and live. I converted. I live."

Miguel hung his head. This story was a common one. It was the reason the two cardinals were at odds. Cardinal Talavera, Archbishop of Granada, remained loyal to the Treaty of Alhambra guaranteeing religious freedom to Jews and Moors. Cardinal Cisneros held that God commanded every soul to believe in His Son. Thus, it was not a matter of choice. Because of Cisneros' violations of that treaty, the Moors rebelled more than once. Each time Cisneros' soldiers put down the rebellions. Cisneros levied a heavy hand.

"And your family?" Miguel asked.

Jalaf shrugged his shoulders, shook his head. Miguel knew that meant either execution or expulsion. He wished he could return to Granada and learn about Jalaf's family.

The two men rode in silence for the next several hours up and over craggy hills and valleys. It was clear to Miguel, Jalaf knew to avoid the main roads, roads that would shorten this journey by many hours. Yet they would spend a chilly night somewhere in the forested mountains.

ATLANTIC
OCEAN
HISPANIOLA
Santo Domingo
CARIBBEAN
SEA
San Sebastian
SOUTHERN SEA
(Pacific Ocean)
TIERRA FIRME

Chapter Six

1509 - San Sebastian Settlement, Gulf of Urabá, Tierra Firme

"This is exactly what you wanted!" Captain Ojeda told Francisco, "You were nothing when you left Spain. You remained nothing in Hispaniola. You begged the gods to be rich. You killed to be powerful. You demanded to be important. Here is your chance!"

Captain Ojeda boarded the caravel and commanded the canvas sails be hoisted immediately. Captain Alonso de Ojeda, an experienced Spanish explorer, conquistador, and governor, was not a tall man. His fine deportment, steeled confidence, and smart leadership won the confidence of King Ferdinand "the Catholic," as the soldiers called their monarch. Behind Columbus' back, King Ferdinand commissioned the conquest of additional lands in the New World. Who else would the king commission but Captain Alonso de Ojeda? With his connections in court and his experience sailing with the Admiral of the Western Seas, Christopher Columbus, on Columbus's second journey, he was a natural selection.

But now the expedition was in ruins. The new settlement, named San Sebastian, was low on supplies. In its first six months, it failed to develop a trade with locals and they'd yet to find the plethora of gold and silver rumored to be here; which was critical to funding more expeditions. Its self-proclaimed governor, Captain Ojeda, was now sailing back to Santo Domingo, Hispaniola, for supplies, leaving Francisco, a young uneducated soldier in charge of the new struggling colony.

Francisco swallowed back his doubts as he watched the ship cut through the sea, waves slapping against its hull. He watched it grow smaller, then rowed back to shore and his two hundred sixty surviving settlers. This was his chance. Ojeda was right, this is what he begged for. But it was nothing like what he was promised. There was no gold. Natives were hostile. Supplies would last no more than a month. But by then Ojeda would return, right? This expedition would succeed. Francisco would make it succeed. He had faced challenges more difficult than this. He would die before he would quit. As he approached the shore, men were waving and shouting the dire news. He climbed from the boat only to be met with word his exploratory party of twelve men failed. They were sent along the eastern shoreline where a heavily jungled river met the shore. They were attacked and the only two surviving men returned with nothing but failure. No gold. No food. More death.

Francisco knew death, he saw it in the swine herds back home. He saw it serving those many years as a soldier in the Spanish army, and he was living it here in the New World. His father, Gonzalo Pizarro, was an army officer. His mother was a servant back in Spain's Extremadura, the arid harsh lands of central Spain. Since his parents were never married, Francisco was an illegitimate son. There was no future for him in Spain, nor for his other illegitimate brothers. Francisco had no formal education, he could not read or write, but that did not keep him from dreaming. Now he was living that dream. He would make this dream a reality. He would find gold. He would conquer this land.

Francisco entered the large tent where the two surviving soldiers lay. A bloody bandage covered half of the first man's head. The one visible eye stared up at Francisco pouring forth loathing. Why did this man survive? He knew why. Sometimes a man needs more than courage to survive, sometimes he needs hate. He and Francisco had argued about the risk of exploring so deeply into the jungles. They came to blows before Captain Ojeda halted the brawl. The man wanted to wait until the captain returned with supplies and more men. But Francisco sided with the captain and threatened the men with the sword if they refused. Francisco felt the man's hate.

Francisco turned to the next man. A large patch of blood soiled his sleeve and neck, but there was no visible laceration. Francisco knew this man would not last the night. The poorly educated makeshift doctors would never find an antidote for the poison the natives put on their darts. The local natives learned they could not penetrate the armor or the chain mail. Their attacks were becoming much more deadly as their knowledge of the soldiers' defenses improved.

Francisco put his hand on the man's shoulder, squeezed, and left the tent. This would be a grueling thirty or so days. Francisco could not sit and wait for the captain's return. Idle men consuming limited stores was not leadership. He put the men to completing the fort which was begun by Ojeda. The heavy growth of strong trees at the jungle's edge provided an abundance of lumber. The first several days gave Francisco the hope this settlement might not end as several of Columbus's early settlements ended—with total extermination of the settlers. As days turned to weeks, any kind of injury turned to infection. Disease swept the camp. Spirits ran low, as did the stores of provisions.

Nights became horrific. Chants from the nearby natives competed with the welcome chirps and caws of the prolific parrots and other colorful fowl. Death visited the fort almost nightly. If not visited by the Chiqueños, the settlers could depend on putrition to steal a life or two. Even without a wound to initiate an infection, sores developed in their toes, crotches, and armpits. Putrition, as they called it, developed into large pustules that broke, oozing pus which spread and dried, burning the flesh. Clean water was not to be had without great risk of leaving the protection of the fort. Settlers feared coming in contact with the infected and abandoned the afflicted to their own care. The occasional rainfall cleared the air of the stench of death, but added to the miserable humidity oppressing the settlers.

Ojeda had now been gone thirty-seven days and hope was slipping. Sixty-three of the initial three hundred settlers and soldiers were dead, fourteen from silent native attacks as the men worked the timbers outside the fort. The natives were invisible. They appeared, launched a volley of poison darts, and disappeared silently. Their victims died both slow and painful deaths. During one such attack, three of the natives were captured and brutally killed by Francisco's soldiers. They were brought back as trophies. The trophies did little to frighten the natives. Attacks continued. Of the other forty-nine dead, disease killed forty-one and a remaining seven died from accidents while one other drowned swimming to the ship in fear of the apparent plague that swept the camp.

Picket posts rising twelve feet above the steep mounds of dirt surrounded the settlement and provided some sense of security. Francisco led a small party of twenty men from the fort east along the shore. Mild waves lapped at the beach. In desperation to secure something edible to add to the dwindling stores, they penetrated the jungle with machete and swords drawn. Each man wore helmet and shield, secured over a thick leather shirt. They padded their breaches and wore chain mail to their wrists and heavy scarves around their exposed necks, to protect from poison darts which would come from any direction. They had long since given up worry about animals. The natives stripped the area clear of all wildlife, with the only exception being the deadly snakes. Francisco realized they would never find the gold and silver without the help of the natives who knew this land. He now saw the foolishness of Ojeda's command to show strength and superiority when they encountered the natives of this land in the first days of their landing.

On day two after their arrival, in full armor, Captain Ojada led twenty soldiers from the shore, inland through an open meadow to a break in the thick jungle. They followed a shallow river up a small rise toward the massive hills. There they met a tribe they called the Chiqueños. The Chiqueños were a small people, the tallest standing only a few inches over five feet tall. The men and women wore only a woven cloth around their waist. Francisco struggled to identify the old men from the young, for they all wore a black tail gathered from the long locks that grew around the back of their heads. Those he thought were the young, wore a white paint below their eyes and carried a long narrow tube and a small bag hanging from their waist. The women wore their hair straight, falling over their bare shoulders. The women stood side by side with the men, many with squinting eyes and fixed hard lips looking more fierce than the men.

Who Ojeda took to be the tribal leader, stood forward to challenge the advance of the Spanish. He did not step aside when Ojeda approached. Captain Ojeda, with experience encountering the natives with Columbus on his second journey and two subsequent journeys with other captains, began a negotiation by offering strands of beads and small mirrors. In exchange he hoped to receive any gift that would prove the existence of gold or silver. There was none. As Ojeda struggled to communicate with hand gestures, he pulled a golden comb and showed it to the chief. It impressed the chief, who accepted it as a gift in trade for a woven basket. Ojeda hadn't meant it for a trade at all and when he tried to take the comb back, the chief took offense. He expressed his displeasure and three of the young native boys came forward with their tubes brought to their lips.

All of Ojeda's men knew what this meant, but Ojeda did not back down. He made another attempt to take the golden comb back and the young Chiqueños launched their darts. When the darts bounced off Ojeda's shiny breast plate, he pulled his sword and severed the hand holding the comb. The hand and the comb fell to the ground. The entire tribe and group of soldiers stood stunned.

Ojeda reached for the comb and a second volley of darts launched toward the soldiers. Only one found flesh. Swords flew from their sheaths, and before Ojeda could call his men back, bodies lay bleeding in every direction. The company of soldiers retreated back to the shore. Construction of a fort and protection for a new settlement began in earnest. Francisco felt that the Chiqueños were so stunned, they did not retaliate in fear of these new intruders. But as the weeks passed, an occasional attack showed the settlement would not be an easy one to protect.

Oh, the cost of that golden comb, Francisco pondered almost every time one of his men died from the poison on a tiny, feathered dart. He was convinced the Chiqueños recognized the peril he and his men faced. Where in the first few weeks, wildlife was plenty and the stores were supplemented with wild boar and deer. Now there were none to be found. The Chiqueños drove them off or killed them, Francisco was certain. Survival depended on Ojeda's return.

Two months passed. Provisions were all used up. Several desperate soldiers left the protection of the fort, and secured a plant they thought they saw cooked at the Chiqueños village. They complained of stomach pain after eating it. In the morning, all seven were still, skin pale, eyes bulging open, and dead.

In desperation, Francisco and his twenty men now searched for any animal or any fruit that might sustain them until Ojeda might return. The armor and additional protection packed around any bare skin protected them against everything but the sweltering heat. When the group reached a crystal clean pool fed by a hundred-foot waterfall, men rushed to rinse their heads, and parched throats. Pizarro's command to stop came seconds too late. Darts found the uncovered heads to a man. From nowhere came not just darts, but arrows flew from every direction. In the chaos, soldiers exposed themselves, and each time met a deadly end. Within minutes, only one man stood alongside Francisco; the rest lay prostrated in various stages of death. Chiqueños rushed from the depth of the jungle with clubs and spears completing their work of death. Francisco and his last surviving soldier fought to no avail. There were too many coming too fast. They both turned and ran, darts and arrows bouncing off the backs of their armor.

They reached the fort only to pick tiny darts from their padded protection. Francisco knew it would only be days until all would be lost. He had just lost eighteen more men, bringing the total dead from disease, poison, infection, and starvation to two hundred forty men. In council with the remaining sixty, they agreed to abandon the settlement by night and retreat to the two small brigantines sitting silently in the harbor—a move he regretted they had not taken a month ago. Back then he knew they would soon have help. He couldn't fail on his first conquest. He could not. He now knew he was wrong.

When Ojeda returned, if he did, he would see the two ships gone, and know Francisco Pizarro failed.

Fortunately, there was no moon as they rowed the small boats from shore to the ships. Francisco figured the Chiqueños were watching and recognized they won. They had waited him out and they won the battle by attrition. The slight breeze, welcome during the night, magnified in the morning. The breeze became gale-force wind and as the two ships pulled anchor to leave, Francisco's sails filled, immediately pushing him free of the small harbor. The second ship, by a powerful gust caught a shoal, tipped to starboard, and hung up on an unseen reef. The growing wind pounded it. Cries for help were lost in the wind. Soon, the stranded ship began to come apart as the storm smashed against it. Francisco's ship, with a crew of twenty-eight ragged, starving men, raced north toward Hispaniola, lowering masts to half, preventing the storm from tearing the ship to pieces.

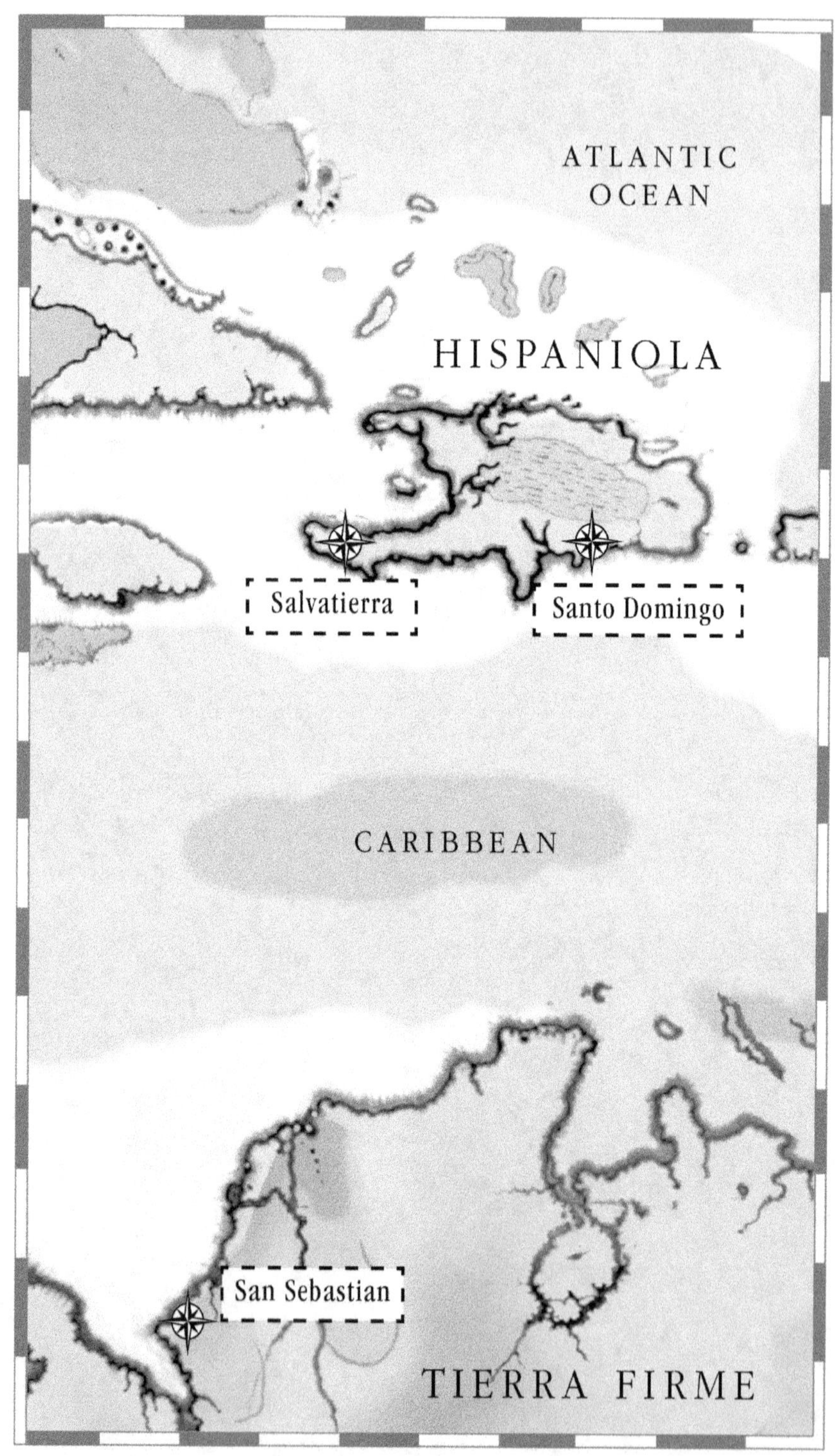

ATLANTIC
OCEAN
HISPANIOLA
Salvatierra
Santo Domingo
CARIBBEAN
San Sebastian
TIERRA FIRME

Chapter Seven

1509 - Salvatierra, Hispaniola, Caribbean

A puff of smoke shot out from the ship, accompanied by the blast of the eight-pound deck cannon of the Santa Maria. The shock reverberated across the small inlet fed by the lazy river that wound its way through the struggling farm. The ship had scarcely furled its sails and dropped anchors before it announced its arrival.

"Haste! The old Bachelor desires us to send our supplies at once," Vasco said. "He plans to lade tonight and sail tomorrow with the morning tide."

Vasco's mayordomo, Pablo, stood arms folded, unshaken by the cannon blast or the words of his master. "No need to worry sir. As for the provisions required of you, we are ready. Your Indians are now transporting your contributions to the shore."

Several large barrels sat on the beach ready to be loaded on the boats. Four Tiano Indians, two on each side of a large cask, with poles on their shoulders, carried the cask suspended on the ropes looped under it. Cracked and callused feet brushed through the sand as they struggled to carry this additional barrel to the shore.

Pablo turned to Vasco, "You are not much the farmer sir. If Governor Don Diego were not forbidding you to sail, your heart would carry you to the Santa Maria."

"The Bachelor would never permit me to sail away, despite Don Diego's decree," Vasco said.

"Don Diego is a fool. So is the Bachelor Enciso. You should be the captain of the Santa Maria. Or the governor," Pablo said.

"Of truth what I would not do to be free of the farm—"

"Or the creditors?" Pablo added.

Vasco nodded, "They are as much the prison that awaits me." The men watched the four Indians drop the cask onto the sand and struggle to stand it upright.

"What would you not do?" Pablo asked. He looked Vasco up and down, looked over to the beach, to the ship, and back to his master. "Go to the rancho, collect your essentials, return in an hour, or better, after dark."

Vasco knew a plot was hatching in Pablo's head. Pablo had been a loyal friend ever since the two men survived the disastrous voyage of Captain Batista four years earlier that landed the crew rich, but starving on the coast of Hispaniola. Pablo was a great negotiator and communicated brilliantly with the natives to help the bedraggled sailors make the long overland trek to Santo Domingo.

Vasco invested his loot in an encomienda he believed to be rich farmland near the town of Salvatierra. Despite all his hard work and Pablo's inventive husbandry, Vasco fell deeply into debt. He was now facing serious charges from his creditors. Since Pablo now owned the farm and Vasco owned the debt, there was little to do but face harsh consequences. It was a mystery to Vasco how the punishment for unpayable debt is debtor's prison. How did the new governor Don Diego expect debtors to pay their debt from prison?

Don Diego, Christopher Columbus's only legitimate son, was the third governor sent by the monarch to govern Tierra Firme, this newly conquered world. Don Diego had a strong hand, a moral justice, a conviction to set these failing colonies aright. Yet he was determined to continue many of the failed policies of the old world, such as imprisoning those who could not pay their creditors. And now he sent an armed caravel to accompany the Bachelor as Vasco called him, Captain Martin Fernandez de Enciso and the Santa Maria, to ensure that no debtors would sneak aboard and flee the island and their debts.

The sun was long set when Vasco returned to the beach. He arrived dressed in his finest breaches, stockings, boots, blouse, and jacket. Two of his Indian servants carried his armor and fine Toledo sword. Even in the faint moon lit night, Pablo recognized the pride Vasco so comfortably wore. He was a tall man, fit and strong. A short, well-trimmed black beard framed his tanned face. His eyes sparkled with ceaseless optimism and confidence, which attracted soldier and native alike.

Pablo stood alongside a large empty cask standing on its end, the top open. Pablo's smile, lost in the darkness, could not have been more broad.

"Master, your accommodations for the night, and the day," he said.

Vasco, mouth open, looked into the large round cask and back to Pablo. "You plan to pack me like a hog in a barrel?" Pablo said nothing. He just instructed the Indians to pack Vasco's armor and other belongings into the bottom of the cask. He added a bag of breads and cheese and a skin of wine, then invited Vasco to climb in.

Vasco, watching the packing without a word, finally asked, "If this barrel is packed upside down, it will become my tomb. I will be squeezed to death."

"No more than your creditors will squeeze you in prison," Pablo said. "I have arranged for your release after two days at sea when it is too late to bring you back."

"My release from a self-imposed prison?"

"Armando Gonzalo will be onboard."

"How will he know this cask?"

"I have instructed the porters to keep this end up. Leoncito will find you."

"My pup?"

"Both your pups."

Vasco smiled; his white teeth reflected the little moonlight bouncing off the water.

"Armando will see to it they are both onboard," Pablo said.

"I give you twenty thousand ducats for your brilliance," Vasco said as he climbed into the cask.

"And when may I expect this generous reward?"

"Truth, when I am governor of Tierra Firme," Vasco said, almost proclaiming it so. He folded himself into the cask and Pablo sealed his friend and master's troubles safely behind him.

A brisk wind, a perfect tide, and a brilliant sunrise met the Santa Maria as sails hoisted. The winds were fair all day and into the evening. This was not the first time Alessandro was on a ship; but the last time, four years earlier, he was only two years old, and his young mind failed to remember that far back. Everything was new. He made friends with everyone. His sidekick, Vasco's pup less than six months old, already weighed more than Alessandro. But the size and bounding energy of both the boy and the pup wore on the crew.

The hound promised to become a powerful war dog, as feared and lethal as his sire, Becerillio, Juan Ponce de Leon's famed killer. Under Alessandro's care, the pup, even with the name Leoncito, Little Lion, the dog was nothing more than a furry playful friend.

As the second day onboard dawned, Alessandro led Leoncito below decks to find their master. Within minutes, letting the hound utilize God-given talent, Leoncito sniffed, shuffled, and sat proudly at the foot of a large cask. Gonzalo, who brought the two onboard with him, quickly broke open the large cask.

A stiff, tired, sore, and jubilant stowaway climbed from captivity, and carefully extended each limb, willing it to release the blood back into the veins and awaken the muscles. A deep breath pushed eight hoarse words free, "Truth, I never want to do that again." With fingers clenching and releasing to help the circulation of blood get on its way, Vasco squeezed and released the thick brown hair of his pup and then the short black hair of his little friend. "We are free again," he said.

"I beg watch the Bachelor when he learns you are on board," Gonzalo said, "from a distance." Gonzalo began pulling the armor from the cask and handed Vasco his sword. He pulled it from its sheath and gave it a quick slice through the warm moist air of the cargo deck. He continued shaking free the kinks of his fleshy armor as Gonzalo helped him put on the breastplate and backplate. Vasco's steel plate was crafted to perfectly fit his body—his body from years earlier. It now was a bit tight, and Gonzalo did not hesitate to remind Vasco he had been living a bit rich of months late. He cinched it tight. Vasco exhaled. Next were the pauldrons to protect his shoulders and the rerebraces to protect his upper arms.

He attached the cuisses to protect Vasco's upper legs and then the greaves for the lower legs.

"You know, if Bachelor Enciso, in surprise or anger, throws you over, we will simply bid you farewell," Gonzalo said.

Alessandro watched with curiosity as the two men interacted. Gonzalez showed respect but did not fear his friend Vasco. He was comfortable tightening the armor a bit much. He looked to enjoy inflicting a bit of discomfort. Vasco, though a bit uncomfortable did not lash out.

In his young mind, Alessandro compared Vasco's patience with Gonzalo to Enciso's anger. Earlier in the day, a servant got in the way causing Enciso to no more than bump into a railing, and Enciso beat the man. Alessandro enjoyed watching people and wondered how they could be so different.

He watched Leoncito's eyes go from each piece of armor to Vasco's face as the armor was secured to his master. Alessandro wondered what might be going on in the young pup's mind. Was it the same as was dancing in his own?

Gonzalo attached the vambraces, protecting the forearms and then the gauntlets to finish the scene. Alessandro stood silently holding the morion, the distinctive Spanish helmet with its wide brim and comb-shaped crest. As his master took on the shape of a steel statue, Gonzalo reached down and took the helmet from him. Alessandro was happy to give it up. The bright red plume came to life as Gonzalo straightened it and fluffed the matted barbs. It almost looked proper again.

With sword in hand, Vasco moved slowly and stiffly, still working out the kinks from being folded so long. He was surprised his innards were not screaming for relief.

With a nod of approval, he marched up the steps to the quarter deck, followed by his small retinue.

Vasco approached Bachelor Enciso, who stood speechless and open-mouthed in shock. Vasco removed his hat and bowed almost to the deck. Seconds turned to minutes, then Vasco broke the silence, "Vasco Nuñez Balboa at your service."

Silence again for several minutes. Enciso stared as if collecting an entire vulgar vocabulary and peppering it with spice. He then expelled each and every word with its own accent. At last, when his rage and colored vocabulary seemed exhausted, Balboa deflected the tirade with a single remark, "Well, Senior Bachelor Enciso, after all the wrangling by you and Governor Don Diego, the island has lost a bad citizen, while you have gained a good soldier."

Vasco looked from Enciso to Leoncito and Alessandro, then back to Enciso. "No, by faith, three good soldiers, for my two young companions will serve valiantly as well."

Enciso finally got hold of himself long enough to cobble together more than a profane tirade. "Yes, the island did lose a most certainly bad citizen, and the reefs of Roncador will receive that citizen where marooned he may subsist on such as the sea may yield. And that kindness from me is more than the scoundrel deserves."

Balboa responded with another bow.

Enciso took several deep breaths, "What impudence to force yourself upon my company, when, as you cannot deny, you owe me two hundred ducats!"

"Nor do I deny it," answered Balboa, his genuine smile never faltering. "By faith, consider the fact that I now pledge to serve you with the sword in an attempt to liquidate that obligation. You yourself know there is no opportunity in Hispaniola. If there were, you can trust I would remain to meet my creditors. Though I succeed not as a farmer, with this in hand, as a soldier I will."

Balboa pulled his sword. Holding the blade in his hand with the hilt held high, he said, "Take me with you, good man. Give me opportunity, and from the spoils I win from the heathen, you will recoup the two hundred ducats and I shall not rest until all my creditors likewise are repaid."

Alessandro watched this exchange with such interest, when Leoncito let out a slight growl he realized he had nearly strangled the innocent hound standing at his side. He whispered a light "sorry" to the animal and released the death grip which had been tightening throughout the conversation.

"I do not know," Enciso said. "I never knew you to be anxious to discharge a debt." He paused and looked at the crowd of men gathered around the two men. "Since you are here, and will pledge your loyalty, promising support and obedience to my commands, I will allow you to remain."

"I thank you, your excellency." Balboa bowed low again, turned on his heel, and walked through the crowd of men.

Enciso watched him leave and shook his head. Alessandro watched Enciso, curious that he was so willing to accept his master Balboa into the crew. His young mind wondered. Leoncito dashed off with Balboa the minute the conversation ended. Alessandro knew Balboa was indeed expert with the sword, but he only heard about it, and other than practice, had never seen it in action. Maybe Enciso knew what he was doing. Enciso stared down at Alessandro. Their eyes met. Alessandro tried bravely to stare back. He couldn't. Enciso's angry eyes were too scary. He turned and walked quickly after the men following

Balboa off the quarterdeck.

Above the sound of the ocean crashing against the hull and the boots bounding away on the deck, Alessandro heard the words, "I may regret not throwing the impudent rascal overboard."

Might he still? Alessandro wondered.

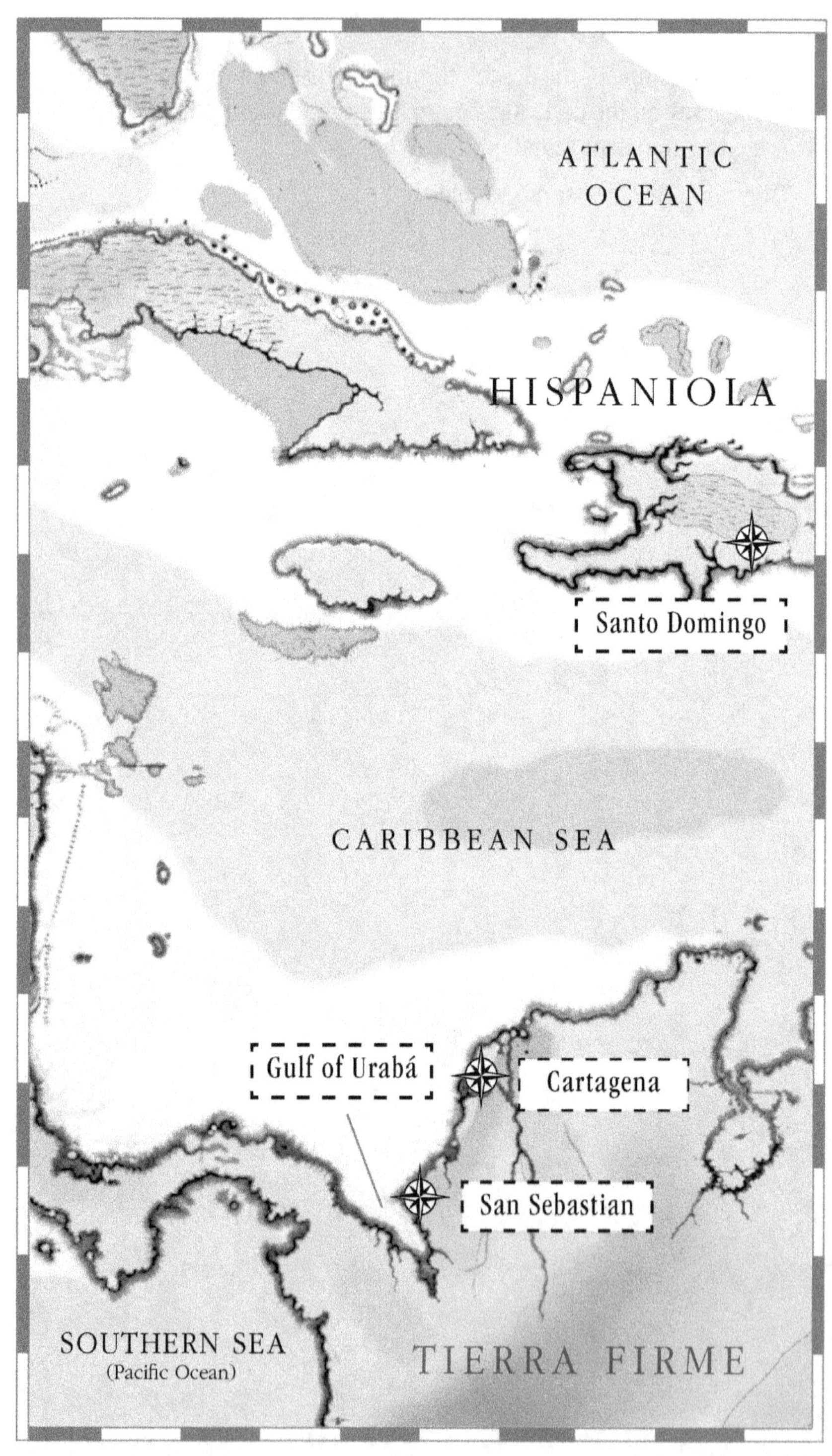

ATLANTIC OCEAN
HISPANIOLA
Santo Domingo
CARIBBEAN SEA
Gulf of Urabá
Cartagena
San Sebastian
SOUTHERN SEA
(Pacific Ocean)
TIERRA FIRME

Chapter Eight

1509 - Onboard the ship Santa Maria, at sail in the Caribbean

"Forget about the steel Vasco." Gonzalo said as he helped Vasco out of his armor. "Our voyage is to deliver provisions to a colony; not conquer. This expedition is for the relief of Ojeda. Did your time in the cask erase that fact?"

"A fool's errand it is," Balboa said. "Why our sovereign king gave Ojeda and Nicuesa these two lands to conquer and settle was folly. Neither man has the skill or temperament to lead men or appease the natives."

"Yet your farm helped supply their expeditions," Gonzalo said.

"Only to settle some debt," Balboa said.

"You doubt these colonies can survive?"

"In those two territories? Certainly, Tierra Firme is rich with possibilities. Captain Nicuesa gets the land west upwards to Cape de la Vela, and Captain Ojeda the land east near Gracias a Dios. Both areas are flush with riches and with savages. But neither Ojeda nor Nicuesa are flush with wisdom," Balboa said.

Gonzalo could not disagree.

The sailors understood their mission was fulfilling a charge from Captain Ojeda to his partner the Bachelor of Law, Captain Enciso, to bring provisions after a number of months. Those months passed and the provisions were late. Very late.

Balboa knew there was little chance Nicuesa and Ojeda were still alive. He also doubted with supplies so delayed whether either settlement had survived. But he was free from debtors' prison and ready for a new start.

Balboa, freed from the confines of the armor, again stretched and worked each joint and muscle to release the residual tension and pain from the many hours he had spent in confinement inside the cask. He was also free of the plagues and poverty of Santo Domingo.

"Ah then, by faith, dear Gonzalo, you will see it is good that I preserved my sword, for with its fine Toledo steel, we are off to carve a fortune with it in a new land where gold abounds!"

The young boy Alessandro caught up with the group of soldiers that gathered to congratulate and welcome their new shipmate. Many of them knew Balboa's history on Hispaniola and the exploits that landed him there. Balboa was a survivor. He also knew Tierra Firme. Four years earlier, Balboa was one of Captain Bastido's soldiers who successfully traded with the countless tribes living along the northern coast of the large new continent Tierra Firme. Captain Bastido captained two ships along its coast for months, trading for gold, silver, and pearls. Each and every soldier became individually rich. They also nearly lost their lives when the small armada suffered from an infestation of shipworm, which at first crippled their ships then destroyed them off the coast of Hispaniola.

Balboa never hesitated to recount this story with any new potential listener. But with this telling, he was going back to Tierra Firme and he felt confident that though more than four years had passed, his familiarity with the natives could help re-enrich not only himself but everyone on board. With his experience, he may not need his sword at all.

Balboa continued his story with more fervor, "When our longboats, crowded with our surviving men and hard-earned wealth…" Balboa held an open hand high imitating it full of gold, "we had naught but riches to buy our way across that wretched island. Seized by that wicked governor of Hispaniola, the wretched Bobadilla, we were imprisoned and stripped of our remaining gold." Balboa's voice raised; his hand tightened into a strong fist. "But not this time." He brought his fist down, slowly opened it, and caressed the hilt of the sword with his fingers.

Gonzalo was patient with Balboa's dramatic telling. He heard it enough times he was confident he could tell it as accurately, even more accurately, since with each telling, Balboa added some new tidbit of adventure, and each one more fantastic.

"My good friend," Gonzalo interrupted, "when we reach the Gulf of Urabá, we will see if your Toledo steel will turn us into rich men."

"The Gulf of Urabá?" Balboa's fingers tightened on his sword. "East or west?"

"Ojeda's territory is east," Gonzalo said, "you knew that. Nicuesa's territory is west."

"By the gods, we will have our hands full," Balboa said.

Like Gonzalo, Alessandro had not only heard Balboa repeat the stories of the Bastido expedition, its triumphs, tragedies, and betrayals, he lived part of it.

As the days wore on and the Santa Maria neared the northern coast of the great new continent, Tierra Firme, even without Balboa boasting the fact, to the men it became evident that Vasco Nuñez Balboa was the most qualified to lead this expedition. He sailed these waters with Captain Bastidos on one of the few successful expeditions where everyone became rich, and nobody died from the poison darts of the natives.

The captain, Bachelor Enciso, as the men called him because of his Bachelor of Law degree profession, captained this ship because Enciso financed his partnership with Alonso Ojeda. The Bachelor, like most all the men, was anxious for titles, lands, and riches. But he wore his position as captain with pride.

"Ojeda's a fool," Balboa said, "and we are no better if we think the natives will trust a Spaniard now."

The Santa Maria now sat at anchor several hundred yards offshore from Cartagena, a village with which Bastida's ships traded profitably years earlier, with just enough distance where poison darts, arrows, and angry natives were out of reach. Days earlier, the landing party led by Captain Enciso were welcomed by a war party. Three crew members were dead and two more, suffering the effects of the poison, would not make it through the night.

Enciso nursed a large gash to his left arm where a lance penetrated a gap between the pauldrons and rerebraces, his shoulder and arm shield. The lance that did the damage was a steel tipped Spanish lance, a lance Enciso recognized as formerly belonging to Ojeda's men.

"I doubt the natives in San Sebastian are on good terms with Ojeda either. With Bastido, we found no friendly natives along the eastern Urabá. Faith, we should abandon this folly here, and find Ojeda. If not poisoned, he is starving. You see that we will not restock provisions here in Cartagena," Balboa said.

Enciso nodded and called to hoist sails. Just as they did so, they saw a speck on the southwestern horizon. Sails of an oncoming ship grew, though ever slowly. All eyes watched as the ship approached.

"Captain Ojeda's frigate, the San Martin," Enciso said. "Ojeda's coming to us. We lingered too long."

Balboa knew Captain Ojeda left Santo Domingo with two caravels and a frigate with over three hundred men some nine months earlier. Enciso's relief provisions were at least thirty days late, maybe even sixty. Nothing was heard in those nine months. He could see the concern in Enciso's squinting eyes and pitched lips.

The sea was calm enough. Both pilots navigated an efficient approach. Balboa was impressed by the navigation skills as the two ships came side by side. Little Alessandro with his massive pup Leoncito at his side, stood, arms on the rails waiting as anxiously as the rest of the crew to learn what was happening.

The Bachelor, Captain Enciso hailed the captain of the San Martin. A tall man, in full metal armor, hailed back.

"I am Captain Francisco Pizarro of the San Martin, from the colony of San Sebastian. Captain Alonso de Ojeda sailed for Santo Domingo two months past and never returned. Partners of the captain failed to bring provisions. My twenty-eight men are all who survive."

Balboa stepped up alongside Alessandro eager to watch this interchange between the two captains he anticipated to be an interesting one. Enciso captained the ship that was late, and now the settlement had failed.

Pizarro stood tall and lean with a commanding presence. His weathered face bore the marks of the harsh failed expedition. Yet he was not weary. His piercing, intense eyes seemed to demand respect. Balboa saw in them an ambition and firm determination. Balboa turned to Alessandro and asked, "What are you thinking?"

This was not necessarily a game between Balboa and Alessandro, but it was their customary way to start a conversation. And it had its own unique practical function. The six-year-old orphan and the thirty-five-year-old explorer and conquistador could have either a unique superficial, or deep philosophical discussion. It started when Balboa first met Alessandro and his tiny family in Azoa, when his ships were eaten and sunk in the Gulf of Ocoa. Alessandro's father, Diego de Niño, a tall, smart black Spaniard, learned of the New World and joined Columbus' second expedition. He met a beautiful Tiano princess, took her as a wife and stayed to help colonize Hispaniola. It was rumored he was a cousin to one of Christopher Columbus' captains,

Pedro de Niño, who captained Columbus' Santa Maria.

When Captain Bastida's expedition landed so fatefully on the Gulf of Ocoa, on the island of Hispaniola those four years ago. Alessendro's father helped Bastido's men retrieve the spoils of their journey. Before he accompanied them across the island to Santo Domingo, Alessandro's mother fed the starving men. While in Alessandro's home, Balboa thought it quite comical how his mother would turn to this little two-year-old toddler and ask, "What are you thinking?" At first, he wondered what kind of gibberish would flow from the baby. Balboa realized that though he did not understand a word, the little boy did, and for some reason his mother did. There was a special understanding between the two.

Alessandro looked up to Balboa, still thinking, then said, "I think I do not like him."

"Who, our captain or that captain?" Balboa squinted, turned from the boy, and looked closer at Pizarro.

"Both," Alessandro said.

"It's neither," Balboa corrected.

"I do not like neither captain," Alessandro said.

Balboa turned back to Alessandro. "We shall see."

Enciso brought Pizarro on board and received the whole report. Pizarro held nothing back. He was firm, confident, and precise. He is a man of action, Balboa decided. Balboa remained silent through the report until Enciso insisted they all return and rebuild San Sebastian and make it a successful colony.

"Dear Bachelor," Balboa began, "we recognize the importance of the demarcation between Captain Ojeda's territory and Captain Nicuesa's, but if you choose to return and die east of the Urabá where likely you will make a good porridge for the natives, I beg the indulgence to leave me first on the west of the gulf."

All eyes turned to Balboa. Mostly the crew were tired of Balboa's arrogance, which stemmed from his successful interactions with the natives along these coastlines. But after hearing the detailed account from Pizarro and his losing over two hundred and seventy men to the ravages and savages of the jungles, Balboa's confidence appealed to the men.

Yet, as Ojeda's partner, Enciso held rank to which both Pizarro and Balboa submitted without complaint. That too impressed Balboa. This

Pizarro, with plenty to grieve about, yielded command to the Bachelor.

Both ships sailed southwest to return to San Sebastian. As they entered the harbor, Ojeda's third ship, which wrecked on a shoal the fateful night of Pizarro's escape, lay on its side in fractured pieces. Partly burned, it gave no evidence of any survivors.

The small fort of San Sebastian was also nothing but ashes. A war party lined the shore, anxious to receive the returning Spanish ships. Both of which anchored outside the reach of the natives' poison darts and arrows.

Soldiers on both ships expressed eagerness to seek revenge. Those with experience held no enthusiasm for blood, for blood's sake alone.

Balboa stood alongside Alessandro and Leoncito again. They looked across the harbor at the burned fort, the shell of a ship and a welcoming party anxious to finish a work of annihilation.

"What are you thinking?" Alessandro asked this time.

Balboa looked down at Alessandro and Leoncito. "Maybe we should ask Leoncito if he wants a fight," Balboa said.

"He does not," Alessandro said, eyes fixed on the war party, his arm over the hound's neck.

"No?" Balboa asked.

"Why would he? That Captain Pizarro said there is no gold here. You said these natives were not friendly to you, so Leoncito wants to go somewhere friendly," Alessandro said, eyes not leaving the war party.

"And you? You think that as well?" Balboa asked.

Alessandro just nodded his head.

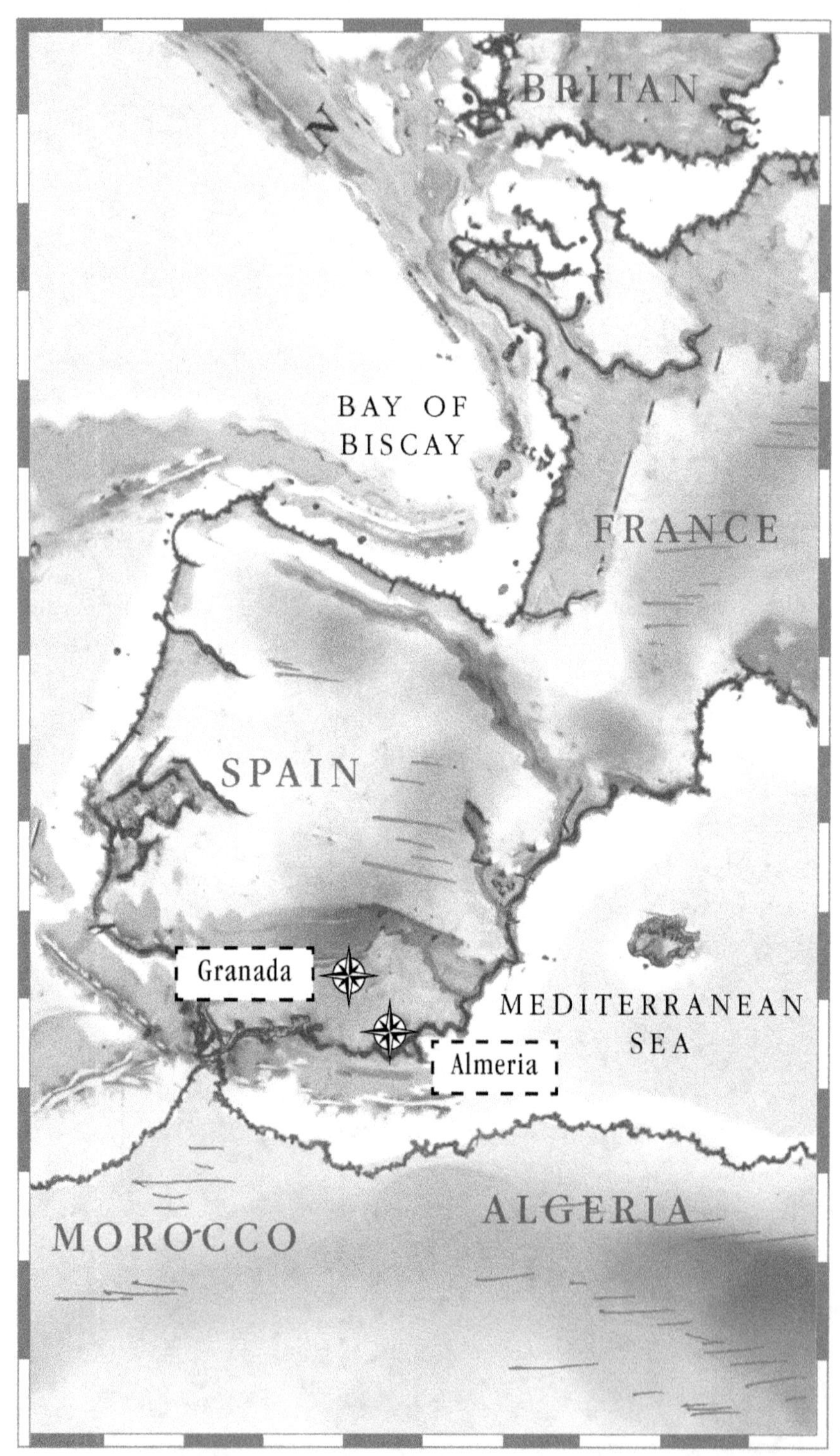

BRITAN
BAY OF
BISCAY
FRANCE
SPAIN
Granada
MEDITERRANEAN
SEA
Almeria
MOROCCO
ALGERIA

Chapter Nine

1509 - Sierra Nevada Mountains, Spain

"Almeria? Why Almeria?" Miguel said.

"Shortest and safest route to Rome," Jalaf said.

"You, are taking me to Rome?"

Jalaf looked Miguel up and down, shaking his head. "Not taking you anywhere." He pointed toward Almeria. "I leave you there. The Isabella will take you to Rome."

The Isabella was a new galleon named after the recently deceased Catholic monarch, Queen of Castile. How fitting, Miguel thought. The only person who stood between Cisneros and Talavera while she lived, gave her name to the ship that might deliver Miguel to and from the Pope to provide Talavera's release. Yet, how did Jalaf have this escape and delivery all figured out?

Jalaf interrupted Miguel's thoughts. "You, my friend are a newly converted Moor. A Morisco like me." Jalaf handed Miguel a large golden cross hanging from a long, jeweled chain. "They will be looking for the Basque, Miguel de Ziortza de Bolibar, the heretic."

Miguel opened his eyes wide in shock. Who is this Morisco? Who knows so much about him? He wondered, "And who might I be now?"

Jalaf's smile signaled there was a play at hand. Miguel almost regretted asking.

"Ali Abdallah al-Mutayyam." he said.

Miguel nearly slipped off his horse he turned so quickly to face Jalaf. "I am a follower of Allah, who is madly in love?"

Jalaf nodded.

"And with whom am I madly in love? Allah?"

"Sukayna."

Miguel paused. That could be true. He only saw her one time, but those eyes penetrated his heart. Jalaf noticed Miguel's eyes dancing as they pondered those moments he spent in the shop where Sukayna outfitted him. Jalaf laughed out loud.

"I only met her once," Miguel insisted.

"That is all it takes with Sukayna."

Miguel believed it.

"How else do you think she captured my heart?" Jalaf almost whispered it to himself.

How much of his heart did Sukayna capture? Miguel wondered. "Is she your…?"

Jalaf raised his eyebrows, nodded, then said, "but it will be your heart the cardinal's men will capture if they recognize you.

"Might they be expecting this lover boy to board the Isabella?" Miguel asked, still wondering how Jalaf knew so much.

"No. They will be expecting the heretic."

"In that case, I am Ali Abdallah al-Azzim," Miguel said.

"You? The great, magnificent greatness? As you wish." Jalaf bowed. His smile never faltered.

Cisneros suspected Miguel and his accomplices were cunning enough to stay clear of the primary thoroughfares between the two cities. He was confident he and his men would be waiting when the heretic fugitive attempted to flee the peninsula heading to Rome. An overland trek to Valencia or Barcelona and then by sea might be safer, but could cost the heretic several weeks, and by land the entire journey would cost him months. Cisneros felt sure Miguel would not suspect they could be ahead of him. For security, Cisneros dispatched soldiers to Valencia and Barcelona to watch the ports.

On this journey, the majesty of the land was lost on Cisneros. Its rugged beauty and untamed wilderness during other journeys fascinated him. This single-minded quest made him oblivious to the small villages and hamlets they passed. The Sierra Nevada mountains loomed over the landscape, their snow-capped peaks visible in the distance.

Their journey clung to the Camino Real de Granada, the well-traveled road that linked Granada to the coast. As the road wound through the fruitful lands, the air filled with the sweet scent of blossoming fruit trees. Cisneros did not notice. The Vega de Granada, a fertile plain irrigated by the Genil River, came and went without its colorful fields observed either. The road became steeper and narrower, and the landscape grew increasingly rugged as they approached the rising Sierra Nevadas. The journey, which on a normal occasion might require three to four days, had to be made in less than two. It was after dark when they stopped for the night at a small village tavern.

They rose early, invigorated by the brisk morning air, and pushed on. By mid-day, they crested the mountains and began the descent into the dry, barren plains of the Almeria region. The sun beat down on them mercilessly, and the wind carried dust and sand that stung their eyes. They paid it no attention. They rode on, spurred by the sight of the distant sea, glistening like a jewel in the sun. As they approached Almeria, the landscape grew more populated. The bustling port town filled with sounds and smells of trade and commerce as they rode into the city, their horses lathered with sweat and dust. They wound their way through. The Isabella stood majestically in the harbor. Boats tendered back and forth, preparing it to sail with the tide.

Cardinal Cisneros dusted himself off and approached a tall, robust man barking orders to a team of men loading a boat with tall crates and casks full of the area's prized wines and popular textiles.

"Where do I find the captain?" Cisneros asked. No greeting. No pleasantries.

The man kept shouting orders to the men. He pointed up the hill toward a tavern that overlooked the port. The cardinal turned and marched toward the tavern, leaving his men and horses at the water's edge.

Patrons of the tavern moved aside as the cardinal stormed into the tavern. Even dusty, he still commanded respect, respect he failed to receive at the dock. His black cloak, edged with rich red trim, contrasted his white cossack and collar. He wore the short cap he used to replace the zucchetto, the broad-brimmed hat he used during his flight from Granada. After the long, hard journey his steel-gray eyes maintained a strength uncommon to a lesser man.

When the crowd cleared, the captain, who was discussing business with a fellow mariner, looked up, smiled, and stood welcoming the cardinal to his table. The bartender offered a drink, which the cardinal waved off.

"What an honor," the captain said. "To what do I owe it?"

"A passenger," Cisneros said.

"You?" the captain asked.

Cisneros shook his head, "A heretic. I want him. He will be coming to sail with you to Rome."

"I know nothing of a heretic. Our passengers are pilgrims and merchandise," he said.

"Archbishop Talavera's guard is fleeing the inquisition."

The captain raised an eyebrow. This was news to him. He knew enough of the cardinal not to question how the man escaped. Even this far away, news traveled that Cisneros arrested Archbishop Talavera and most of his associates. They also heard that the arrest came at the accusation of the Grand Inquisitor Diego Rodríguez de Lucero, a man everyone, Christian, Morisco, Moor, and Muslim alike hated.

"You think he would dare sail with me?" the captain asked.

"The archbishop thinks a papal bull is forthcoming that will forgive his transgression. The heretic will think he is on God's errand. He might be careless."

"We sail at dawn. When might this heretic come?"

Cisneros was relieved that indeed he and his men reached Almeria and the captain before Miguel and his accomplices. The captain motioned to one of his men, who leaned down to lend an ear to the captain. He shook his head in understanding and rushed off.

The captain looked back up to Cisneros, who had refused to sit at the table. "If he is here, you will have him before dark. If he is not, we sail, and he remains your problem."

The warmth of the sun purged the chill of the night on the mountain. Jalaf and Miguel continued off the hills toward Almeria. Miguel asked one more time. "If we will soon part ways, may I ask again, who are you?"

"Why?"

"Why?" Miguel said, "A Morisco, trusted by the royal guards, sneaks a physician into the cell of the key witness expected to betray Talavera. At great risk you freed me, fed me, healed me, and prepared me in fake preparation for a trial; no, an exhibition; and you orchestrated a daring escape which will certainly bring the wrath of the Holy Roman Catholic Church down upon you. And as far as I can tell, you were baptized but never converted. I am curious to know who this Morisco, my current savior is."

Jalaf acted as if Miguel did not ask the question. He rode in silence for several minutes. He finally answered. "If you were any good with a sword or even the slightest fleet of foot, I would not need to risk my neck." The smile never faltered.

Miguel could not believe his rescuer could dish out such an insult and keep that smile beaming. Who is this person? Miguel still didn't know.

Dressed as a Moorish nobleman had its advantages. As they rode through the scattered homes approaching Almeria, proper people gave him the respect he would expect. If they only knew he was just a simple Christian pilgrim striving to serve a man of God, the Archbishop Talavera, the finest man he had ever known.

Was Jalaf also serving the archbishop? Miguel had accompanied Talavera to Almeria several times. Together they taught many of the Moorish nobles and merchants. Miguel preferred to teach the more humble peasants. He felt like one of them, and appreciated their simple view of life. Yes, he felt they needed the good news of a promised Messiah as taught by the prophet Isaiah, but they honored and respected Allah and lived a life respecting the two great commandments. Much better, he thought, than many of the Christians.

Jalaf stopped at a large bazaar that filled the wide plaza. They dismounted. Jalaf gave charge of their horses to a young man, and they went immediately to a food stand. Miguel knew this food stand. It would be a test of Sukayna's disguise. Both Miguel and Talavera frequented this popular food stand. Its owner served a blend of fresh vegetables with a thick peppered beef broth with small chunks of beef folded into a small bread dough and baked in a brick oven. The fresh pie was a favorite of both travelers and city residents. Other food stands, inns, and taverns offered this and other popular items, but none surpassed this stand.

It was evident Jalaf was well known here. He called the proprietor by name. "Ismail, my friend, feed this pilgrim here the best you have. He is off to Rome to see the Pope."

Miguel knew this proprietor as well. Why did Jalaf have to draw so much attention?

A test, yes, a test. Miguel did not hide. Ismail looked directly into Miguel's eyes, considered for a few moments, squinted an eye, and laid a large platter of the folded pies in front of Jalaf and Miguel. He looked back at Jalaf and winked. They stood at a tall table and ate. Miguel saw how Ismail monitored the two men. Miguel concluded he was still trying to recall his face. He recognized Miguel but could not quite decide how. Ismail, not realizing Miguel was watching out the side of his eye, leaned to another man, whispered something, and pointed toward Miguel and Jalaf. The man dashed away from the food stand.

Jalaf ate more than his share of the platter. Yet Miguel felt satisfied. An uneasiness about Ismail tinged his satisfaction with the food.

In the portside tavern, the captain and the cardinal discussed outfitting as many ships and armies as possible to prepare for a siege on Oran. The captain's messenger stole back into the tavern and whispered in the captain's ear. A triumphant smile filled the captain's face.

"Even you do not deserve this much providence," he said. Cisneros did not beg the question.

"Your man, with a single Morisco, and disguised as a Morisco, just left two tired Arabians in Diego's livery. Do you want them now or later?" The captain's smile never wavered. He brought his mug to his lips and drank deeply, rewarding his discovery.

"I will send my men. Where is he?" Cisneros asked.

Chapter Ten

1509 - Almeria, Spain's Southern Coast

The massive walls of the Alcazaba fortress never ceased to intrigue Miguel when he would accompany Talavera on his pilgrimages to other cities in the Muslim dominant areas of the Al-Andalus. The rugged hillside gave the walls an appearance of a snake winding its way up and over the terrain. The fortress suffered several series of destructions over the centuries as armies came and went. Portions of the walls were in various stages of repair.

"Did you say we sail this week?" Miguel said.

An energetic exchange between Ismail and a soldier began as Jalaf took a large bite of the last pie. The exchange of words was not clear to Miguel and when he asked Jalaf if he understood, Jalaf simply held up a hand to silence Miguel's inquiry. It may have been the first time he witnessed Jalaf's eternal smile flinch.

Jalaf swallowed, "You sail," Jalaf said, his attention elsewhere. He turned quickly back to Miguel, "time we go."

The two men hastily made their way past the fortress and down toward the center of the city, which leveled out and met the calm sea. Several ships sat in the large, deep harbor. Miguel watched small boats tender men and supplies toward the largest of them, the Isabella, the galleon taking him to Rome.

Jalaf looked directly into Miguel's eyes. The smile seemed forced. Its meaning unreadable to Miguel. "May your Christian God protect you," Jalaf said.

Three heavily armed men lurched from inside a small butcher shop, swords drawn. Two more immediately appeared behind them. Miguel looked at the men and back to Jalaf just as a heavy cloak was pulled over his head. All went black. Miguel felt strong cords tighten, locking the darkness.

Without a moment's pause, he landed hard on a wooden surface, which began a bumpy trip over the rough stone road. Miguel surmised he was in some type of cart heading up away from the port. His hope to seek an audience with the Pope faded in the darkness.

Suddenly, the cart's direction changed. It plunged downhill. With each bump, Miguel slid forward until his head pressed hard against the wall of the cart. Or so he imagined. The minutes stretched into what felt like hours. The cart leveled out and the path or road or whatever the surface was, felt much softer. He could feel the cart slow and weave. We're now on sand, he thought. Lapping waves confirmed they were near the sea.

Large, powerful hands grabbed him by the feet and pulled him off the cart, dropping him onto the soft ground. Dragged across the sand, he couldn't imagine what surprise awaited him. Deep grunts accompanied several hands hoisting him into another cart. No, a rocking boat which immediately shoved away from the shore. Oars dipping in and out of the water moved rhythmically with the movement of the boat. He was being tendered to a ship. He knew it. But what ship?

The oars stopped and Miguel felt the boat bump into what he knew would be a ship. He wasn't returning to Granada, that was certain, at least not soon. The absence of any conversation during this trek in the darkness added to Miguel's confusion. Was he kidnapped by Moors, Castilians, Corsairs, Muslims, Christians, Cisneros' inquisitors, or Ottomans? The ropes holding him bound tightened suddenly. They hoisted him up out of the boat and dropped him on what he figured was a deck. He laid motionless. Every sense struggled to capture a clue.

Cardinal Cisneros slammed his fist hard on the table, knocking two mugs to the floor, and tipping another. Foam flowed across the table, drenching the captain's shirt.

"How?" he yelled at the guard who just reported that as they readied to apprehend Miguel, four men charged out, bagged both him and his associate, and hauled them out of the city toward a second bay along the shore. The guard, nursing a badly bleeding arm, told how when he and his men attempted to stop the apparent kidnapping, three of the assailants, excellent with the sword, killed two of his men, badly wounded another, and left himself lying in his own blood.

With no feeling of concern for the dead and wounded, Cisneros demanded more information.

"I followed as best I could. They loaded your heretic onboard a Moroccan galley. He is gone to sea."

"Pirates. Barbary," the captain said. "They are the very reason the Isabella travels so heavily armed."

Cisneros' face matched the red in the trim on his cloak's collar. He rose, walked to the door, slammed his fist again, returned to the table, and struggled to breathe evenly. Minutes passed. Nobody dared to break the tense silence.

Color returned to his face, starting at the brim and worked its way down. When the color reached his mouth, a twisted grin seemed to lift his chin. He slowly turned his piercing eyes to the captain. "I will sail with you tomorrow."

The captain raised both eyebrows, but nodded his head slightly, his lips pursed.

Had this journey taken minutes, or hours? Finally, the ropes were cut, and the cloak pulled free, spinning him to his back. Many hours, he confirmed. It was pitch black. One small lantern set on the binnacle provided the tiny, shadowed light that confirmed Miguel was with people he preferred not to meet.

"Corsairs." He whispered so lightly he wasn't sure his word had formed.

"Up!" The command was Arabic. Moroccan, he thought. Did they think he spoke Arabic? Did they know who he was? Was this a kidnapping? Why did Jalaf rescue and then betray?

"Up!" This time, the command was Castilian. Stiff, sore, bruised, and weary, Miguel slowly climbed to his feet. The salvation for his battered body was the padding provided by the fine clothes given him by Sukayna. A man grabbed the cross hanging from the chain around his neck and yanked it free. A gift from Jalaf, his ticket to sail on the Isabella, the cross was now testimony against him.

"A Christian." The back of the man's large hand knocked Miguel to his knees. "Strip the imposter." Wearing now only a pair of trousers, they dragged Miguel below decks and slammed him on a hard wooden bench next to a man asleep, his head resting on the oar pulled from the sea. Now in complete darkness, the very senses he called upon earlier to gather intelligence about his future, announced he was the newest galley slave in a dark, dank, filthy pirate ship.

The sun barely broke the eastern sky when the Isabella pulled anchor and raised the sails. Cisneros stood boldly on deck, clean and refreshed. He had a new plan. Again, he inwardly complemented himself for his cunning. He was not going to Rome. Rome had nothing for him. He was going hunting. They took his prize from under his nose, and he was going to get it back, whatever the cost.

Using the power of his influence with the king and position in the Church, the captain acquiesced to Cisneros' demands to sail westerly to Gibraltar and back along the African coast. The captain felt helpless to resist being bait for the Barbary pirates. He assured Cisneros there was no need to invite an attack. It would come sure enough if they clung so close to the southern sea routes.

When the pre-dawn light tumbled down from above, Miguel saw he was one of twenty-four oarsmen, two per six rows on each side. His companions, all still sleeping, appeared to represent diverse peoples. His bench companion looked to be many years Miguel's senior, with large powerful arms. The crepuscular light softly glistened off his deep ebony skin.

Voices from above, all in Arabic, summoned the crew to position. They're preparing for a chase, but chasing who? Miguel asked himself. Soon, the oarsmen were awake, fed, and readied to work. In the morning light that dimly lit the galley, Miguel tried to cautiously assess his fellow slaves. He was seated in the third row. Men in front of him shared the marks of the lashes they'd received. His own stripes from Cisneros's soldiers marked him as belonging here. The men wouldn't question that. Yet, he wondered why the very chains that held his companions were mistakenly left unlocked for him. Laziness in the dark of night?

Miguel had little experience on board a ship and never as a galley slave, but he watched carefully and soon learned how to avoid the lash. Several days passed. Listening as intently as he could, he almost smiled when he learned their target was the very ship Jalaf said would deliver him to Rome, the Isabella. Miguel recognized the Isabella would be a prime target since it would be transporting treasure from the New World to the church in Rome. He knew if this ship caught the Isabella, it would not be an easy task to capture it.

From the mainmast, a lookout spotted a set of sails. Cisneros didn't care which flag it might be flying, as long as it was the one that might have taken his prize. Knowing Miguel was posing as a Morisco and a light-skinned one, his Christianity guaranteed he would become a slave. Cisneros expected Miguel was a galley slave and, if God willing, on the approaching ship. The Isabella was well armed with both men and steel. Even the captain knew his crew would triumph in a sea battle. Yet, there was always the unforeseen miscalculation.

A soldier standing alongside Cisneros used the glass and recognized the oncoming ship. Cisneros looked briefly toward heaven, mouthing a thank you.

"This is our ship," he told the captain. "Be prepared to cripple and board her. Sweep the deck clean and leave it sinking for all I care. I just want one man. God willing, he sits in chains below decks."

On what Miguel felt would be the sixth or seventh day, days that appeared to be spent waiting for signs of the prize, the men above decks spotted the Isabella. Immediately they put the ship to chase. Sharp commands, whip cracks, groans, and sweat consumed the galley. Miguel steeled himself to taste his first sea battle.

The distance between the galley and the Isabella narrowed. He couldn't see it, but by the cries of the men above, they were closing in. Then, just as suddenly as when the men pulled the cloak over his head in the market, a cannon ball ripped through the starboard side of the galley, tearing two men into pieces, scattering steel, wood, and flesh everywhere. Splinters lodged in Miguel's neck and cheek. The slave master lashed harder. The slaves rowed faster to avoid the fierce lashes. Two cannon blasts from above declared this battle was to the death. Another ball from the Isabella cracked above decks. An enormous boom smashed on deck. A fallen mast, Miguel thought. The battle to the death seemed to favor the Isabella.

Another blast tore through the galley, cutting the slave master in half. His vile whip landed at Miguel's feet. His sword, still sheathed, lay next to the lower half of him. Miguel's Christian cross, given him by Jalaf, laid in blood pouring from the slave master's severed arm. The next blast might be the one to finish the battle. Without the oarsmen and a mast, maneuverability became impossible. Whose side did he want to be on? He looked the sword and bullwhip up and down. If Jalaf was right and his skills as a swordsman were inferior, his skill with a bullwhip would challenge Jalaf's intimation he was a weak adversary.

Two more blasts from above and the shouting appeared to be in the corsair's favor. Another broadside blast tore through the galley. He knew this ship was not sailing away. Yells and shouts declared a hand-to-hand battle above decks. It was time to choose a side. But which? He was a heretic, running for his life after abandoning Talavera, who might at this very time be burning. Should he defend the inquisitors? He was no longer under the protection of Sukayna's disguise. If Cisneros' men were above deck, how would he choose?

He stood, kicked loose the poorly fastened chains, grabbed the sword, and coiled the bullwhip, tucking it into his pant. He turned and looked at his bench mate with whom he communicated solely by eye gestures, and read the plea for freedom. Miguel quickly retrieved the keys to the chains that kept the few surviving slaves in their positions. Another blast shattered the beam supporting the deck. It knocked Miguel from his feet, pinning him beneath the fallen beam and imprisoning him into the trench of human refuse. It held him tight.

All hope left the oarsmen when they lost sight of Miguel. The man with the keys was gone.

The battle raging above decks ceased. The creaking of the broken deck caused by the shattered support beam echoed through the galley. The sound of boots crossing the deck stopped at the top of the stairs. One step at a time revealed the long cardinal robes of the galley's visitor. With the added holes in the walls of the ship, the light below decks was sufficient for the cardinal to eye each and every surviving oarsman still chained to their benches. Not finding who he sought, he took particular interest in the bloody remains of bodies ripped apart from the direct cannon blasts. He reached down and picked up a golden cross lying in a pool of blood next to a severed arm. Slowly, he shook his head, eyes closed, then pulled a kerchief to his mouth and let it filter the repulsive stench of gunpowder blended with blood and human refuse. He turned and marched back above decks.

Shouts from above and then two more blasts from the Isabella's gun decks breached the starboard side, sending water gushing into the galley. The water was enough to lift the fallen beam, releasing Miguel and washing him across the galley, crashing into the port side wall. He fought his way to his feet as the water reached waist depth. He tried desperately to regain his bearings. Plunging below the surface of the rising water, he unlocked the chains of his bench partner, handed the key to the man, and tried to climb above decks. The galley listed to starboard. The damage was fatal. These were indeed Cisneros' royal guard. They outnumbered the corsairs four to one. The main mast lay motionless on its side. One by one, the corsairs fell to the overpowering royal guard. There was no hope for the galley. Another blast from the Isabella tore across the deck. The captain of the Isabella called his men back on board and they left the ship to sink. Miguel struggled to climb his way up and onto the shattered main deck, sword drawn, whip ready to engage, but with no one left to fight.

The men from below, now free, scrambled above decks only to realize their freedom would be short-lived. They watched hopelessly as the Isabella retreated into the eastern sea.

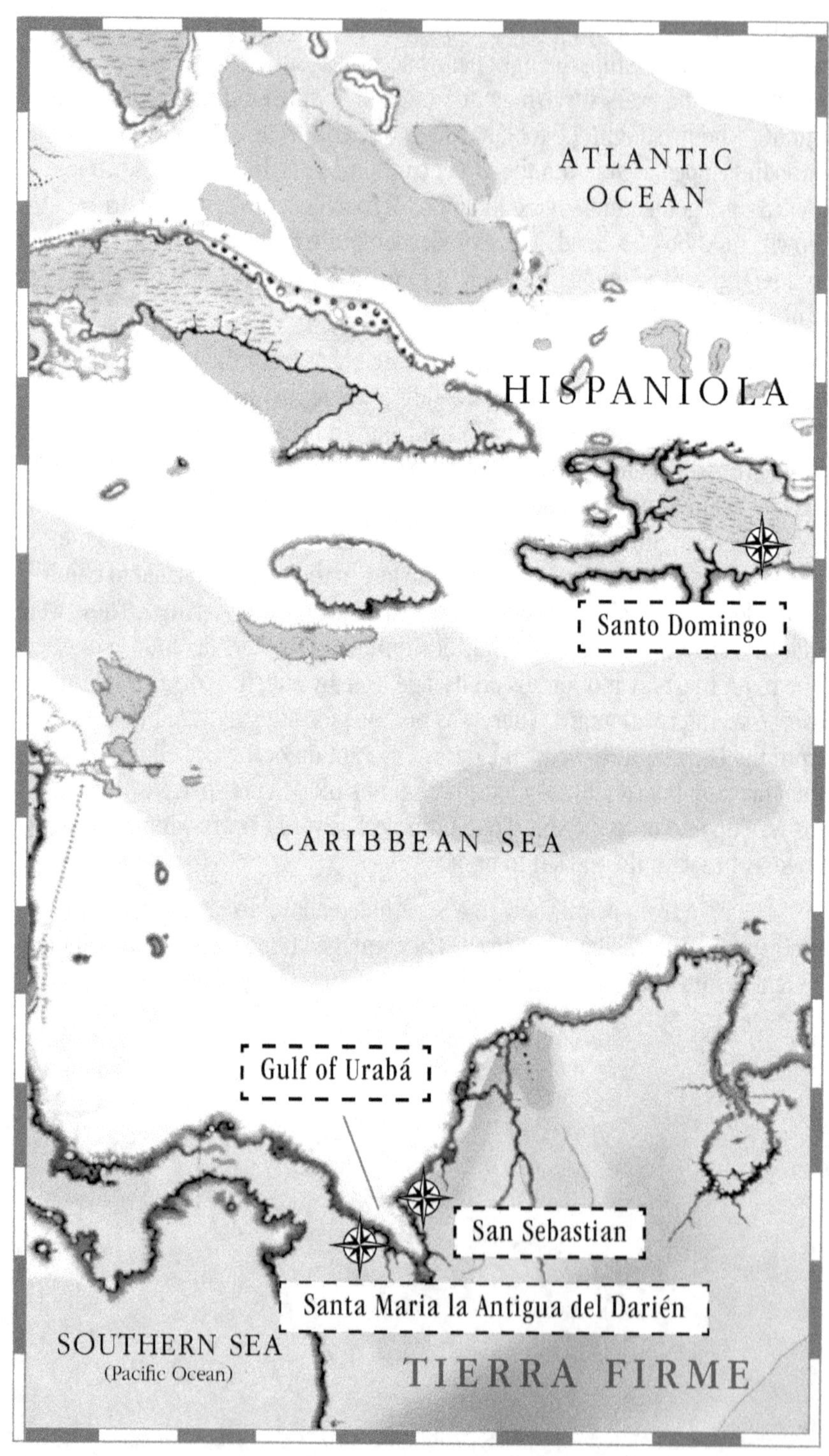

ATLANTIC OCEAN
HISPANIOLA
Santo Domingo
CARIBBEAN SEA
Gulf of Urabá
San Sebastian
Santa Maria la Antigua del Darién
SOUTHERN SEA
(Pacific Ocean)
TIERRA FIRME

Chapter Eleven

1509 - Onboard the Santa Maria - Caribbean -
Western shore of modern-day
Isthmus of Panama.

After considerable debate, the Bachelor agreed the best course was to proceed to an area Balboa described as native friendly where the Bastido expedition had traded most favorably, and the jungles were less formidable.

Captain Enciso's Santa Maria and Captain Pizarro's San Martín dropped anchor. No war party, no sign of natives at all was both a relief and a concern. No one spoke, they didn't need to. They all knew the instant they set foot on land a party of invisible natives could attack without warning. Yet, there had been a village here very recently. The jungles hadn't had time to consume it.

Two scouting parties searched the buildings, the nearby forest, and the abandoned fields. Comfortable that no immediate ambush awaited them, the two parties spent the next several weeks converting the abandoned area into what they claimed would be the first permanent settlement on Tierra Firme. Captain Enciso claimed and named the new settlement Santa Maria la Antigua del Darién. The settlers simply referred to their new settlement as Darién. Provisions would not last indefinitely, however.

Balboa's failed attempt at farming the past four years was not wasted. His hard-earned experience paid off. As Balboa organized the new colony, Enciso, a lawyer by education and an administrator by connections with influential members of the Spanish court, was overwhelmed. One decision after another displeased the new colonists, who for the most part were soldiers anxious to fight, conquer, and take the plunder. They did like to eat and thus when Balboa organized the farming, they followed his leadership. Large, cultivated fields were left behind by the village's previous inhabitants.

As the months passed, scouting parties ventured into the dense jungles seeking both gold and striving to learn about the native population. Minor skirmishes with small bands of local natives ended harmlessly. They found no gold.

After two months, three relief ships arrived with provisions sent by partners of Diego de Nicuesa in Santo Domingo. Upon learning Nicuesa had not settled there in Darién, the captains of the relief ships in concurrence with Balboa, who over the months had demonstrated far more influence with the men than Enciso, chose to sail north in search of Nicuesa.

With provisions and more colonists to help bear the burden of the promising harvest, and the realization they were not alone, the small community sensed a possibility of success. Though the natives had yet to create problems, the heavy oppressive heat daily extracted its wages for civilizing its shores. Disease took its toll. In the first month, nineteen men became sick of what they called jungle rot, only three survived. By the end of the second month, thirteen more were buried in the nearby plot named Jungle's Revenge.

Chapter Twelve

1509 - Santa Maria la Antigua del Darién (Darién)

Shirtless and barefooted, Alessandro pulled the invading vines from the edges of the furrowed field. It was one of six fields left bare of crops when the previous inhabitants abandoned the settlement. Balboa claimed the fields had grown maize previously. The stocks of corn grew fast, in less than two months it was reaching Alessandro's shoulders. But the vines also grew quickly. Without regular tending, the vines would quickly smother the crops. Leoncito waited patiently for his cherished friend to finish his duty and go play.

At last, the two launched back into the jungles. They bounded through the thorny underbrush. Also on the march were caravans of leaf-cutter ants toting their banners of bright yellow membrillo flowers. The jungle was lively this morning. Howler monkeys barked and chachalacas blasted forth their deafening cry. The noise of the jungles bounced through the cuipo trees that towered into the canopy.

Something moved in the canopy above him. He gave up trying to count how many different birds inhabited these jungles, but this was not a bird. It crawled rather than flew or jumped. It was fur he spotted. Grayish-brown fur covered the whole body. Alessandro climbed the tree as quickly and silently as he could. He was now just feet away. The fur grew darker on the animal's throat. He hoped it was the throat because what he thought was the head was not much bigger than the neck. Its face was pale compared to the dark fur on the forehead and sides. Though he thought he was still, the creature paused and looked directly at him. It moved so slowly, Alessandro didn't worry that it was afraid, nor that it would suddenly spring at him. A dark stripe of fur ran beneath its eyes. The fur looked so soft he was tempted to reach out and touch. That thought vanished when the creature reached toward Alessandro with its three long toes. They looked more like claws than toes or fingers. The creature pulled a large leaf from the limb supporting

Alessandro and drew it into its mouth and kept chewing.

Far below, Leoncito watched quietly and patiently. When Alessandro gave commands, Leoncito obeyed. And this time, silence was the command obeyed. The slow-moving creature soon lulled Alessandro into boredom. He scooted down to Leoncito waiting patiently. With Leoncito, Alessandro felt no fear in these jungles.

Only a few days ago, Leoncito warned off Alessandro's fearless adventuring with a low growl. The growl was unnecessary. Alessandro saw the moving fur of the large spotted cat. The jaguar paid no attention to Leoncito or Alessandro. It had more important prey on its mind. The two carefully trailed the cat as it tracked a large cavy rodent, the capybara. The large piglike capybara was in a party with several others, slowly rummaging in the dense grasses along the edges of a small calm opening in a river that Alessandro had not explored before.

Alessandro soon lost interest in the jaguar and its soon-to-be breakfast. Some three or four hundred feet across the water, he saw several natives fishing in the slow flowing shallow river. He knew if the jaguar changed its mind and wanted a slender brown boy for breakfast, Leoncito would let him know, and would certainly let the jaguar know this particular brown boy was not on the menu. Alessandro's interest was in what he hoped were new harmless friends.

Carefully, Alessandro dodged pit vipers and poison ants. He gave wide berth to the spiny trunk of the sandbox tree, whose sap caused the blindness of two of the soldiers who mistook its pumpkin shaped pods for fruit. Following the painful rashes and blindness, both soldiers died. Regardless of the sandbox tree's healing properties Balboa described, all the settlers decided they'd stay clear.

Alessandro paused in a blind where the natives would not see him. He sat and watched. Three young natives he guessed to be not much older than he was, were spearing fish. None of them wore clothing, which was not new for him. Back home in Hispaniola, some of the few surviving native clans remained outside the Christians' efforts to civilize them. Balboa laughed at the friar's efforts to convert the natives and teach them modesty.

As Alessandro watched, he envied their apparent lack of fear and inhibitions. They looked like family or at least friends. Something he never experienced.

His father was a powerful black Spaniard, his mother a native Tiano. They were thus hated by both peoples. But not by Balboa, who was now

Alessandro's only family.

As he watched, movement behind the three young fishers caught Alessandro's attention. Not because of danger, for Leoncito didn't move. A young woman, possibly three or four years older and at least a foot taller, cleared the jungle and joined them. Her long black hair flowed over her shoulders and accented her shapelier figure. Alessandro's lungs sucked in a bug when the beauty of the naked woman caught his breath. He choked it out and dove to the ground to evade their notice.

He waited, heart pounding, hoping a poison dart wouldn't be his next surprise. He preferred to be eaten by the jaguar. Nothing happened. Howler monkeys screamed above him as if telling him he was doomed to die, or the coast was clear. He waited for a warning from Leoncito. Leoncito was more interested in the jaguar.

Alessandro kept his discovery to himself. He knew the soldiers were well aware of the many bands of natives scattered in these jungles. One tribe who appeared not to be a threat began a correspondence with the soldiers within the first few days. One of the contentions within the ranks of the soldiers was their desire to find and conquer the natives and take their gold and provisions. Enciso showed a cool head and, at the urging of both Balboa and Pizarro, chose to strengthen their own position before putting the settlement at risk. Pizarro already suffered the destruction caused by an angry local population. He wanted the wealth as much as the others, but having lost ninety percent of his men in San Sebastian, patience was wisdom. But not for long. As weeks turned to months, patience waned.

Alessandro returned to the river many times hoping to encounter the natives, especially the older girl. Each time he sighted a member of the tribe, he tried to follow and find their village. They were too swift and cunning. He wasn't sure if they knew he was there or not. He hoped today would be the day. He followed the previous path toward the river as he did each day. Whereas weeks ago the spotted jaguar crossed his path, this time it was bronze skin and long black hair. It was she. He wanted to get closer. Wanted to look into her eyes.

She stood, her back toward him, a long lance in her hand. Like a flash of lightning, the lance flew into the river. Just as fast, a large pipon dangled from the lance's sharp tip. Leoncito, anxious for a bite, made a slight whimper but remained at Alessandro's side. The girl turned. Both dropped to the ground and remained motionless. Minutes passed. It seemed like hours. His hand rested on Leoncito keeping him silent. It was late in the afternoon.

The howler monkeys were silent, and the countless flocks of birds seemed to hold their breath as well. It seemed the only sound of the jungle was his pounding heart.

He lifted his hand from Leoncito's neck and began to stand. A familiar growl, almost imperceptible to anyone else, shot shivers up his back. He turned. Ten feet in front of him stood the girl, dart ready to fly from the reed she held to her lips. Her fiery black eyes burned into his. He froze. Leoncito saw the figure but didn't feel danger, for he froze in place as well. She lowered the reed, looked directly into his eyes and, like a ghost, disappeared.

Thunder clapped, shaking the whole forest. Instantly, a bolt of lightning blasted through the jungle forest, shattering one of the giant trees to splinters. Alessandro's thick black hair stood straight up.

In the many months living in Darién, as the men began to call the settlement, they had regular storms. It was a tropical rain forest after all. However, this storm seemed to grow faster and harder. Back on Hispaniola, Alessandro's family lived through a hurricane that nearly destroyed the island. He was too young to remember much, but he did remember how his father assured they would be ok, and his mother held his shaking little three-year-old body.

No mother and father were here this time. Alessandro, Leoncito at his side, charged through the jungle toward Darién. A torrent of water plunged through the canopy. Streams, easily jumped over earlier, became rivers. Alessandro held tight to Leoncito's neck as the bounding hound plunged through the powerful deluge. Both boy and dog lost their footing. The wet fur became slippery. With all his strength, Alessandro tried to grip his hands around Leoncito's neck. The power of the growing river was too much. Water and mud broke the pair apart.

Swimming was not an option. Alessandro tumbled over and over. Broken branches, stones, and logs battered his body. With what he thought might be his last breath, the torrent plunged him under. There was no up or down, just spinning, rolling, bouncing. Something pushed hard against his neck, forcing his chin against his chest. The breath he held exploded from his burning lungs. Expecting his next breath to be mud, his lungs filled with air and rain, powerful, almost painful rain rinsed his face clean. His eyes blinked open as Leoncito dropped him to the ground. Even as the storm continued to pound, the mighty animal stood above Alessandro, sheltering him from the worst of the driving rain.

So often Alessandro explored shirtless, with only a pair of trousers that reached his calves. The shirt he wore this time saved his life. Unless, he thought, Leoncito had grabbed him without impaling him with his giant teeth. He reached up to the collar of his shirt. It was not torn. Maybe the dog did control his mighty jaws. Why not?

When they reached Darién, the crops, so promising, littered the colony. The fields were washed clean. There would be no harvest.

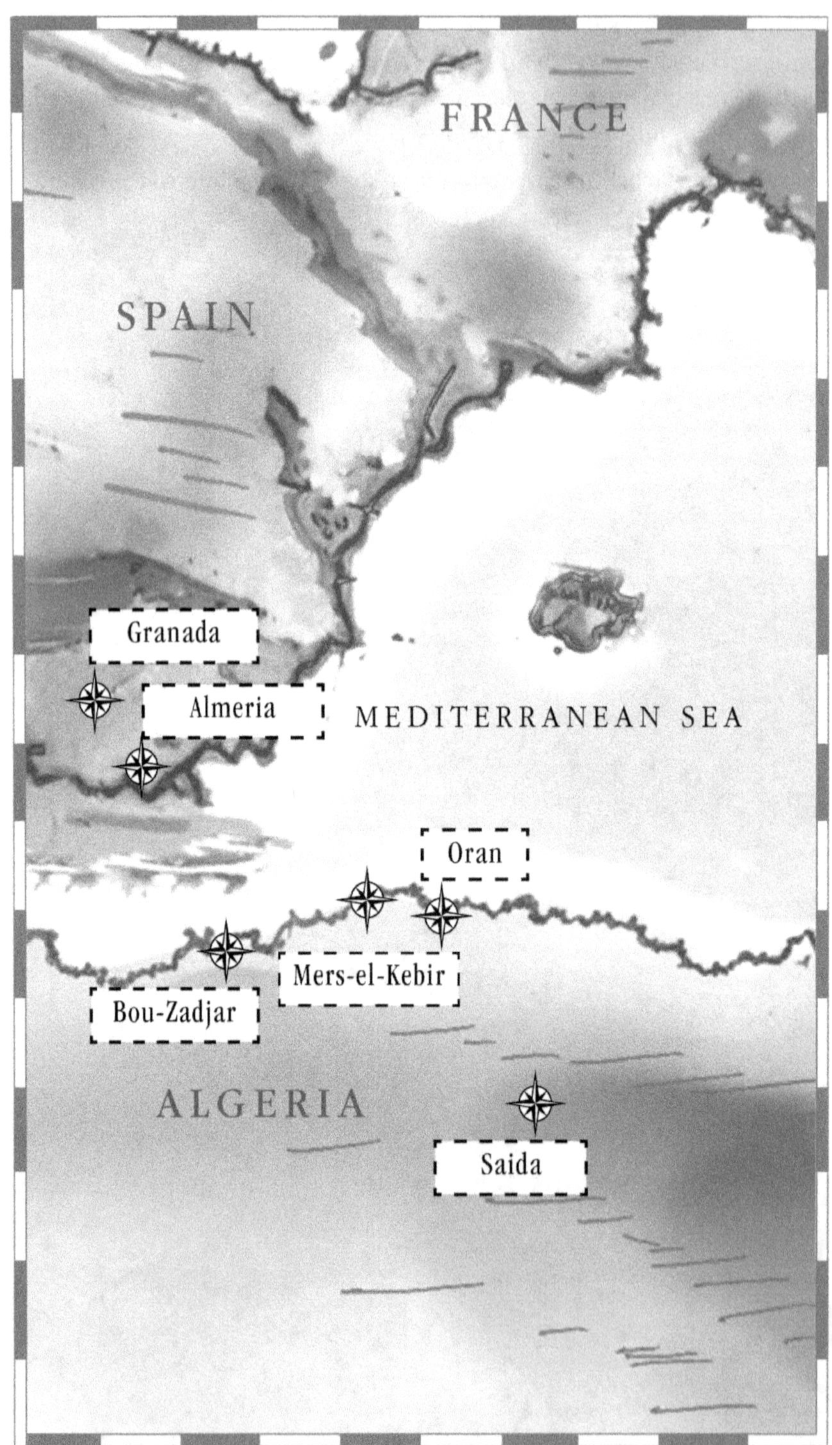

FRANCE
SPAIN
MEDITERRANEAN SEA
Granada
Almeria
Oran
Mers-el-Kebir
Bou-Zadjar
ALGERIA
Saida

Chapter Thirteen

1509 - Mediterranean Sea

Cisneros stood resolute as the sinking pirate ship became nothing more than a speck on the horizon.

Was it God's will for the heretic to die so easily? Maybe jailing the archbishop was enough for God's justice. Maybe his languishing in prison was God's will. Maybe keeping Miguel from reaching the Pope was enough. Maybes flooded his mind and slowly melted his anger. What did God want? Did God want anything? The answers never came. He finally turned his attention to what he wanted God to want, and that was the conquest of all of North Africa. He would conquer the unbelieving Muslims, convert them to Christ. That was God's will. He released his grip on the railing, allowing blood to return to his fingers.

He climbed up the stairs to the helm and faced the captain, who stood next to his helmsman. "There is a change of plans. I am not going to Rome," he said to the captain.

The captain just spent a week trolling the Mediterranean as bait for the very pirate attack he just fought and won, and now the cardinal demanded more. He stared back at the cardinal, who did not see the ice in his eyes.

"You will leave me at Mers-el-Kébir. We will part company there." Cisneros made the statement as a fact. Not a request or a demand. He then turned and proceeded below decks and retired to a cabin he had taken from the captain's first mate.

There was no objection. The helmsman looked to the captain for instructions. The captain motioned with his head toward the African coast. The helmsman set course toward the northern coast of Africa and more roaming Barbary pirates, to Spain's sole foothold, the recently conquered Algerian city of Mers-el-Kébir.

"At least we will be free of the unbearable cardinal," the captain said. It wasn't much of an excuse for sailing back into harm's way, but it was all he had.

By the time the Isabella disappeared into the eastern horizon, the nineteen surviving oarsmen climbed up on deck, breathing the first free air many of them may have breathed in years. Miguel took a quick mental inventory. With five dead slaves and the slave master dead below, he counted another twenty-three bodies severely hacked to death lying still on the deck, blood painting its surface dark red. He couldn't guess how many men might be lying on the bottom of the sea. But the battle was a complete rout by the crew on the Isabella, his Christians. He didn't blame them. This ship lacked the leadership and the manpower, or much less the intelligence, to attack such an overpowering target as the Isabella.

He turned to the men standing motionless behind him. Looking from face to face, he saw they were just like him—wrongfully put under another man's dominion.

He started with Castilian, "Are any of you of Castile?" Not even a motion of a head. "Aragonese?" Another answer-less inquiry. He tried Basque, his mother tongue, though not a one of them looked fair enough to be Basque. "Basque?" Nothing.

Then in Arabic, "My agreeable companions, share with me your homes of origin that we may enjoy our fellowship in the next few hours before we swim with the fishes." Smiles climbed into about half the faces. He turned to his large bench companion. He nodded. And asked with one word, "Home?" The blank stare registered the question but gave Miguel to wonder if he was mute rather than just unable to communicate.

"Mali," a tall slender man with bulging forearms motioned toward the man.

"Mali," Miguel said. The man nodded. Mute.

Miguel looked back to the tall man. "Israel," he said. Miguel repeated, "Israel? Do you have a name?"

"Joseph," he said.

"A fine Hebrew name," Miguel said as he bowed in appreciation for the candid response. Being a Christian, he was the minority here, but maybe he shared that title with Joseph.

He went around the group and learned these men represented the many countries in northern and central Africa, as well as some of the eastern Mediterranean lands. He even had an Ottoman. Miguel wondered how each of these men's stories brought them to this fate. A fate none of them chose.

He leaned past the tall man, looking into the western horizon. He squinted, closed his eyes, wiped them clean, and stared again. The speck was definitely not a sparkle created by the late afternoon sun. It was a sail. And it was growing.

"Gentlemen, we may have company." He pointed west with his head. The men turned, and for several minutes watched the sail grow. Then, as innocent children, looked back to him. After all, he was holding the sword and the snake-like bullwhip. And he spoke languages most of these men didn't know. Miguel realized he was captain of this sinking ship. He leaned down and pulled a shirt from a man with a severed leg lying in his own blood, and pulled the shirt over his shoulders. Fortunately, little of the blood stained the shirt.

The sail continued to grow. Still speaking Arabic, the lingua franca of this ship, Miguel encouraged the men to gather weapons and prepare for whatever this unknown visitor might intend. With the galley filling with water, the foremast cracked, and the mainmast down, all they could do was appear to be strong. Miguel wanted to laugh. What could they do? Fight for the right to be left alone to drown?

The ship slowed, struck sails, and coasted alongside the galley. Two hooks thrown expertly over the side secured the two ships together. Miguel stood, open stance, somewhat blood-stained shirt, ragged trousers, bare feet, but defiant and courageous in every way. Again, he wanted to laugh at himself. At any other time, he would be willing to fight. It was Talavera who insisted he run. A disastrous choice.

Miguel stood facing the new ship's captain. The deck was at least four feet higher than the slowly sinking deck of Miguel's only ship he had ever captained.

This was a time he wished to be eye to eye. The captain's eyes were nearly as captivating as Sukayna's. A woman captain! A striking woman. Black braids fell from under the corsair's cap, which was edged with a white fur Miguel didn't recognize. The tight black leather jacket was open in the front, allowing her generous chest and white silken ruffles to betray her stern pose. Around her waist was a woven silver belt. The tunic that hung freely from beneath the belt was also black, but not leather like the jacket. The tunic stopped halfway down her calves. Black boots met it there and tightly followed the gentle curves of her calves down to her ankles and feet.

She stared at Miguel, assessing his situation. It surprised Miguel she was not laughing. Certainly, he and his new little army of soldiers held no threat.

A soft whisper bounced from man to man. "Al-Hurra."

Miguel knew that name. Everyone who sailed the western Mediterranean knew that name. Right now, Miguel felt maybe drowning might be the better of the few choices he had left.

"Are you the captain of the Little Goke?" she asked.

So that was the name of the ship. He never asked. The Little Goke. He supposed the Big Goke was somewhere faring much better, and she asked in Arabic.

"I am," Miguel said. He hoped he sounded confident.

"Are you the Christian?" she asked.

The Christian? Why not a Christian?

"The Christian?" he repeated.

She reverted to Castilian. "Yes, the Christian. I assume since you look nothing like these men, and you speak at least twelve words in both Arabic and Castilian. You must be the Christian."

Did she know about his kidnapping?

She did not wait for his answer. "I assume you are." She looked around the deck and seemed to count the bodies. She motioned with her head toward the carnage. "You seem to be as poor with the sword as I was told." A very slight motion of her gloved hand pointed to the whip hanging from the belt he took from the slave master. "Are you any better with that?"

Miguel's confusion held his words at bay. He only nodded.

"I am trying to decide if you live or die. You are not making it easy. I understood you could speak. You seem to be as mute as the man next to you."

She quickly pulled her whip, gave it a crack, and sent its biting tongue flying toward Miguel. His whip was off the hip and free so quickly, the two tangled in mid-air. She gave it such a quick yank she pulled Miguel to his knees. He dropped the sword to the ground to catch his balance. The two untangled, and another crack announced a second attack. Miguel ducked, rolled to his feet, and launched a sting toward this woman. She met it easily. This time Miguel was sure-footed enough he stood strong as the two tangled whips stayed tied together. He did not know if he should pull and try to dislodge her stance or just watch her play out her hand.

She smiled. "Very good. I accept your surrender. The Little Goke is taken. Bring your men on board. You are now all mine. You belong to me. I have work for you. If you succeed, I will grant your liberty and you can be on your way to Rome; and in a proper ship."

With a reverse twist of her hand, the whips freed themselves. She coiled hers, then motioned to one of her men to get the men off the sinking ship. Miguel stood so shocked it took Mali to push him toward the ship. Coming to his senses, he rushed to the sinking captain's cabin, which had taken one ball in the early cannon volleys. Debris was scattered everywhere. But with a quick search, he grabbed the fine boots given him by Sukayna, along with the tunic and turban. With arms full, he was the last one off the Little Goke.

Al-Hurra was gone when Miguel cleared the rail and stood firmly on deck of al-Hurra's ship. Not a single sword was drawn. They escorted his men to sleeping quarters rather than a hold or brig. Everything felt wrong. A ship of corsairs captured his ship. His ship? He laughed to himself. She accepted my surrender? It was more a rescue, or maybe a recruitment. He kept the whip and the sword. He turned and watched blood mix with sea water as the Little Goke succumbed to the pull of Neptune.

"Which God saved you?" It was a voice Miguel knew. He closed his eyes, bowing his head as it shook.

"Was it your Jehovah or my Allah?" the voice continued. Miguel was certain that voice was accompanied by the eternal smile. Miguel slowly turned. A rescue, he concluded.

"I prayed to them both. You are trouble enough, it needed both gods," the voice said.

There stood Jalaf. The eternal smile filled his face. Miguel wondered if he should use the whip on Jalaf or hug him. He looked Jalaf up and down. This was no longer a Morisco. Jalaf stood as a full royal Morrocan. Yet a colorful one.

Cascading out from under the white turban flowed a bright yellow cape, reaching halfway down his back. Contrasting the bright white shirt, a bold red vest hung partially open. Hanging over his shoulders, a deep blue cloak reached just inches above the deck. Vibrant yellow blousy pants matching the cape tied tightly at his ankles and covered the tops of rich black boots. Miguel, a galley slave, captured by the notorious al-Hurra, the woman pirate, standing barefooted, with a borrowed blood-stained vest and filthy pants, had no right to make a comment. He did anyway.

"You look like a peacock. Where is Sukayna when she is the most needed?"

Miguel wouldn't have imagined it possible to fit any bigger of a smile on Jalaf's long, narrow face, yet his comment scooted the remaining cheeks aside to do so. It was as if Miguel gave Jalaf the ultimate compliment.

"And you, my friend," Jalaf began, "need Sukayna more than I. Come with me. We will get you cleaned up. Again."

The 'again' was a deliberate addition. Miguel's association with Jalaf may have begun weeks earlier, but he had never learned enough about him to understand the meaning of this reunion.

"Very cunning, to secure the kurbash from the slave master. I feared you might embarrass me, though. With some practice, you might master it," Jalaf said.

Miguel followed Jalaf below decks, still confused by how small he could feel under Jalaf's casual insults. *Jalaf has no idea how proficient a whipmaster I am. He's never seen me use a sword,* he thought. *Al-Hurra thinks me a fool with one. Yet, I did become captain of my own ship, and surrendered it the same day. Who is this Jalaf?*

Jalaf opened one of two large, finely carved doors. He pointed inside and said, "You will find this more agreeable than your previous accommodations. I will return after looking after your men." He pulled the door closed after Miguel entered. *My men?* Miguel shook his head.

Miguel had not actually seen himself since long before abandoning Talavera. In the large, polished mirror hanging securely against the paneled wall, he looked himself over. *Disgusting.* He never favored much facial hair, preferring to shave as often as possible. But his several weeks of growth, and the finely trimmed beard wore by Jalaf, encouraged him to keep it. When he did sport a beard, it was thick and almost as curly as his soft brown hair. He washed up quickly, dressed in the wrinkled but otherwise clean clothing provided by Sukayna. Was he to wait here or go looking for Jalaf? After all, he was a slave, captured at the hand of the terror-of-the-western-Mediterranean. He had never been on a pirate ship, other than the one on its journey to the bottom of the sea. It surprised him at its fineness. Jalaf kept good company. He was obviously connected to al-Hurra. She did not fear Miguel or his men.

Jalaf seemed to have his own cabin. Thoughts and questions raced through his mind.

On the wall next to the door hung a sword arsenal. Miguel admired the hilts of several highly polished swords. Each one hung with care to accent its particular style. The cutlass was naturally the center of the collection with its curved blade and cup-shaped guard, but to its right and left the dao and the dadao hung like brothers, hilts wrapped tightly in matching black leather. The scimitar hung directly above the cutlass. That is odd, he thought. But what stood out like an adopted stray was the falchion, a long single-edged, single-handed sword with its quillon'd cross guard for the hilt. He wanted to lift it off the wall and give it a swing or two.

What was missing from the collection was the Nimcha with its long, curved blade so common in Morocco and Algeria. With his assumption of being held captive on a North African pirate ship, he found it interesting there were no short swords or daggers so commonly worn as a secondary weapon for close fighting.

A knock startled him, interrupting his admiration of the display.

Jalaf entered the cabin, eternal smile and all. "Do you like my sister's collection?"

Like a bleating lamb from a hungry wolf, all thoughts of swords immediately fled the cabin. Miguel turned to Jalaf so quickly he almost lost his footing.

"Your sister's collection?"

"Of course, it is her cabin. You will figure it out soon enough. I assume you are more alert and wise than any indications have showed so far. Although your quick act of taking the kurbash from the slave master was a good move. It saved you embarrassment with the sword."

"Your sister? Al-Hurra is your sister? I am in her cabin?"

"Maybe you are not that sharp. I tell you now, so you will not discover the truth around your men and ruin my reputation. It is a truth you and I must protect."

Miguel stood stunned. "You said your family…"

"They became refugees. Expelled from Granada. Where do you think refugees go?"

"You converted?" Miguel asked.

"They baptized me. You know very well how that works for us Moors and the Jews. In fact, I believe one of your men is Jewish."

"Joseph?" Miguel asked.

"That is good. See, I am right. You are wise. Getting to know your men and their origins. That way, you will know their allegiances, their motivations, their tendencies, and who you can trust."

"Do you trust me?" Miguel asked.

"Not yet. But you are a simple man and Archbishop Talavera trusted you, and I trust him."

"I may not be as simple as I appear."

"No?" Jalaf said. "Are you hungry?"

Miguel nodded.

"You are simple enough. Follow me. The captain wants you to dine with her," Jalaf said, stepping over the threshold into the hall.

Miguel took a step toward the door. "Does she know?"

Jalaf never turned. "That you are simple? She will soon enough."

"That I know she is your sister." Miguel nearly reached exasperation.

"Of course she does."

Of course she does? Miguel struggled to fathom the entire circumstance. He quietly followed Jalaf above decks.

The evening sun launched orange, red, and yellow sparkles dancing across the wake of al-Hurra's ship, the al-Namir, which calmly cut a path through a relatively calm sea. Several of the former galley slaves were on deck assisting other crew members. They looked content doing so. Their cleanliness showed they too transitioned from slave to crew. Their clothing varied as much as Jalaf's. Not so colorful, but certainly not to the par of Sukayna's standards. Many of the men were shirtless but with flowing blousy pant tight at the ankle. The color variety declared loudly they were not cut from the same bolt of cloth. Most of the men kept their beards, but they were now clean and trimmed.

What kind of ship is this? A floating bazaar? Was all this plunder? Who on board had the skill with barber shears? Miguel asked himself these questions and felt he might do for a little cleaning up. As Miguel passed, the men al-Hurra indicated were his, they acknowledged him with a respectful nod. Was it Sukayna's outfit or that somehow they credited him for their good fortune?

Arriving at the upper deck, the captain stood peering off to the south. Faint evidence of land gave her the bearing she was looking for. She turned to face the two men as they approached. She also took advantage of the time to freshen up following the great capture. Miguel wondered if she had a second cabin.

She stood taller than Miguel thought earlier. When they wrangled with the whip, she was standing on the deck several feet higher than him. He had no way to assess her height. Her long black hair hung loose and tickled the light gray fir of either a very large fox or a small wolf, which gave its life to comfort her shoulders. A long, flowing blue tunic was gathered at her waist by a wide brown belt which accentuated her bust and hips. Hanging from her belt was the short sword he noticed missing from her cabin. The sheath was trimmed in gold and diamonds. The hilt, small as if designed for a petite feminine hand, rivaled the sheath for beauty. From elbow to wrist, leather armbands let the sleeves of the blue blouse out up to the shoulder and under the fur. She was feminine enough with the deep dark eyes and her olive skin framed with fine textures. It would almost be worth it for a fly to join the spider for dinner just to see her up close before dessert. The quick thought raced through Miguel's mind. If these two are brother and sister, they do not use the same valet.

"Sayyida al-Hurra, at your service," she said, bowing to Miguel. Her open palm invited the men to sit. Miguel's suspicious eyes never left hers as he sat.

"My brother tells me you have important business with Pope Julius in Rome," she said. "Are you helping him with his new war or his new basilica?"

"Your brother is correct. A bit of a misunderstanding landed me here in your fine company," he said, not leaving her gaze. He wanted to say her brother betrayed him and sold him to foolish and incompetent pirates, so he could afford the ridiculous wardrobe he wore, but he held his tongue.

"That misunderstanding is fortunate for us both," she said, waving for a steward to deliver three fine plates of breads, cheese, grapes, and roasted chicken. He then delivered three vessels full of wine. She motioned to eat. Between bites, which Miguel took slowly and intentionally to mask his raging hunger and to savor each bite, he said, "Fortunate? This fine meal and the company is, yes, fortunate. For me…now.. anyway."

"There was no time. As you learned in Granada, immediate choices are often required. You prepare to make a choice throughout your life. Once you make the choice, there is seldom an opportunity to choose again. In this world, the wrong choice is usually your last one. You are usually dead. Ask Qasim, captain of the Little Goke." She left that statement to marinate a bit.

Then she continued, "Ismail is a cousin of mine. He alerted Jalaf that our common foe waited for you at the Isabella."

Miguel thought it was Cisneros who came into the galley as the Little Goke was sinking. Being trapped under the beam, his view was blocked enough, he could not bring himself to believe it. Now he did.

"Ismail made a decision. He sold you to Qasim. Qasim was greedy and foolish. By the gods I found you."

"By the gods?" Miguel nodded toward Jalaf.

Sayyida smiled, "Well, gods must work with what they have. Sometimes they cannot be choosy. My brother knew Qasim valued his new prize enough not to damage you before reaching the flesh markets in Algiers. Jalaf came to me to reach Algiers before Qasim."

"A prize?" Miguel repeated between careful bites.

"A Christian, strong, fluent in Castilian and Arabic. He did not care you are not much with a sword, but he did not know your surprising capacity with the kurbash. Despite that, yes, a prize."

Miguel choked back the continued misconception about his swordsmanship. Sayyida winked at him. Did she believe Jalaf's claim?

"It was by the gods that we came across the Little Goke. You and your men will help me with a minor problem and then I will see personally to your safe arrival in Rome and an audience with Julius."

A minor problem. How minor? Miguel wondered.

Miguel's subtle probes into the nature of the minor problem met with more cunningly subtle misdirection. This Sayyida al-Hurra is very artful, he concluded. Too many questions crowded his mind, so he settled on an easy one to end the evening's discussion.

"Ismail chose quickly to sell me to pirates. Why not warn Jalaf to hide and wait for another ship, or leave from a different port?" He wanted to ask her why her wily brother did not just bring him directly to her.

"Cisneros' spies watched the entire transaction. An actual kidnapping, bargain, and product delivery were essential. I believe it possible the Isabella lingered in the open to lure Qasim and the Little Goke just to insure your death. Now, free of you and the threat of your meeting with the holy pontiff Julius, Cisneros has no interest in Rome. His interests lie in expanding his personal conquest of all Northern Africa and the wealth he gains by plundering villages, capturing natives, and cattle. He and the Isabella will be at Mers-el-Kébir, not at Rome."

Miguel's mind finished the race a single step ahead of this cunning queen of the western Mediterranean. He realized the minor problem she mentioned earlier consisted of a sea battle, and land war against the mightiest military in the Mediterranean.

Chapter Fourteen

1509 - Mediterranean near Bou Zadjar - Algeria

The next morning, despite sharing a luxurious cabin with his peacock of a rescuer, Miguel's fitful rest brought him no peace. The ship sat at anchor in the small harbor of Bou Zadjar. Al-Hurra presented a plan to the ship's crew, which now included Miguel and his men. Miguel realized the plan was put into action long before even Talavara's arrest. The inclusion of his additional men gave the plan a new twist.

Surrounded by her own well-rehearsed and outfitted men, numbering about sixty-seven as Miguel counted them, along with his tiny army of emaciated former slaves, al-Hurra stood confidently. She looked from face to face. She was their general. They loved her. Miguel watched the connection. She would not be a pirate for long. One day, she would rule far more than a floating stage. He felt it. When her eyes eventually met Miguel's, she began.

"Miguel, you will be my captain on the ground. With your men, you will rescue fifteen hundred men and women snatched from their homes to be sold as slaves. The Spanish captured Mers-el-Kébir to bring Christ to the people." She smiled at her mocking words. "They plunder villages. They claim the humans they enslave bring the people to Christ."

This talk was no surprise to Miguel, but it still bristled his skin. The Moors and the Jews had plenty to grieve about. Too many times those griefs reached a combustion point, and like gunpowder exploded. Al-Hurra seemed to sense Miguel's bristle, and she pulled back on her tone.

"Cardinal Cisneros and his generals are creating great wealth at the cost of the lives of our people. In recent raids, they have taken some fifteen hundred captives to be sold as slaves, and nearly five thousand head of cattle for the meat markets." Miguel loved how animated her hands became as she spoke. When she said the numbers, her tight black gloves gave each finger its own freedom to accentuate the facts. "From Mers-el-Kébir, they also launch attacks on Oran, which, if they capture, the Oran harbor will strengthen their foothold in my land."

All eyes remained fixed on her every word. Her intensity was not an act. She looked like a general in every way. Dressed in nearly all black, her cap lined with reddish fox fur was the only variation. The textures varied, giving her definite form. The shine of black leather on her wide girdle that rose from her hips accented the soft linen blouse that complemented her bosom. Her sleeves, also black, buttoned down the outside. From her fur-lined cap, the long black hair hung comfortably, framing her deep olive complexion. Now in the morning light and not being threatened by immediate destruction, Miguel recognized she was a young woman not much older than he was and, fortunately for her, she looked little like her younger brother.

Al-Hurra planned to connect with several other pirates, including Khayr al-Din, to create a small armada to attack Mers-el-Kébir from the sea. Miguel realized al-Hurra was deadly serious when she said her rival-partner was al-Din. In Granada, al-Din was referred to as Barbarrossa who's name rivaled al-Hurra's in striking fear in Mediterranean mariners.

She finished her show, and it was a show. Miguel liked her plan, with only one exception. That being his responsibility to take his tiny conscripted special force and battle the ruthless North African sun while they trek across country visiting villages to recruit tribal warriors to the cause of rescuing their own friends and family members savagely taken by the Spanish. He held out little hope. After all, if there were tribal warriors willing to fight, would they not have done so when the Spanish attacked?

Al-Hurra gave Miguel and his men four weeks to make the hundred-mile trek down through the vulnerable tribes around the Sebkha of Oran, the inland flatland salt sea. It was obvious to Miguel that al-Hurra didn't fear an attempt by Miguel and his men to escape. On foot, with only enough provisions to carry out the mission, escape into any direction would result in their capture by tribes who would likely re-sell them into captivity. As a condemned fugitive he couldn't run to the Spanish in Mers-el-Kébir. Miguel's challenge was to become a chameleon and be whatever he needed to be at the time.

"All she has been waiting for was the right bait," he whispered to himself as she outlined the plan. "Jalaf's call for help provided her the bait she needed. She has no intention of us surviving this rescue. The rescue of just another legion of slaves? Did she care about them? Who better to serve as a distraction to Cisneros and the royal army than the heretic?"

He saw the clever strategy. He himself, now slipping from Cisneros' grasp twice. Nothing could be more tempting. And if the Isabella and Cisneros were in Mers-el-Kébir, al-Hurra could not have planned it better. The complication was Miguel's overland trek from Bou Zadjar to Mers-el-Kébir, around Oran's Sebkha salton sea.

Chapter Fifteen

1509 - Algeria, North Africa

As Miguel's men left al-Hurra's ship, they practiced with sword, sling, whip, and even hand-to-hand combat. Various skills were evident as they practiced—skills they brought with them from their various native lands. He hoped these few days wouldn't be just the light before a very dark storm when they reached Mers-el-Kébir.

Miguel started with his mute former bench companion he called Mali. Fed, clothed like a warrior, and unchained, Mali's sheer presence demanded respect. His deep black skin shined in the morning sun. He held his pike and sword with confidence. A test of his agility and response to a little sparing with Miguel proved he could be taught and had some natural ability.

Joseph, Miguel's sole Jewish soldier, was an early victim to the conquest of his Iberian homeland by the Christians. His resentment for the treatment of his people fueled an intensity that easily compensated for lack of actual physical skills. Joseph's native Hebrew intrigued Miguel as it had when he and Cardinal Talavera taught among the villages where remnants of Joseph's people remained. Though Miguel never mastered Hebrew as he had Arabic, he knew enough so that he and Joseph could communicate crudely.

Each of Miguel's tiny band of warriors brought with them a history of mistreatment and loss of identity, family, and hope. In his years with Talavera, he saw the mistreatment between the Spanish Christians and the Moors and Jews. The clash was not between Christianity, Islam, and Jewish religions, or theology. It was the age-old battle over control and domination. Religion was only the weapon of choice. Miguel was well aware of the conquests where the Muslims conquered centuries before. Liberty was always the first thing lost.

Talavera insisted the conflict was never between Christians and Muslims, nor was it between Muslims and Jews. It was between good and evil. Evil was the manifestation of one people thinking they were superior to another. Those people then felt they could control others. Talavera told the stories of Jesus, no home, foxes have holes, he said. He was creator of the world, yet condescended to be born in a manger, grew up in the trades, became a carpenter, his earthly father eventually died. He dined with sinners, the poor, the lame, and the humble. Now the earth is His footstool.

Jesus taught, I want you to be like me. Miguel asked himself, in serving al-Hurra, would I be like Jesus? Yes, because I would be serving the least of these—the captives.

Miguel thought back to Christ's parable about the wise king. Talavera taught the parable with such passion, yet in all his studies, Miguel could not find it in any of the four gospels.

There was a wise king with a peaceful and prosperous kingdom. The people of the kingdom lived in peace one with another, even traded and supported each other in good times and bad. His people prospered, their flocks and herds flourished. His people were a good people. They served God. But neighboring kingdoms prospered less. Their kings levied heavy taxes and built great palaces and the people suffered. Their kings and priests taught the people that their suffering was the fault of neighboring kingdoms. They became jealous and angry. From time to time they waged war. But the armies of the wise king always prevailed.

The wise king grew old. He saw how good kings ruled with honor and loved their people and the kingdoms prospered. He also saw how a wicked king can rule in wickedness and his people suffer.

Instead of appointing one of his sons to rule in his stead who might turn to wickedness, he organized his people to rule themselves. This was unheard of. "How could they rule themselves?" his people cried. "Appoint a new king" they said. The wise king taught his people that by the voice of the people they could chose good men to be judges. He reminded them how the neighboring kingdoms suffered at the hand of wicked kings. He taught that by the voice of the people, they could make laws—laws recognized and accepted by the people. And when these laws were violated, the people's judges could mete out just judgments.

The people organized. They chose their judges. They created and accepted the laws. They continued to prosper. But the day came for the wise king to die. He requested his people to gather. When they had gathered, he told them of his love and trust. But he gave them a strong warning saying, "Only a good people can rule themselves. No laws made by man can long preserve the liberty you will enjoy. It will be your own wickedness that will take your freedoms from you."

When Miguel asked Talavera about what happened to the kingdom where people governed themselves, Talavera simply said, "When the people obeyed God they prospered, and when they did not, they suffered." Miguel wondered if a people like that existed and if they did, could they ever govern themselves.

Then he wondered how these men, each with their own particular lives seemed to look to him as their trusted leader. Could they govern themselves? Were they actually governing themselves, by choosing to follow him?

Then he thought back to his time with Jalaf, who Miguel now realized was an incredibly astute spy and agent for whichever entity suited himself at the time. In al-Hurra's plan, Jalaf would slip into Mers-el-Kébir and assess the friends and the foes. Miguel wondered what costume might give him the most invisibility as a spy. Likely a new brightly patterned one representing the fine parrots of the southern jungles.

If Cisneros' forces were powerful enough to capture fifteen hundred native tribesmen and take upwards of five thousand head of cattle, as al-Hurra claimed, he knew there was no hope his little band could attempt a rescue. An attack would be nothing more than suicide. But if al-Hurra was successful with her assault from the sea, he believed with the help of God something miraculous might happen.

Miguel and his little band began their trek toward Mers-el-Kébir. With each village they encountered, his anger grew. The invading Spanish forces looted communities with no thought for the surviving residents, who usually consisted of the old and the infirm. Supplies to replenish his own provisions, were scarce. In the second village, several of his men imparted small rations of their own food to a group of elderly women left to starve.

With each day, the urgency to rescue the captives and return them to their homes grew. Miguel sensed the compassion of his men. He grew up yearning to fight in the great conquests. He had taken every opportunity to learn from masters in every discipline of battle. Regardless of how Jalaf assessed his skills, he felt competent enough with his sword. Yet he did not fight personally in the conquests of Granada. Sometimes he wondered if Talavera recruited him years earlier as a personal guard to keep him out of the battles. Yet, Miguel's ability to quickly master the local languages of the people he and Talavera served was more valuable to Talavera than his skill with the sword.

The little band of warriors seemed more like ministers than warriors with each plundered village they visited. Ahabib, Miguel's sole Egyptian, stopped to help a bent old man with a bundle of sticks. Ahabib became a galley slave when he was sold to an Ottoman merchant because his family failed to pay a required rent on a farm of pomegranates. Ahabib bowed in reverence and said, "Shaykh muhtaram, my esteemed elder. We come seeking help to free your countrymen. Are there any men here able to join with us?"

Miguel was not close enough to hear clearly, but he understood enough to know this village was like the others and had lost its able men to Cisneros' purging the country of so-called heretics and paying for the invasion by selling the heretics as slaves.

Ahabib led several of his fellow warriors to a small freshwater river that wound its way from the hills of M'Sila. They fetched water and filled large pots for the few remaining residents. Two aged men stood at the open door of a whitewashed mud building, which looked to be a gathering place during earlier times. Up and down the long row of short buildings, old men and women stopped and watched the visitors.

Ahabib approached another short, bent grandfather who waved him close and, with the help of a roughly carved staff, tilted his head back enough and looked up at Ahabib. Ahabib waved at Miguel to come listen to what the old man was saying. Listening intently, Miguel and Ahabib made new plans.

Week after week, they fought the oppressive heat. The little band finally reached the Saïda, a fertile valley on the southern slopes of the wooded Tell Atlas Mountains that rose steeply from the valley floor. Saïda was fed by the Wadi Saïda, the small river which wound its way from the forest through the fields. This community seemed alive. Men were in the fields, a small market bustled with activity, children ran and played. Desperation, they felt in other small villages, no longer hung in the hot summer air.

As Miguel's men entered the small community, the people looked on, well aware of visitors, yet they showed no fear. That surprised Miguel. His nineteen strangers, armed with swords, pikes, and kurbash, entered a place where safety could not exist. Marauding tribes, pirates, and armies had left their mark all across North Africa. Why not here?

The answer came soon enough. Three tall black shiny Arabian horses, mounted by black leather clad warriors casually entered the road cutting off Miguel's men. The warrior in the middle calmly sat with reins loosely in hand, as if he were ready for a nice chat with a friend. The two men on each side were less relaxed, each with a bow and arrow nocked and ready to pull.

No wonder the people were at ease, Miguel thought. With protectors like these, a ragged, tired misfit band of whatever Miguel's men might be, they were no match for these horsemen.

Miguel bowed. The slightest commotion behind him caused him to turn and look. Three more warriors, also on horseback, stood behind them. And three more on each side. Miguel's little band was not only surrounded, but they were also clearly out matched. How long had these men been watching or following? He knew it was unlikely they just showed up at the villagers' beckon call.

"Why is a Christian leading an army of…" The leader looked from man to man, just as al-Hurra had, assessing the virtual threat. "What is this band?" he finally asked. He knew there was no threat. Not giving Miguel a chance to answer, the warrior to his left raised the bow, pulled the arrow back, and let it fly at Miguel. Just as quickly, Miguel pulled the whip from his belt, let its tail free, and snatched the arrow from the air mid-flight. The rest of the men stood in shock. Both at the flown arrow and Miguel's quickness and accuracy.

"Well done, Christian," he said. "Why are you here disturbing my people?"

"We seek your help," Miguel said, again bowing. The tail of his whip laid relaxed on the ground.

"My help?" the man said. "Yes, I can see you get some food and direct you back to…" The horseman looked back at each of the men. It had now been several weeks since they had been freed from the ship's galley, but they had not yet escaped the fallow look of a slave. They were not so emaciated as Miguel thought they might look, being underfed, but their sinewy muscled arms and shoulders had yet to become fleshy from good food and relaxation.

"Back to your conquest," the man finished.

Miguel raised his head and confidently looked the man in the eyes. "The pirates Sayyida al-Hurra and Barbarrosa lay siege to Mers-el-Kébir. Some fifteen hundred of your people are held captive along with thousands of cattle. This small band is all there is to return your people and their cattle to their villages."

"My people?" The man smiled. "They are not my people. Look around you. These are my people. If I help you rescue a people you so mistakenly call my people, who will protect these, who are my people?"

Miguel recognized he held no justifiable grounds other than pity for making the request for help. Talavera held deep personal beliefs that there is only one people. All were God's sons and daughters, and the responsibility of Christ and His life on earth was to unite all the tribes, nations, and cultures into one in their worship of the Father. Talavera taught sermons about unity both public and private. Yet, he was not blind to the fact there was not unity among the priors, priests, bishops, and cardinals; even the archbishops were divided. Now here, Miguel realized he was trying to unite one people with another. What a fool, he thought to himself.

Miguel coiled his whip and secured it to his belt. "Forgive my ignorance. May I learn from you the skills to protect any people from the despots of another until we may unite in peace?" Miguel hoped this request made sense. He worried it sounded rather altruistic, too lofty; unite in peace? He slowly shook his head.

"You impress me with your words. I understand each one. But I have no idea what you just said," the man said. "You, a Christian, want to free the villagers taken as slaves by other Christians and you beg the help of Muslims to do so?" He motioned for the man on his right to loose another arrow, which he did. But the arrow never reached Miguel who did not even try to defend himself. Quick as lightning, and as unexpected, Mali snatched the arrow from the air.

"You want me to teach you?" the man said. "Why should I?"

"My friend lies in prison for teaching Christ to the Moors in Granada. He is the Archbishop Talavera. He is held captive by another more powerful archbishop, Francisco Cisneros, because my friend will not force the Moors to convert and worship Christ instead of Allah. I seek an audience with the Pope in Rome to free my friend."

The man turned to his men and said, "Bring them to the mosque." He turned his horse to leave. Mali stepped forward and offered the arrow back to the second archer. The archer snatched it from him and rode away.

Two horsemen escorted Miguel's men through the village. It was built alongside the river, which at several points sent small falls cascading over rocky outcroppings. The village of Saïda enjoyed a coolness from the many trees and the tumbling waters. It in itself was an oasis, a stark contrast to much of the area they traversed over the past many weeks. Miguel feared the siege promised by al-Hurra would be long over by the time he and his little band ever reached Mers-el-Kébir.

"Here you shall wait," the horseman indicated, then he galloped off.

The large grassy area was fed by a small tributary that wound its way through the wide flat expanse of a beautiful, lush forest. It was more a natural garden than a forest. Several rock buildings surrounded the meadow-like area. Cultivated fields could be seen through the trees, which provided enough shade but didn't crowd the open welcome feeling. The men found comfort relaxing along a shaded wall that sat just tall enough to serve as a bench. The peaceful air was only disturbed by the sound of a collection of goats being urged through the garden by two small boys chattering to each other about some game they would enjoy once they completed their chores. Miguel smiled at the boys when they gave him a curious look and then went back to their own concerns.

A man with a slight limp crossed the grassy area accompanied by a young woman who appeared to be not much younger than Miguel. They pulled a small cart carrying a clay pot and a basket covered by a brightly woven linen cloth. The man bowed to Miguel and offered him a cup, then with a long-handled scoop, filled the cup with crystal clear water from the pot.

"I am Abu Ahmad Zayyan. I welcome you to my home." He continued offering each of the men the refreshing water. The young woman followed behind him, carrying the basket and provided freshly baked breads and goat cheese.

"This is my daughter, Fáthima," he said, introducing her with great respect. "She is one most gifted with the tasks of home and field."

Each man thanked both Abu and Fáthima as they received the much-needed refreshment.

Abu looked the men over. He spoke to them as a group, though he stood nearest to Miguel. "You look like a collection of ocean shells washed upon the shore and collected to ornament a table." He paused and smiled to accent the comment as a favorable one. "Led by a Christian?" he nodded to Miguel, "and a Jew," he motioned to Joseph, "Egyptians," he looked to the stout black Mali, "deep African," then looking toward three men seated on the ground, "and Ottomen?"

Miguel shook his head ever so slightly and said, "Very good."

As quick as lightning, and more surprising, Abu pulled Miguel's sword, which hung on one side of his belt. He cut the leather tie that held the whip on his other side, and it dropped to the ground. The man held the sword to Miguel's chest. The men were in such shock none dared move. Mouths full of food gaped open in stunned silence.

Just as quickly, Abu tossed the sword in the air, catching it by the blade, and offered the hilt to Miguel.

"And harmless," he said, smiling. Not a word was spoken by any of the men.

"If I am to make you ready to fight, let us start now." He reached into the cart and pulled a shiny Nimcha with its long-curved blade. He handed it to Joseph. He then lifted a longbow from the cart, tightened its string, grabbed several arrows, and handed them to Mali. Mali smiled so broadly Abu laughed out loud.

Then he pulled a whip and held it like a master. He motioned with his head toward Miguel's whip lying on the ground. Miguel picked it up. With another motion of the head by Abu, Miguel set his sword into the cart. Abu stepped back a few paces and loosed the biting tongue. It snapped and snarled as it flew. Again, as quick as lightning strikes, Abu's whip bit the tip of Miguel's ear pulling a drop of blood with it. Miguel touched his ear in shock and looked from the blood on his fingers to Abu, whose raised eyebrow invited Miguel to challenge him. A second quick strike bit at Miguel's shoulder. He stepped back, brought his whip to life, and deflected the next attack. The two men swung, dodged, snapped, tangled, and untangled, each landing a successful nip here and there. Miguel received two or three painful bites for every one he delivered.

The rest of the men stood motionless watching the duel. It was fast and fluid. Miguel felt betrayed by the skills he had been so proud of over the years. He felt Abu was playing with him and could have delivered serious injury at any time. There was no fury. He realized the limp and apparent fragility of the older man was a ruse. Abu was a seasoned warrior, a master, yet he was the one left behind to care for a hodgepodge of former slaves. Sweat dripping from his brow, Miguel welcomed a nod from Abu when he coiled his whip to end the duel.

"Well done," Abu said, then turned to Mali who held the bow like a precious crystal vase. "Now you." Abu took Mali's elbow and turned him around facing a tall woven cloth draped over a bundle of what looked like straw. Abu motioned for Mali to draw the arrow and loose it at the cloth. He did so, and the arrow found its home in the center of the cloth. Mali smiled at Abu and then Miguel.

"Thought so," Abu said. "You do not speak?" Mali shook his head. "Tuareg warrior?" Mali nodded. "Taken captive in battle, they made you mute and sold you?" Mali nodded. Abu handed him another arrow. Mali landed it gouging the side of the first arrow.

Abu said, "I cannot do anything with that." He turned to Miguel, "You will learn from him."

Abu motioned for Joseph, who stood holding the Nimcha, its blade glistening in the strips of light cutting through the trees. Abu reached into Fáthima's nearly empty basket. He tossed a small loaf toward Joseph, who easily caught it square in the middle. The loaf sliced in two, and Joseph quickly struck one half in pieces again before it hit the ground.

Abu looked at Miguel. "Galley slaves?"

Miguel just raised his eyebrows and shrugged. "I never said that."

"How else would a Christian gather this band of misfits? Each has the signs. Their hands, their backs, they scream a galley's life. You do not." He pointed with his eyes toward Miguel's un-callused hands. "You speak perfect Arabic, and I guess Castilian. Hebrew as well?"

Abu motioned toward Joseph. "Salim, the man you met in the village, could not decide if he should kill the Christian or not. He will expect my advice when he and his men return," Abu said.

"Did Salim tell you why we are here seeking his help?" Miguel said.

"I want to hear it from the Jew."

Miguel, in his somewhat broken Hebrew, asked Joseph to come closer. Joseph held the Nimcha loosely but confidently and approached without arrogance or fear. Joseph started in rough Arabic, but Abu stopped him with an upraised hand. In fluent Hebrew, Abu and Joseph conversed as casually as two old friends. Joseph related the journey to Abu, who paid particular attention to each word as his eyes scanned the men, how they stood and listened, taking in their mannerisms, reading each one.

Miguel paid close attention, understanding Hebrew better than he could speak it. Abu asked why a Jew would follow a Christian when the Christians not only drove the Jews from the Iberian Peninsula but now the Moors as well.

"He is not a Christian," Joseph said flatly. Both Abu's and Miguel's eyes opened wide at that statement.

"No?" Abu said.

"Just a man," Joseph said.

Abu went from man to man, assessing each for their strengths and weaknesses. To a man, Abu identified areas where this little band could become a unified team. They were not all warriors, nor could they all become so. Two somewhat tall Central Africans displayed no skill with weaponry. Abu walked with them from the grassy meadow, he led them to a small corral with six beautiful wild horses, jet black. He left the two men there and returned to the group.

"Tuareg tribe. Tuaregs are masters with the horse," he said.

Evening came and Salim had not returned as Miguel thought he would. Abu led the men to a covered platform with nothing more than eight tall posts supporting a roof made from thatch much like most of the structures in the village, but with no walls. "You will remain here tonight."

Abu left the men and the weapons he provided. Fáthima brought another large basket of food, including breads, dried meats, and cheeses. The men ate quietly.

The men woke to find another basket with food. With it was a goatskin bag full of wine. By mid-morning, they all cleaned up at the river's edge and were becoming restless when Abu, his limp more noticeable than the day before, came from between two whitewashed buildings pulling the cart. Mali quickly stepped forward to pull the cart, relieving him. Abu motioned for the men to follow him. They crossed a stone bridge and ascended from the river's edge, and reached a plateau where a stream wandered aimlessly back and forth, creating small patches of brush and grass. Several of Saïda's residents were hard at work clearing rocks and redirecting the flow of the water. Miguel paused to watch how the residents were efficiently irrigating the field. Abu directed various pairs of Miguel's men to join in the work.

Miguel wondered if the time on the galley stripped these men of their independence. None murmured. They joined in the work seemingly without objection or question. Throughout the day, Abu returned and escorted pairs of his men away and put them to work on other tasks. Until he took Miguel and Mali late in the afternoon, Miguel's resentment was growing, sensing Abu's abuse of a new brand of slaves who had voluntarily submitted to domination.

Abu ignored Miguel's questions about what Abu was doing with his men. They entered a long narrow building with no covering on doors or windows. A slight breeze blew through making it comfortable. Then Miguel recognized this new work was part of a larger plan. Abu introduced Mali and Miguel to Haynid, the craftsman responsible for making the bow and arrows that Mali so appreciated and demonstrated the day before.

For the next several hours, Haynid patiently taught Miguel and Mali the craft of making these fine weapons.

When evening came and the men united again at the meadow, they recognized each set of men were put to work in the manufacture of weapons, and their use by weapons masters. Miguel realized he was directed by God to Saïda not for warriors, but for weapons and training. Does God care about weapons? Miguel wondered. What does God expect us to do?

The routine continued day after day. Joseph and the Egyptian spent their days at a forge crafting a variety of swords. Joseph told of the hard work, but proudly showed the Nimcha he made. Abu assured Joseph it now belonged to him. The skills his men were gaining in the manufacture of weapons and their use from various masters from the village, were paid for by their service in the repair and development of the lands and buildings.

Chapter Sixteen

1509 - Saïda, Algeria, North Africa

Days became weeks. The men were well fed, respected, and productive. Miguel learned about the men's backgrounds, their trials, and how they'd been taken from family and home and put into servitude. These were not all innocent victims. Several admitted to the justice having been sold to pay the price of their crimes, some which were committed in desperation, others by greed. They were becoming a unified band.

He wondered if the siege promised by al-Hurra began and had ended, if the fifteen hundred captives were already on slave ships bound for places unknown, or if Jalaf was back in Granada with Sukayna finding another victim to send off on a wild journey. Miguel's desire to get to Rome hadn't waned. Yet he didn't feel he could abandon these men and find his way to Rome, nor were his goals their goals. Each of them certainly wanted to return to their homes. In the evenings as the days wore on, the men became more comfortable with each other. They talked of the future, of the day, and Miguel watched as they celebrated each other's success. He had never seen such a diverse group. They represented seven nations, five languages, and at least four religions, yet they united with one another on a mission none of them actually comprehended. Miguel was still trying to compose some vision of what this little band was supposed to do.

Several times, Abu assured Miguel and his men that soon enough they would know. Yet Abu insisted he himself waited for Allah to make His will known.

Several more weeks came and went before Salim and his horsemen returned. Abu was ready to disperse Miguel's men to various chores for the day when the horsemen arrived. The sun rising behind Salim made him an unsettling vision. He and his men appeared to have ridden through the night. They all looked well worn, and the horses breathed heavily. Several were lathered from a long, hard journey. Salim dismounted and almost instinctively, the two Tuareg stepped forward and took the reins without any resistance or encouragement from Abu or Salim. Several other men dismounted, and the horses were led away. Miguel thought it odd the men trusted their mounts to these strangers.

"You trust these men?" Salim asked, quickly turning as he realized his horse had just been led away by some of them.

"They are all we have, but they are ready," Abu said flatly.

Out of breath, Salim said, "The Spaniards have captured and will sell thousands from tribes along the coast. They are preparing an attack on Oran to seize the harbor. We can cut the legs out from under them if we act fast. Are there fresh mounts?"

Abu's smile, powered by the pride a teacher has for a star student, accompanied a wink at Miguel that said, "This is what we have prepared for. At last, Allah will be with us. Allah expects us to do our part."

Abu led Salim and his men across the rock bridge and up the trail toward the higher meadows the same way the Tuareg led the spent horses. They approached three sturdy corrals containing several dozen magnificent pitch-black horses. Four beautiful white mares ran free down a long pole-fenced field.

Miguel's men spent many days up with these majestic animals. These Arabians were good natured, high spirited, and alert. Miguel recognized why Arabian horses served so well in raiding and war. They were easy to handle and they recognized the competence of their riders. Though they were somewhat shorter than the Andalusians Miguel grew up with and admired so well, they were powerful and strong. Many times over the past weeks, Miguel contrasted his more muscular Andalusians with their long flowing manes and tails and their elegant movement to these beautiful Arabians, which seemed to understand their job was to get to work. Abu insisted that having been bred for speed and endurance, these desert horses would embarrass his Andalusians if given the chance.

Miguel liked Abu. He was comfortable. Many times, they contrasted the lives they each lived, the histories of their peoples, their individual approach of worshiping God, the injustices Miguel's Christians perpetuated on the Jews and the Moors. Yet, Abu recognized his people were not immune from the challenges of tyranny and despotism. Was there a people free from such a history? They talked about Cisneros' injustices against Talavera. More than one discussion ended with Abu challenging Miguel's loyalty to a church whose leaders competed with one another for power and riches. They agreed that men from all kindreds tended to dominate one another when possible. That is what kept Abu's people employed, he jested, war. The constant need for horses, weapons, and battle skills.

Salim stepped into the corral, took a steely eyed stallion with both hands by the jaw, and stood face to face touching his forehead to the broad forehead of the horse. He ran his hand down the neck. The sun reflected off the smooth handprint as it worked its way down to the shoulders. Salim was bonding with this horse. Salim looked over to the Tuareg who stood watching every move like a mother watching out for her toddlers. He smiled and nodded to the two men who had obviously been caring for the pride of Saïda. Miguel's men learned early on this tiny village was a respected source for the finest horses in North Africa. These several dozen with which Miguel's men worked were just a few of the many being bred and trained in the surrounding fields.

"You came to my village seeking my help," Salim said as Miguel and the other men reached the tall rails of the fence and watched Salim's men admire the horses they obviously helped breed and train.

"I did," Miguel said.

"Abu says you are ready. Are you willing to fight your own people to rescue mine?"

Miguel knew this was exactly what was required of him when al-Hurra extended the bargain to free him and his men if they helped her rescue captive slaves. He prepared these many weeks to answer that question for himself. Now, he answered it to the men he knew wondered within themselves.

He looked Salim in the eyes. The man stood with his arm resting on the shoulders of the magnificent beast, fingers playing with the short mane. "I do not fight my own people; I fight for the right of men to be free. Tyrants are not my people."

That very afternoon, after preparing man and beast, the small cavalry wished farewell to the many friends they made in Saïda and rode north toward Oran. Surprised but pleased, Miguel rode side by side with Abu, who selected one of the beautiful white Arabians as his mount. "This is a battle I want to watch," he said. "It will be a testimony to my ability to make something out of nothing. Like your Jesus making fine wine from water."

Miguel had no response, but recognized Abu was well read. Where did he learn of Christ?

Abu continued, "You are a complex man. Unlike any Christian I have known." Abu kept his eyes forward, looking into nothing. The horses, at a light gallop, sensed enough of the momentum and purpose they needed little direction. Miguel sensed Abu concentrated his thoughts on his companion.

Miguel rode a gray stallion, light gray front legs, neck, and mane. Both back legs faded from medium gray to nearly black tail and hocks. Its gait was smooth and rhythmic. Miguel looked over at Abu and back to the trail ahead of them. They left the fertile well irrigated farmlands and began their trek up the Tell Atlas Mountains. Miguel didn't respond to Abu's statement. It wasn't a question.

"You hope your Pope will liberate your archbishop. What if he refuses?" Abu asked casually.

Miguel looked over at Abu. This time, Abu expected a response. He asked another question before Miguel could answer. Miguel pondered that question himself from the very moment the archbishop made the request.

"How do your Catholic leaders differ so much on such fundamental truths?" he asked.

In the many discussions over the past many weeks, that question had risen countless times in one form or another. Yet Abu never received an adequate response. Miguel didn't have an adequate answer.

Salim estimated it would take four days to reach Oran. He and his men took only two days returning, but the toll on his horses was too great to repeat and then expect a performance once they reached Oran.

Accurately predicted, late on the fourth day, the small calvary reached a summit and looked down on the walled city of Oran. In Saïda, Abu spent several evenings during their preparations, describing the battles where the Spanish conquered the city of Mers-el-Kébir from the local Algerian Zayyanid dynasty a few years earlier. When Abu described the treachery of Cardinal Cisneros and General Pedro de Ruiz, Miguel recognized he and Abu had a common foe. Abu was part of the ruling Zayyanid family. Badly wounded in the battle for Mers-el-Kébir, Abu retreated to Saïda and created the small deadly mercenary force led by Salim, a force now joined by nineteen free men. Abu had a horse in this race, as Joseph described it.

BRITAN
BAY OF BISCAY
FRANCE
Zoirtza-Bolibar
SPAIN
Pamplona
Barcelona
Granada
MEDITERRANEAN SEA
Almeria
ALGERIA
MOROCCO

Chapter Seventeen

1509 - Pamplona, Basque Country, Navarre, Northern Spain

Maria's elbows rested on the back of the colt. With a hand on each side of the letter, she read it once again. Her fiery brown eyes refused the tears begging to fall. She leaned the letter back and looked past it to the messenger. He was a vibrant young Gitano she traveled with when her passion for adventure drove her from the Extremadura two years earlier.

"When?" she asked.

The way that one word escaped her lips told Vano the answer would complete a puzzle her mind would quickly solve.

As the oldest son, Vano would soon lead the Gitanos. He proved himself astute, cunning, and charming. Oh, what he would give to keep Maria with his clan.

"Three weeks, maybe four," Vano said. "You are going, I feel it." It was a statement, not a question.

Maria folded the letter, tucked a long rebellious strand of her walnut brown hair behind her ear, and stared back at Vano. A tiny smile began to form. The corner of her bottom lip pinched between teeth. Her eyes darted from the letter to Vano's eyes. "Am I going alone?" she asked.

The question was answered. He knew it. He knew he could not let her go to Rome by herself. Vano did not need to protect her, but it would be kind to protect those who might trouble Maria along the way. Certainly, she was still quick with the blade. He smiled inside, remembering how she took to the short blade when a sword master traveled with his Gitano family one summer. Besides, it had been a few years since Vano visited Rome. It would be nice to see it again. Rome was teaming with opportunity.

Yet, there was no adventure in Rome to exceed that of a thousand-mile journey with Maria. His family of Gitanos prospered as they traveled through northern Spain. Their colorful wagons, brilliant dancers, their food and music drew locals from the dreariness of daily labor to the entertainment of the nights, infusing their drab lives with splashes of vibrant color, exotic foods, and tales of the world. And Vano's father, with his deep powerful voice, could entrance the children. He could teach the word of God with fantastic stories about enormous floating ships that carried every animal in the world, of a young boy slaying a giant with a sling and a single stone, and God destroying whole cities of people who refused to worship Him.

Many a clergy member envied Vano's father's ability to captivate audiences with stories from the Latin Bible; which, of course, was against the law for a non-clergy to possess. The clergy often brought local constabulary to disrupt the Gitano camps. Yet even with Ferdinand and Isabella's efforts to expunge such undesirables from the united kingdoms of Aragon and Castile, the vibrant Gitanos flourished in this the Northern Basque Country and Navarre.

"Will you require a chaperone?" Vano asked.

"Can I trust you with my virtue?" Maria shot back.

Vano was reasonably certain that even traveling a thousand miles together, he would have almost no chance of turning her heart to him. In all his efforts the past several years, they became so incredibly close, yet he could never penetrate her heart. It was locked. He envied the man who might one day unlock it.

"Do you believe I can behave?"

Her smile relaxed, her teeth released the lip, and a tiny wink set the plan into motion.

"By land or by sea?" he asked.

"Do I get Andixpi?" she asked.

"Andi? You ask too much."

Andixpi, shortened to Andi, was the pride of Vano's family. She was a tall, fast chestnut mare. Andi's dam foaled her the night Maria joined Vano's family. Being raised on a horse farm in Extremadura, Maria naturally helped when a complication required a quick hand to turn the foal during the birth. Vano's father offered the foal to Maria, but she declined. Maria did offer to give the new arrival the name Andixpi after her mother, who died years earlier. Feeling the new filly was too valuable a gift, combined with her own personal insistence in maintaining independence, she never wanted to be indebted in any way to anyone. Because of this, the request to borrow Andi would be a complement to the family.

Maria and Vano arrived at the Gitano camp in the valley outside of Pamplona. Vano's father joyously hugged Maria, nearly squeezing her breathless. The release was as welcome as the gentle embrace from Vano's mother.

"Father, before you ask, no, I have failed again. Yet, there is hope. It starts with you lending Andi to Maria for a short ride," Vano said.

"A short ride?" he asked.

"Well, to Rome, then to Granada, then home," Vano said.

"Ah, will that give you time to make my Maria our daughter-in-law?"

Maria blushed, even though this was the ongoing banter between father and son. There was no doubt Maria was a favorite of both men.

"Rome?" Vano's mother asked.

"Cisneros," Vano began, "he arrested our Cardinal Talavera for heresy. Only Pope Julius can demand his freedom."

"Talavera requires this of you, Maria?" Vano's mother asked.

Maria opened the letter and read, "I am sorry to ask of you so great a task. My dear brother Hernando is being held by the Cardinal Cisneros. His personal guard, along with all the friends and family, are under arrest, including myself. We are to recant and denounce my brother or suffer the flame. The Bishop of Malaga delivered the writings of his scribe that condemn us all. Without leniency from Julius, Hernando will meet the flame also. By the time you receive this letter, my voice along with Mother's and Juan's, and our other friends will be silent." Maria paused, looked from the letter to each sober face, then continued, "The letter is signed, Magdalena Talavera, your dearest friend."

"But he is the Archbishop of Granada, appointed so by Isabella herself!" Vano's mother displayed a passion rarely seen by the clan.

Vano's father calmly laid his hand on her arm. Addressing Vano, he said, "God wills this of you." He then turned to Maria and said, "You know Andi is yours. She has always been. She was given to us for this very purpose. If I could provide more than Andi, I would."

"What about me?" Vano said.

"I am sorry, my son. I have done what I could for you. I beg God for forgiveness in my failure."

Vano's mother released his hand from her arm and swatted her husband. "He means that you are offering your son to travel with Maria, which, too, is a generous offering."

His father turned to Maria with a tiny wink. "Is it too much a burden to care for my son on your journey?"

"I think I would quite like that responsibility," Maria said.

"Cardinal Cisneros has the ear of the monarchs and a power he will kill to protect. Make your plans known to no one. By this letter, it is clear the cardinal will destroy any who meddle in his plans," Vano's father said.

Maria loved listening to Vano's father. He was wise and calm. Mostly, he loved and feared God more than man. "The world will always produce men seeking dominion over others. There is nothing those men will not do to maintain that dominion. I leave you with my blessing. I feel this journey may be but a tiny part of God's quest to make men free. Not just one man, but all men."

Maria could not even fathom what that meant.

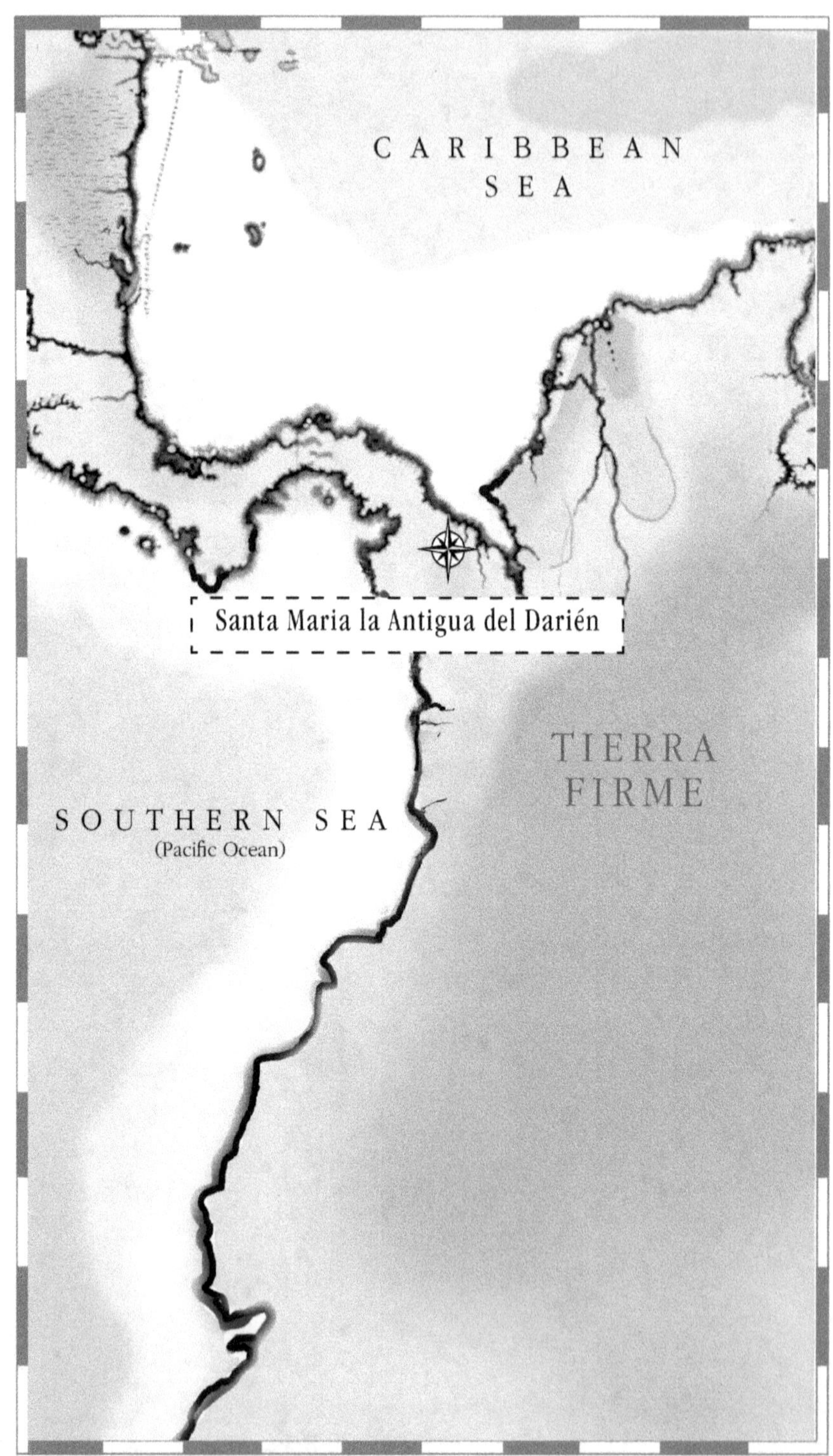

CARIBBEAN
SEA
Santa Maria la Antigua del Darién
TIERRA
FIRME
SOUTHERN SEA
(Pacific Ocean)

Chapter Eighteen

1509 - Darién, Eastern side of current Isthmus of Panama

Crops and hope were both washed clean by the storm. The flash flood also undermined the foundation of the fort and many of the houses. Optimism was as scarce as the gold. In the many months the company worked to establish a colony, there was no success acquiring anything but toil and death. Interaction with one local tribal chieftain turned up no gold or provisions.

As the weeks passed, soldiers became more restless. They had no interest in farming; they did not sign on to this expedition to be colonists. Provisions were now exhausted again.

Enciso had long since lost respect from angry soldiers.

"Now we know why this village was abandoned!" a soldier said. "The natives know they do not need to fight and die."

"Like Pizarro here said, they have all the time they want to wait and watch us die of starvation and the rot!" another said.

"With no crops and no hope, I say we leave!"

"I say we march into the northern village and demand their gold and food!"

Balboa stood, arms folded, silently watching a mutiny unfold.

"What are you thinking?" came the innocent voice. Balboa looked over to his two pups, both growing faster than he imagined.

"I am thinking it will not take much to light this powder keg," he said.

"The Bachelor will go wild and punish them if he hears this," Alessandro said. Balboa nodded.

"But who will he use to punish them?" Balboa said. After a few minutes of listening to the men carry on with bluster and threats, he asked, "What are you thinking?"

"They like you more than the Bachelor," Alessandro said. "If you want to stay, they will stay."

"Do you want to stay?" Balboa asked.

"I think so." Alessandro wanted another encounter with the beautiful young native girl.

Balboa unfolded his arms, stepped forward a few steps. "By the gods," he started, "if I have not heard a more short-sighted vision. You all want easy wealth. You left the hell of Spain to get rich and powerful. Well, me too. But the riches that come so fast, go so fast. Look at me. With Bastido, I became a rich man. No men died and it was all taken by worms and a wicked governor. Years later, my own debt forces me to hide in a barrel to escape prison. The great Columbus is cheated and sent back to Spain in chains. For what? Because the governor sent by the king to govern was a better thief and liar. And what did the king do? Removed the chains, gave him more ships, and sent him back. Riches come and riches go. Greatness comes when we conquer the land, this land. From this land, we will venture into fame, glory, and wealth."

"And Captain Enciso?" a soldier asked. "He is no more than another wretched Governor Bobdilla who will take everything from us and then take some more."

"We will not follow the man," said another.

The conversation stopped. Balboa's eyes left the soldiers. He squinted, focusing far into the northern horizon. All eyes turned to see what caught Balboa's attention.

The speck became a dot which became an object, then sails, and finally appeared the supply ship sent several weeks ago searching for Captain Nicuesa. All conversation of mutiny faded. The group made its way to the shore to welcome the arriving boat. Enciso and his tight group of loyal followers were already there.

Captain Gibson climbed from the boat along with six of his men. Two others, who looked sun beaten and shaggy, stepped free of the boat.

The captain bowed to Enciso and said, "Captain Nicuesa is settled well north in a failing colony named Nombre de Dios. We found these two no more than eighty leagues from here. They were left behind by Nicuesa during an expedition a year earlier. They have an interesting story."

The taller and thicker man spoke first. His shirt was worn and faded, his breeches equally so. Both men were due a shave. Balboa wondered why the captain had not cleaned these men up before arriving. The man spoke, "Our captain sent a group of us ashore to explore the potential for gold and to assess the native population. A storm separated our group and when we finally returned to the shore, Nicuesa was gone. None of his ships remained."

The second man, just as ragged, spoke with a slightly mumbled accent that Balboa didn't immediately recognize. "In d year, wa bin stranded, wa d only tu alive. Udda sevn dead."

Nicuesa left nine men behind and two survived for a year? Balboa found this extremely enlightening. Balboa knew Darién was officially in Nicuesa's promised territory. Thus, if Nicuesa returned, he would rightly be governor of a colony he had no claim to, other than because the king said so. He wondered if Enciso was thinking the same thing he was. How do we keep Nicuesa away?

It was clear to Balboa, Captain Nicuesa was as inept with his failing Nombre de Dios as was Captain Ojeda with his failed San Sebastian. Captain Enciso, right here in Darién, was no better. All it took was money and connections to get the great monarchs handing out titles and lands. And with those titles and lands come the ownership of the peasants and slaves that live and work on those lands. Balboa resented that he bought his own land in Hispaniola. He worked his land. And with a few servants, that he had to pay, he not only did not become nobility, he had to run for his life. Oh, the injustice.

"Pray, tell me," Balboa asked, "how do two fine gentlemen as yourselves survive this harsh land for more than a year?" This was a question he knew everyone wanted answered.

The taller stouter man simply said, "La Carreta."

"Natives?"

"Who knows how many warring tribes inhabit these jungles," the man said. "They hate each other. Only the Carreta were friendly. They are experts at crops, they hunt brilliantly, and they are rich."

Three words resonated with the gathered crowd. The first was friendly, the next was crops, but when the word rich rolled off the man's tongue, hope returned, and mutiny fled.

Chapter Nineteen

1510 - Santa Maria la Antigua del Darién

Alessandro sat cross-legged on a large stone jutted into the harbor. He counted the armored soldiers standing at attention along the shore. Sixty-three, unless the mosquito that entered his ear caused a miscount. A lone boat lowered from a newly arrived ship. Captains Enciso, Balboa and Pizarro met the boat at the shore. Two men climbed from the boat and the oarsmen rowed back to the ship.

Several more trips brought more men from the ship. The soldiers remained at attention on shore. Alessandro saw they were anxious for this command to be finished. He didn't know why they were so careful about who they allowed to land. Usually, new arrivals were welcomed. The boats stopped shuttling men to shore. None of the men coming to shore looked strong or healthy. Several needed help from the shore up to the village. Two soldiers carried a small crate of supplies from the settlement down to the shore. Once it was in one of the boats, soldiers rowed it back to the ship. Most of the soldiers relaxed and returned to the village.

That was the cue Alessandro and Leoncito needed to abandon their perch and wander away. Nothing to see. Maybe something to hear. He crept within earshot so he could hear Balboa.

"If we let him land, he will claim his royal-right to rule. Even Enciso knows we have not settled in an area where your Ojeda was given the grant. None of us are where we belong," Balboa said to Pizarro.

"Are there enough men loyal to him to enforce his threat to have us in chains?" Pizarro asked this, dismissing the threat. He shook his head.

"Give them enough food and rest and they may try," Balboa said.

"You are too trusting. The way he treated his men, there are not enough loyal ones to crush a turtle. Our men will be your trouble."

"Our men?"

Pizarro took a deep breath and positioned himself like a parent explaining a simple concept to a child. Alessandro recognized this posture. He knew it irritated Balboa, and it fueled the mistrust planted in his heart the first time Alessandro saw Pizarro.

"This is the first and only successful settlement on Tierra Firme. Climate and contention between ourselves are our only enemies. We acclimate slowly. Crops do not sustain growth. Conquests do not sustain the greed. I know. It does not sustain me. Anger becomes as oppressive as the heat," Pizarro said.

Alessandro expected Balboa to roll his eyes, but he didn't.

Pizarro continued, "The Bachelor rules with a firm hand and severe penalties. We can not even trade individually with local tribes. All plunder remains under Enciso's dominion."

He paused, took a deeper breath, and advanced the point of his lecture. "The men hate the Bachelor. You do nothing about it. He has no more right to this land than you or even I do."

Another breath, Pizarro continued, "If you let Nicuesa off that ship, your damned loyalty to the monarch will doom this settlement. Right now, I doubt how long my men will support your men, or Enciso's men. The only conclusion is to keep that man off my land."

Alessandro wanted with all his heart to know what Balboa was thinking. For one thing, however, this was a time Alessandro agreed with Pizarro. He did not even know this Captain Nicuesa. But everything Alessandro heard was that he was brutal and jealous because his settlement up north failed, and Darién did not.

Negotiations continued for several days. Soldiers patrolled the shoreline. Alessandro wanted time with Balboa but too much was demanded of Balboa's time. With things so tense, Alessandro found no enjoyment in the jungles either.

Two weeks later, a boat was loaded with supplies and rowed to a ship so small, many of the soldiers doubted its ability to even sail this far. When it brought a small group of settlers no one trusted it to ever make it back to Hispaniola let alone Spain. It had sat empty for months, so when the boat took supplies to it, Alessandro's interest piqued. He wandered to the shore. Eighteen men went from Nicuesa's ship to the small one. They hoisted sails and the ship disappeared into the horizon. Alessandro had not immediately noticed, but several dozen men appeared alongside him watching it vanish.

Captain Nicuesa, who was appointed by the king to govern this land, had not earned it and would never govern it. The decision to prevent Nicuesa's landing was final.

Chapter Twenty

1509 - On board the Basala, Sayyida's ship, Mediterranean Sea

"The Isabella is joined by two galleons," Baba Aruj said.

"Only two?" Sayyida's answer was more a statement than a question. "He is amassing a fleet. We will see the horizon filled with sails."

"Your small armada will be ripped to pieces, and you want me to be destroyed with you?" Aruj said.

Baba Aruj watched the two galleons on the distant horizon. Aruj and Sayyida stood on the deck of the Basala, Sayyida's own feared pirate ship. Aruj was most commonly called Barbarossa by the non-Arabic speaking Europeans due to their sloppy pronunciation and the Italian slang for his red beard. The oldest son of a wealthy Ottoman mariner, Barbarossa picked up the nickname when his privateering activities merged with his refugee transport business. He became a fierce enemy of the Spanish traders.

Aruj's ship was a fast three decker galley rigged with square and lanteen sails. It also featured thirty-two slaves manning its eight oars on each side. Aruj, like Sayyida and his three brothers, operated their many privateering businesses out of the North African ports coveted by the Spanish. Many of the ports' residents were the very Jewish and Moorish refugees rescued by Aruj and his brothers. There was no love between the Barbary pirates and the Spanish.

"Do I assume the two galleons are more Spanish?" Sayyida asked.

"More likely your friends the Knights of Saint John, if the giant red cross on the sail means anything."

Sayyida took the glass from Aruj. She watched the ship closely. It didn't seem to be in a hurry, which was good news. "Cisneros is calling in favors. He will take no chance losing Oran," she said.

Aruj smiled, his red beard waving in the breeze. "I believe you still have a score to settle with the Knights, no?" he asked.

She returned his smile. "Can you keep the second ship out of my way?"

That was enough. The two parted company. Aruj tendered back to his ship. These two Knights of Saint John galleons would not be supporting Cisneros' attack on Oran.

Chapter Twenty-One

1509 - Oran, Algeria - Northern Coast of Africa

A great mixture of would-be soldiers protected the gates of the city of
Oran. In the preceding few years, General Ruiz, Cisneros' general, and his
army led many raids into local villages and captured man, woman, child,
and cattle. To avoid being captured, people from neighboring villages, even
from diverse tribes, sought protection from the raiding Spanish within the
safety of the walls of Oran. The guards welcomed Salim's forces into the city.

As best as Miguel could assess, there were some eleven thousand
additional potential warriors expected to gather to protect the city. How could
his tiny band of less than twenty make any difference? But that was not his
responsibility. Then he learned the plan. He and his men needed to free the
captives held near Mers-el-Kébir. The expected Zayyanid warriors weren't
there yet, and the nearest villages had been decimated by General Ruiz's
forces, thus the success of any defense depended on timing. Would Cisneros'
armies arrive to support the general before the Zayyanid warriors arrived to
defend Oran?

Miguel wondered whose army God, the very cosmic timekeeper, would
favor. All Miguel knew was he needed to devise a way to free over a thousand
men so they might join in the defenses in Oran. Yet, he didn't even know
if there were weapons enough in and around Oran to give these men any
advantage over the steel and armor of the Spanish.

Based in Mers-el-Kébir, forces from Cardinal Cisneros' three thousand
cavalry became confident and somewhat careless about sallying out on
horseback and raiding the villages. Having such superior weapons in their
swords and muskets, along with their armor, the local villagers were unable
to put up much resistance. Miguel donned a Spanish soldier's uniform and
mounted a tall dappled gray Andalusian. Both were captured from a fallen
Spanish soldier during one of the Spanish raids. He and his men worked

their way out of Oran and circled south to approach the coastal Mers-el-Kébir from the west. Local spies reported the captured soon-to-be-slaves were guarded in a walled encampment. After hearing how the small pirate armada led by al-Hurra was successfully harassing the Spanish fleet, Miguel wasn't surprised the captives had not been moved.

The hilly, rocky, mountainous terrain protected Miguel and his men from an open approach, yet he knew a lookout would be watching for any unwanted visitors. Positioning his men out of sight, he approached the first camp, his outward confidence masking the nerves ready to snap. Serving with Archbishop Talavera, Miguel had enough direct experience with Spanish soldiers, and hoped he could act the part.

Three sentinels met Miguel as he pulled up and hailed the leader. He deepened his voice and made it somewhat raspy. The reins were held loosely in one hand, while the other casually rested on the horn of his saddle. Could he hide his nervousness anymore?

He began, "That fool Captain Gonzalo let his men get sloppy. Three hundred captives were lost when Zayyanid mercenaries ambushed his camp. They fell upon the guards who fled in panic. I have been sent to assess your security."

The guard looked to the others for some kind of reassurance. They didn't know Miguel, but he looked official and sounded convincing. After a nod, they motioned to let him in. Miguel remained on his horse and rode along the perimeter of the camp where the captives were being held.

He stopped to talk with a couple of guards trying to learn their routines. Then the sound of a large cannon blast echoed up the hill from the direction of Oran. A second blast, and then a third, broke the relative quiet of the camp. Who was firing on who? Miguel wondered. If that blast came from a ship in the harbor near Oran, that sound was traveling five or six miles. That is a serious cannon, he concluded.

The guards, along with everyone else in the camp, turned to face the sound of the cannons. Blast after blast echoed up the hills.

"He did it!" a guard said to another. They seemed to congratulate each other. Miguel couldn't reveal he knew nothing about who did what, but the elation in the voice of the guard pierced his heart.

"The blockade is breached!" the other guard said.

Cannon blasts repeated in such frequency Miguel knew this was at least five or six cannons. These men knew about al-Hurra's blockade? Was it her blockade? Of course they would. Who is the 'he' of he did it, Miguel wanted to know.

"Do you understand your commands with these swine when he breaches the blockade?" Miguel asked, hoping to appear like he knew the plans. Listening closely, he finally learned they had no commands. All these soldiers knew was that a blockade by an armada of pirates was harassing the supply ships, making it difficult for them personally. Rations were few and ships were unable to take the captives. That meant the inglorious work of guarding them continued. From time to time, the captives rose up and attempted escape. Each uprising cost lives. Miguel listened and prodded here and there to keep the men talking. They appeared to appreciate an officer they assumed to be of some rank listen to their reports. The camp experienced occasional uprisings and the guards were mostly unhappy.

The blasts increased. It was now evident to Miguel a genuine sea battle was being fought. The battle was not a siege on Mers-el-Kébir; Oran, a city only six miles down the coast was the target. No question about that. Would al-Hurra hold her own? His heart sank when the soldier said he was told Cisneros himself would be leading the battle. Miguel desperately wanted to race back to Oran and warn them they would be facing the cardinal himself. But what did he know? He was hearing second hand from the rumors spread by disaffected soldiers. But if Cisneros led the attack, his men needed to know. These soldiers guarding captives in the hills didn't have instructions on what to do during an attack. It was time to give them some.

"Where is your commander?" Miguel demanded. They told him and he worked his way past the walled compound toward three large tents. From the distance, he saw several soldiers looking off toward the sound of the large guns, which continued to send powerful blasts echoing up the hillsides.

These men assigned to watch the captives knew they were missing the very purpose they had chosen to become conquerors. Miguel knew the life most soldiers left behind offered them no future. They were second, third, or fourth sons, or even bastard sons who faced no hope of an inheritance. Joining the ranks of the conquistadors gave them a chance to participate in the conquest and the plunder. These men were missing both. They guarded the captives soon to be sold as slaves. They would get none of the money and none of the plunder if Oran should fall. As he got closer, even from the short distance, Miguel saw the anger in their faces. He kicked his horse to a full run toward the tents.

"Captain!" Miguel said as he charged the men pulling his horse up short. He watched to see which man responded to his call. All the men turned, but it was evident the snarled, gray bearded soldier with leathered cheeks and piercing eyes led this group. As if he was this man's superior, Miguel addressed him directly.

"General Ruiz commanded me to leave the siege and relieve your men to join him at Oran! He fears the local armies might overpower his ground force. My men will watch the captives."

He could tell the captain wanted with all his heart to believe Miguel. Nothing would please him and his men more than to participate in the siege and its plunder.

"Go man! Do I have to report you and your men as cowards?"

Miguel hoped the captain wouldn't wait for Miguel's men to arrive and relieve these men of their duty. His men were far from looking like uniformed Spanish soldiers.

The captain barked out orders to the men standing around him. This was a fight he and his men wanted to be in the heart of. His men scattered and soon gathered from their posts. Proudly filled with enthusiasm for the rewards of a sacked city, they marched toward the coast road, which they would follow to the battle. Miguel hoped the blasts of cannon, which had not ceased through this whole exchange, was indeed the sea battle al-Hurra had gathered her fellow pirates to engage. If it wasn't, he was making a terrible mistake sending reinforcements for a conquest of the city.

Miguel rode the perimeter of the walled compound. No sign of guards on the ground or the several towers overlooking the interior. He quickly climbed the wooden ladder leading up to the tall lookout. His heart rejoiced and sank at the same time. Inside the walled compound, a city of emaciated, conquered men and women stood facing the sound of the battle. From his vantage, only a few dozen feet above the compound floor, Miguel looked into the eyes of the few closest to him who stared back to see who the new taskmaster might be. A tall man, one of the few that appeared to have his wits about him yelled up to Miguel, taunting him. "Are we now left here to starve?" he shouted. "You Christians have destroyed our homes, our lands, and our families! Now you leave us to die?"

Miguel smiled. This was the very leader he doubted still existed. "You, who condemns my soldiers, your name!" Miguel yelled back. The man paused. He levied his accusation in Arabic, an accusation he bellowed many times before. Miguel was certain it always fell on deaf ears. Miguel's response was in perfect Arabic. It surprised the man.

Hesitantly at first, then proudly, "Ali Abdallah Muhammad IV."

Perfect, Miguel thought. The man stood taller, his stance more secure as he identified himself so defiantly.

"You are right! We have destroyed your homes and families," Miguel said. "Not as Christians, but as greedy fallen men! Only followers of Christ are Christians. They follow Christ, they do not enslave other men."

The eyes of the crowd shifted from the echoes of cannon fire to Miguel on the tower, conversing with the man who appeared to be the leader of this unfortunate mass of human cattle.

"I need you to provide me one great service!" Miguel said.

"Die?" the man asked, so defiantly Miguel's heart nearly lost its compassion.

"Gather your sick, your weak, and your weary! Take them home! Take them all home. Praise your God in Heaven for His deliverance. Teach your children that only those who follow Christ are Christians. For He is your only deliverer!" Miguel made this pronouncement feeling what he had not felt in a long time, a confidence he was doing the right thing.

The captive leader, Ali Abdallah Muhammed IV, stared at Miguel unable to speak. Miguel climbed off the tower and signaled to his men. They left their hiding places and lifted the large beam that secured the tall wooden doors. As the large doors pushed open, they stepped back out of the way. Miguel didn't feel he even needed to have a hand on sword or whip. The man stopped, looked deeply into Miguel's eyes and gave a slight nod of the head, then examined each of Miguel's men.

"What do they call you so I may commend you to Allah?" Ali asked.

"Allah will know who you are praying about," Miguel said. "We might be surprised how much your Allah and my Christ know us. May they both bless you Ali Abdallah Muhammed IV."

Miguel bowed. Ali led his people away.

Joseph, who was standing at Miguel's side, looked at Miguel and with the little Arabic he understood asked, "Do you include my Jehovah with your Christ and his Allah?"

Miguel smiled and winked as he said in Hebrew, "Today, they are one."

Miguel stood still as the people walked, hobbled, limped, or were dragged out of the compound. As the last of Ali's people left, four men who looked like they could be brothers, approached Miguel. "We are not ungrateful. But what about our cattle? We will starve without them."

Miguel could not imagine rescuing five thousand head of Arabian cattle. The men guarding the cattle would never be fooled so easily. They would not be soldiers, they would be experienced Spanish caballeros, experts with animals, and there would be more of them than his men and four underfed peasants could handle. Miguel paused; his eyes looked over the mass of retreating captives. He turned back to face the questioning men.

"How many of these men can you recruit to trust us?" Miguel asked.

"How many do you want?" the man asked.

"How many will it take for you to start and manage a stampede?" Miguel's subtle smile carried the message well enough.

"Please wait here," the man said. He then spoke to each of his companions in a dialect Miguel did not understand. They scattered into the fleeing crowd.

Cannon fire paused for several minutes and the quiet unnerved Miguel. Who was the victor? Was there a victor? Was the battle over? Miguel wondered.

The four men returned to Miguel at the large open gates, each with a collection of ragged former captives. Miguel stood there with ropes and chains he gathered from inside the compound. A group of around forty men stood with as much concern as recently released prisoners facing chains could possibly demonstrate. Miguel looked from the four men to those they brought back. He shook his head slightly and smiled at his own men. The immediate trust shown to a former enemy supported his hope that all men were alike if given a chance. They just wanted to live with liberty to pursue their own lives and provide for those they love.

There was no time to waste. If the battle was over, whoever the victor, the brigade he had just dispatched to join in the battle and plunder would return. Miguel handed the chains and ropes to the apparent four leaders. With a nod, Miguel's own men scattered back out of sight.

"Secure these men in a train with enough rope and chains to convince the Spanish vaqueros that you are in my command," Miguel said.

The man who Miguel assumed was the elder brother, if they were brothers, nodded and huddled with his three likely brothers. Speaking in the dialect among themselves, they appeared to be convinced of Miguel's intent. The elder brother nodded to Miguel and the four men quickly worked through the small crowd issuing instructions. They secured themselves.

"We place our lives in your hands to get us in," the man said. "Once we are in with our cattle, I will take the lead. These are our cattle." Once his fellow psudo captives were ready, he handed the lead rope to Miguel.

Miguel took the lead rope and mounted his horse and led the men up and over a ridge away from the now empty compound and the city. The roar of cannon fire began again. The echoes up the coast were deeper and harder. This was no longer a sea battle. Miguel knew the Spanish Armada breached the pirates' defenses. Miguel prayed the city would hold up under a direct attack; and he just sent a brigade of reinforcements? He shook his head.

The cattle were restless and the vaqueros, all on horseback, attempted to calm them. They walked their horses slowly, chanting out a low sweet type of lullaby Miguel assumed was some tune familiar to the animals.

"We are here to help you calm the cattle," Miguel said to a vaquero sitting squarely on his mount watching over the massive herd. "Scatter these slaves throughout. They know these animals."

The man who Miguel assumed led the vaqueros looked Miguel up and down, then over the captives who acted the perfect submissive wretches they pretended to be.

Miguel didn't need to tell the captives to mingle in among the cattle. Each man, appearing to be restrained with ropes and a few with steel fetters, worked into the massive herd. The cattle seemed to settle. They appeared to recognize their former owners, Miguel thought. Miguel now realized their leader had instructed his men to mingle close to the vaqueros on horseback. He saw tiny nods, winks, tiny head movements. This was becoming an orchestrated, though spontaneous event. These men were cunning. Miguel struggled to restrain his smile all the time he was eager to see how a stampede might look. Once the captives were in position, their leader nodded to Miguel. Miguel pulled his whip, cracked it, and wrapped it around the lead vaquero, pulling him from his horse. He then pulled a second man to the ground. The movement was so fast neither man had time to understand what happened. The former captives loosed themselves from pretended bondage and pulled men from their horses. Within seconds, more captives were on horseback than vaqueros. The cattle were on the move.

One of the brothers struggled to bring a vaquero off his horse but as the cattle crowded the horse Miguel was sure he would be crushed by the stampeding animals. A quick jump onto the back of the charging steer then onto the back of the horse surprised the vaquero who in the shock was easily pushed into the charging cattle. Each of these submissive, forlorn captives of just minutes before shocked Miguel with their vitality and expertise with a stampeding herd.

Miguel knew there was no way so small a group of men could keep the herd together. Being proven wrong could not have been sweeter. The grasses of the mountain meadow served well to keep these cattle fat and strong. They were using their power right now. The pounding of cannon fire was erased by the pounding hooves of the herd. They were easily pushed into a powerful movement, but with precise direction. These men knew just how to stampede them in the right direction away from Mers-el-Kébir.

Miguel began to feel it might work. The freed villagers would not starve tonight. He was eager to return to Oran, where Cisneros' armada was now attacking the city. He questioned his loyalty to his country and king. Accused of being a heretic, was he now a traitor also?

Suddenly, three large balls connected with tight leather cords wrapped around Miguel, throwing him hard to the ground. "Bolas," he groaned, "I should have known." A bola dug deep into his back. His breath gone, the pain nearly drove him to unconsciousness when he tried to refill his lungs with air. The cattle stampeded past, running in every direction. He was down and could not see anything but dust and hoof. Again, he was bound and helpless. The earth finally stopped shaking and dust began to settle. Cannon fire continued to echo. He thought it was not as profound, maybe because each heartbeat shot pain through his back.

In the settling dust, five furious vaqueros stood above him. No weapons were in hand; they didn't need them. The bolas were thrown by an expert. Miguel knew the vaqueros' skill with bolas could bring down a charging bull so proficiently, the bull could not move an inch. Unfortunately, he was weaker and smaller than a bull.

"You will hang for this." The vaquero speaking sported a long cut along his forehead, which bled enough to redden his hair and cloak. Miguel knew he was right. A heretic and a traitor.

Two men yanked Miguel to his feet and quickly tied his hands and feet, nearly knocking him back down. They released the straps holding the armor-plated vest. When it fell to the ground, a short but solid vaquero sent a powerful fist into his stomach, bending him in two. Pain clouded his eyes and ears. Two vaqueros who managed to remain on horseback returned to the tents where the vaqueros were dragging Miguel.

"The cattle are scattered from here to hell and back," said one. Then, without warning, the man fell from his horse, dust rising when he hit the ground.

The second man dropped as well. The shock paralyzed the men surrounding Miguel. In very broken Spanish, the words "Release my friend," climbed their way out of a man holding a proven-to-be-deadly sling. It was loaded with a rock they believed could knock them down just as quickly as it had their two companions.

More menacing was the large powerful black man with arrow nocked and ready to fly. His smile disarmed the vaqueros as much as the weapons held at the ready. They backed away. Hands held clear. "He is yours."

Miguel blinked his eyes to reassure himself he believed what he saw.

Joseph motioned with his head for Miguel to come forward. As he did so, the two Tuareg horsemen with several horses, including Miguel's, rode up to the gathering. Joseph quickly cut the bands holding Miguel and helped him to his horse. He readied his sling again, giving Mali a chance to mount. Quickly, they turned and charged off the hill and down toward Oran where the cannon fire continued to disrupt the otherwise peaceful hillside.

Smoke rose above the trees as the men pushed across the rocky hillside and into the craggy forest that battled the rocks for the right to exist. Their horses struggled for a footing as they approached the city. Just before they reached the summit, the cannon fire ceased. Each man listened intently, expecting the blasts to start again. They didn't. The silence was more ominous than the non-stop barrage.

They cleared the sparse trees and stood atop the bare topped mountain overlooking the harbor and city. To a man, all hope fled. Eight vessels stood defiantly in the harbor. From the distance, Miguel identified three galleons, two frigates, and three caravels. Smoke billowed heavenward with flames consuming two more. They were too far away to confirm, but with men pouring out of the small boats and disappearing into the city, Miguel knew the northern walls of Oran had been breached.

"Your peacock is Morisco again." Miguel slowly turned away from his focus on the battle below and squinted at the Tuareg seated on the single gray mare. The Tuareg repeated himself, "Your friend, the peacock, said you would know. He will be Morisco."

"He spoke to you?" Miguel asked. "Where?"

The Tuareg motioned toward the city with his head.

Joseph, speaking in Hebrew, asked, "And you?"

Miguel squinted, then said, "Today, I am the heretic and a traitor."

Joseph smiled.

Yes, these are my men, Miguel thought. They worked their way off the rocky mountain toward the city by way of the southernmost walls. Their fears were confirmed. The northern walls were breached, and Cisneros' forces poured into the city as fast as his men could get to shore. Some thousands of men from Mers-el-Kébir who had been the ground force during the siege were already inside the city. The sound of musket fire revealed the battle would now be man to man. Was he ready to battle his own? Were they his own? No, he was not one of Cisneros' men nor Ferdinand's. He was Talavera's.

He led his men into the city. This was a bloodbath. Except for one last section of the city, the Spanish forces washed through the streets. Bodies, hacked and bloody, lay everywhere. For every one of Cisneros' soldiers lying dead, twenty or more of the Oranian and local tribesmen had been killed. And it was not just the warriors, but citizens of the city unable to flee. Women, children, and the elderly were slaughtered. How quickly the superior armor, muskets, and swords permitted the Spanish to overwhelm the city's forces.

Miguel reached into his heart and answered Joseph's question again. "Today, I am a Spanish Christian." He turned to Joseph and Mali and his two horsemen. "We must find Abu, Salim, and their men and help them escape. The city is lost. Those captured will be taken and sold as slaves. Valor and courage demand we survive to fight another day."

He removed the armor and sword from a dead soldier and assumed the role of the soldier once again.

"Stay clear of the armies, rescue those you can, and get them free from the city. I go looking for my peacock," Miguel said.

A small band of soldiers charged past a deserted mosque and into the square where Miguel and his men were ready to scatter into the city to find their friends. Without warning, a soldier fell, an arrow in his neck. Then a second one with a stone to the eye. Within only seconds, six Spanish soldiers lay dead. Miguel hadn't even drawn his sword.

Miguel looked at his men who had just eliminated a small garrison in seconds and said, "If I live and meet you again, please hesitate long enough to recognize my face." He recognized he could now marshal with the Spanish, but he would also be a target for Abu's men. But he needed to find his peacock. Was Jalaf here in the city? Did Jalaf mean as a Morisco he would be fighting with the Spanish? No, Jalaf would be fighting for himself.

Miguel's newly acquired armor, dirty and covered with blood, bought him access to the final forces mounted to capture the last unconquered sector. Miguel thought these were probably Abu's forces providing the final resistance. All around him, the Spanish gathered captives, herding, and guarding them. How many would remain here as slaves to the Spanish and how many be taken and sold on distant shores?

Miguel watched as a soldier raising a freshly loaded musket ready to fire, dropped it, fell to his knees, and rolled to his back. An arrow was stuck deeply into his throat. Miguel recognized that arrow. Indeed, these were the warriors from Saïda. Yet, there was no way they would survive this last stand, despite their deadly defense. Each attack left more Spaniards dead, despite their armor and superior numbers. The Spanish knew they had conquered. Oran with its perfect harbor, its ideal access to the important trade routes, and its perfect location closest to Spain now belonged to them. This last pocket of resistance was merely an annoyance. Why waste another man?

"They are bringing cannons. The resistance is lost." The voice was a matter-of-fact whisper. Miguel could not believe what he just heard. Not the words, they were most believable; it was the voice. His head shook as he turned.

"You might want to rescue your men," Jalaf said. "Before the cannon destroys them."

Jalaf stood in a dark brown roughly woven priestly cloak, hood over his head. Around his waist, a thick white rope gathered the excess fabric bunching it in several places. A large golden cross hung from his neck. His hands were held in the fashion of humble prayer; fingers touching his chin moved slowly in the sign of the cross.

"Drop your sword. It is of no worth to you anyway. Raise a hand in peace and follow me," Jalaf said, giving no time to refuse. The two men, Jalaf in a posture of humble prayer, one hand raised signaling peace, and Miguel, with hands outstretched to show he was unarmed, stepped out into the line of fire which ceased. They stepped over and around butchered bodies of both citizens, warriors, and soldiers. Nothing Jalaf had ever done made sense to Miguel. This march into death was no exception. He stopped some ten feet from the barricade, standing between the two forces.

"To the captain of the forces of Oran!" Jalaf yelled. "In moments, cannon will arrive and destroy this last vestige of resistance. In the name of the Father, the Son, and the Holy sense of self preservation, you may now surrender to this man, who I believe you trust will honor the terms of your surrender."

Miguel turned to Jalaf so quickly every man watching knew this was a surprise to Miguel.

Behind Jalaf and Miguel, the Spanish forces parted, permitting three twenty-four-pound cannons to the front line. The powder-men began loading and preparing to fire.

"This man will negotiate your surrender. Do him no mischief. He is harmless," Jalaf said. Then addressing Miguel, he said, "From Tunis, you will find passage to Rome." He put his hand on Miguel's back and pushed him toward the resisting forces of Oran, barricaded and trapped.

Jalaf turned to retreat to the Spanish line of attack where the cannons were readied for a final assault. He said over his shoulder to the resistance, "If you cannot agree on terms of surrender, which will certainly be violated by the Spanish as they have always done, you may keep my friend there as a hostage. As I said, he is harmless." Jalaf's tone was deadly serious, as he added, "He is also useless, unless you find freedom to fight another day more palatable than certain slavery or destruction."

Miguel walked slowly toward the resistance. Jalaf went back to the army now ready to finish the battle.

When Jalaf arrived at the Spanish line, he humbly said, "They have five minutes to agree to your captain's terms of surrender. If they kill him instead, you may blast them all to hell."

The captain stared at the barricade and said, "My captain? I am the captain!" He turned back to Jalaf, but Jalaf was gone. He yelled to the gunner on his left and the other on his right, "When powder and ball are ready, on my signal!" He waited several minutes. He didn't know how many. "Fire!" he yelled. The air erupted with the blast of three cannons firing at once. The earth shook and the barricade exploded, including the front walls of the buildings behind it, throwing wood and stone every direction. Smoke hung in the air and the Spanish army charged into the chaos.

A hundred horses charged up the ravine out of the view of the attacking army. One man shed his armor and slipped into the robes of a fallen priest.

The tiny remnants of a once sizable Zayyanid force, at one time numbering over eight thousand men, chose Jalaf's exhortation to choose freedom to fight another day. The well over twelve thousand Spanish forces with an armada of eight warships had taken the vital port city of Oran in less than one day. Thousands of the Algerian forces and hundreds of Oran citizens lay dead in the streets. They were the fortunate ones. The survivors were certainly to become slaves to the conquering army.

With the last of the resistance destroyed, Cardinal Cisneros climbed from the large Spanish galleon and into the boat manned by eight oarsmen. Head held high, a hand on the golden belt securing the bright white cassock around his waist; he would have strutted like a rooster if the boat were larger. His mozzetta, the short black cape, contrasted sharply with the long brilliantly red cappa magna over-cape. When the zucchetto, his wide-brimmed hat, caught the breeze, he reached up to secure it, making sure the large gold ring on his right hand broadcast his authority as God's representative in this struggle.

Cisneros' general met him as he stepped from the boat to the shore of his conquered city. Soldiers lined the route as he marched from the water's edge through the shattered walls and into the center of the conquered city.

Chapter Twenty-Two

1509 - Oran, Algeria - North Coast of Africa

"All are dead save these," the soldier said.

Cardinal Cisneros sat on a makeshift throne, a large white stone that once served as the cornerstone of the now demolished Oran mosque. Cannon fire reduced it to rubble. Cisneros considered it a sign of God's sanctioning the destruction of these people.

"These only are the surviving leaders of the Zayyanaid forces?" Cisneros' grin was forced. His total defeat of the local forces gave him great satisfaction. His mood swung wildly as he received reports from his several captains of their successes and failures during the great battle. His anger at having lost some fifteen hundred captives and over five thousand head of cattle from Mers-el-Kébir during the siege burned inside him. It was a lack of leadership his general would pay for.

Three men stood, bound in chains both hands and feet. The tallest of the three stared defiantly at Cisneros, his black eyes fierce enough to burn holes through the cardinal's bright red cappa magna, which in its pristine unwrinkled condition was obviously preserved to be worn in the cardinal's triumphant entry. Cisneros recognized the defiance. "These three will be mine. They will serve the Church as penance for their crimes."

"Crimes? The crimes of fighing for liberty?" a hooded Miguel in a long black priestly cloak whispered to himself. "Yours? No, they will be mine."

The cardinal was flanked by seven priests standing in reverence to the cardinal. These priests were present to bring order and hope to the people of Oran, offering redemption through baptism. They knew, however, that most of the surviving citizens of Oran would soon be on ships to the slave markets throughout the Mediterranean, many of whom were the very refugees who refused Cisneros' mandatory baptism in Granada.

"You did not escape." The whisper came from a knight standing on Miguel's right.

Without raising his head, the hooded man in the priestly cloak smiled, and wondered how he did that? The knight in full Knights of St. John uniform stood beside him.

"Who are you now?" Miguel muttered, slowly and carefully observing Jalaf's new costume. The Knights of St. John's battle uniform consisted of a white tunic with a black cross on the front and back. Over the tunic, the black mantle with its white cross on the left shoulder identified their membership in the order. For protection in battle, the breastplate and backplate were held together with leather straps. But Jalaf did not bother with the armor. He didn't bother with the typical battle uniform.

Jalaf wore the dress uniform. Over the white tunic, a bright red mantle which rivaled the cardinal's red cloak for brightness, displayed the black cross on the shoulder. Jalaf also dispensed with the metal gauntlets and greaves that would have protected arms and legs during battle. They were unnecessary now the battle was ended.

When Miguel and his men descended from the cliffs to the city, Miguel saw the bright red cross on the sails of one of the ships in the harbor which told him Cisneros obliged the Knights of St. John to support the siege with man and fire power. Who else supported Cisneros's conquest? Naturally, Miguel thought, adding another Christian friendly port to the western Mediterranean would bring more security against the Barbary and Ottoman pirates and give the Knights more power against the Turks. The Knights of St. John were the Christian version of the privateering Barbary and Ottoman corsairs, sanctioned by the pope himself hundreds of years earlier. They were a deadly and powerful force, and a natural ally to the Spanish armadas.

"Philippe Villiers de L'Isle-Adam," Jalaf whispered.

Miguel jerked so quickly to face Jalaf he nearly lost his hood. "The grandmaster?"

"Why not? As my close follower, you may address me as Philippe."

"I hate to waste time asking, but how…?"

Cisneros stood, ushered the three captives guarded by eight soldiers toward the sea to be taken to his galleon. The battle was over, and soldiers ransacked the city. Discipline was lost in the chaos. Though deadly and catastrophic for the citizens of Oran, the mass turmoil facilitated Miguel's and Jalaf's unencumbered movement through the city. The two men followed

Cisneros' guards through the city. Jalaf quickly darted away from the crowds, Miguel at his heels. The two men arrived at the shore well before the captives, whose progress was hindered by the chains, and the crowded streets littered with fallen and mutilated bodies.

In grandmaster confidence, Jalaf commanded two soldiers tending to the cardinal's personal boat to be ready to transport the most important conquests to the cardinal's ship. He stood at the ready when the captives neared the shore. He waved them toward him as he whispered to Miguel. "Do you have a sword under that cloak? Not that it will do you any good, but how about the whip?"

"Whatever your cunning mind has dreamed up this time, you will not be disappointed." Miguel resigned himself to follow Jalaf's lead. It might be painful, but he would likely live.

Jalaf hailed the captain of the guards. "The cardinal commanded me to personally escort your prisoners, freeing you to partake of the spoils." Jalaf stood resolute and spoke with such authority standing in the dress uniform of a knight grandmaster, and accompanied by a priest, the men leaned toward their own lust and greed and accepted the offer to relinquish the responsibility of the prisoners and join in the debauchery.

The soldiers secured the three men in chains into the boat. Four oarsmen, a lead soldier, the knight, and the priest climbed in. The soldiers pushed it off. Jalaf saluted and stood at the bow as the boat moved away from the shore toward the cardinal's ship.

"Good men, the cardinal wishes to remain in the city for some time and then on to Mers-el-Kébir. We are to deliver these prisoners to the Knights of St. John's ship for safe transport to Barcelona." Again, Jalaf's command, even with a slight Moorish accent, was credible enough. The oarsmen steered toward the large galley flying the black flag with the bold white cross. Its mainsail boasted its importance with a bright red cross.

Miguel sat at the stern of the boat. Jalaf stood at the bow, looking forward. Miguel's mind raced to possibly outthink the man leading him and the cardinal's captives to a very unfriendly ship. He raised his hood enough for the captives to see and recognize his face. Abu's cautious yet confused smile confirmed that he and his two companions, Salim and another warrior who Miguel did not recognize, were either being betrayed or rescued. Miguel was satisfied they knew something unexpected was about to happen.

The cardinal's boat reached the Knights of St. John's ship. Phillipe hailed his fellow knights.

"The good cardinal commissions us to deliver his personal captives to Barcelona. An added portion of the plunder is ours for such an act!"

Three knights, dressed in battle dress complete with armor plates and helmets, looked down into the boat. One yelled, "Why might we want to assist the cardinal again?"

"Because the cardinal will pay double our share and reward us with five hundred slaves to dispose of as we wish!"

"And," Jalaf said, "I am Philippe Villiers de L'Isle-Adam the Grand Master and Captain of the Gregory. This is my ship and I accepted the terms offered by the good cardinal! Drop the ladder."

The Spanish leader and his oarsmen untied the chained men and let each climb from the boat to the knight's ship. They struggled to manage the rope ladder with hands and feet in irons. Once they were secure onboard, Jalaf commanded Miguel to join them.

"You, my good priest, will attend to their spiritual needs during our journey. Of all men here, you will not stand for heresy." Miguel climbed the ladder, followed by Jalaf.

Jalaf turned to the men on the boat. "Please tell the good cardinal, I will personally deliver these men to their fate, and he will deliver the promised gold and slaves to me."

The oarsmen pushed back from the ship and rowed back toward the harbor.

Jalaf, now speaking Arabic, said to a knight standing at the helm across the deck of the Gregory, "To Rome. We must deliver my captive to Rome."

The helmsman's tunic, mantle, and breastplate did not sit right. It was too loose and baggy for the slight frame. The helmsman yelled to the slave master below decks. "Drop oars! Be moving! Half speed!" The voice did not fit right either. The knight was a woman.

Miguel lowered his hood, his head shaking at one more mysterious rescue. He looked to the men in chains whose smiles were also mixed with confusion.

"Remove these chains! My guests do not wear chains," Jalaf commanded. He turned to the three captives, "Welcome aboard the Gregory."

Two decks below, the oars splashed into the calm water and the ship pushed forward away from the fallen city. After several minutes with sails hoisted and the oars pulled in, the Gregory sailed east with the evening sun lowering behind them.

"To Rome?" Abu asked as the chains fell from his ankles.

"Only if you wish to visit the Pope," Jalaf said. "My sister will drop you anywhere along the way, if you prefer freedom to baptism." His smile never faded.

Salim bowed and quietly said, "Algiers."

"Not in this ship," Abu said. "Leave us at Tenes, the old Phoenician port. The tribes are friendly and there will be no resistance. From there, we can return to Saïda and prepare for war."

Miguel knew Abu was right. War was coming.

"Your band performed well," Abu said. "I invited them, if they survived the siege, to come to Saïda and live in peace with us. If that peace might last. They are good men. I fear many want to return home. I hope one day we do not face each other as opponents. I trained them too well," Abu said. "With the ruse from your good… what is he, anyway?" Abu motioned toward Jalaf. "Your partner?"

Miguel smiled. What kind of answer would Abu believe?

With a comfortable wind the Gregory neared Tenes as the sun broke over the horizon. The peaceful night was a major contrast to the battle waged and lost.

Abu, Salim, and the third man climbed down into the boat, waved goodbye, and rowed to shore. Tenes was nothing but the ruins of an early Phoenician port city. Now it looked to serve as nothing more than a fishing village inhabited by Moorish refugees from Granada.

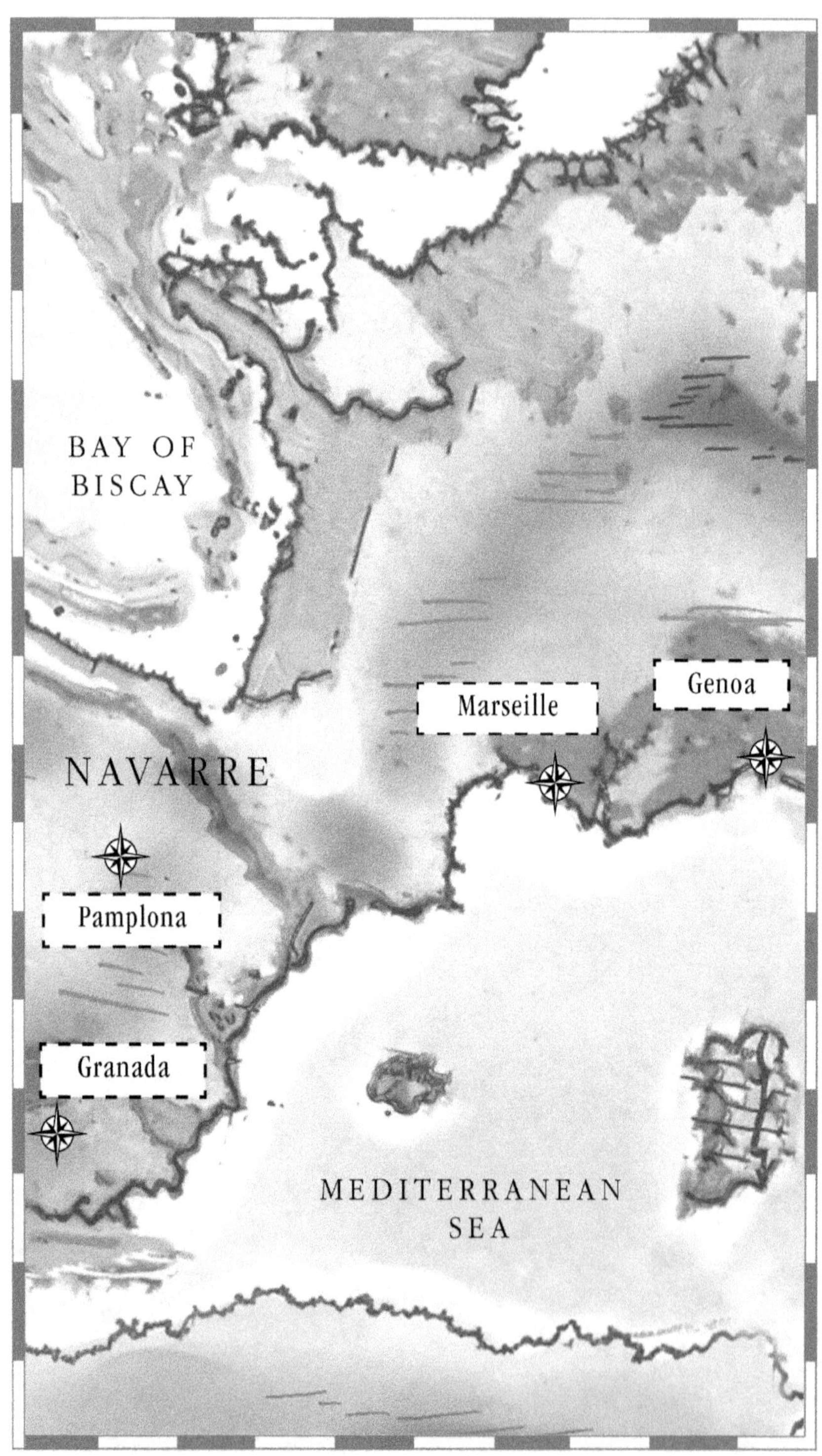

BAY OF
BISCAY
NAVARRE
Marseille
Genoa
Pamplona
Granada
MEDITERRANEAN
SEA

Chapter Twenty-Three

1509 - Navarre, Northern Spain - Pyrenees Mountains

Andi did not disappoint. The beautiful mare never hesitated, even through the rugged Pyrenees. Maria's once carefree approach to life now seemed guarded to Vano. When she first traveled with the Gitanos a few years earlier, she seemed more fun. He credited her current state to the seriousness of her quest to reach Rome and help free the brother of her dearest friend. Vano hesitated to delve too much into the fear that her friend likely had already suffered at the hands of the inquisitors.

They reached a quaint Pyrenean village nestled in the foothills. The air was crisp, and the scent of pine trees seemed to permeate the surroundings. After the previous several nights sleeping in an abandoned barn or under the protection of beach and fir trees, they welcomed the chance to shelter in a small inn. They were up early. The cold spring air was refreshing, and as the morning sun dried the night's dew, the warmth seemed to melt the stiffened joints. Maria said very little. Her focus seemed to be far off in the distance. Vano wondered if Maria even noticed the warm glow of the sun cast on the stone cottages and cobblestone streets.

They began ascending through the forested trails. The sound of birdsong accompanied the rhythmic hoofbeats. The air was filled with the earthy fragrance of moss and pine. At any other time, Vano decided, a journey like this, where alpine lakes shimmered reflecting the surrounding peaks, and mountain meadows were dotted with wildflowers, would be all pleasure. Maria's determination and concern dampened this panoramic canvas.

Having caught a glimpse of the elusive Pyrenean brown bear earlier in the day, the two riders were grateful to reach a charming mountain village where they were offered a warm welcome. Vano noticed Maria's appreciation of the flower-filled balconies on the stone cottages. They seemed far more interesting to her than the majestic beauty of the rugged untamed wilderness. He smiled, realizing his father's astute understanding of Maria's needs. He had insisted that unless Vano could provide Maria with stability and security, she would never be his. A home, a home like these, represented stability. But could Vano ever leave the free life of a Romani?

Vano's French was better than Maria's, so he negotiated the accommodations on the rare times when they stopped at a cottage or tavern. The combination of a young Gitano escorting what by any man's standards was an attractive woman and insisting on separate rooms was frequently met with surprise when an inn keeper attempted to lodge them together.

After many weeks of rugged travel, the couple reached Marseille. Another night in the wild was unacceptable. They entered a tavern they hoped was friendly. Maria attracted more attention than Vano cared to permit. Vano quickly stepped between a man and Maria and stopped an unwelcome advance with the tip of his sword. He was knocked aside by three other men. Vano was now on his back, a sword at his throat. The tide turned. Maria now faced three unruly men. However, Maria had long learned that the same ale that gave men the false confidence in their capacity also slowed their reflexes. And these men were just bullies. They had probably left the army in disgrace and wanted to prove their manhood. What skills Maria had not learned in the tough Extremadura, she learned in the camps of the Gitanos. When Vano's father teased about Maria watching out for Vano, it was not totally a joke. Maria learned well.

Vano hoped the inn keeper or some other valiant sole might intervene. No one seemed to dare stand against these men.

Maria's loose linen dress was gathered at her waist with a wide leather belt engraved with a scene of horses splashing through a river. The shawl that wrapped her shoulders hung loosely down and past the belt, obscuring the long knife protected inside a leather sheath engraved with the image of what looked like Andi's head. The sheath was a gift from Vano's young brother, who missed her when she left the clan to serve a community of Jewish conversos with Cardinal Talavera's sister in Avila. Vano's eyes darted from the men, to Maria, to her hand calmly hovering above her knife.

The larger of the three men, with grimy teeth bared, moved forward. Though his massive frame dwarfed hers, Maria was not a tiny or frail woman. She was only a few inches shorter than Vano's nearly six feet. But under the flowing dress, Vano knew she was all woman, with every curve proving so. She had always dressed to hide that fact, but there wasn't a thing she could do to hide the smooth golden cheeks and perfectly formed nose and mouth. But it was her eyes that could change like the weather. Fiery storms or calm seas broadcast in her eyes the forecast of her moods. And her eyes were predicting an upcoming storm. They danced from man to man. Then they appeared to relax. How could they now be at peace?

Vano, with a sword at his throat, remained on the floor watching more in interest and less in fear for Maria's safety. He smiled as she pinched her lower lip between her teeth. Slowly, her left hand tucked a strand of hair back over her ear. Her eyes became calm as a summer morning; confident, not fearful, or angry.

The man lurched forward. As his hand touched her scarf, a foot-long knife impaled the palm of his hand. Just as quickly, the knife was at his throat. Maria pushed forward, keeping the point tight, drawing drops of blood. She positioned the knife to the right of his windpipe. If he tried to swing with the left hand, she would impale it too. He just attacked with the right hand, so she reasoned the left was weaker and slower. If the bleeding hand moved, she would let the knife fly, ripping the blade through his throat.

The man backed up, his bloody hand held out wide pulsing blood to the floor. The man holding Vano at bay, distracted, lost focus. Vano was on his feet instantly. Three bullies became cowards. Maria's quickness and steeled eyes had so disarmed the men, a simple motion of her head had them all on their knees. She removed the knife from the man's throat and kicked him in the face, knocking him backward to the floor. Vano stood at her side, his sword in hand and at the ready, but he knew it would not be needed.

"Shall we go?" she said. They backed out of the tavern and returned to their horses.

"I would still like to eat," Vano said, returning the saddle and mounting up.

"That little demonstration did nothing for my appetite either," Maria agreed.

In the darkness, the sound of the horses on the empty street echoed off walls, then disappeared into the sea. The calmness of the waves splashing and washing up onto the deserted sands betrayed the vibrancy of life away from the shore. One more light up ahead invited the two forward. They crossed through the city and headed south toward the point where the rocky shore worked its way west. They hoped to find a more welcoming inn with warm food and a soft bed. Marseille was a formidable city, but they anticipated an opportunity to rest up, eat up, and clean up before crossing inland over the hills and into Toulon. They did not fear spies or trouble from the Spanish, but plenty of highwaymen commonly waylaid travelers. They thought an out of the way route, though a few miles longer might provide more safety.

They added their horses to three others who stood tethered in front of the small inn. Vano entered first. Looking around he saw only what seemed to be fellow travelers seeking a quieter abode. He bowed to the inn keeper, motioned to one of the many empty tables and, with a nod from a robust woman, pulled a chair and they sat.

"Meal an a bed?" the woman said as she laid a old chipped plate on the table. No answer. The condition of the chipped plate did not slow Maria from taking the warm loaf and tearing it in half. This was the Maria Vano knew. Down to business, no pretense. When the woman placed two large bowls of piping hot stew before them, she said, "Stayin' the nigh?"

Vano nodded.

"I've a nice room, top a da stairs."

Maria held up two fingers rather than interrupt her full mouth, which was too busy to talk about anything so unimportant.

"Two? You are not…?"

Maria shook her head.

"Love, how far away do ye wan 'im?"

Maria smiled. "The barn?"

Vano's eyes gave both women enough to laugh at.

"He's harmless," Maria said. "This is delicious, but I would love a bath."

"Tha a can do." The woman turned, leaving the two to devour the stew, the bread, the cheese, and the full cask of wine.

Vano looked Maria over closely. "The barn?"

Maria just tipped her head.

Vano returned to the horses and led them to the barn amply supplied with feed. The barn offered more than most of the nights he and Maria had traveled these past several weeks. Would not have been that bad, he thought.

"You have done well, girl," Vano said to Andi. He unbuckled the girth and lifted the saddle off her back, then unfastened the throat latch and lifted the bridle over Andi's ears and hung it on the post. He rubbed his hands down Andi's neck, patted her shoulders, and repeated the care with his own horse. There was still a long journey ahead. Their equine companions now secured for the night, he stepped back into the small yard. A large fist met his face, and all went black. The barn it was.

Chapter Twenty-Four

1509 - Marseille, France

Vano woke in the darkness several hours later. He massaged his jaw. Finding it still moved, his attention turned to the pounding in his head. It must have hit something hard when he fell. He found a large cut. Dried blood matted his hair into a thick mass.

He felt around searching to locate his sword where he set it when preparing the horses for the night. When he found it, Vano strapped it on.

Both his horse and Andi's breathing remained undisturbed. The sound of sleeping horses gave him the tiniest slice of peace. When he stepped out into the yard, a second time in how many hours he wondered, he wished he had even a sliver of moonlight. There was none. Pitch blackness enveloped him. It was different from the darkness in the barn. Though the air was clean and moist from the sea, the darkness felt heavy.

Did anyone inside the inn care he didn't return from the barn? Whoever knocked him out was not after the horses. They did not care about his sword. There was only one thing of value. As if he just finished a marathon, his heart pounded, and his lungs struggled for breath.

A few street lanterns in the distance gave shape to the dark hilly cityscape, but the inn was black. The complete absence of light smothered all hope.

Frantically, he found his way to the inn and slammed the door open. Stubborn embers from the large hearth silhouetted overturned chairs and tables. With no evidence of life, Vano pushed past and up the stairs. Heartbeats drowned out the sound of his boots on the wooden steps. A tiny light shone beneath a door. He pushed it open. A once mighty candle struggled to light the room with its last remnant of wick and wax. The kind, robust woman lay bloody on the bed, her large bosom rising and falling with each breath. She was alive. Vano grabbed the lantern lying on the floor, lit it with the dying candle, and charged from room to room. Nobody.

He returned to the woman. It was evident her head received a terrible blow. The blood from her scalp made a bigger mess than the wound. He gently awakened her, helped her up, and brought her a basin of water and a towel. By the sound of the cocks outside, dawn was nearing. The woman recognized Vano's eagerness to learn what happened and what might be Maria's fate. She looked into his eyes with compassion, her eyes holding back tears. Was it pain or sorrow? He wondered.

"They followed you. Your lady embarrassed them. They could not let it be," she said. She continued to clean the dried blood from her face.

Why did he dare leave her alone? Could he have stopped the intruders? Would he be lying dead right now? Where did they take Maria? His mind raced.

"They will hurt her," she said. As she spoke, her trembling hands relaxed and her voice became firmer.

"Who? Who are they?"

"Brigands. A bad lot. Deserters."

"Where? Where do I find them?"

"The calanque de port pin," she said. "They haunt the hills there."

"Where is that cove?" Vano insisted.

"Over the mountain to Cassis," she said.

"Might they have remained in Marseille?"

She shook her head. "They keep their women at the calanque. A protected cove."

The sun brushed darkness aside, but it failed to settle Vano's racing heart and mind. He helped the woman wrap the gash in her head, which now bled again. He kissed it tenderly, bid her farewell, and raced to the barn. Quickly, he saddled both horses, mounted Andi, and charged up over the mountain toward Cassis. This was a part of France he did not know. But now he knew he was right to have planned to stay away from the coast roads. The plan he should have implemented yesterday. Marseille had been a mistake.

He could outrun any brigands along this route, but did he want to? No, they would kill him, take the horses, and both Maria and Andi would be captive.

He stopped each time he reached a cottage where he thought he might learn details about the marauding brigands. He knew this sort would be a collection of failed, dishonorable soldiers or criminals, many with considerable skills. The local country folks certainly knew these men, for they likely were forced to provide food in exchange for supposed protection.

Little by little, he garnered a picture of the cove the woman described.

By the nature of the terrain, he realized it would be situated to make accidental or unwelcome visitation impossible. From the hillside, he could see down to the waterline. Cassis was nothing like Marseille, but it looked to be a productive fishing village from where Vano stood. Somewhere, he hoped, between where he stood and Cassis, was a cove so heavily hidden and protected, a group of unsuspecting criminals were preparing to die.

Before leaving the inn, Vano searched for Maria's knife. It, and the few other belongings of hers that were not tied to his horse, were all gone. Considering her deadly quickness with the blade, they certainly got it from her before it went to work on her kidnappers. There was not enough blood to indicate there had been a struggle.

He wanted to charge down each ravine and rescue her. He knew the longer they kept her the likelier someone would suffer. And Maria would certainly be among the someones. His heart nearly pushed aside hope. In the distance, he heard what sounded like a wagon pulled by horses. Vano climbed off the road, staying hidden from upcoming riders. Maybe, he hoped, he could follow.

But he was not so fortunate. A man drove a small wagon carrying two women. The man wore a weathered gray shirt, blousy sleeves, and black trousers, a faded brown cap from which long white hair reached his shoulders. The woman, not much younger, must be his wife, Vano thought. She wore similar wrinkles as did the man. Her dress reminded Vano of the woman at the inn, but it was not as full. It was the younger woman sitting next to her that captured and kept Vano's attention. A long black braided tail fell over her shoulder, contrasting against a lively blue blouse. Her flowered pink coif was uncommon, he thought. Normally, the white linen cap was more in keeping with the peasant class. Maybe she was just independent.

His focus didn't last long. Riders charged from both directions and surrounded the small cart. Six men on horseback, swords drawn with three innocent travelers, did not urge Vano into a daring rescue.

He remembered they had not killed him the night before when they had the chance. He hoped they might only take the women and not kill the old man. But would they only take the women? His hope of finding Maria held back an impetuous charge.

After a few words Vano could not hear, two horsemen in front, two in back, and one on each side ushered the wagon forward. This was Vano's chance. He kept distant enough and followed. It was only a mile or so when the cart was guided off the road into a ravine. Vano would have passed that ravine without ever noting it was even there. Brilliant, he thought. He gave them several minutes to be out of sight. He climbed higher on the hill to see if he could see anything below. Between himself and the sea, there was nothing but forest. If he charged in, would he ever get back out? Would the horses be a hindrance or a help?

He secured the horses. There was enough grass, they would have plenty to eat and would be content. He worked his way along the ridge parallel to the road that penetrated the thick forest. The sound of the wagon and horses echoed between the trees. He knew he was close. As they climbed deeper, so did he. Soon, he saw the brilliance of the camp's location. A beautiful meadow opened to expose a well-organized camp. Small buildings formed a square maybe a hundred feet wide and deep. Horses were tethered along the north edge of the meadow. Beyond it was sheer rock rising some hundred feet. The view of the sea was nonexistent. Smart, he thought. Mariners would never see the camp. He knew there were guards watching the entrance, and entering from where he stood would be slow and noisy. But which building held Maria? He watched and soon guessed the closest to the seaside. They dragged the two women toward it and locked them inside.

Men and horses in view indicated to Vano this small colony might support a dozen or so men. He just followed six men who, in mid-day, brought the three new captives. How long would they allow the man to live? Would they abuse and let victims free? Would they keep the young woman and kill the others? Was there a ransom element?

Two men approached the females' building. They pulled the young woman out and dragged her screaming and fighting across the center clearing. Any thought to wait until dark vanished. A slight moist breeze blew up through the trees from the sea.

This was not going to wait. Vano climbed down through the trees. He watched as they dragged the young woman past a building with open walls that appeared to be where meals were prepared. A small trail led into the trees and down toward the sea. The cries of the young woman continued. A loud slap silenced her. Anger fed Vano's determination. He knew both men were too much for the girl to escape. How many men would it take to subdue Maria? More than two.

Sobs replaced the screams. The men were anxious with their prize and did not see Vano step from the trees.

"Not today," he said so calmly, the men hesitated one second too long. Vano's sword flashed. The man holding the young woman's kicking legs fell instantly to the ground. Vano's sword pushed the man off the woman, the man's shoulders chasing the partially severed head. The other man reacted too quickly, Vano's lunge missed, offset by the young woman struggling to cover herself, tangled in his feet. She quickly scooted out of the way.

The two men faced each other. Vano recognized the man as the one holding him at bay the other night. He wondered if the man regretted not wetting his blade with Vano's blood when he had the chance. He wanted to look to see if the hand of the headless man wore a bandage. There wasn't time. The man charged. He was quick and caught Vano in the arm, drawing first blood. The eyes were the window to the man's strategy. From his father, Vano learned the connection between the eyes, the mind, and the hand. Both the movement and intensity of the eyes broadcast each attempted strike. Vano also learned to prevent his eyes from betraying his move.

Both men demonstrated exceptional skill with each attack and defense.

Three consecutive and lightning-fast lunges backed Vano onto rocky ground. With a last-second block, Vano redirected a lunge, sending the man's blade into Vano's arm rather than his heart. Two large red spots continued to expand across Vano's body. It was the sword; Vano was watching the sword. The man's skill had thrown off Vano's focus. Vano now watched the eyes. Vano's sword moved before the man even began the strike. The lunge missed wildly, which surprised the man. Vano saw the next one coming as soon as the message was sent from the man's eyes. Again, Vano sent the man's strike into the air. It was Vano's turn. One more errant strike from the man and Vano attacked, driving the man's sword in every direction as he tried to defend Vano's calm and methodical assault. The man's breathing was short. He was tiring. Vano shortened it even more, quickly brushing the man's attack aside and plunging his sword into the man's lungs and back again into his heart.

The man's eyes opened in shock and his breathing stopped. He tumbled to his side neatly by his headless companion.

Vano took a deep breath, then exhaled slowly. He wiped the blood from his blade and offered a hand to the young woman.

"I am truly sorry you had to experience this."

She stared at him, but said nothing.

"Are you hurt?" He saw she was whole and now covered, with no bruises evident. The flowered coif was gone, and her long black hair reflected beautiful red accents in the afternoon sun that cut through small clearings in the canopy.

The young woman stood motionless and silent.

"Were others in the building with you and the older woman?"

Nothing.

"Is she your mother?"

Nothing. Her eyes seemed to plead for something. Was she mute? Deaf? Then, in a delicate voice, she spoke. A giant grin filled Vano's face. In his very challenged Italian, he began the questions over. She was not deaf, mute, or French. She was Italian. But he was past the pleasantries.

"Were you and your mother alone in that building before they dragged you out? Was that woman your mother?"

Vano's Italian was good enough she forced a smile. "Three women, and yes my mother."

Vano quickly described Maria. The young woman introduced herself as Sofia Lorenza and confirmed the other young woman inside fit Vano's description of Maria. She also confirmed two guards remained inside the building at all times.

Vano concluded the women weren't likely to remain as personal slaves to these men. They were merchandise. Probably used merchandise if the men had their way. He looked through the trees toward the sea and calculated its distance. The market for female slaves was at the shore. He knew it. The men he just bested took everything he had. He was not anxious to fight another dozen.

Soon, someone would come looking and know they had an intruder. Sofia and Vano dragged the two dead men deep into the trees and covered the blood with dirt and rocks. Vano led the young woman out of the ravine and directed her how to get to his horses. She seemed to understand well enough. He hoped.

He worked his way down to the shore and found the cove to be a perfect inlet from the sea. Two men waited there, as if for an incoming ship. A large ship could enter, as the water seemed deep enough.

What was transpiring back up the hill, he could only wonder. He counted to himself. Two men disappeared with a fresh young woman. Three additional women were under guard from two other men. With these two in the cove, that accounted for six. The headless man didn't wear a bandage on his right hand.

Still too many to confront alone. Could he get a knife to Maria? She was worth two men. And what about the man driving the cart? Was he Sofia's father? Probably. Was he under guard and still alive?

Vano spent the afternoon and into the evening exploring the cove. Up and down the ravine he went, looking for guards, exit and entry points, escape routes. He found the spring that provided their fresh water and took advantage to freshen up, treat his wounds, and prepare for an active night. Two more guards roamed the upper edges of the cove, making a total of eight. When he discovered their intricate system of trails, he knew he could strike and retreat. But if he left a witness, he would be swarmed and killed.

From a rare vantage point, he saw the sails of a ship approach the cove. A delivery or a pickup? Time to move. He decided elimination of each adversary as the opportunity afforded would be his strategy. He would give no quarter. With no intent for a fair fight, he felt like a coward, but it was the only chance the merchandise would return home safely.

Two men speaking loudly enough to confirm there was no suspicion they had an intruder, wound their way toward him from the shore. The lead man described a woman the second man was going to enjoy. They reached a bend in the trail and the lead man dropped to his knees. Vano pulled the sword from the man's chest and had it to the second man's throat so quickly he did not have a chance to resist.

"Now, my friend, if you wish to live, how many men are below?" Vano asked.

The man remained silent. Several voices from behind Vano ended the little chat that did not have time to begin. Quick slashes left the man speechless. His hands grasped his bleeding throat too late to make a noise. Vano quickly pulled the men into the trees and ducked out of sight. As he hid with the two dead bodies, he reached down and pulled Maria's knife from the first man's belt. Sophia, the young woman he rescued was right. These were Maria's abductors. He tucked the knife into his belt.

Beams of the late afternoon sun were blinding when he looked down toward the water. He wanted to see what kind of group waited below. He could not worry about that. From up the trail, two men led three women with two more guards following behind. The ropes securing the women's hands dropped to their ankles, allowing only short steps, then back up their waist and back to the next woman. Smart. They shuffled along. Vano wished he could see Maria's eyes to measure the storms mounting inside her.

He waited till they passed before he moved. Then more voices and two men brought the father. Four men dead, four with the women, two with the man, how many more need to die?

He paused once more. There was at least one more. He had not yet seen a bandaged right hand.

If the women got on that boat? His pounding heart seemed to shorten his breath. Could the father help? A thought dashed into his mind—advice his father gave while cleaning up the blood and bandaging a few cuts received after some local villagers ganged up on Vano and left him bleeding and bruised. "My boy, do not fight against the odds. Change the odds." As those words tripped through his mind, he turned back up the ravine to the camp. How many more men could there be? Or hostages? All was quiet. From one bend in a trail, he overlooked the bay. A ship sat at anchor some three hundred yards from the shore.

Squinting against the sun that was struggling to stay above the horizon for a few last minutes, it appeared a boat was lowering. The camp seemed to be deserted. Vano dashed from building to building to confirm no surprises awaited him. He reached the building with the open walls. Hot coals. Vano scooped a pot full and poured them into the first building. By the time the third building received its fair share of bright orange embers, the first building was in flames. Vano raced to the corral, opened the gate, and shooed the animals free. Spooked by the rising flames, they knew just where to run. Still no bandaged right hand.

Back into cover, he climbed and fought his way back down to the water. Passing the small clearing, he saw the boat leaving the ship toward the shore. But the men on shore were not watching the boat and the receipt of their merchandise. All attention was back toward the camp. He was too far to hear the words, but instantly men abandoned the small beach and charged toward the camp past Vano.

One, two, three, four, five. The odds were improving. It was now a race to the beach. When the men passed, he quickly left cover and charged full speed down the trail. Too soon.

"You!" The man pulled a sword with his left hand. The right one, bandaged tightly, pulled a knife. Vano did not have time for this. Odds be hanged. He pulled his sword, stepped forward, and lunged. The man easily dodged as Vano's blade found nothing but air. When the man in arrogance slowly turned to face Vano. Vano was gone. Completely out of sight.

The man would come charging, Vano knew this, but would he alert the men charging toward the burning camp or chase him alone?

Vano cleared the forest and charged across the sand. Two men were left behind to meet the approaching boat. In the seconds he had before the boat and the bandaged hand cut him off, Vano had to even the odds once again. He pulled Maria's knife and threw it wildly toward the man standing between him and the women. When it landed wide to the right, the man smiled, pulled his sword, and turned to face Vano. The second man readied for a two against one battle.

But Vano did not miss. Maria had her knife back quicker than the strike of a rattlesnake. With the ropes quickly cut, she not only evened the odds she turned them around. Before blades had a chance to disturb the lapping of the waves on the beach, the first man fell, life blood soaking into the sand.

The last man standing had seen Maria with a knife the night before. He turned and dashed into the trees.

With flames shooting above the forest and men falling into the sand, the approaching boat stopped. A simple collection of human merchandise did not look so simple. They began to row back to the ship.

The moment the odds changed, the bandaged hand was no match for Maria's knife and Vano's blade. After a flurry of steel, the man laid dead. It would take more than a bandage before he attacked another woman.

"Gather the ropes and get into the water. They will be back," Vano said. Maria immediately understood. She urged the two women into the water, followed by the old gentleman.

The older woman refused to move.

"What?" Vano said, sword in one hand, knife in the other, but upturned in exasperation. The woman was speaking in Italian so quickly neither understood.

The other young woman interpreted, "She says she will not leave here without her daughter." Vano's impatience with her softened immediately. "Oh, yes she will," he said. "Tell her Sofia's waiting for us in the forest above the road. She is in the least danger. Now move!"

With relief washing over the worried mother, they all ran into the water. Just as quickly, they swam to the far edge of the cove and climbed out into the thick trees. They watched men pour onto the beach from the camp. Two dead bodies, the captives gone, the boat being raised up onto the ship, the men from the camp thought they had been betrayed by the men on the ship. At least that is what Vano hoped they thought.

"Let's go find Sofia," he said. He led the small group slowly and quietly around the cove and up to the road. The moon offered glimpses of light through the heavily forested hills.

Vano wondered about the men. The one survivor from the beach would never admit his cowardice. The two who had taken Sofia were missing, along with the horses, four others dead, and the camp burned to the ground. How long would the rest of the men risk staying in the area?

The party carefully following the road, they entered where Vano thought he directed Sofia to hide with the horses. She understood perfectly. There she sat with Andi, Vano's horse, and four others.

"They came wandering past, so I invited them to stay," Sofia said. The message translated, they mounted and raced through the darkness, hoping to leave the bastards and their sort to the French.

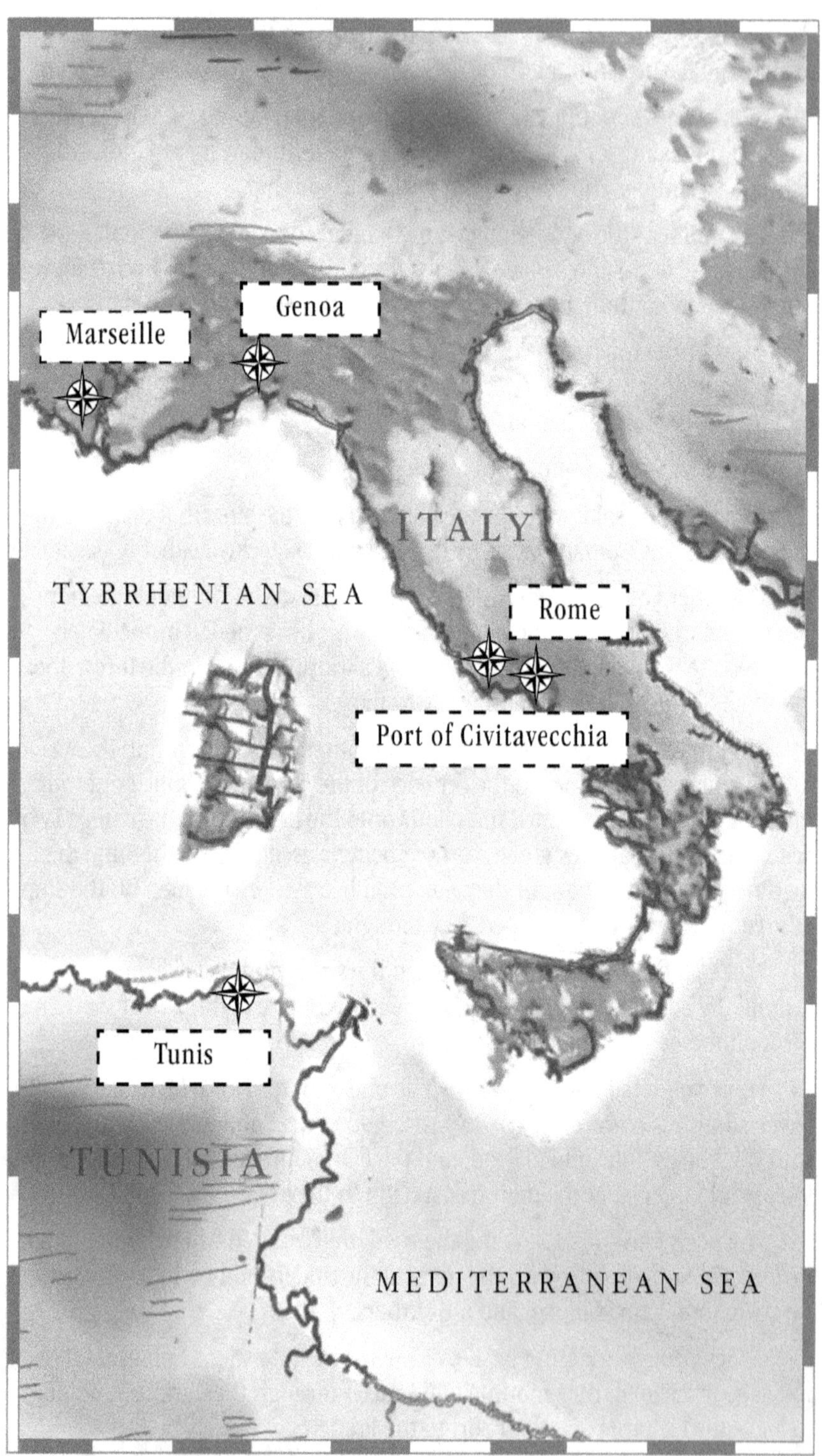

Marseille
Genoa
ITALY
TYRRHENIAN SEA
Rome
Port of Civitavecchia
Tunis
TUNISIA
MEDITERRANEAN SEA

Chapter Twenty-Five

1510 - Genoa, Italy

Lower lip pinched between her teeth, eyes fixed on the people entering and exiting the tavern, Maria touched the handle of her knife, pulled her scarf over it, and gave Vano a nod. As they journeyed the past many weeks, they remained away from cities and highways certain to be littered with highwaymen.

The caution exhausted the two travelers, but the dangers were all too real. This was the fifth inn they considered since they arrived in Genoa that afternoon. One of the greatest port towns in all the Holy Roman Empire, Genoa offered countless options. The clever owner of this tavern named it the Inn of San Lorenzo, after the centuries old Cathedral of San Lorenzo which stood majestically only a few hundred feet away.

Horses, carriages, and wagons littered the courtyard of both the inn and the cathedral. They hoped the piety of these patrons might offer more security for travelers.

The aroma of baked breads and roasted meats wafted in from a kitchen Vano assumed was at the back of the tavern. If all went well, they would secure their horses at a livery and stay a night or two to rest up before the final three-hundred-mile leg of their journey to Rome. The markets of Genoa certainly offered everything Maria and Vano needed to prepare for an audience with Pope Julius.

The inn was bustling with activity. Yet, the patrons appeared more civilized, respectful. It felt right. Maybe it was just its proximity to the cathedral. A good choice on Maria's part, Vano thought.

Vano's eyes and ears were drawn to a very animated discussion between a young monk seated at a large table near the window that overlooked the cathedral and two men dressed like the Moors back in Granada. The monk sat in his dark brown robe, hood pulled back, exposing his tonsure.

The robe looked a bit worn, but the sharpness of the tonsure indicated that if this monk was a traveler, as the robe indicated, he at least had time for the clipping of his hair so the bare scalp remained clean. By its tan, this monk had not spent much time inside. The monk and the lively discussion caught Maria's attention as well. They sat nearby in hopes to listen in. The discussion revolved around the power of the Church to control the word of God. Though speaking in Latin, and with two totally different accents, Maria and Vano understood well enough. The two men debating with the monk were Moors exiled from their homes in Granada. The monk was on a pilgrimage from Germany, visiting the many great cathedrals on his way to Rome.

"The monk is not convinced of his own words," Maria whispered.

Vano leaned in. "Why do you think that?"

"He's searching. Listen. He says salvation comes by faith without works."

Vano nodded.

Maria continued, "But the monk insists a man must repent to be saved."

"That is what Christians believe. How is he searching?"

"The Moors insist repentance is works. The monk cannot refute that."

Vano listened more intently. How did she get that from this lively debate? As wise and intuitive as Maria was, this sense of religious understanding was a side of Maria he had not seen. Is she a theologian? Where did she gain such scriptural insight?

"The Holy Catholic Church teaches that our Pope Julius II is the mouthpiece of God," she said. "This monk is saying the Bible is the mouthpiece of God."

"Is it not?" Vano asked. Vano's people, the Roma of Spain, lived the Gitano life to the fullest and many claimed them to be nothing but vagabonds and thieves. But Vano's father was a highly religious man, despite differing in opinion to many of the teachings in the Catholic Church. The details of his father's teachings never interested Vano when he was a youth. He was a young adventurous male with a world of new and exciting discoveries ahead of him. Attending to religious dogma was not an interest. Though he could read and write both Spanish and Latin, his father's illegal copy of the Latin Bible made him a heretic, though nobody paid much attention to it, including Vano.

It was Maria's attention to the debate between a monk and two Moorish refugees right now that interested him.

"So, how do people know the Bible without the Church?" Vano asked. It was a rhetorical question, and a discussion his people shared many times. Thus, it was a contentious point between his father and the Church.

Maria smiled vaguely, but was more intent in the other conversation than her own. Suddenly, her eyes darted past Vano. He watched her eyes widen. Her head tilted forward almost imperceptibly. Pupils dilated, she blinked several times, and her fingers tucked the renegade hairs back behind her ears. She straightened the wrap that hung over her shoulders. Vano slowly turned around to see what elicited such a response.

Standing just inside the tavern door, a man stood, gently closing the door behind him. Not much older than himself, or the monk or even Maria, the man turned to face the woman serving a table of refined Italian gentlemen. Their attention had also been caught by the newcomer. While Maria and Vano had spent the few minutes listening in on the monk's debate, the tavern appeared to have filled up. Vano quickly scanned the room, trying to see who the man might be looking for. He caught Maria's frozen face staring as if she were a fine marble stone, carved by the master himself.

On this new arrival's right hip, a fine Toledo sword hung lazily and on the other a kurbash, coiled loosely, hung comfortably like a dog resting on the lap of his master. Interesting, Vano thought. Unless he is left-handed, his weapon of choice is the whip. The man's white tunic was embroidered around the sleeves and the hem, where it hung loosely above tall brown leather boots. A faded red cape draped over his shoulder whispered it spent considerable time in the sun. It, too, was finely crafted with gold embroidered patterns along its seam. But it was the curly brown beard and wavy hair that framed a confident sun-tanned face Vano figured caught Maria's eye, and was likely jingling the keys to her heart. Vano hoped not.

Maria's breaths became short, almost chokingly. Vano could not resist a smile. The man approached the table, bowed, and in awkward Italian asked if he could take the last available seat in the tavern. It was the only thing between Maria and the monk. She sat frozen.

Vano looked into the man's eyes, which had now resorted to his. "I think she would be honored to have you join us." Vano stood partially and motioned to the empty chair.

The man offered a respectful bow. Maria broke from her paralysis and nodded.

"Thank you," he began, and just as he did the tavern door burst open. Standing as if expecting the room to rise and welcome the emperor, a smile, carrying with it a slender bronze-tanned Arabian knight, extended his arms in welcome. He wore a bright white silk turban accented with brilliant red piping that crisscrossed in a diamond pattern. A bright yellow scarf draped up off his shoulders and over the turban. Below it, a rich blue cape hung regally. Three wide leather belts around his waist each served to hold various sized swords in sheaths accented in gold and gems. Loose shiny white pants tucked into jet black boots laced halfway up his calves.

With a quick glance, he spotted the visitor at Maria and Vano's table, but before he could approach, a second person entered. With this one, Vano took short breaths. She was stunning and scary. The two new arrivals confidently crossed the room and stood at the edge of the table. Vano's attention was not focused on her white tunic, the jeweled belt and short knife, the dazzling diamond earrings, or golden bracelets up and down her bronze bare arms. It was her eyes. When she lowered the veil, it was her smile.

The woman took Vano's hand and the man took Maria's. She said, "I see you have met our friend."

Vano thought, we have not met anyone. The friend simply stole any hope I had for Maria, which he admitted to himself was slim.

"Jalaf of Granada most recently," Jalaf bowed, and "Sayyiada al-Hurra of Tetouan." Jalaf bowed again. The two Moors seated across from the monk, startled at the name al-Hurra, quickly rose, and offered their chairs to the two new arrivals. Vano eyed the Moors with a squint, recognizing they believed Jalaf's claim. Vano was not fluent in Arabic, but he knew al-Hurra was as much a title as it was a name. He was seated with a queen. Should he bow? Maybe even for her beauty?

Jalaf and al-Hurra took the seat opposite the monk. But not before Jalaf scooted the monk's table next to Maria's. The monk found this interesting enough, he scooted with the table.

Vano waited only seconds before he tried to tie the loose strings. "Pardon us," he looked to the monk, "we have rudely disrupted your conversation. I do not know why it must be me to do so, but I apologize. My friend and I have traveled from Zaragoza." He pointed to Maria. "She needs no bodyguard, but as you can see, a Romani like me could not resist an adventure to travel with such a companion." He bowed to Maria's obvious beauty, even in her disheveled state.

"You know the Aljaferia?" Sayyida asked.

Vano nodded with a smile. "A magnificent palace. It does your people great honor."

"It gives your monarchs their self-induced majesty they believe they deserve," Sayyida said.

"With its name, I assume the palace was of Mudejar design and construction?" the monk asked.

Sayyida nodded, her slight smile appreciating the monk's understanding and tone.

"And I," Jalaf announced, "was named for the palace, but in respect to the builders you may call me Jalaf."

The man who caught Maria's eye, as well as most everyone else in the tavern, turned to Jalaf and said, "Your humility astounds me still."

"And we," Jalaf said, "to fulfill an oath, and unlike your pleasurable journey, Sir Gitano, at great sacrifice and burdensome duty, do accompany this troublesome Christian heretic on a quest these many months, avoiding the very devil himself, to seek audience with His Eminence the pontiff Pope Julius II in Rome."

The man meekly shook his head, "Forgive my friend here, though I hesitate with the word friend. Abductor may be a better word. I am Miguel Ziortza-Bolibar, traveling on duty to a more righteous cause." He bowed to the monk and then again to Maria, on whom his eyes lingered an additional few moments.

Vano whispered to Maria, "Ziortza-Bolibar. That is your country."

Maria nodded slightly and whispered, "And he is going to Rome."

The monk respectfully listened, smiled, bowed, and then rose. "I find the company of Moriscos," he looked to the two Moors who remained close by, having taken two seats recently vacated at an adjoining table, "an Arab queen with her royal guard, a loyal Gitano, his charge, and a heretic, a fine complement for the evening. As I have traveled these many miles from the north, visiting many churches both great and small on my way to Rome, I have not encountered such an interesting collection of travelers. It is my pleasure to mingle with such an esteemed company. I am but a young Augustinian monk seeking answers. Perhaps we may discuss them together. They call me Friar Luther, Martin Luther of Wittenberg, Saxony-Anhalt, Germania."

The monk was right, Vano thought. What a unique collection of people!

The dazzling queen Sayyida, spoke first. "My dear friar, if your feet are willing to accept my invitation to rest on board a stolen ship rather than walk to Rome, it would be my pleasure to have you accompany us. My ship, needing some repair here in Genoa, will be ready by week's end and we sail to the port of Civitavecchia."

"That is very kind," the friar said, "I have not sailed on a stolen ship with a Christian heretic and a Muslim queen. If not restful, I would find it interesting."

Sayyida turned to Maria and Vano. She did not need to ask. Her eyes spoke for her. Vano understood immediately. "I am Vano Medrano of the Seville Romani. My friend, who seems to have been struck dumb, is Maria. Originally of Trujillo, recently of Zaragoza."

Sayyida took Maria's hand, "And, my beautiful friend from my homeland Zaragoza, Genoa cannot be your preferred destination."

Maria seldom ran short of words. She bowed her head, just in case this striking and confident woman was indeed a queen. She finally said, "Before giving her life to protect a great man wrongfully accused and imprisoned, my dear friend begged me to implore the Pope for clemency."

"Rome seems to be popular tonight," Sayyida said. "You Christians!" She closed her eyes, shaking her head.

Jalaf did not waste the opening. He looked into Maria's eyes. "Despite your choice of traveling companions, please sail with us."

"Thank you, but no," Vano said. "We are on horseback. Our feet need no rest."

"I insist," Sayyida said. "It will be nice to converse with another woman. I often forget there is goodness in the world."

Vano began to object, "We—"

Miguel knew what was coming. He said, "Like the good monk here, your horses will appreciate the rest. I have learned if al-Hurra wishes it, it is best to oblige."

How much has he obliged? Vano wondered. A simple nod and the arrangement was made. At week's end he and Maria would sail to Rome with a queen, a Morisco, a heretic, and a monk.

Food arrived at the tables and the group ate heartily.

Miguel was fascinated watching this unique collection of people assessing, glancing, noticing, and appraising each other. Short conversations about their homes and their journeys, the food and plans for the night, sprinkled between mouths full of a savory stew and excellent wine from the local Italian vineyards. When they could, without risking rudeness, his eyes rested on this fascinating woman Maria from Zaragoza. How had he never known her? Zaragoza was in the embattled country of Navarre. His hometown of Ziortza-Bolibar, also in Navarre, was mostly Basque. Was she Basque? He noticed Sayyida kept an eye on Maria as well. A competition? A relief for female companionship? He smiled.

Plates and bowls emptied, mugs refilled, the conversation slowed. The monk's eyes were alive. "This will be an interesting journey." Luther turned to Vano first. "You kindly apologized for interrupting a conversation. Permit me to start a new one." He turned to Miguel. "As a heretic, how do you view the Church's role in a man's pilgrimage toward salvation?"

Miguel wondered, what kind of a monk was this Martin Luther? He was from Saxony, so likely did not know who the "devil himself" was that Jalaf referred to in his so typically flamboyant introduction. Was Luther another Johann Tetzel, the inquisitor? Traveling through Saxony hunting heretics? He learned from Talavera and Abu truth always served best, so he answered honestly.

"Until the teachings of Christ are accessible to the people, who can read the words of Christ themselves, the responsibility lies with the priests to teach," Miguel said. Was that the answer the monk wanted?

Luther nodded, "Indeed. But should the people be permitted to read and know for themselves?"

These were loaded heretic questions. Miguel wondered if a trap was being set. He wanted to look around to see if a garrison of Church guards cunningly sent by Cisneros himself to trap him lurked nearby. Truth, he said to himself again.

"When I was taught from the Holy Bible, I learned what the teacher wanted me to know. When I read the words myself, I learned what the Master wants me to know." Miguel wondered how that would sit.

Luther's smile could mean anything. Did he say too much?

"You have read them yourself?" Luther asked.

Miguel nodded. "I learned to read from the holy scriptures. One day, I hope to have them for my own."

Even Jalaf remained silent. All at the table were captivated with this simple exploration between a sincere appearing monk and an alleged heretic.

"May I ask again; how do you view the Church's role in a man's journey toward salvation? Is the church's duty only to declare the word?" Luther asked.

"Forgive my being blunt, Friar Luther. You seem sincere, which in my experience is rare, but I interpret the scriptures differently than I have heard many priests, even cardinals and bishops, teach them."

Luther nodded. Miguel continued.

"The Church places itself, even the pope, between the individual and God, between the individual and grace. I believe Christ taught very clearly that only He should be between us and God. He taught that no other means but by Him could we come to the Father. Forgive me, but I do not believe that a pope, a bishop, or cardinal, or even you can come between me and my Father who is in heaven."

If there was ever a declaration of heresy, there it was. And right now, he was declaring what Archbishop Talavera was rotting in a prison for teaching to the Arabs. But it felt good to declare it.

Vano watched Maria follow the discussion between the monk and the heretic. When the monk repeated the question, her eyes readied for a storm and her bottom lip found its way between her teeth.

"This will be a most enlightening voyage," Luther said. "I thank God for bringing me here tonight to meet you all." He turned to Sayyida. "He brought you all here in an answer to a prayer I have repeated my whole adult life." He took her hand and kissed it gently.

Maria released the lip and breathed deeply.

Chapter Twenty-Six

1510 - Onboard the Gregory.
Sayyida's captured Knights of St. John's ship.

A soft, warm breeze filled the sails. Andi gave no thought to climbing the ramp up onto and then below decks. Maria was certain neither horse had maritime experience, but it appeared to her that Andi was excited about the journey. Maybe Andi knew it was saving her three hundred miles.

While waiting for the kind invitation to sail with the queen's collection of passengers, Maria spent the days she and Vano lingered in Genoa preparing to make the right impression when she met with the Pope. She still was not certain she could secure an audience with him. But Talavera's freedom was worth the attempt. If the archbishop was even still alive.

The ship began to move. Maria was confident with her skills, her knowledge of horses and men, and even enough theological understanding she seldom felt nervous, but with this Miguel it was different. He was respectful. He was confident, declaring beliefs that could take him to the pyre. He was respected by Sayyida al-Hurra, who, in the days in Genoa, she learned was a queen and a feared corsair. And he was handsome. His light brown wavy hair was neatly trimmed just above the collar and he wore a well-trained beard. His leather belt, free from the sword and whip it held the night they met, pulled a white tunic tight around his waist. Bold golden bands sewn into his sleeves accented what she was certain were powerful arms. The gold bands repeated at the wrists. A finely embroidered cape hung over his left shoulder. Did Jalaf dress him too?

She stiffened, took a deep breath, and stepped up alongside the heretic. "Have you sailed with Sayyida long?" she asked.

At the sound of her voice, he turned. He was not a giant of a man, but as he looked down and she tilted her head, the lock of renegade hair caught the wind and fell into her face. Do I move it? She asked her self. Does it

163

demonstrate I know nothing about hair? Maria was now dressed like a proper lady. She took Sayyida's advice to allow Jalaf to escort her to a local tailor. By the looks of the heretic, she concluded Jalaf was his valet as well. But even Jalaf did nothing to rein in her rebel lock of hair.

"Pardon me," Miguel said. She tucked the hair up under the cap from where it escaped. "With Sayyida? Not as long as with Jalaf. I owed her a favor, which I fulfilled. She now returns the favor delivering me to Rome."

Her regular breathing returned. "Did you say you are from Ziortza-Bolibar?"

"By birth, yes. But in life since then, Navarre, Aragon, Castile, Granada, Algeria and now Italy," he said.

"Basque?"

He nodded, then asked, "Is Zaragoza home?

"Now. I left Extremadura and traveled with Vano's family for a while. I am essentially Romanian."

He said nothing, just looked into her eyes, captivated by their mystery.

"You talked like a heretic. Seemed to please the monk. Are you?" she asked.

"A monk?" he teased.

She squinted.

"Maybe the monk is the heretic," Miguel said.

He never denied it, she noted.

With Genoa behind them, accompanied by flocks of gulls and full sails, the ship cut through the Tyrrhenian Sea. The eastern sun climbed, bringing with it the Mediterranean heat. The rugged coastline faded in and out of view. Small villages and cities dotted the shores.

The monk, finishing a spirited conversation with Jalaf, crossed the deck. "Your companion there…" Luther pointed toward the helmsman where Jalaf and Sayyida were giving some kind of instruction, "tells me you have a talent for trouble, heresy being the least of them." He lifted his wide-brimmed galero which shaded him from the sun and wiped the collecting perspiration.

"We can just say trouble seems to follow my dear companion and, for some reason, I find myself always close by," Miguel said.

Maria turned her concentration from Miguel to the monk. "If you have traveled mostly by foot from Saxony, your feet must appreciate this ship," she said.

"I cherish the chance to spend a day or two with fresh ideas," Luther said. "This heretic, I fear, may have emboldened me with his courage."

"Do not credit me with courage," Miguel said. "I watched the most courageous man I knew, arrested by powerfully evil men, and I ran. My sword never left its sheath. As our very Savior declared to his disciples long ago, when the shepherd is taken, the sheep will scatter. I know what Peter felt like when he wept bitterly. Please do not think of me as courageous."

Maria knew few men with this much meekness, yet confidence in their weakness. She thought of Magdalena's brother, the archbishop. He was this kind of man. He was a man worthy of a dangerous journey to solicit help from the Pope. Now, possibly, she had met two men with such courage. Maybe a third in the man struggling with the sweat running from his bald head through his tonsure and down his cheeks.

"Are you the heretic because you have read the Bible, or because you think it may not agree with the clergy teaching it?" Luther's question was sincere and without any tenor of accusation. Maria liked this man. She watched Miguel squint one eye. As if he was picking a stray nut stuck in a tooth, his tongue lifted his mustache. His squint faded as he looked directly at Luther.

He did not answer, she noted. "Do you think it agrees?" he asked,

Luther's bushy eyebrows arched slightly, "I teach it. Are you asking if I teach what I believe is in the holy book or what the Church tells me to teach?" A chuckle accompanied the question.

Miguel nodded.

"This pilgrimage? They sent me to Rome so I can become more in line with the Church. They hope our Eminence Julius II can help me see the light, as they call it."

"They?" Miguel said.

"My superiors at the monastery," he said. "They hope I can overcome my demons."

Miguel thought a moment, then started a new line of questions. Maria realized there were plenty of questions to keep this journey lively. "Do you believe," Miguel asked, "the war in heaven described by John genuinely resulted in demons, fallen angels as some call them, actually coming to earth?"

Oh my! thought Maria, where does this man's mind find so twisting a path? From heresy to demons?

"As far as I trust the translation, I do," Luther said.

"You question Jerome's Latin bible?" Miguel asked.

"Don't you?" Luther said.

"It raises enough questions I hope to have time one day to explore. You, my dear monk, will find the next two days might be more exhausting than if you walked," Miguel said.

"You, my dear friend," Luther said, "will learn that this invigorates me."

"It tires me!" Jalaf said as he and Vano approached the group. Directing himself to Luther, he said, "Your new friend will not invigorate you for long. He just hopes you can convince him to not become Muslim. In Granada, he taught my people alongside the archbishop, but he did not take time to learn that my people have Allah. They do not need your Jesus or the Jews' Jehovah. Several months fighting alongside my people in Algeria turned his heart, for sure. So, if he's no longer a heretic, he is at least a traitor, or as you call it, an apostate. Either way, stay clear of the whip, but do not worry about the sword." The smile never wavered.

Like a statue, Maria stared speechless at Jalaf. Slowly she glanced toward Miguel. "You…taught…alongside the archbishop?" Her words were hesitant, just barely above a whisper. His look that resembled a man trying to decide whether to throw Jalaf overboard or just impale him with the very sword he just insulted, turned to genuine curiosity at her question.

He looked to Maria, his eyes trying to focus on the words rather than the captivating eyes. "Archbishop Hernando Talavera? Yes, I did," he said.

The breath escaped her lungs so quickly, had the sails needed any help they would have had it. "You know him?" The words required a second breath, which had not come quickly enough. She placed her hand on his arm.

Vano, Jalaf, and Luther remained motionless, watching the emotion on Maria's face. Miguel only nodded. He, too, was stunned by her intensity.

"Is he alive?" she asked.

"I pray so," he said.

"They arrested him."

"Yes, I know, I was there."

"He was the man you abandoned?" Her voice stepped up a notch. So did her intensity. "Why are you not doing something?"

Jalaf gently took her arm. "He is. Why else are we going to Rome? Why would anyone go to Rome, but to foolishly beg something from the Church?"

She stared at him, then at Miguel. "Who are you?"

"Why are you going to Rome?" Miguel asked, becoming the inquisitor. He looked over to Vano, who obviously wanted to stay out of it, then back to Maria. She was breathing hard.

Vano kindly entered the conversation, "Maria, read the letter."

Maria pulled the letter from inside her belt. Her hands were shaking. She took in a breath and relaxed, then opened the letter and quoted. "I am sorry to ask of you so great a task. My dear brother Hernando is being held by the Cardinal Cisneros. His personal guard, along with all the friends and family, are under arrest, including myself. We are to recant and denounce my brother or suffer the flame. The Bishop of Málaga delivered the writings of his scribe that condemn us all, and without leniency from Julius, Hernando will meet the flame also. By the time you receive this letter, my voice along with Mother's and Juan's and our friends will be silent. The letter is signed by Magdalena Talavera."

Miguel closed his eyes. Tears gathered and struggled their way over his cheeks to hide in his beard. He wiped them off.

"You are his personal guard are you not?" she asked. "And you left him? You left the archbishop to die? You let them murder Magdalena? You abandoned them and ran to Africa?"

With each questioning accusation, the pitch increased. As if Vano knew the blade tucked inside her belt was itching to illustrate her disdain for this pretend seeker of spiritual wisdom, he stepped between Maria and Miguel. He gently took the letter and handed it to Miguel.

"Did you mean it? Are you actually going to Rome to help the archbishop?" Vano asked, "Have you repented and now want to intercede on Talavera's behalf?"

Miguel's hand, combined with the pained expression, was enough for Jalaf to hold his tongue.

Miguel took the letter and re-read it slowly. Then he said, "I am sorry, but regret and repentance are twin warriors. When they win a battle, pride, fear, and cowardice die."

He handed it back to Maria. Her eyes bore into his soul as if to add one more warrior to the battle; disgust. Her lip nearly pierced in two.

Maria turned and, with as much dignity as she could muster, she fought the urge to run screaming or to return and remove Miguel's yellow liver.

The men said nothing. Just watched her slide away. Vano squinted at Miguel and shook his head.

"You never told her?" Jalaf said.

Miguel shook his head.

"There is more to this," Luther said. "Did you know these two are on your same quest?"

"The fool that I am," Miguel said shaking his head.

"This is another gift for me," Luther said. "I have three kindreds accompanying me to see the Pope; a Romani, an apostate heretic, and a flaming fire."

"Friar Luther, have you read the Quran?" Miguel asked.

Sayyida left the helmsman. Having witnessed something very unpleasant between her passengers, and watching her sole female companion melt below decks, she casually disappeared.

When she caught up with Maria, Andi was enjoying a very vigorous combing. Sayyida approached and leaned against the opposite side of the magnificent mare.

"Was it my brother, the monk, or the man who draws your eye that angered you?"

Maria's lips tightened. Her eyes glared. "I hate him!"

"Hate? My brother does not engender that much emotion so quickly."

"Not your brother. Miguel. He abandoned the archbishop. My friends are likely all dead!" She told Sayyida about the confrontation and the realization that she was on this journey because of Miguel's cowardice and his valiant warrior regret and repentance excuse.

"I see." Sayyida slowly nodded her head. She ran her fingers through the beautiful mane. "And my brother did not tell you?"

"Tell me what!" Maria snapped at Sayyida.

"Hold on to your anger. If there's somewhere to direct it, it is not toward Miguel."

Maria softened slightly. Andi relaxed a bit, appreciative that Maria's brisk brushing lightened.

Sayyida described Miguel's arrest, the beating, the rescue, the escape, the kidnapping, and his slavery. She went on to share his valiance, and humor in the surrender of the Little Goke, Miguel's captivity, his saving the captives from Mers-el-Kébir, Cisneros' siege, and the fall of Oran.

With each story, Maria's disgust weakened. Eventually, it became embarrassment. How could she face him now? He was not the coward she just declared. She laid her head on Andi's shoulder, wetting it with her tears.

Sayyida paused, giving Maria time to absorb the truth.

"There is nothing to be ashamed of. Your indignation was justly placed. And now with the truth, you can invite the two warriors you described into your battle."

Maria said nothing.

"May I fix that lock?" Sayyida said, reaching over and tucking the renegade hair up into the long braid from which it had escaped.

Sayyida turned to leave. "When you are ready, I will stand by you." She left Maria to her horse. She patted Vano's horse, which had watched the whole event jealous of the attention his traveling companion just received.

Maria buried her head in Andi's neck. Her shoulders shook as she sobbed.

Chapter Twenty-Seven

1510 - Rome, Italy - Yes, that Rome, Italy

A cool spring rain freshened the air, rinsed the cobblestones clean, and was followed by a gentle breeze carrying with it the sweet but subtle scent of cherry blossoms. The delicate pinks and whites dotted the countryside and ornamented the young trees lining the road.

Of the travelers only Vano as a child had been to Rome, the center of Christendom, the ultimate end of the pilgrim's trail. The four travelers, at Miguel's insistence, journeyed the several miles from the harbor to the city in a comfortable coach. Vano's and Maria's horses, secured to the back of the coach, followed oblivious to the excitement inside. They crested a hill and saw the glory of Rome. Each heart beat with anticipation. An audible gasp filled the coach.

Luther insisted they stop when the coach reached the gates of the city. He climbed down, dropped to his knees and with arms raised, cried, "Hail, holy city of Rome!"

Luther's seven-hundred-mile journey from the monastery in Saxony, up and over the Alps through the harsh winter was now about to bear fruit.

The four pilgrims, as they now considered themselves, shared the anticipation of this singular opportunity. They talked about the sites they planned to visit, worship and honor. Though Jalaf and Sayyida had downplayed the holiness of the city, they were respectful enough to the importance the pilgrimage meant to Christians. The one issue with which Jalaf had the most fun was the Christian worship of sacred relics. "You preach the resurrection, yet the heads of Peter and Paul are in the Basilica. What happened with their bodies?" It was Maria's stinging glare that backed him off.

Leaving the coach and stabling the horses, they moved through the throngs of people toward what would be the highlight of a pilgrimage, St. Peter's Basilica. They crossed the venerable Ponte Sant'Angelo, the famed, five arched Roman bridge spanning the Tiber River. The river ran peacefully beneath it.

"It is taught that this obelisk rests directly over St. Peter's tomb," Vano said. "It was a Roman chariot race course then, and that is where he was crucified."

Only Maria paid attention. Vano seemed to know more than a casual visitor would. Luther and Miguel each had their attention focused elsewhere. Maria had her thoughts focused on 'how do we get an audience with Pope Julius. Is he even in the city?'

Each day, the bishops and cardinals surrounding Julius found new reasons the Pope was not available. Hope faded for the group with each failed attempt. Desperation sucked enjoyment from what should have been a joyous pilgrimage into the very center of Christendom.

After an unsuccessful week, Miguel entered the inn and found Maria refusing some kind of proposal. He laid his hand on the hilt of his sword and strode up and stood alongside Maria seated uncomfortably next to the man.

"I am a sculptor, not a painter," the man complained.

Maria held her scarf tightly around her shoulders. Miguel sensed no danger and his hand relaxed.

The man looked at Miguel and said, "Help me here. She declines my offer to serve as my model."

"You are a sculptor?

"They call me Michelangelo."

Miguel plopped onto a bench, mouth wide open. "Il Divino?"

Michelangelo closed his eyes and shook his head. "Michelangelo, only," he said.

So I am not the only one obsessed with her beauty, Miguel thought. I am vindicated. "Maria, do you know this man?"

"No and still no," she said.

Miguel wanted to laugh. Two men pushed through the door and looked around. Miguel raised his hand and motioned Vano and Luther to join their table.

"I do not sense enthusiasm from today's pilgrimage," Miguel said to the new arrivals.

Luther said nothing. Vano eyed the man seated next to Maria.

"Our Maria here refused this artist's invitation to model for him," Miguel said.

All eyes turned to the man and then to Maria.

"Brother Luther, Maria, Vano, permit me to introduce you to His Eminence Pope Julius' artist. La Pieta we so admired in the chapel today is the work of this man. Friar Luther, meet Il Divino."

The man shook his head, lowering his eyes. Luther paused only a moment. "The Divine One?"

The man looked up to Luther, "Michelangelo only, a sculptor. There is no divinity in my name."

Luther bowed to the great sculptor. "Your gifts are from God. That is evident in the divinity of your depiction of my Lord and Savior in the arms of His mother. I knelt, tears wetting the stones at its base." Luther placed his hand on Vano's shoulder. "As this good man can attest. We visited many sacred relics today. Peoples' coins are wasted on them. As magnificent as they are, none touched my heart as your creation stirred me.

Michelangelo's somber countenance slowly softened. Luther took his hand and kissed it gently. Maria's scarf loosened.

"Did Maria tell you why we are in Rome?" Miguel asked.

Michelangelo shook his head and said, "To see our Pope, to offer penance, purchase forgiveness, avoid purgatory, seek answers, pray to dead bones? Am I close?"

Luther's gentle smile erased the sour tone. "All of those and more. A great man of God lingers in prison unjustly. These, his friends, seek relief from Pope Julius."

"And you?" Michelangelo asked.

"I doubt even the Pope can offer what I seek," Luther said.

Michelangelo looked from one waiting face to the next. Then he looked deeply into Luther's eyes. "Come with me," he said, and ushered them from the tavern and led them across Sant'Angelo to the chapel.

They entered the sacred chapel. The power of the paintings on the walls sucked the breath out of them. Depictions of the apostles and the events of the early Church brought life to an otherwise bare hall.

Above them, large curtains shielded their view of the ceiling. Michelangelo led them across the open hall and began climbing a ladder that led up above the large curtains. Breezes drifted through the chapel, giving the curtains enough movement Maria felt like they were climbing into clouds. No one spoke. When Maria reached the top rung, Miguel took her hand and helped her onto the scaffolding suspended on rods protruding from holes drilled into the walls. His touch was as magical as the scene above them.

Small windows that lined the sides of the upper chapel above the curtains lit the most magnificent painting Maria thought she had ever seen. She felt she was looking up into heaven. She saw God the very Eternal Father, reaching down to endow Adam with life.

She was blessed to learn to read and write, and at the violation of the Church's edicts, she read the Bible. She read about the creation of Adam and Eve, believed what was written, but she never understood the verse like she did now. The words reverently escaped her lips, "God created man in His own image. In the image of God created He him, male and female created He them."

Miguel turned and stared, as did Michelangelo. Maria did not realize she spoke those words out loud. She wanted to blush, but she held back. The realization that God was in the very image of the man He created overwhelmed her.

"He is perfect," she said.

Michelangelo managed a tiny smile. "Thank you."

"No, yes, I mean, you painted Him perfectly, but He is perfect." Her eyes stayed glued to the painting.

"You expected Him to be spirit. So did I. How do you paint a spirit? No one can. You paint God as a man, a perfect man. There is no painter's emulsion to portray God."

Vano was not looking at the depiction of Adam in his innocence reaching to God, nor was he looking at God reaching out to the man God just formed in His own image. He was looking at the woman protected under God's left arm.

"That is Eve. She is anxiously waiting to be next," Vano said.

Michelangelo's eyes seemed to radiate. The tiny smile broadened ever so slightly, but Maria saw him stand a little taller.

"And these others behind Eve are excitedly waiting their turn," Vano continued. "Did we live before?"

Maria struggled to pull her eyes from the painting to see if Michelangelo's interpretation of the holy word was affecting them as it was her.

Luther's palms were pressed together, his eyes closed and lips moving. Is he praying? She wondered.

Words seemed inappropriate.

"Il Divino," Miguel whispered, "you are divinely blessed."

The beautifully perfect representation of the creation of Adam softened Maria's resistance to Michelangelo's invitation to serve as a model. Would she be as beautiful as Eve?

Luther muttered mostly to himself. "It is wrong."

All heads turned to Luther. Michelangelo's growing confidence deflated.

Luther's muttering turned to a whisper, "It is wrong."

"It is wrong?" Michelangelo's words pleaded for clarity.

Luther's head jerked up, and his eyes fixed on Michelangelo. "No, no, no. We are wrong. You are not wrong. We are wrong. We are doing it wrong." Luther was nearly breathless. "We have it all wrong!" The words tumbled out like the rushing of wind on the day of Pentecost. "The Church has it all wrong!"

Luther looked directly into Michelangelo's eyes. "You teach truths I doubt even Julius understands."

No one spoke. Luther looked from face to face.

"I have spent my life searching. I trudged seven hundred miles over the frozen winter Alps to receive enlightenment here in God's city. I tried to worship at the sacred relics and paid for each opportunity. I knelt and prayed on each of Pilate's sacred stone steps, climbing on my knees in humility, giving penance, seeking forgiveness. And here, I climb a common ladder made from non-sacred trees, and I see a non-clerical man who reads the word of God, understands God better than the monks, the priests, the bishops, the cardinals and even the Pope himself. Yes. We have it all wrong."

Luther's chest filled with breath, but more, it filled with confidence. "We must liberate these people."

Luther's enlightenment overwhelmed the magnificence of Michelangelo's masterpiece. "The sermons you teach in this one depiction of scripture, reveals more about man's relationship with his creator than a life spent sitting on the pews attending mass."

His head shook and his lips pursed in contemplation. He looked past everyone into nothing. Luther refocused and looked back at the group. "In less than a week, I have been invited to bed by seven different harlots. Three of whom offered a special bishop price because… I am a pilgrim."

Shocked by the unexpected revelation, Vano nearly stepped off the scaffold. The abrupt change in subject flipped Luther's epiphany upside down.

"Celibacy." Luther shook his head and, turning to Michelangelo, asked, "Did you find that in the holy word?"

Maria liked the monk. He was frank. Meek. A genuine man. Luther's shoulders relaxed and he stood at ease and turned his attention back to the painting as if he had not just given the group a trip through his mind.

"I have concluded my work in Rome. Michelangelo, you will never know the greatness of the work you have performed. I will forever be personally grateful." He returned his attention to the painting. Maria wondered if Miguel, Vano, and Michelangelo were bracing for another subject change. It did not come.

"Five hundred years from now, if Christ has not returned by then, this sermon will continue to inspire His followers."

He put his hand on Michelangelo's arm. "You have changed my life. How can we now help these lost souls with their quest to meet the Pope?"

Michelangelo put his hand over Luther's and said, "Meet me here in the morning. Julius will entertain their requests." He then ushered the group back down the ladder.

As they left the chapel, Vano asked Michelangelo, "What if the Pope refuses an audience?"

"I will stop painting." Michelangelo closed and locked the tall chapel doors. As he turned, he winked.

The next morning, the group gathered with renewed hope and anticipation for an audience with Pope Julius.

Miguel took a second serving of a steaming grain cereal topped with berries fresh from the markets. "It is wrong, you said. What did you mean?"

Luther looked refreshed, energetic, and in fresh clean tunic. What did he see on the chapel ceiling that she did not, she wondered. They had all cleaned up in preparation for an audience with Pope Julius II, the only hope for Archbishop Talavera's freedom. But Luther was extra bright and alert.

"I was not exaggerating about the harlots' invitations, nor the cost to worship," Luther said.

"Seven? Really? I only got one," Vano asked. He tore the fresh loaf in half and subconsciously offered a piece to Maria.

"Are you disappointed? Outdone in the flesh market by a monk?" she teased.

Vano shook his head and muttered, "It would have been a nice gesture."

Luther smiled at the two friends. "Our pompous Pope Julius is spending a fortune for an extravagant remodel of this church. The contradiction between the enormous wealth of the Church and Christ's emphasis on simplicity and care of the poor offends me."

Vano got past his disappointment at being less attractive to the harlots than a monk, and said, "Julius wants to build something so grand that a thousand years from now pilgrims will line up and pay to kiss his shiny foot. A giant bronze statue of Peter sits there for a thousand years. Pilgrims come from all over to kiss his foot." He paused to emphasize, "But it is not just the foot that offends me. Christ chose Peter. Who chose Julius?"

"Christ said 'You are Peter, and upon this rock I will build my church,'" Luther said.

"For Talavera's freedom, will you kiss Julius' foot?" Vano asked.

Maria snarled at him.

"I will," Miguel said. "But I would prefer to bathe the Savior's feet with my tears. Not Peter's, nor Julius'."

"You will not have to," Luther said. "Julius worships his chapel too much and I believe Michelangelo's promise. Your archbishop will be free."

"You said we are doing it wrong," Miguel returned to the original question he posed to Luther.

Luther looked firmly into Miguel's eyes. "One of Christ's last conversations he had was with the Judean Governor Pontius Pilate. The governor scoffed at the word truth used by the Savior. I think Pilate doubted you can ever know truth. But Jesus taught earlier that continuing in His word makes you one of His disciples and then you would know truth. He taught truth would make you free. That is what the Church is doing wrong."

"We are not teaching truth?" Miguel asked.

"Michelangelo, a common man, though I admit with a very uncommon talent, studies for himself. He is a disciple. He knows truth. The people need the word. They need to read it themselves. But if they do and they learn truth, what happens to the Church?"

"Every one that is of the truth heareth my voice." Maria quoted from the interview Jesus had with Pilate. All eyes turned to her.

"A woman who can read and think might topple the Church," Miguel said.

Maria smiled, but the men stared at him. "How so?" Vano asked.

She cherished Miguel's response. "Christ loved the Marys, He loved Martha, He forgave the adulteress, His hem healed the woman with the issue of blood. To Christ, women are sacred. Did you not see how Michelangelo painted Eve?"

No one was more surprised by this mini-sermon than Maria. She stared, wondering about this man. Is he for real?

"Amen," Vano said with his first smile of the morning.

"And women will be the first to teach the children," Luther added. "They will read about tithing, not indulgences. They will read about humility, not pride. They will read about forgiveness, not penance." Luther's voice grew in confidence with each word.

"I may not be the only heretic here." Miguel winked at Luther.

Sunlight streaming in through the tavern's doorway cast a shadow from the figure stepping inside. Maria noticed he, too, was cleaned up. The personal care which Maria had not dared comment about the day before was no longer an issue morning.. Michelangelo motioned with his head for the group to follow him to the chapel where she anticipated the Pope would receive them. This was it. Talavera's life depended on the next few minutes. Was he still alive? Would she and Miguel help free him or be condemned with him?

Despite the light from the morning sun, the chapel felt stagnant. Maria hoped that when the billowing curtains shielding Michelangelo's ceiling from premature viewing were removed, the chapel would liven up and showcase the glory Michelangelo intended.

Pope Julius II, the 212th leader of the Catholic Church, sat on a high back throne-like chair with gilded pummels on each side. His posture exuded a position of power, of strong personal resonance. Maria was surprised he was sitting in his choir dress rather than his full regalia. The white papal cassock shined in the limited light and flowed to the floor. The bright red velvet cape-like mozzetta was lined with white ermine fur. The zucchetto, his skullcap, matched the mozzetta. The white contrasting with the red asserted his imperial ambitions. Many claimed he chose the name Julius trying to emulate the Emperor Caesar. His warlike passions did little to diminish those claims.

Only the collection of bishops and cardinals who surrounded Julius were not sneaking glances upward, curious about what was behind the flowing curtains. If they could only see, Maria thought.

Their opportunity to petition the Pope finally came. Without any pretense, kneeling, or even a bow, Michelangelo introduced the pilgrims.

"Your Eminence," he said, "from Granada, Navarre, and Saxony, these pilgrims, my friends, come to worship and beg a blessing from Your Holiness."

Luther knelt, took the offered hand, and kissed the ornate papal ring. Maria wondered if anyone recognized how this display of respect so contradicted his earlier disgust for the life of the Pope. She understood Luther respected the position, yet not the man in it.

"Your Eminence," Luther said. "My friends come on behalf of the recent confessor of Queen Isabella of Castile, the Archbishop Hernando Talavera. Unjustly, they feel, he was imprisoned for teaching Christ to the Moors in their mother tongue, and refusing to denounce them when they refuse baptism."

Julius tilted his head, looking closely at Miguel, Maria, and Vano who all knelt and meekly listened. "You," Julius motioned to Miguel, "who sent you?"

Miguel remained on his knees. "I served with the archbishop many years and when he was arrested, he begged me to seek your just and wise intervention on his behalf."

"But we all must be baptized," Julius said.

Beads of sweat formed on Maria's brow. It was not the Lord's prayer that raced through her mind. Help him, dear Lord. Give Miguel the words. Please.

Miguel remained on his knees. He looked earnestly to Julius, "You, as the very vicar of Christ, knowing the great weakness and frailty of men, understand how doing the will of God may be misunderstood by lesser men. Lesser men who envy the success of more humble, righteous disciples of Christ. Archbishop Talavera, appointed by the queen herself and anointed by the Church, sought only to love as Christ loved. And as Peter, whose holy position you now hold, was commanded to teach every nation, Archbishop Talavera only seeks to obey your admonition to teach, baptizing in the name of Christ."

The Pope did not look at any of his counselors. He focused on Miguel. The bishops and cardinals all fixed their eyes on Julius. Maria knew some of these counselors would seek clemency and others justice.

"Who is the lesser man?" The Pope asked.

Did he know Cardinal Cisneros? Of course he does. Maria knew that. Julius was already considered the warrior pope; he was Cisneros' kindred spirit. Both men would rather use the sword than the word. Maria knew the next word out of Miguel's mouth would free or condemn Talavera.

"We are all lesser men. For this purpose, we seek your inspiration." Miguel skirted the direct question.

"Who condemned and jailed your archbishop?" Julius asked. The request held a tinge of impatience.

"Sadly, the man jealous of Archbishop Talavera's ability to quell uprisings among the people. A man unleashed by the death of the queen whose ambition is to reign above his station. Cardinal Cisneros."

Julius laughed. "I respect your attempt to be so generous in your protection of the good name of my dear friend Cardinal Cisneros."

Maria knew all was lost. They were friends. Talavera would die in prison or be burned by fire.

The Pope demanded a parchment from a chamberlain who humbly stood by. With quill and ink, Julius wrote feverishly, requested his seal, and stamped the document. Everyone waited. Silence was only broken when the Pope commanded Miguel to approach. Miguel knelt again and kissed the offered hand.

"Take this back to Spain to my friend the cardinal. If he is off on another war, see to it the bishop releases your friend."

Miguel accepted the document. He looked to the Pope and reverently bowed. The words 'thank you' rolled sweetly from his lips. He bowed again in supplication to be excused.

"May God go with you," Julius said.

Two bishops, both in fresh black cassocks and white caps, escorted the group out. When they reached the outer door, they paused and reached to look at the Pope's document. It was only then they read the pardon. Luther's face, red enough to light a fire, seared into the two bishops. Maria feared the two clerics might combust. She came closer to read. Then she saw it. This was no pardon; it was an indulgence. An indulgence requiring a payment of two hundred ducats.

The bishops remained calm, expecting a payment. Miguel put his arm around Luther and spoke to the bishops. "When is payment expected?"

"Before you leave with this document," one said, rolling it up and holding it out of Miguel's reach.

"Thank you. Please remain here. We will return," Miguel said.

Michelangelo joined the group. He asked the bishop holding the rolled-up sheet. "How much did he demand?"

"Two hundred ducats."

Michelangelo's shock confirmed it was a sum the Pope anticipated they could never pay. He turned to the group.

"About the value of my painting you admired yesterday. He wants you to pay for the Creation of Adam."

"We will return shortly," Miguel said. With Luther in tow, he walked back to the tavern where they had spent the recent week.

"Two hundred ducats?" Luther was disgusted.

Miguel pulled a satchel from behind the bed where he carefully hid it when they first arrived in Rome. He pulled forth a large heavy bag and counted two hundred ducats. Luther's eyes widened.

Miguel smiled. "Sayyida said she knew the Pope better than I did. She insisted I take this if I hoped to free the archbishop."

"A Muslim paying two hundred ducats to free a Christian?" Luther almost mumbled the words.

"A daughter of Allah freeing a son of Elohim, is how she put it. I asked her the same question," Miguel said. "Besides, she took it from one of Cisneros' own ships, captured during the siege. By now his soldiers, unpaid and unfed, are making his conquest a bitter success."

Moments later, and to the bishops' surprise, Miguel counted out each ducat. He reached for the indulgence complete with a pardon, the Pope's signature, and seal.

"Let us go home," he said. They turned their backs on the bishops standing dumbfounded, paralyzed by surprise. Maria wondered what their instructions were if they actually collected the two hundred ducats. She was certain they expected to return the pardon to Julius. She agreed. The best thing now was to go.

Michelangelo shared in the surprise. "I am sorry. I never anticipated two hundred ducats. I thank you for purchasing my painting. I am happy you are not taking it with you, but wish you could stay to enjoy it." He winked at Luther, entered the chapel, and walked away toward the ladder.

"It will inspire the world for ages," Luther said, "as it has me."

To go home was the predominant thought. They gathered their belongings and gathered on the portico of the Basilica of San Lorenzo. Luther wanted to see the thirteenth century frescoes which were renowned for their depiction of stories of St. Lawrence and St Stephen.

Content he saw as much of Rome as he needed to see, Luther wished his friends well. "When you tire of the intrigues of the Church in Granada, I welcome you in Wittenberg. Saxony is beautiful, maybe safer for a heretic," Luther said.

Miguel handed Luther a small bag of coins. "Our friends have provided, courtesy of the cardinal." Miguel padded the satchel hanging over his shoulder. "We will part company here and wish you well on your journey home."

Luther nodded, thanked them again, and began his northbound trek. The remaining party watched as their friend gradually disappeared into the throngs of worshipers, pilgrims, merchants, and monks.

"It will be a shame for him to burn," Vano said.

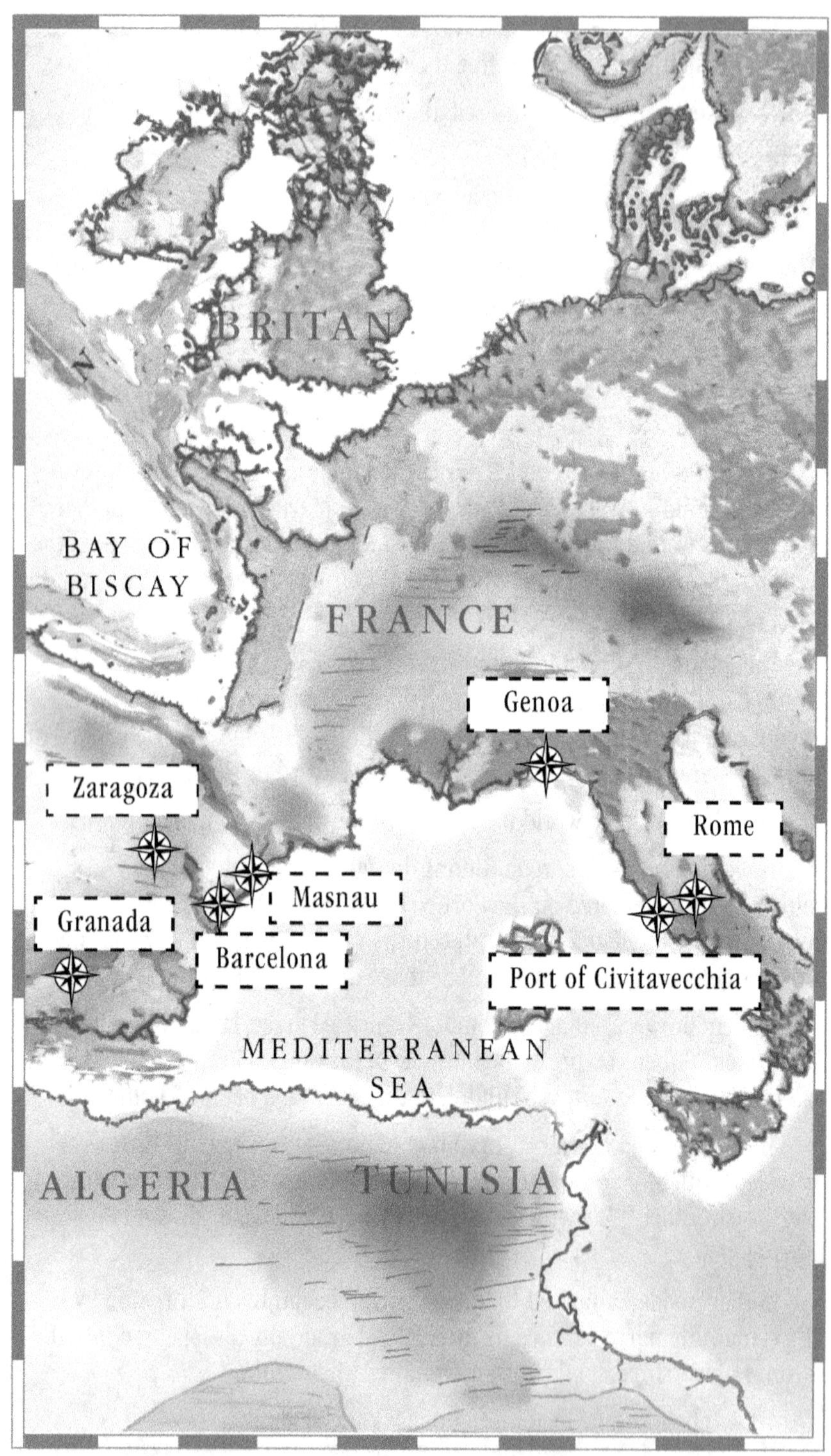

BRITAN
BAY OF BISCAY
FRANCE
Genoa
Zaragoza
Rome
Masnau
Granada
Barcelona
Port of Civitavecchia
MEDITERRANEAN SEA
ALGERIA
TUNISIA

Chapter Twenty-Eight

1510 - Port of Civitavecchia - Port of Rome

Wind filled the sails, and hope filled their hearts. The next stop was Barcelona, and days later they would be in Granada.

The Pope's order for Archbishop Talavera's release was as sacred a document as the holy scriptures. The epistles of Paul to the churches in ancient days, traversing the Mediterranean, could not be held in more regard. Though it was nothing more than an indulgence that cost two hundred ducats, ducats to help build a monument for the Pope, it meant their friend would be free.

The only disagreement Maria and Miguel had to this point was the matter of who paid their passage. Miguel insisted he pay. Maria resisted due to her stubborn independence. Miguel explained the money he carried was not ill gotten, but honestly won when Sayyida sacked one of Cardinal Cisneros' own treasure ships. What better use of that money than to undo an injustice perpetrated by the cardinal himself? Miguel eventually won the day. But the victory did not taste as sweet as he hoped.

On the second day, their ship was accompanied by three brigantines, each bearing the large Red Spike Cross representing the Knights Hospitaller of Saint John. Miguel wondered if they were out searching for the Georgia and the sacred prisoners Sayyida took from under the very nose of Cisneros. And now Miguel and Maria were about to snatch the archbishop from the cardinal's grasp.

If this was not an errand of the Lord, nothing was, Miguel thought.

"What brings that smile to your face?" Maria asked. Miguel stood, one hand resting on the railing and the other on the rigging.

"You," he said. "The archbishop asks me for help. I meander my way across North Africa as a fugitive, a galley slave, a soldier, a knight, all the time me being a captive by somebody, and you…" he paused and tucked the rebellious lock of hair back over her ear. He loved touching her. "You get a letter from a friend. You charge from country to country fearlessly putting your life in God's hands. And now, you stand there biting your lip like a little girl, blind to the fact that Vano wants to marry you."

She quickly set her lip free. Her eyebrows rose. "He is not subtle and I am not blind. But I could never ask for a better friend. And he would be a marvelous husband."

"I would? Yes, I would," Vano said as he approached the two from behind as they looked out to sea. "Let us get started. I can call the captain."

The rebellious lock broke free and fell over her eye. "A marvelous husband for a very lucky Gitana. Any one of them would take him off my hands in an instant," she said.

"Oh, the pain," Vano said, holding his broken heart.

Miguel loved his two new friends, and he loved they were not married. Maria's eyes were dark, but in the morning light here on deck they glistened green. He thought back to Sukayna's eyes, those dark pools, inviting, intriguing, captivating. Could she really be Jalaf's wife? Was he serious when he claimed that was all it took to capture his own heart and make her his wife? If so, how could he stand to ever leave her side? Because he loved Talavera. That is how. Miguel almost felt guilty for not recognizing Jalaf was on the same mission, just playing a different role. And so was Maria and Vano, and Sayyida. God must want Talavera free very badly. But why go to so much effort? Why not just stop Cisneros, one of His professed servants, from jailing him in the first place?

Miguel recalled how Talavera taught that the only limit to God's almighty power was His commitment to honor man's free will. God will not force us back to heaven, he taught. And therefore, He will not stop us from mistreating one another. Every time Miguel tried to argue the unfairness of it, Talavera so confidently stated that in the end, Christ, because of his suffering and resurrection, He has power to make it all right, regardless of our earthly experience. Miguel remembered adamantly insisting there better be a long time between death and hell for Christ to make it all right, or he would rebel.

Miguel was ready to sit at the feet of Talavera once again and learn from the master. He missed the hours spent debating how the scriptures differed from the priests' sermons. During the year away from Talavera, Miguel concluded that indeed, he himself was a heretic.

"What happens next after we liberate Talavera? He can not possibly continue in Granada," Maria asked.

"An enemy like Cisneros will not quit until he is destroyed," Vano said.

Miguel nodded, pondered, then said, "He will go with me back to Navarre. We can stay north of the Pyrenees, out of Satan's reach."

"We may accompany you. Maria is returning to Zaragosa and my family is up there. I want to introduce you to my sister," Vano said, watching Maria closely. He was rewarded with Maria's slight scowl.

"When you escaped from Oran, Sayyida led Cisneros' men to believe she was transporting his personal captives to Barcelona following the conquest of Oran. Did I understand that right?" Vano asked.

Miguel nodded, not wishing to avert his eyes from Maria's hair dancing in the breeze. She was biting her lip again.

"We should not go to Barcelona," she said. "Can Andi swim?"

Miguel caught on quickly. "We will leave the ship early, but we will not need to swim." He excused himself and sought out the captain.

Masnou was nothing more than a tiny fishing village with a port fit for small craft only. The captain pulled the ship as close as he could to the long, sandy shoreline. Despite the strong objections of Miguel, Maria, claiming victory, sat bareback atop Andi. With a vigorous kick, Andi lunged into the water. Yes, she could swim. Maria held to the loose halter as Andi pulled her to shore.

Vano was right behind her. Miguel, having been taken to shore in the small boat with all their gear, stood waiting the arrival of his two companions. His resentment for Maria winning the tug-o-war over bringing the horses to shore vanished the second she stepped from the water. She sent all her outer clothes with the saddles and other belongings. Her wet linen under-tunic clung to her body and did her figure more than justice. He wondered if she heard the wind escape his lungs leaving him breathless. As much as he hated to do it, he wrapped a dry cloak over her shoulders, leaving his arm resting there a moment or two. He took the lead rope from her hand and led Andi up the beach.

They eventually secured a horse for Miguel and were on their way south, bypassing Barcelona and anxious to avoid any of Cisneros' men.

Maria got past her objections of using Sayyida's ill gotten money. It afforded them comfortable inns and good food as they traveled toward Granada. Conversations gravitated to Maria's poor family conditions in Trujillo, her self-directed education, her time with Vano's family, and her relationship with Archbishop Talavera's family.

Miguel realized he was attracted to her confidence, her independence, and her grit. It did not hurt that aside from Sukayna she may be the most beautiful woman he had ever known.

After a week traversing the country, they pushed up and over the Sierra Nevadas and stopped on a ridge overlooking Granada. It had been over a year since Miguel, with Jalaf's help, escaped the pyre. All he could do was hope Talavera was still alive and the parchment with the Pope's seal could free him. There was only one person in this city, well, maybe two, he could trust. The late afternoon sunlight bounced off the stone works of the Alhambra, bathing the massive palace in rich orange.

"Time to see a tailor about these rags," Miguel said.

Miguel had been in large cities like Toledo, Madrid, and most recently Rome. He anticipated the energy of Granada, which in his memory was as vibrant as the others, would welcome him home. It did not. Rome was a bustling city, but the feeling of it was worldly. It was not the spiritual center he hoped it would be. He missed the spirit of Granada, the love of the archbishop, and the people they taught. But that was gone. He thought back on his time with Abu in Saïda. It was not a large city. It was only a village, but it had a spirit about it that he now missed. What happened here? He was so caught up in his thoughts, Maria had to nudge him after her third try to get directions.

"Are you lost?" she asked. "We passed through this market twice."

He realized he was lost. He quickly gathered his thoughts and looked for something familiar. The cathedral of Granada poked its dome above the market. He recognized where he was and quickly left the market square and led Maria and Vano through the winding alleys to the livery where Jalaf arranged for his escape. He remembered the man who led him from the city. The man never spoke to him, and Miguel was not sure what reception he could expect.

They dismounted. Miguel stepped inside. A young man attending to a tall white mare looked over his shoulder and nodded.

"Is this where I might find Ubayd?" he asked. The young man said nothing. He lifted the front leg and dug dirt from the dirty shoe. Was he deaf?

Or just rude?

"Ubayd was a friend of mine," Miguel said.

The young man looked closely at Miguel, but said nothing. Miguel closed his eyes, took a deep breath, and realized the young man was not deaf. He was a Moor who spoke no Spanish. Miguel wanted to slap himself for his foolishness.

"Hello, I am Miguel. Ubayd was very kind to me many months ago. I was in a hurry and failed to thank him. I have returned to do so." This time he spoke in Arabic, to which the young man responded.

"He was taken away. There is no need to thank him now."

Miguel did not pry. "Might you care for three animals while we pay our respect to others to whom I owe gratitude?"

The young man stood and followed Miguel out. He opened the livery door and brought the three horses in from the street.

"How long?" he asked.

Miguel said, "Overnight, maybe longer."

The boy bowed and led the animals away.

"I hope he was not the tailor?" Vano asked.

"The tailor is next," Miguel said.

"Do you trust him?" Vano asked.

"The tailor or the boy in the livery?" Miguel said.

"Either," Vano said.

"I do not know who to trust. Let us see if you trust the tailor," Miguel said.

They worked through the alley and stood in front of the shop where those many months ago, Miguel was captivated by a pair of eyes he had not forgotten for an instant.

"From what trouble can I rescue you, this time?"

All three of them recognized that voice before the big smile dragged it from behind a long curtain. Maria received the first hug, Vano a vigorous embrace, and Miguel a disdained look as Jalaf eyed him up and down. He motioned to the sword hanging on Miguel's hip.

"You still wear that thing? Hope you are improved this time around. There is going to be trouble if that smile means you are here for the archbishop," Jalaf said. "Sukayna is not here, but she has been praying to your Jesus for your success. The archbishop is not well. They treated him worse than us infidels," Jalaf said.

Vano said, "You infidels have not treated him well?"

Jalaf ignored the question. He grew more serious than Miguel had ever seen him. "Cisneros' bishops have strict commands to force him to confess and recant the writings."

"What writings?" Maria asked. She looked to Miguel for an answer.

"Archbishop Talavera felt strongly that conversion was an individual decision, that a man cannot be forced to believe a thing he does not understand. He must understand before a choice is valid. That is why he had me teach the priests the language of the Moors, so we can teach them in their own language," Miguel said.

Vano breathed out, "Ooh, and he wrote that down?"

"I wrote that down, and more," Miguel said. "The Bishop of Malága betrayed Talavera and gave my writings to Cisneros."

"You have something besides that sword to free the archbishop, I hope?" Jalaf said. Gone was his jolly self, but not his joy in poking at Miguel's swordsmanship.

Miguel pulled the indulgence out and handed it to Jalaf. Jalaf read it quickly, looked up into Miguel's eyes, and said, "This piece of paper is all you brought back? With what my sister gave you, I could have bought two popes!" He shook his head in disappointment.

"Where is Talavera now? Can we visit him?" Maria asked.

"You can. And maybe the Gitano. Miguel will be arrested on the spot."

"They think I am still alive?"

"No. But they believe in the resurrection." Jalaf smiled.

"Who is the new archbishop?" Miguel asked.

"Who else? Francisco Jimenez de Cisneros," he said.

"Where is he?"

"Navarre, I hear. I do not usually keep track of him."

"Navarre? Why?" Miguel got anxious. He had watched Cisneros' brutal conquest of Oran. What would he do to Navarre? Navarre was Miguel's home, and an independent country nestled between Castile on the west, Aragon on the east and France on the north. And Miguel's Basque Ziortza-Bolibar sat perfectly in the middle. The small independent nation had been the object of conquest for centuries. If Cisneros set his eye on Navarre, it was time to demonstrate the sword he wore was not just an ornament.

Over the previous weeks, many discussions revolved around the strategy to secure Talavera's release. They were convinced Cisneros would only honor the indulgence if it were presented publicly. Yet, publicly meant embarrassment for Cisneros. With Cisneros absent, would the bishops honor the Pope's decree? A papal bull demanding a release would have been better, yet the Pope favored Cisneros style, as evidenced by his appointment as Grand Inquisitor years earlier.

It was now or never.

Miguel won the argument of whether the three should approach the bishops as they were, dressed as pilgrims from Rome, or as Jalaf offered; as the Three Magi from the East.

Vano wanted to be outfitted by Sukayna, who he understood to be of surpassing beauty. Both Maria and Miguel voted that down. But where was she? Miguel wondered. He did not wonder long. There she stood.

Vano's breathing became audible. "She belongs to Jalaf," Maria whispered. Miguel smiled.

"My prodigal has returned," Sukayna reached up, and with both hands pulled Miguel's head down and kissed each cheek. "Oh, the stories my husband tells about you."

Maria's wide eyes were met by Sukayna's. "And you are as lovely as he told me you were. I felt fortunate he chose to return home to me," Sukayna said as she gave Maria a warm embrace.

Then she turned to Vano. "Welcome to my home." She quickly hugged and kissed both cheeks to the approval of all but Jalaf.

"My humble tailor shop caters to many men of the cloth—as well as their mistresses," she winked at Maria. "The bishops are not all corrupt. They let me minister to Hernando despite Cisneros' threats."

Miguel had not heard anyone call Talavera by his first name in years. It was almost disrespectful. But he recognized this beautiful woman was not ministering to an archbishop, she was ministering to a man. A man mistreated and betrayed by the very church he had given his life for. The words of Christ drifted through his mind, "I was in prison, and ye came unto me…come ye blessed of my father, inherit the kingdom prepared from the foundation of the world, inasmuch as ye have done it unto one of the least of these, ye have done it unto me."

Jalaf handed the Pope's indulgence to Sukayna. "Will they honor this decree?" She read it slowly.

"Bishop Martinez will. He hates what Cardinal Cisneros has done. With this," she held up the indulgence, "he has the backing of Julius."

"How soon?" Miguel asked.

"Right now," she said.

The busy market, which just minutes before bustled with commerce, now seemed hollow. The late hour sucked the busy merchants and shoppers into homes, taverns, brothels, and churches.

It was happening. Miguel wondered if Maria's heart was pounding as hard as was his. At one point, they cut between two shops and up a steep step. Miguel took Maria's hand as she made the step. He unconsciously did not let go for several seconds. She did not pull her hand away. They reached the large plaza where Miguel last saw Talavera taken away. Where he began his journey to Rome. It was empty. The only sound was the clatter of their own boots on the stones.

Without hesitation, Sukayna pushed into the cathedral. Evening mass was about to start. The congregation included only a few dozen parishioners and, from the look of them, Miguel assumed these were newly baptized converts trying to prove to the Church their sincerity.

Bishop Martinez paused. Two altar boys knelt at the altar. Miguel did not recognize either one. But then they probably grew several inches in his absence. Mass would have to wait. Sukayna led the group directly to the altar. She knelt in reverence, crossed herself, and on one knee took the hand of the bishop. What must the bishop be thinking about this disturbance? He, Vano, and Maria knelt as well. The bishop motioned for them to rise. Sukayna whispered something to the bishop and handed him the indulgence.

He unrolled the parchment and read it silently. Miguel watched his eyes pause at the signature and seal, then return to the top and read again. As he read, the serious firm lips softened. When he reached the signature again, a smile forced its way onto his round, wrinkled face. The tall, stiff shield-shaped white mitre almost danced on his head. The smile became contagious.

"This warms my heart," he said. He immediately excused the parishioners, who happily and speedily exited their pews and disappeared into the waning light of the setting sun.

He gave instructions to the two altar boys who also took leave of their responsibility. Bishop Martinez led the group from the cathedral and through a nearly abandoned section of the city. Miguel knew where they were headed.

Standing on the site of the eleventh century Zirid fortress, the Nasrid dynasty in 1238 built a citadel that was now the oldest part of the Alhambra—the Alcazaba. Miguel knew this fortress well. It not only held administrative and sleeping quarters for the guards and their families, inside the military enclosures were the famed underground chambers they called the mazmorras. These dungeons were notorious. Used for ages, they were the most secure part of the Alhambra. Prisoners were typically forced to perform manual labor during the day, and then lowered back into the dungeons at night.

Miguel hadn't imagined Cisneros so vile as to condemn the archbishop to this fate. As they wound their way through the labyrinth of halls and streets of the Alcazaba, fury fought desperately with guilt that he had not used his sword to commend Cisneros to the grave rather than run.

Bishop Martinez then turned suddenly and entered a section of the Alcazaba Miguel did not recognize. They stepped into a large hall lit by torches on each wall. Two guards stood at attention guarding a large wooden door hinged on one side with thick steel hinges that looked to carry the rust of centuries. Other large doors on the opposite wall hung partially open. The expected dank smell of ancient stone cells was not there.

The guards remained at attention, but visibly relaxed when they recognized the bishop and Sukayna. There was no threat tonight.

"The Good Lord has chosen to release our prisoner," the bishop said. He held up the indulgence for the guards to see and read. Miguel wondered how well these men could read. Immediately, he saw the bishop's wisdom. The more public he made the indulgence known, the more difficult for Cisneros to reject it. Though it cost two hundred ducats, the Pope included Archbishop Talavera and his associates in the pardon.

They pushed the large door open. It was not locked. Maria and Sukayna hurried through before the bishop could enter with the lantern.

Stripped from his priestly robes, the prisoner struggled to grasp the meaning of the visit. He was an old man. So different from the vibrant, wise, and kind Archbishop of Granada, Hernando Talavera was a shell.

One on each arm, the two women gently helped Talavera to his bare feet the way a mother lifts and cuddles a newborn. Soft words slowly escaped his dry and cracked lips. Like an unattended garden is soon consumed by noxious weeds, his tonsure was lost to patches of long gray hair reaching his shoulders. His face was hidden behind a thin gray beard. Miguel wanted to beg why any decent human let this man remain ungroomed. The earlier fury and guilt melted into heartache and then determination. Tears pushed through the war of emotions.

Before Talavera's eyes adjusted to the light, the subtle scent of jasmine announced Sukayna was one of the two women helping him up. His eyes could not have been more blessed to see his other benefactor so equal her in beauty.

His eyes finally rested on Miguel. He blinked, squinted, and blinked again. "Miguel?" A broad smile parted the gray, hairy face. He lifted his arm toward heaven. "Praise my Lord and God. You are alive!" Just as quickly as his smile arrived, he wrinkled his brow and squinted at the bishop.

"God's will be done. You are safe now." The bishop held up the parchment, not trying to open it. "God has spoken through our Eminence Pope Julius II. You are finally free."

Talavera looked back at Miguel, who snatched him from Maria and Sukayna and held tight. Both men wept, shoulders shaking. As tears slowed, the emotional war inside Miguel mounted again. This once strong disciple of Christ, though not a large man before, felt like a skeleton in his arms.

"Let us go home," Sukayna's tender words echoed in the small stone chamber. She and Maria each took an arm and almost carried him from the cell. The guards bowed in respect as they exited the hall.

The bishop showed the papal indulgence and told those they encountered the good news of the Pope's release as they wound their way through the Alcazaba. What little strength Talavera had before left. Now back in control of his emotions, Miguel scooped him into his arms like he would a young child and proudly marched him into freedom.

"Where is home?" Vano asked.

Chapter Twenty-Nine

1510 - Granada, Spain

"Come with me." Bishop Martinez took Miguel's arm and led him and the group down a dark street, back toward the square past Jalaf's and Sukayna's shop into a quiet residential area built against the back walls of the city.

"You must not be part of this," the bishop said to Sukayna. "The cardinal permitted your care of the archbishop as a gesture of his mercy. His anger at this release and pardon will know no bounds. If you are to remain in Granada or even alive, you need to distance yourself."

The lantern lit a cozy walkway through a garden to a finely carved door. He knocked gently and pushed it open. The large, finely appointed room was welcoming. The bishop lit two other lamps and turned off the lantern. A soft cushioned couch welcomed Talavera, as Miguel carefully laid him down. He immediately sat up and clung to Miguel's arm, then pulled him onto the couch.

"You are here! You are here!" Talavera said. "God delivered you!"

"No, I delivered him," Jalaf said. "God delivered you."

All eyes turned to Jalaf. He winked.

The bishop stepped into an adjoining room, spoke with someone, and quickly returned. The sound of footsteps outside faded into the distance.

Minutes later, stomping boots announced the arrival of two visitors. The door pushed open. In stepped a short, muscled man wearing the Moorish peasant pant, with an open linen vest that exposed a powerful chest. He was followed by a woman several years his senior. Her bright floral dress may have provided more light than the lamps hanging on the walls.

The man stopped in mid step, squinted at Miguel. His eyes slowly scanned from head to foot. The slightest of smiles stole onto his face. The recognition was mutual. Miguel nodded a gentle thank you, both for his attention those many months ago and for the aid he was about to provide the archbishop.

Jalaf watched the two men renew an acquaintance.

With the same earnest attention, but gentler, he applied various balms to Talavera's frail body. Leaving Sukayna with Talavera, the elder woman took Maria from the room. They returned just as Talavera sat cleaned, shaved, and dressed in fresh linen robes. Platters of fruit, cheeses, and breads were complemented with a warm vegetable and lamb stew. Talavera visibly gained strength as Sukayna and Maria nourished the frail man. Yet, the frailty ended at his eyes. They were as firm and strong as the fortress from which he had just been extracted. They burned with power, with understanding, with peace. No one spoke. He put his gentle hands on Sukayna's and Maria's. He whispered a thank you to each.

The bishop stood, arms folded at the door. He had not eaten. The woman stood at his side. This was her home, Miguel realized. Talavera reached forward to the bishop, who stepped over and knelt before Talavera. In that instant, Miguel saw the respect and love between the two men. It was this bishop who had defied the cardinal and permitted the care Sukayna provided. It was this bishop who prevented his incarceration in the underground cells where the only access was to be raised and lowered with a rope.

The voice was meek but clear. "Bless you, my son. From the day you arrived, you have proven a true disciple of Christ. He alone will claim you His." Talavera pulled him close and kissed his forehead. The bishop returned to the woman's side.

Talavera reached for Jalaf, who, along with the others, blinked back tears of joy. In the first show of humility Miguel ever witnessed in Jalaf, he knelt. "Before you bless me, you should know I am playing both sides. I petition Allah and Jesus to get my miracles done. Caring for Miguel required both. If he could use a sword, either Allah or Jesus alone could do the job."
"Could they be brothers?" Jalaf asked, almost sincerely.

"Miguel and Jesus? Brothers?" Talavera asked with a wink. "I think so."

"Allah and Jesus," Jalaf clarified. Sukayna swatted him.

"You must be my Maria," he said, taking both her hands. "Magdalena talked so much about you. You look exactly as I imagined you, complete with the rebellious lock and the quivering lip." He reached up and tucked the lock up over her ear. She freed the lip that had been tucked between her teeth.

Miguel loved how Talavera's gentle hand rested on Maria's cheek. Like that of a loving father proud of a daughter.

"Magdalena prayed you would get her letter in time. She is gone now, taken to heaven like Elijah in her own chariot of fire." He blinked away tears. "Introduce me to our friend," he asked.

Vano bowed, "Your Eminence, I am Vano of the Saragosa Romanis, blessed to accompany your disciples."

Miguel had now witnessed two rare demonstrations of humility. He wondered what it would be like when these two stood before Jesus Himself.

"Thank you. The Romanis are a unique type of disciple. I once traveled with a Roma family. Their daughter nearly kept me from the priesthood." Talavera's serious tone weakened just enough for a broad smile to sneak through. A memory he tried to bury must have broken free, Miguel thought.

His voice grew stronger. The company of people, the love which filled the room, the food, and certainly the spirit of God was enlivening the once powerful archbishop who had been on the brink of death.

"My dear Miguel," he said. "My belief in you was not false hope." Miguel took Talavera's hand as he knelt and bowed. He did not notice how Talavera's eyes shifted from Miguel to Maria and back again. A tiny smile betrayed his soberness.

"I sense your journey was led by God," he paused and winked at Jalaf, "and your guardian here, for a bigger purpose than me. I am not long for the world." Talavera took several deep breaths, as he closed his eyes for several seconds. The strength from just minutes before seemed to drain out. "Tomorrow, I want to hear it all."

Sukayna took command as she evidently had done for months caring for Talavera in his prison cell once Bishop Martinez arrived. They helped him into a small bedroom. She had him comfortably laying on the simple bed. She kissed his cheek before she ushered everyone back to the front of the house.

"You may all stay here," the bishop said. The woman nodded.

"Maria will come with us," Sukayna said. "I do not trust these two with her." She grabbed Maria's arm and the two stepped out into the darkness. Vano and Miguel said nothing. They just looked at each other. They had just spent countless nights together and now they were untrustworthy?

"My wife has spoken," Jalaf said. He marched out, following Sukayna and Maria.

"Come with me," the woman said. The bishop nodded to her and left, closing the door behind him. They followed the woman through a kitchen that consisted of a clever stone fireplace designed with an oven at waist height, and a stone platform to the side of it with a steel top featuring a cavity to build a fire. A large hood above the fire caught the smoke and ushered it from the house. Miguel paused to admire the inventive design. The woman watched him proudly.

"I designed it. The bishop had it built for me," she said. He nodded approval.

They exited the kitchen into a garden. It was too dark to appreciate, but the leaves and branches brushing his arms and shoulders proclaimed a healthy garden pathway. The woman pushed open a door and fumbled in the dark for a moment. A small lantern brought the room to light. Four beds, one on each wall, filled the single room. Windows on each side of the door were the only accents to the bare stone walls.

"The beds are clean. I will have food ready in the morning." She left the lamp on the only small table in the room. "Thank you for this," she said. With tears in her eyes, she closed the door.

"We will see what that kitchen you admired can do," Vano said, dropping onto a bed.

Miguel loosened his belt, removed his sword, kicked off his boots, and blew out the lamp.

Miguel rose before the sun and at first light was out exploring. He was right, the garden they passed last night was heavy with growth. Even overgrown, he thought. In the back of the garden, he found a small washhouse providing everything necessary to refresh himself. Two large gardens were full of vegetables. On one end of the property, he found at least a couple hogs, several goats, and chickens everywhere.

He wondered how Jalaf was doing with two extraordinarily beautiful women. Was Maria biting her lip? Had Sukayna helped her tame the wild lock of hair yet? He hoped not.

Before long, his nose called him to breakfast. One of the oven's chimneys poured the scent of the baked goods into the garden. Bread. Fresh, hot bread.

Miguel stepped through the kitchen admiring every inch of it and absorbing the individual scents from the pots, pans, and oven, each flavor parading through his senses.

A small dining area which he had not noticed last night already sported its first guest. Archbishop Hernando Talavera, with hands folded on the table, smiled at Miguel's approach.

Liberty alone injected light into his eyes and confidence into his voice. Yet his hands trembled, and movements were intentional and abrupt. Miguel sat across from him, staring into his face. Where a bright smile once poured forth the Gospel of Jesus Christ to Jew, gentile, and heathen, the smile was there, but the brightness of his teeth bore a year's worth of neglect.

"We will take you home," Miguel said.

Talavera laid his trembling hand on Miguel's. "You will not be the one to take me home. I am old. I am sick. My Lord will take me home. But let us not talk about that now. Tell me about your friends, your journey."

Where to start, wondered Miguel. "I want to join you in the ministry. You always discouraged me. But I can teach, you know that. I can help people come to Christ."

Talavera watched as Miguel became more intense. A smile seemed to trickle down his arms into his hands. He squeezed them.

"I met a monk," Miguel said.

"In Rome? I imagine so."

"He thinks like us. He loves the Church, but hates the lies. Hates the wickedness. He is not afraid. He is like you. I want to be like you. I want to fight along with you."

"We will be crushed. Oh, if we could make a difference. The bishop showed me the indulgence. You bought my liberty with two hundred ducats. The Pope never pardoned me, did he?"

Miguel shook his head.

"You have an enemy in Cardinal Cisneros. You and the others must leave here and fight another day, in another way," Talavera said.

Talavera breathed in slowly. It was a shallow, pained breath. His eyes struggled to focus. After a few moments, his attention returned.

"Where did you get two hundred ducats? That might be a story worthy to share?"

"Sayyida al-Hurra. A long painful story."

"Sayyida? Jalaf's sister? The pirate? Bless her soul!"

"Her soul? I am not convinced her soul is in near the jeopardy as the souls of Cisneros, Julius, or Bishop Martinez." Miguel softened his voice as he motioned toward the woman.

"What are you thinking? She is his concubine?"

"Many of the priests and bishops in Rome have a mistress of some sort," Miguel said.

"Cardinal Cisneros demands celibacy. Bishop Martinez insists the Bible does not." Talavera called softly. The woman quickly came. Miguel noticed how the strain and the effort to call the woman wore on Talavera. He is old, he is sick, Miguel realized. Talavera took the woman's hand.

"Anna Maria, my friend here appreciates your kind attention for the good bishop. Share with him your relationship, if you please."

Miguel's face flushed at Talavera's insinuation that Miguel thought she was a mistress.

Anna Maria smiled proudly. "I am his wife." She put her hand on Talavera's shoulder. "Married by his authority." She squeezed. Miguel's surprise brought both Talavera and Anna Maria a chuckle.

"That is not a fact to be shared too broadly."

"For either of your sakes," Miguel said. "The monk I mentioned is just a younger version of you. He cannot seem to align himself with many of the clergy's teachings."

"Many of us cannot. But we are loyal to our Christ. You can be loyal to Christ in other ways. Tell me about Maria."

Miguel stiffened, and his eyes opened wide. Anna Maria and Talavera both chuckled again.

"She is lovely," Anna Maria said.

"She bites her lip," Miguel said.

Anna Maria swatted his shoulder and returned to the kitchen. "Do not say more till I am back." She soon returned with warm bread, a pot of hot oats, and goat milk.

"Now," she said, "tell us this amazing story."

"She is your sister Magdalena's dear friend who loves your family. She answered Magdalena's plea to seek your pardon from the Pope. Sayyida, Jalaf and I met her and the Gitano in Genoa. Actually, that is where we also met the monk. He was having a spirited debate in the tavern where we stopped."

"Does Maria belong to this Vano?" Talavera asked.

"He wants her to," Miguel said.

"How about you?" Anna Maria asked.

"What about me?" Miguel turned to Anna Maria, almost ready to excuse her from the conversation. Her impudent smile softened him. She is a romantic, he thought. She fell in love with the bishop, convinced the archbishop to marry them. She loves love.

"She and Vano's family are very close. She is too independent to settle down. Vano told me how quick she is with a short blade, and deadly if she chooses to be. I keep my distance."

"She is in love with you," Anna Maria said.

"Pardon me?"

"Last night. Even in the short minutes she cared for the archbishop, her deference for you was evident. She did not want to leave with Sukayna. A woman can tell."

Talavera ate only a few bites. He continued to tremble, making it difficult to eat. Anna Maria sat and helped steady his hand.

Vano, refreshed from a safe and lengthy night's rest, joined them and sat. Anna Maria quickly provided a plate.

Talavera caught Vano's eyes. "We met briefly last night. I apologize for not expressing my appreciation for your help. Though I would much like to spend time getting acquainted, I must beg of you the fulfillment of an important chore."

"Please do," Vano said. "The way Maria and this rogue respect you, I feel it would be an honor to serve."

"Get out of here," Talavera said.

Anna Maria dropped the oat filled spoon. Miguel choked on the swallow of goat milk and Vano's eyes opened so wide so fast the wrinkles on his forehead nearly knocked his hat off.

"Not just you. The three of you. Will you please help my dear friends get as far from Granada as you can? The cardinal is due to return from Navarre.

He cannot harm me again. But you three, and I fear Jalaf and Sukayna, are in grave danger. Cisneros will not attempt a trial or a public burning of heretics. He will simply have his guards eliminate you. Immediately."

Talavera bowed his weary head, slowly lowered his eyelids, and pulled in as much air as his aged lungs could.

Anna Maria took his hand and steadied him. This was not the vibrant Talavera Miguel served those many years. Miguel never knew Talavera as a young man. As Talavera's young mischievous altar boy, Miguel thought Talavera, then in his sixties, was old. But now it was more than the years. Prison broke his health. But his soul and mind were impervious to Satan's wrath.

"I am not leaving," Miguel said flatly. "My blade is not so weak, as Jalaf says. Cisneros is my enemy, not Vano's, nor Maria's."

Miguel turned to Vano, whose mouth was full. "The archbishop is right Vano. You must get Maria back home. She and you are not in this fight. And it is a fight. Sayyida gave us enough coin to get you comfortably home to your people."

"I think Maria might not leave you so easily," Vano said. He picked his teeth clean with his tongue. Anna Maria smiled and nodded.

Talavera tried to stand. "I think I need to rest. This is more than my old sick bones have endured all year."

Miguel and Anna Maria helped him back into bed. They propped him up comfortably. He then shooed them from the room.

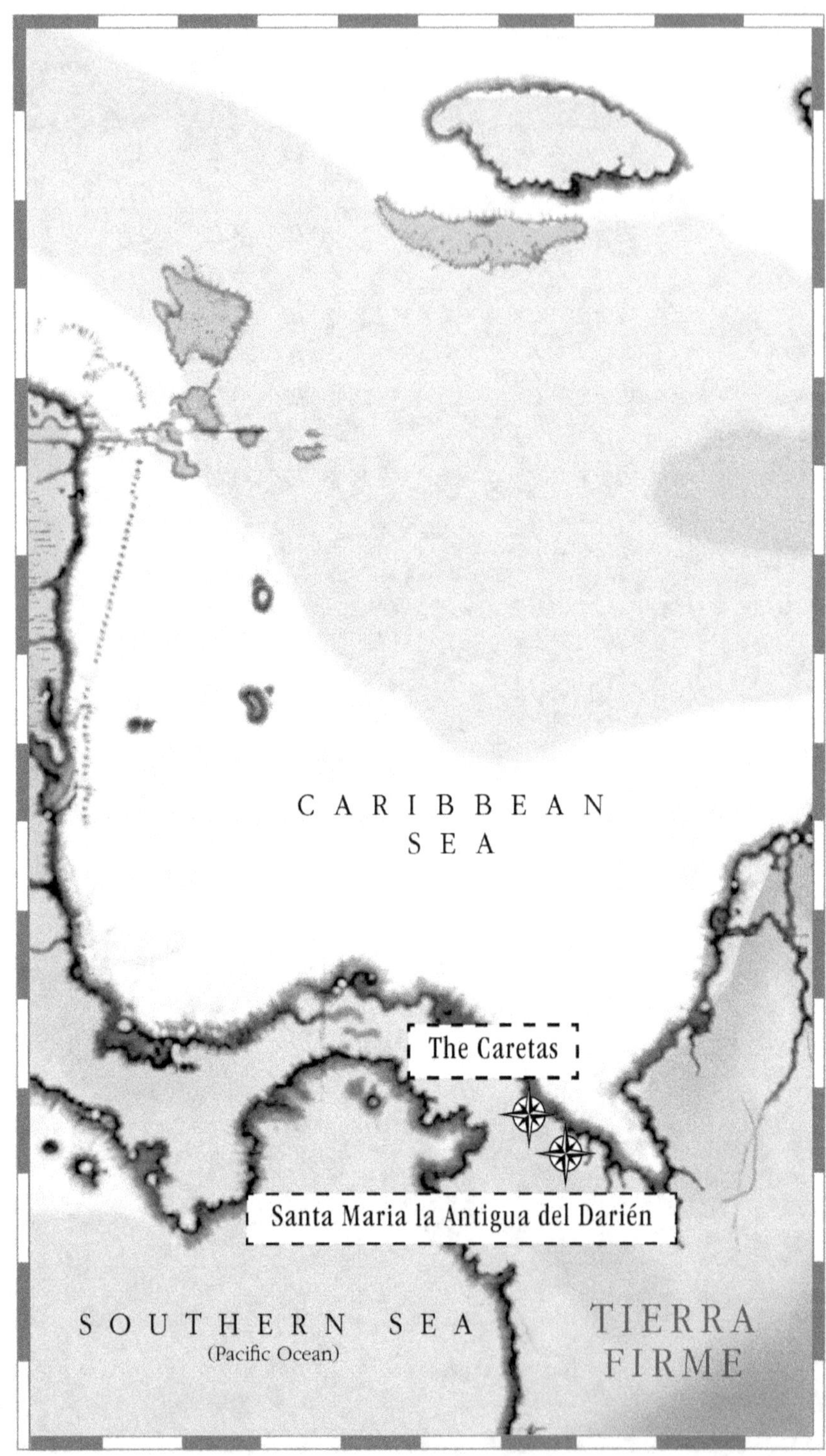

CARIBBEAN
SEA
The Caretas
Santa Maria la Antigua del Darién
SOUTHERN SEA
(Pacific Ocean)
TIERRA
FIRME

Chapter Thirty

1510 - Santa Maria la Antigua del Darién

Mornings were usually sunny, but this morning a spirit of adventure added an energy that made it even brighter. The soldiers donned their full armor. The clanging of swords, shields, and helmets echoed through Darién.

"What are you thinking?" Balboa asked. Alessandro stood on a rock bringing the boy and man face to face. He secured Balboa's breast shield to the back plate, a task he performed countless times. Alessandro liked it when Balboa was dressed in his armor. It gave him a sense of pride and safety.

"I want to come. They say it is a friendly tribe," Alessandro said.

"And your armor?"

"Leoncito."

"He will take the poison dart for you?"

"He will warn me."

"You are sure?"

"He did before." Alessandro regretted it as soon as the words left his lips.

Balboa knew Alessandro spent time in the jungles. He reported on the jaguar, the tree sloth, other discoveries, and the flash flood. Until now, he had not reported any contact with natives apart from some locals already trading with the settlement. They proved to be harmless and poor.

"Before?" Balboa's question was as natural as a parent would pose to a child he trusted, but at the same time knew he was still a boy.

"Once," Alessandro lied.

Balboa doubted the answer with a raised eyebrow. Alessandro handed Balboa the helmet and belt.

"Tell me," Balboa said.

"They were fishing, that is all. Across the river." Alessandro hoped the answer sufficed. It did not.

"How far?"

"A few hours," Alessandro said.

"Did they see you?"

Alessandro knew the older girl definitely did. She would have killed him if it was not for the storm.

"No." His heart raced. Why did he have to ask so many questions?

"Maybe." His heart slowed, but not enough. He hated to lie. One thing his mother said from his first recollections came to mind. 'No such thing as one lie. Always at least two, one to you and one to the other.'

"Yes." The word was so quiet maybe only Leoncito heard it.

"I need a promise," Balboa said.

"What?"

"For any reason, any reason at all, I say run, you run. You get back here and hide."

"I promise." Was that forgiveness for the first lie too?

The expedition set off from Darién. The two men who were rescued by Nicuesa's provision ship led the force of forty-three soldiers, including Balboa, Enciso, Pizarro, a priest, and Alessandro with his armor, a growing and protective Mastiff who, if anyone doubted, was worth two or more of any other soldier.

The excitement of the expedition waned quickly as the heat and humidity took their toll. The men were out of shape. Months of lazily farming and building a settlement on reduced rations had not done much for their health and stamina. Alessandro was not out of shape. He, of course, wore nothing but the trousers and leather shoes Balboa insist he wear in the event of an emergency. It was soon evident that Nicuesa's two soldiers who lived with the natives for nearly a year had never traveled these jungles. The fellow soldiers recognized the expedition was a fool's errand. The jungle's canopy made it difficult to judge direction or time. Nor did that matter. They were lost. They reached a small stream, which they followed for several hours anticipating it would lead them to the settlement.

As the group stopped to rest and grumble, Balboa stepped over to Alessandro, who at Balboa's insistence maintained a short distance between himself and the group.

"What are you thinking?" Alessandro asked.

"I think you know where we should be going," Balboa said.

Alessandro smiled. "It is that way." He pointed to the northwest toward the mountain.

"The Chicamba say that is Ponca's kingdom and we should stay away," Balboa said.

"Not that far. But we will have to cross the river."

"You came that far?" Balboa said.

"It is not that far if you go straight." Alessandro's effort to wink generated a comical half smile that closed the deal.

"Have Leoncito direct me with a bark when I lead poorly. We will protect the ego of these men," Balboa said. He winked back.

Balboa took the lead and pushed through the foliage, wielding his machete generously. At an occasional yelp from Leoncito, Balboa changed direction. Hours passed. Suddenly, Leoncito bounded past the group and halted in front of Balboa who stood motionless. Just as he stopped, a poison dart bounced off his shielded chest. He held up his hand in surrender. All the men stopped.

Nicuesa's man called out, "Chima! We come in peace." The man turned to Balboa, "Chima is the chief's name," he said.

The many tribes had their own dialects and languages. Hand gestures served as the common language. When Nicuesa's men spoke, it sounded like a poor choppy version of Spanish. Its lack of fluidity brought little comfort to the men. With the exception of the howler monkeys and parrots, the jungle was silent. The men called out again. After what seemed like most of an hour, two men, dressed in nothing but spotted jaguar skins about their waist, slowly approached. They were flanked by six muscular warriors armed with bows and nocked arrows. Everyone knew there were many others, invisible and deadly.

Nicuesa's men bowed. As they did, they told Balboa and Enciso this was Chima the chief. Balboa lowered the machete, took it by the blade, and offered the handle to the chief. He bowed and signaled for Nicuesa's man to speak.

Nicuesa's man introduced Enciso as the governor and Balboa as the alcalde who had come in peace to trade with the tribe. Balboa knelt and offered a gilded mirror to the chief, who took it respectfully.

The chief and Nicuesa's man spoke briefly. The chief turned and walked away. The bowmen did not follow. Nicuesa's man said, "He wants us to follow." They went deeper into the jungle. Though paths had not been hacked clear, the natives knew this jungle. The way seemed easier. Even the steep climbs up rugged hills and climbing over fallen trees took less strain on the men. They entered a large clearing surrounded by buildings made from what looked like mud covered by a lime white covering. The roofs were tall and steep, made from tightly woven reeds. The center building, which they assumed to be the chief's home, looked to be about forty feet by sixty feet. Large windows for ventilation and light ran along each side. Rolled up woven reed mats hung above each window.

The placement of the other buildings demonstrated planning and organization. Chima, the chief of this people, exited from the large building, still in nothing but the jaguar skin about his loins and a cape secured over his shoulders with buttons that looked like the long toes of the sloth Alessandro had seen those many weeks ago.

Chima carried with him a tall earthen bowl from which he drank and then handed to Balboa. Balboa motioned for Enciso to drink first. Balboa then took his turn. Enciso's eyes watered, and he breathed deeply trying to suck in as much oxygen as possible. Balboa accepted the bowl and drank. Before the effects of the drink took effect, he reached for another swallow. Chima allowed a smile to appear for the first time.

Nicuesa's man translated as Enciso began a request for provisions which were badly needed. His request was neighborly, but he held no authority to demand. After all, they were visitors. A small token of supplies was delivered. It was so small Enciso took offense and demanded more. Chima refused more, saying that was all they had. The translator called Chima a liar and told Enciso and Balboa there was much more.

At this, the priest in his long black cassock and wide brimmed white zucchetto stood forward. He held a crucifix in his right hand and a breviary in his left. Through the translator, he introduced himself as a representative of God and the Holy Roman Emperor. He declared that this people, the Carreta, led by Chima himself, must renounce all other gods and convert to Christianity. And if he refused, he would be considered an enemy of the Church and enemies to the rightful king, and in the name of the king they would declare war on the Carreta people. And as an enemy to the crown, they must forfeit all their gold.

Alessandro saw Balboa shake his head. Captain Pizarro flinched, ready for a fight which triggered a chain reaction among the men as they brought themselves to attention. Alessandro had not ever heard of one people commanding another to renounce their beliefs and follow another. He knew he was baptized as a little child. But he made no choice about it. All he knew was that it meant he was a Christian. His experience with church was scarce. He saw priests pray. He prayed regularly with Balboa, but hardly ever thought anything about it. All he knew was Balboa believed in Christ and therefore he did too. Many times, he heard Balboa wish he had a Bible and could read it for himself, and if he could, he would teach Alessandro from it.

Chima stared at the priest. He reached out to touch the gilded cross, which held a red jewel on each of its four tips. A soldier standing close by pulled a sword so quickly, Chima recoiled and two archers loosed arrows at the soldier. One arrow shattered when it hit his shield, the other cut through the skin on his cheek drawing blood immediately. Another soldier lunged forward, cutting the arm of another archer who hesitated one second too long. Pizarro leapt at the soldier, knocking his sword to the ground. The air filled with tension.

"Why, after all we have done for you, do you bring these men to hurt my people?" Chima said to the interpreter. "Your visit is over."

Chima turned and walked back toward the large building, which he departed just minutes before with an offering of friendship. Archers closed in behind him.

"They have more provisions. They are hidden for protection. They have gold. They have pearls," the interpreter yelled.

Balboa stepped in front of his men and turned his back to the archers. "We will go now. We are no longer welcome."

Soldiers had just been denied the very thing they left home to take. Grumbling became mutinous. Alessandro was ready to run. He thought if there was a time Balboa might send him scurrying off, it was now.

"Of truth, if you ever trusted me, trust me now," Balboa said. He calmly marched through the men and back into the jungle.

Completely stunned, one by one they turned and followed. Alessandro was the last to exit the tiny grove where he and Leoncito parked themselves for the encounter. Alessandro was not watching the men leave, nor the archers and dart-men. His eyes were locked on those of a girl peering through a window watching as intently as he had. Finally, he slipped from his perch and followed Pizarro who was berating the soldier whose bloody hand held the side of his lacerated face.

"Archers know our shields," Pizarro said. "The first was a warning, the second a demonstration. It is the savages with the blowpipes I fear. You do not see them, and the poison is painfully deadly. I saved your life back there. Never do that again," Pizarro was adamant. The soldier began to wobble. His feet became unsure. Pizarro put his arm around him for stability as the soldier began dragging his steps.

Alessandro urged Leoncito ahead. "Go, get Balboa." The hound bounded out and through the complaining men. Minutes later, Balboa and Enciso were kneeling next to the dead soldier. Balboa wiped the man's cheek, revealing coagulated blood and pus. He shook his head. "Fool."

"Drag him off the path," Balboa said. He returned to the front.

After several hours, Balboa brought his men to a stop.

"Now we wait," he said. "Tonight, we show Chima how much he needs a partnership."

Anticipation kept most of the men awake through the night. A symphony, performed majestically by a jungle insect orchestra, became monotonous. Those awake grumbled at its occasional crescendo. Others worried at the nocturnal hunters waiting for an opportunity to strike. The mosquitoes and their blood sucking relatives did not wait. Miserable hours wore on.

Quietly, Balboa crept among the men, waking them and giving whispered instructions. They were ready to return and encourage the Carreta into a treaty, as Balboa described it.

The night-march depended on stealth, a difficult thing with dozens of men donned in steel. Balboa explained he planned the strike just before dawn, when any guards or spies would be most vulnerable. This gave them the greatest chance for success.

This return march was more difficult without experienced natives as guides. The orchestra changed its melody. The men were grateful to be on the move.

There was no movement in the Carreta village. The stillness made many of the men leery. This was too easy.

Balboa positioned six men at each of the six buildings. He did not know how many others might live outside the construct of these six buildings. He and two others took the main building. Enciso and Pizarro each led a team and each of Nicuesa's men and another soldier the last building. At Balboa's signal, the teams attacked. Their assignment was to secure the buildings inside and out and to neutralize any with weapons immediately, then hold the rest captive inside the building. Any force from outside would endanger the hostages inside. He hoped.

Within minutes, the small force from Darién took the village by storm—a small, somewhat non-violent storm. Balboa's team captured Chima lying between two of his wives, likely having finished off the drink he offered his visitors the day before. There was not much fight in him. They dragged him from the house, now in chains.

Crepuscular light from the eastern sky began to crawl its way into the clearing. It was enough to decipher between man or beast, but not much more. A figure dashed past them and disappeared into the forest. Balboa called Leoncito, pointed, and whistled the command. Leoncito took one glance toward Alessandro, who gave a quick nod, and the two of them charged off into the dark jungle.

Alessandro was glad he obeyed Balboa and wore the shoes he normally shed as quickly as possible. Leaves and branches from plants and trees whipped at his arms and face as he chased after the figure. It was so fast. He feared Leoncito might get too far ahead. He did. Leoncito was now out of sight. And soon the sounds were gone. A path which he thought he was following disappeared, and Alessandro was now alone. Was he now the prey? He slowed his pace, leaning ears in every direction and hoping for the sound of Leoncito, but fearing it might be the sound of the hound having a quick native breakfast.

In the distance, far to his left and toward the mountain, Lioncito howled a short howl. He was not dining on fresh flesh. He was calling Alessandro. That howl was one of triumph. Alessandro worked his way over and through thick undergrowth. There had to be a trail somewhere. How else could the native run through this? Another howl. Not impatient, just enough to fine tune Alessandro's directions.

In the minutes of pursuit, enough light now crept through the canopy.

Alessandro saw his large hound sitting comfortably, tending to his captive who sat against a tree, knees pulled tight against chest, arms wrapped tightly around them. Alessandro approached. Leoncito had not taken a single bite. The captive was trembling. Alessandro's heart softened. He knew fear. Recently, the fear he knew was in the faces of others. Very little was his own while he had Leoncito at his side.

He rested his hand on Leoncito's head, fingers rewarding his valiance. The victim looked up at Alessandro, and their eyes locked. It was her. His heart nearly stopped. He wanted to…he did not know what he wanted. To tell her Leoncito would not hurt her? To let her go? He wanted to look into her eyes and did—for a long time.

"Come with me," he finally said. He knew she did not understand. He knelt at her side and took her hand. It was trembling. It was warm. She did not yank it away. He stood. Taking her other hand, he lifted her to her feet. He wanted to step back and look at her, but those eyes. She was several inches taller than him. Her tangled black hair collected a few random twigs and leaves during her run through the jungle. He wanted to pull them free.

With Leoncito at his side, she had no hope of escape.

"This is Leoncito," he said, pointing at the dog. He wanted to say that Leoncito would not hurt her, but he knew better. Balboa taught the young Mastiff to hunt and to kill, a skill Alessandro respected and hated. Leoncito's sire was Ponce de Leon's famous war dog, Becerrillo. Rumors told that he could tear savages to pieces for fun.

"My name is Alessandro," he said. He pointed to himself. He pointed to her, expecting her to finish the introduction. She stood silent. She continued to tremble. He took in the vision of the girl. He did not know what to compare her to. She was the first girl he ever saw up close with no clothes. He decided she was beautiful. But it was her eyes.

"Come, Leoncito." Alessandro kept hold of her hand and led her back where he hoped to find the village. She walked a little quicker and took the lead. Quickly, they were on a path. "Thank you," he said. She made no effort to take her hand from his and they walked, saying nothing.

The noise of soldiers and natives climbed above the monkey and bird chatter. It all stopped when Alessandro led the young woman, for that is what he decided she was, into the village. Instantly, she broke free of Alessandro's grasp, which had for a long time been nothing more than friendly. She dashed into the large building out of sight.

They all stared at the building. Balboa glanced at Alessandro. Alessandro shrugged. Leoncito stood panting ready for another game of chase.

Several of the native women who were taken from their houses broke free of the soldiers and dashed into the building behind the girl. No one spoke. Three warriors appeared at the edge of the clearing. They stood with arrows fully pulled, ready to deliver death, which had up to this point mostly been avoided.

Chima spoke sharply to them. The translator said the chief told the men to stand prepared but wait for his command before launching a war. The discussion was heated. To Alessandro, Chima did not appear weak or afraid. He did not tremble like the girl did. A second native barked out what Alessandro assumed were demands as part of negotiation. He could not hear or understand it, but he wanted to walk up to Balboa and ask what he was thinking. He just stood still. He also wondered what was happening inside the building. Chima turned and spoke to the women inside the building. It, too, was an animated conversation. Swords remained drawn, arrows pulled, and Alessandro knew somehow that since these three bowmen had not been captured, there were poison dart pipes aimed as well, and probably enough to kill every swordsman.

A warrior argued with Chima and stormed off. Nobody tried to stop him. He disappeared into the jungle. The standoff was tense. Finally, without any notice, the girl exited the building escorted by three other women, one of which had to be her mother Alessandro assumed. She wore a flowing robe of cotton, embroidered in gold, gathered at the waist by a golden girdle. Where the leaves and twigs had been stuck in her tangled hair, flower petals and bright colorful feathers accented a golden crown. It contrasted with the deep, shiny black hair that now flowed over her shoulders. Alessandro's eyes ached they stared so wide and hard. Her feet were covered by soft jaguar slippers.

Chima reached out his hands. At Balboa's instruction, a soldier stepped forward, unlocked, and removed Chima's chains. Chima took the daughter by the hand and put it into Balboa's.

What just happened? The priest came forward. He spoke some words in Latin. Alessandro did not understand the words. He supposed with the exception of Enciso and Balboa, neither did anyone else. The translator did not try to translate.

Then Chima took both hands in his and pronounced some words, the translation of which made no sense to Alessandro. It was something about earth, sky, living water, and union of peoples and replenishing the earth.

Chima turned to the bowmen. They lowered their bows. Balboa commanded his men to sheath their swords. Neither natives nor soldiers knew what to do next. Was this a real marriage? Chima gave instructions to the women and called his people from the buildings. They scattered from the village, returning with provisions. Baskets full to the brim. Three warriors carried over their shoulders large leather bags sewn together with fine black leather strips. They presented them to Balboa. He reached inside and pulled a golden vase easily the size of his head. Then another. Thus, Darién became the first and richest settlement on the mainland.

The translators became weary struggling to help the wedding guests learn what had just happened. The Carreta had just made a sacred alliance with the Spanish. The alliance was sealed with the marriage of Chima's first daughter to the strong, handsome leader, Vasco Nuñez Balboa.

Enciso had no interest in the marriage. As the official here, he was content to manage the gold. With the exception of Enciso and Balboa, both native and soldier drank until they could hardly stand. Most of them didn't. Enciso and Balboa each had their prize.

Alessandro and Leoncito wandered off. They met and mingled with the other young people of the village. "I am Alessandro," he said to a boy about his same size, pointing to his chest. "Kipote," the boy said with the same gesture.

Both the Carreta and the Spaniards positioned guards through the night as drink overcame the celebrators. As the men arose the next morning, Balboa and his new wife had already disappeared. Enciso led the men, fully loaded with provisions and gold, back to Darién. Alessandro bid farewell to his new friends who fell in love with Leoncito and enjoyed wrestling with the big furry beast. Alessandro thought it might be fun to be free of his clothes.

Chapter Thirty-One

1511 - Santa Maria la Antigua del Darién

"Is Cacica sleeping?" Alessandro asked. Balboa sat outside the small building constructed in jungle style, made of poles tightly woven together and covered with a mix of clay and stone. It had an earthen floor and a tall roof with a thatch woven so tight it provided a perfect shelter from the tropical storms.

Balboa looked up at Alessandro who cast a shadow from the morning sun. Balboa shook his head. "She went to the village to help her mother."

"What are you thinking?" Balboa asked.

"My turn," Alessandro said. "What are you thinking?"

"I think we might have trouble with Enciso," Balboa said.

Alessandro could not fully capture all the intrigues of men. But he understood they wanted gold and power. When the men in the settlement began to collect the gold from the Carretas and from other tribes the Carretas helped them conquer, Enciso gathered the gold, insisting as governor it was his responsibility. Over the many months the settlement grew, death became less prevalent, and colonists began to arrive. Darién grew. As it did, Enciso became more unpopular. The Spanish soldiers and colonists respected the power of the monarchs who granted them authority to conquer these new lands. But the two rightful leaders appointed by the king, Ojeda and Nicuesa, were both absent.

The soldiers and colonists held their own election and appointed Balboa as their alcalde mayor and sent Enciso back to Hispaniola with the responsibility of escorting the gold for the king. Balboa sent correspondence to the king describing all the events of the expedition. With Enciso gone, everything seemed better to Alessandro.

Sometimes when Balboa led expeditions they would be gone for weeks.

Alessandro spent the time with his Carreta friends. He loved Cacica. It was now more than her eyes. She was gentle and wise. She made Balboa a more generous man. Yet, Alessandro had to share him with her. He always had to share Balboa. As the alcalde mayor, he shared Balboa with the settlement. As the leader of the expeditions, he shared Balboa with nearby tribes. Now, this morning, he shared Balboa with his worries.

Alessandro recognized the worry on his face and although they were alone together, he wished Cacica was here to help him be happy.

"But if Enciso stayed, we would have more trouble. The men would have killed him. I heard them say so," Alessandro said.

"Where is that hound of yours?" Balboa asked. "You want to know what I am thinking? I think I am hungry. Let us go get some breakfast."

Nothing made Alessandro happier. Balboa secured his sword to his waist, and grabbed a pike. Alessandro retrieved a blowpipe, a handful of darts, and a lance his new friend Kipote fashioned to fit him.

"Those are not poison are they?" Balboa asked.

"Maybe."

The two bounded into the jungle.

"Watch," Alessandro said. He pulled the pipe to his lips and let a dart fly. A bright orange naranjilla dropped to the ground.

"You could be deadly." Balboa picked it up, sliced it open, and sucked the tart lulo juices. Alessandro watched intently, pleased his new skill produced a smile. He dropped a second and then a third. Breakfast was on its way.

They reached the small river where Alessandro first encountered the young Carretas fishing. Alessandro stepped quickly into the knee-deep water with the pike in hand. A quick jab had a bluish gray tilapia flopping in the air, struggling to free itself from the barbs. Alessandro held the point toward Balboa who quickly pulled it free. A second and third strike and breakfast was progressing.

"It is my turn now," Balboa said. "What are you thinking?"

"Captain Pizarro's expeditions always come back bloody. But not yours. Why?"

Balboa said nothing for several minutes. "Maybe he does not know how."

"Maybe he does not want to marry the princess," Alessandro said.

That brought a smile. "Maybe not," Balboa said.

"My mother was a princess," Alessandro said.

"Yes, she was. And a beautiful one like my Cacica."

"But they arrested my father. Will they arrest you?" Alessandro asked.

"I am the alcalde. Who would arrest me?"

"The governor."

"Maybe, if we ever get one. But let us not worry about that right now. Let me try that pipe."

Balboa took the blowpipe and a dart. He pulled a deep breath and sent the dart flying at a howler yapping up the still morning air. Missing by several inches, the dart disappeared into the canopy.

"I plan to lead the men on a long journey," Balboa said. "When we met Chief Ponca on the mountain, his son told us of another ocean and beyond it a mighty nation, richer than any other. If we help subdue their enemy, they will lead us there."

"What does subdue mean?" Alessandro asked.

"It means to stop them from being an enemy."

"Will you marry the princess?"

"No, I think one princess is enough."

"Then who will marry the princess?" Alessandro asked.

"Maybe Francisco."

"Pizarro? She will kill him the first night," Alessandro said.

"You still do not like him. Why?"

"He is mean to Leoncito. If he was governor, he would be like Enciso and try to take all the gold."

"What makes you say that?"

"All he talks about is gold. He will kill for gold. I hear soldiers say he is angry because he failed in San Sebastian and you succeed here." Alessandro watched Balboa's eyes closely. He learned when asking tricky questions, Balboa's eyes sometimes revealed if the answer was a simple one to tell a little boy, and sometimes the answer was a big one to tell a man.

"By truth," Balboa squinted. Here comes a man answer, Alessandro thought. "A man who fails may quit and spend his life ashamed, blaming others, or he will fight on and succeed or die," Balboa said. He kept looking into the distance. Alessandro waited. Maybe more was coming.

"Maybe Bachelor Enciso is like the first man and Captain Pizarro the second," Balboa said. "But I am taking Captain Pizarro with me when I go with the Poncas. He is a good soldier and fearless in a fight. The men know they can trust him to fight hard. His greed for gold is not always a bad thing when it keeps a man in the fight."

Alessandro knew what the fight meant, and he did not like it. It meant people would die, probably lots of them.

"Can I come?" Alessandro said. "I will stay in the fight. I know how to use this." He held up the blowpipe.

Balboa chuckled. "No. It is a long journey. And dangerous. The Ponca say we will be passing through unfriendly tribes."

"Just subdue them," Alessandro said with a smile. He knew enough that this new word subdue was probably a Pizarro type word, a bloody one.

As time wore on, the Spanish demanded provisions and more gold with each visit. The two-sided arrangement became more and more one-sided. Though the Carreta had new friends in the Spanish, enemies from the mountains did not hesitate to raid the Carreta village at will. A show of force was demanded by Chima—a war party to march with his warriors to the mountain and retrieve captives taken by the mountain tribes. As weeks passed, plans were made for the men from Darién to live up to their end of the bargain to help protect the Carreta.

Chapter Thirty-Two

1510 - Granada, Spain

Talavera's strength and vitality hardly improved over the following weeks. Even with better nourishment and rest, he failed to recover. His time awake and alert was taken up with stories and debates with Miguel and Vano. They rejoiced and sorrowed together. Talavera's insistence they leave Granada and that Miguel not join the ministry never waned. Nor did Miguel's stubborn resistance.

The time finally came that Vano felt the need to return to his role as the next leader of his family. He enjoyed the spiritual and theological sparing with Talavera. He was confident the friendships he made were lifelong. Vano refused Sayyida's money offered by Miguel.

The contention between Miguel and Maria over her insisting to stay and his resolute stand that she leave with Vano, inserted a new complication into the relationship. Miguel knew Maria had a strong will but when she exerted her demand that she could not be dissuaded by man or beast, Miguel realized Talavera was the man and she felt he was the beast. It was not a light accusation. Vano left Andi with Maria and headed north.

Vano's advice that Miguel yield to Maria's will and let her follow her own heart seemed noble at first. He soon realized it was not noble but was sage practical counsel. Miguel knew hearts were hard to control. During his ministry with Talavera, changing hearts depended solely on one being soft enough for the Spirit of God to mold and form into a heart meek enough to submit to God's will. But was Maria's resistance to leave a hard heart or a meek submission to God's will. It certainly was Talavera's and Miguel's will that she leave with Vano. But then again, it was Talavera's will that he too leave with Vano. Miguel finally gave in to the fact that he did not know God's will so he could not impose God's will on Maria. He thought about the rich young ruler who asked Jesus what he should do to inherit the Kingdom of

God. When Christ said to give his great wealth to the poor and follow Him, he went away sad. Was Miguel like the rich young ruler, unwilling to do God's will? What was God's will?

Miguel was not prepared for the change in dynamics once the threesome became a twosome. He resisted the urge to consider himself and Maria a couple. Yet, as he watched her care for Talavera along side Sukayna, his heart wanted to seek God's will but his head wanted to resist what that will might be. What if it was right to abandon Talavera? What if it was right to stay and face the cardinal when he returned from his conquests. What if God didn't care. Miguel was unaware that his resistance weakened with each passing day. He found himself anxious when Maria and Sukayna appeared content without his involvement in Talavera's care. Yet he found himself alone with Maria without any purpose. *What do I do with a beautiful woman when there is nothing demanding their attention?* He never formalized that question in his head nor did an answer to it ever surface.

"You talk less of joining the ministry with the archbishop. Has Talavera convinced you God has other plans for you?" Maria asked.

Miguel wanted to answer that question honestly, but he had no answer. He lifted her renegade lock of hair from the side of her face, he paused, the back of his fingers lingered against her soft skin. He released the hair and slowly slid his fingers down her cheek. He said nothing. Maria just stared back at him. She said nothing. She pulled her lip between her teeth. Miguel thought he might finally know God's will.

Talavera's health and strength continued to fail. Breathing became more labored. Resting demanded more of his time. Sukayna, Maria, and Anna Maria took turns feeding him.

Finally one morning, Miguel and Maria left Sukayna's shop together and headed back toward Anna Maria's home to fulfill Talavera's request they bring him a fresh cask of wine the next time they were in the market. They walked slowly, finding no reason to follow a direct route. Very little was said. Miguel held the gate open for Maria and gently placed his hand on her back as she passed him. He chose not to remove it. They walked quietly to the house and gently knocked before opening Anna Maria's door. Talavera sat alert, obviously waiting their visit.

"I asked my Lord and Savior to take me home," he said. "He gave me one last command before He does."

Anna Maria sat at his side, propping him up. Talavera requested to be dressed in his full archbishop regalia this morning. He looked regal, though he could not sustain the look for long, but he insisted one last time.

"Miguel, please kneel here," he said. "Maria," he motioned for her to kneel next to Miguel. He reached out to take their hands.

"May we pray together?" He did not wait for a response. He took as deep a breath as he could.

Both Miguel and Maria bowed their heads and closed their eyes in humility as Talavera began the prayer.

"Dear Father, our God and Deliverer and thy Son our Savior and Redeemer." He paused and took another labored breath. "Lord, hear our prayer. Your Son taught us to ask, to seek and to knock. This we do. Confident you will look to our needs and grant our requests, through Jesus Christ our Lord. You created man and woman in Your own image and commanded that they should become one flesh and become united and never divided. This union is symbolized by the marriage of Christ and His church."

As Talavera prayed, his voice seemed to become stronger. His breathing more consistent.

"Lord, look with love upon this woman, your daughter, and this man, your son. Give them your love, grace, and peace. Father, keep them always true to your commandments. Give them strength, which they will certainly need. Bless them to follow you, so they may be witnesses of Christ to others."

Miguel opened one eye and looked over at Maria to see how she was reacting. Her head was bowed, and eyes closed.

Talavera held Maria's right hand in his right hand and Miguel's right hand in his left. As casually as you might bring your own hands together, he placed Miguel's hand on top of Maria's. Miguel opened his eye again, but this time Maria was looking at him.

"Dear Father God of the universe. Please take this man and this woman and unite them in holy matrimony as thou did with our first parents Adam and Eve, and make them one flesh."

Maria's eyes shot wide open, as did Miguel's. But they did not pull their hands away. Talavera continued, head bowed, and eyes closed. Maria and Miguel stared at each other.

"In the name of the Father, the Son, and the Holy Ghost. Amen."

Talavera, as if he had said a routine mass on a casual sabbath night, slowly raised his head and placed his hands back into his lap. He leaned back into the padded chair and struggled again for a breath.

No one spoke. Minutes passed. Maria finally leaned toward Miguel and asked, "Are we… married?"

Miguel's eyes darted to Talavera, then Anna Maria and back to Maria. "I think so," he whispered.

He faced Talavera. "Did you just marry us?" Miguel asked.

"Oh good," Talavera exhaled, "I hoped you were listening."

Miguel was slow to respond. He didn't remove his hand from Maria's.

"Do we need to agree somehow? Say yes, or I do, or share some vows? What about bone of my bones, flesh of my flesh? Cleaving unto each other? Becoming one?"

"Well?" Talavera asked. "Do you?

"Do I?" Miguel repeated to himself. He looked deeply into Maria's eyes. She remained silent after her initial question. His head nodded ever so slightly, as his lips tightened and slowly became a smile. "Oh yes…yes, yes."

"You had to think about it?" Maria asked.

Anna Maria gently but proudly said to Miguel, "What did I tell you?"

"If that is settled, you two need to be on your way. I am weary. Grand and glorious weddings always take so much out of me," Talavera said, sinking deeper into the large, padded couch. Anna Maria lifted the tall white mitre from his head and set it on a small table.

"We are not leaving you," Miguel tried to resist being sent away.

"Oh, yes," Anna Maria said, "you are. It may be one of the last of our archbishop's commands, and you two just covenanted to be obedient. And… this is my house." She smiled and winked at the last remark.

"What do we do now?" Miguel asked. It was more a rebuke to Anna Maria than a question. But Talavera could not resist an answer.

"I hardly think that is a question I am qualified to answer. I being a celibate archbishop." His chuckle turned to a cough. Maria broke Miguel's and her grasp to help Anna Maria lift Talavera to his feet. Miguel finally came from his stupor.

Once on his feet, Talavera turned to Miguel, "But I do know you might start with a kiss as husband and wife." He bowed. The two women helped him to the bedroom.

Chapter Thirty-Three

1511 - Granada, Spain

"What do we do now?" Maria teased Miguel. "I believe that was the first time in the history of the world that a new husband has ever asked that question of a celibate priest following a marriage ceremony. I bet Adam did not even ask that question of the Father."

"That is not what I asked."

"What did you ask?"

Miguel asked himself that same question all day. Anna Maria insisted they announce their news to Sukayna and Jalaf, then leave immediately and return northward to be with family. Miguel thought she was just part of Talavera's plot to get the conspirators of his release as far away from Cisneros as possible.

How do I protect a wife and a man who is dying because you failed to protect him the first time? Why did Maria refuse to leave with Vano earlier? He certainly wanted her to. Why did I not insist? Well, because I secretly wanted her to stay.

Maria remained astride Andi, while Miguel's mind replayed their relationship vividly. What was she waiting for? He finally looked up, realizing she was no longer an independent woman. She was a wife, a lady, and his responsibility.

"Milady, may I help you?" he said, gently reaching to take her by the waist and lifting her down. "What I asked? I asked how a very blessed man, and his beautiful new wife, can best serve the needs of a dying man who gave his life for Christ."

She smiled. He knew there was not a single word of it she believed. He tucked the lock of hair over her ear and kissed it gently.

He led her through the bright red door to an abandoned home on San

Cristobal Hill. The Albayzin neighborhood was one of the last fully Moorish neighborhoods. This house was one of several abandoned by Moorish families who fled the Christian persecution. Jalaf agreed to care for it when the family left. He insisted it would be the safest place for Miguel and Maria to begin their life together. It was close enough to Anna Maria's home that Miguel consented to his and Maria's relocation.

The next morning, he sat alone on the balcony overlooking the great palace of the Alhambra. The last time he was in Granada, King Ferdinand and his new wife were living there, right below where he and his new wife had just spent their first night together. Miguel was certain the king did not ask what to do now. But why did the king refuse to come to the aid of Isabella's former confessor?

Maria stepped out onto the balcony. Miguel gave a quick glance back. Dressed only in her under tunic, maybe the same one she wore when she and Vano brought the horses to shore, she rested both hands on his shoulders before he could stand.

"What are you thinking?" she asked.

"Well, we have been married a whole day. If you do not know what I am thinking by now, our marriage might be in trouble," he said.

"Oh, so you do know what to do. How quickly they learn." Maria pulled Miguel back into the house.

The following days were spent attending to the needs of Talavera. His health continued to fail. His insistence they leave him alone and flee the impending clash with Cisneros did not lessen. Jalaf did his best to Moorishize them, introducing Maria to the local culture. Miguel saw so much of Sayyida in Jalaf, and wondered why cultures collide. What makes one people have such conflict with another? He and the priests who taught the Moors in their native Arabic, loved these people. He felt there was no justification in the holy word that peoples could not coexist. His time in North Africa confirmed the various gods were indeed one God, just understood and worshiped differently.

The strong independent Maria that attracted him from their first meeting in Genoa did not disappoint. She quickly demonstrated a natural skill to support and strengthen their marriage. He thought back many times to how she was so quick to recognize how Eve was protected by the Father in Michelangelo's painting on the chapel's ceiling. For Miguel, he would be eternally grateful it was Archbishop Talavera who commanded he and Maria to become one flesh.

Sukayna and Maria were everything daughters of God should be, he thought. Maria worked with Sukayna in her shop. With the exception of two possessive husbands, they were inseparable.

This late afternoon, the sun brushed the city with brilliant orange facades and long shadows. Miguel and Jalaf cut through the alley that emptied into the street next to Sukayna's shop.

"She's gone!" Sukayna said. "Bishop Martinez sent a messenger. Cisneros is back. He sent his guards to find Talavera and those responsible for his release. The bishop said to run."

"She went for Talavera?" Miguel asked. He broke into a run through alleys, streets, and back doors. He was grateful Jalaf shared the secrets of the city. He bounded into the garden, only to be met by the cardinal's guards. Two guards dragged Talavera from the house. He pleaded with his eyes for Miguel to run. Miguel looked frantically around. Where was Maria?

"Pope Julius pardoned the archbishop. Leave him be," Miguel said, his hand firmly on his sword.

"The cardinal just wants to speak with him. Leave your steel where it is."

"Not this time," Miguel said. Four other guards stepped out from behind trees and bushes, all with swords drawn. Two more exited the house, each with a hostage. Anna Maria obviously put up a fight. Her dress was torn and her previously perfect hair hung loosely over her shoulder. A drizzle of blood ran down her cheek. The second guard fought to constrain Maria's struggle.

The look on Maria's face frightened him. Their eyes met, and as if they had been married a lifetime, her glare said, we can take these men.

Lightning fast, Maria's free hand pulled the short knife, ran it up the guard's arm, and into his neck dropping him instantly to the ground. That was Miguel's signal. As fast as Maria put her knife to work on the second guard, two guards engaged Miguel as he pulled his sword. Anna Maria was free of her captor, but a third guard cut her deeply as he lunged forward toward Maria, knocking her knife from her hand. It clanged against the stone and the man had Maria on her back his sword at her throat.

The two guards supporting Talavera froze. Blades and blood surrounded them. Miguel received a slice across his shoulder. His quickness prevented it entering his chest. The momentum of his blade accelerated just enough to push off a lunge from the second guard. He brought it back so quickly the first guard misstepped and caught the blade square in the chest, but not before he cut the back of Miguel's hand.

Four more guards pushed into the garden with Jalaf and Sukayna tied tightly with cords. The thought was fleeting but flashed through his mind. Now Jalaf can see what my sword can do.

Miguel lunged with two quick strikes and dropped the second guard. There was no time to choose between freeing Talavera or Maria. The perfect nightmare. It was a choice he never made. Maria stretched her hand, tickling the hilt of her knife that laid just inches out of reach. She finally pulled it into her grasp. She knocked the sword at her throat free and plunged her knife into the guard's groin. He dropped to the ground. A guard swung on her and cut her arm deeply and the knife fell again to the ground. A second swing and the guard ran his blade into her chest. She dropped back. He did not pull the blade, but held it there, pinning her to the ground. Her blood rippled out from the sword's blade turning her chest crimson red. Her arm pulsed blood onto the stones. Miguel now faced three more assailants. A sharp pain shot through his back. He did not see that one.

The cry of pain stunned the guard on his right and Miguel sliced his throat so quickly a second guard paused for one second too long and Miguel took the man's arm completely off. It was again one on one. Talavera was too weak to resist or to do anything but suffer the reality his friends were being slaughtered.

Straining against the cords tight around his neck and hands, Jalaf tried to free himself from the remaining guard left to hold him and Sukayna. Miguel quickly had two more guards flanking him. Pain shot through his leg. The guard, poised to stab him through the back, stumbled when Jalaf kicked him from behind. Jalaf's guard pulled so hard on the cord both he and Sukayna tumbled to the ground. The guard put a boot on Jalaf's neck, assuring this time Jalaf was helpless.

The cut in the leg brought Miguel to a knee. Just as it had a year ago, his efforts came up short. He struggled to his feet. Bleeding and in pain both in heart and body, he poised for a final attack.

"Bring him!" A strong commanding voice called above the battle. "I want him. Bring him and the archbishop. We have some catching up to do."

Miguel realized he was not going to die yet. He knew what awaited him, but this time there was no savior. Jalaf lay unconscious under the boot of a guard. Maybe unconscious, or dead. The guard pulled the sword from

Maria's chest. She was still. Blood pooled beneath her. Miguel chose to continue his marriage on the other side of mortality. He thought of the words he heard so many times 'until death do you part.' If death was parting him from his wife, he willed to die with her. He closed his eyes, breathed deeply, and drove his sword clear through the closest guard. A blade pierced Miguel's ribs and he dropped to the stones. Lying on his side, Miguel moved his head just enough to see the cardinal's wicked smile. He turned back in time to see the boot end the pain and bring on darkness.

Chapter Thirty-Four

1511 - Granada, Spain

Tears poured down the bishop's cheek. He failed. The remorse was crippling. His quick efforts to warn the others made no difference at all.

Bishop Martinez leaned his head against the wall, softly pounding it in hopes it might change reality, a reality that could not be changed.

When Cisneros returned to Granada unexpectedly and sought an audience with his favorite prisoner Archbishop Talavera, he exploded with anger. The bishop was absent and unable to deflect the outrage. When the guards were called, the bishop heard and sent runners to warn Talavera's caretakers. He knew he could not hide Talavera for long. Whatever Cisneros wanted he got. Regardless of who pardoned Talavera, he would never be free. But now everyone who cared for Talavera was included in Cisneros' rage.

The bishop tucked back into the shadows across the cobblestone lane, praying and watching. Cardinal Cisneros was the first to leave the garden. Closely behind, two guards mostly drug Talavera. He was unstable on his feet. The bishop counted at least six guards enter, but he knew several arrived before him. Moments later, two guards, one on each arm, dragged Miguel into the lane. Was he dead? His head hung limp and legs scraped along the stones leaving a trail of blood.

He was about to cross the lane and see to any survivors when Jalaf and Sukayna, bound hand, neck, and foot were dragged out. Six guards so far. How many more? How long could he wait?

A guard stood at the gate sword in hand, looking down the lane which was now quiet. How long? Prayers never ceased. The bishop pleaded, begging his Lord for direction, inspiration, for forgiveness, and for strength. The clatter of hooves on stone broke the trance of his prayers. Two additional guards with a wagon stopped at the gate. They entered the garden. The bishop wanted to know what was happening inside the garden walls so badly he almost charged across the lane and into the garden. He wondered if his prayer was being answered right then. He felt he was to just hold tight.

One by one, guards pulled lifeless bodies and laid them on the cart. After six or maybe seven bloody and lifeless bodies were loaded, they led the cart away. Once they were out of sight, he hurried across the lane and disappeared into the garden. There sat his own Anna Maria, bleeding herself yet holding a lifeless Maria in her arms. He knelt, tore a length of fabric from her dress and wrapped it tightly over her arm and shoulder stopping the blood. The cut on her head demanded more attention, but fresh blood was coagulating quickly.

He stood, told Anna Maria he would return in mere moments, and dashed from the garden. It was mere moments. He was not alone. He brought with him the short bronze magician who cared for Miguel a year ago and Talavera only weeks ago.

After only seconds looking at Anna Maria's bloody bandages, he placed his ear against Maria's blood soaked chest. He snatched her up out of Anna Maria's arms and carried her into the house. He had her tunic torn off and anxiously plugged a hole with a paste carried in a small bag he brought with him. Her bleeding arm oozed blood.

"Is she alive?" Anna Maria asked. Bishop Martinez helped his wife into the house.

"Not for long," the magician said. "She is bleeding more inside than outside." He pushed in more paste and with a finger filled the hole. "The bleeding must stop inside. Her heart or lungs or both have been punctured."

He pulled Talavera's blue finely embroidered chasuble up over her body. Bishop Martinez felt it appropriate. The sacredness of the chasuble was symbolic of the yoke of Christ and is taught to represent charity. This young woman gave her life for a man who was neigh on death anyway. She consecrated herself to seek Talavera's freedom and refused to run. She was worthy to expire under the chasuble.

Pain shot through Miguel's body, yanking him from unconsciousness. With each jerky pull from above, every wound screamed for release. A dim light from above illuminated the dark stone tomblike cell. He must have been unconscious when they secured his hands to the ropes and lowered him down.

Miguel knew exactly where he was. For the past year, he feared this was the very prison where Talavera was held. The relief when they first found Talavera in an above ground cell softened his anger. He realized the cardinal was never going to extend such mercy to him.

When he reached the level of the ground, they dropped him on the cold stones. How long was he unconscious? This time his fate was sealed. Where was Talavera? Another cell? Dead? Where was God?

"I want him alive."

Miguel's eyes struggled to adjust. How long had he been out? When his eyes finally focused, internal fury drowned the pain. Cisneros' eyes lingered on Miguel's.

"He will stand trial for murder and heresy before his execution. Keep him alive until I return." Cisneros turned and left the guards to their work. Miguel drank deeply from the pail. He wanted to wash his face in it. He stopped to take a breath when the rope tightened and yanked him from the ground. He hung and swung back over the pit. His body crumbled as he reached the pit's bottom. The rope remained tight, keeping his arms elevated above his body.

"Until he returns?" Miguel muttered.

Jalaf ran his fingers along the scar that wound its way around his neck. He was secured so tightly, several times during the forced journey to the coast he concluded the guards hoped he died to prevent their need to travel so far to expel him and his wife from the country. If it were not for the specific command from the cardinal, they would have killed him and taken Sukayna for pleasure.

The guards made one mistake. They conspired to profit from this assignment and sold Sukayna and Jalaf to the Knights of Hospitaller from Rhodes. The two exiles were dropped on deck while the guards collected the payment, who rowed back to shore, and disappeared.

"And our friends?" Sayyida asked. "We can get them back."

They stood at the rail of the Gregory as the harbor disappeared behind them.

"Only in the resurrection," Sukayna said. Since their arrest, she had not said but a dozen words. She watched Maria die, pierced through the heart, a bleeding and unconscious Miguel dragged away, and the remaining vestige of hope in Christ among a sea of treachery, washed away. From her stone cell, she witnessed the mockery of a funeral march for Archbishop Hernando de Talavera who died without care, alone in a priest's apartment two days after the arrest. Guards insisted she and Jalaf watch them publicly destroy their shop, demonstrating the consequence of standing against the Church.

"The resurrection?" Sayyida repeated. "A beautiful hope."

Sukayna nodded.

"The more powerful we become, the more jealously we protect our power," Sayyida said.

"And the more power it requires," Jalaf said.

Chapter Thirty-Five

1513 - Santa Maria la Antigua del Darién

The energy in Darién always increased when the men readied for an expedition. From the alliance with Chima and the Carretas, most of the expeditions built on the success of allying with one tribe to help conquer, or at least deter, the aggressiveness of another. Darién was now a prosperous settlement. It was more than just a fort full of dirty, angry, dying soldiers. Tailors, craftsmen, women, and children—actual citizens—lived in Darién.

Balboa and Pizarro handpicked their two groups to search for the rumored south sea and the riches beyond. Alessandro was no longer the quiet little boy who could slip in and out, learning tidbits of hearsay and gossip. In the years of Darién's development, Leoncito and Alessandro increased in size and wisdom. Alessandro mastered the weapons of the jungle and was learning the weapons of the Spanish whenever he could convince the men to teach him. Balboa's support in his progress and Alessandro's persistence finally edged out the concern for Alessandro's safety during a journey. Cacica's brother offered to go and watch over Alessandro, but not with sword and shield. He and Leoncito would travel lightly with the scouts.

The Ponca, once a vicious enemy of the Carreta's, became a trading partner with them. It was their prince, who in disgust of the Spaniards' insatiable lust for gold, agreed to lead them to the south sea. From there, he hoped they would leave his lands and go to the richer and more powerful empires to the south.

They believed the expedition might take months, which would require them to ally with tribes both friendly and hostile. With nearly two hundred men, plus dozens of local guides and porters, they began the expedition.

A brigantine and nine large canoes carried Balboa's men up the coast where Chima added a thousand friendly natives, who served as guides and carriers on their march from the ocean to the mountains. Here in Chima's friendly territory, Balboa left half his men to guard the ships and supplies in case they needed a fast retreat.

The first week was routine. Familiar tribes, hot tropical weather, and exhaustion accompanied the journey. The second week increased the exhaustion as they cut their way through thick vegetation climbing the steep mountains, which served as natural barriers between tribes. It would all be different now. Rumors of invading strangers arrived in the villages well before the invading troops ever did. Along with the news about the invaders came claims they were otherworldly, and any effort to deny them was met with destruction. That news served both the natives and the Spaniards well. It was well into the fourth week when an arrogant tribal chief challenged the approaching group. Balboa quickly put the warriors down when their spears and darts failed to pierce the steel armor and the steel swords left the native warriors limbless and lifeless.

There was no open trail through the mountain wilderness. The men hewed their way through thick vegetation with sword and axe. Though natives carried most of the armor and provisions, many soldiers, even those lightly clad, were overcome with weakness and illness. A third of them fell by the way.

Steadily climbing, the fatigued group neared a high mountain village. It was deserted. Alessandro, traveling with the scouts, warned Balboa the tribe was not far away. The group paused to take advantage of the provisions and to ransack the dwellings for gold and jewels. At once, a flurry of arrows and darts rained down upon the men. In an instant, Balboa charged the warriors who were emerging in mass from the depth of the forest. Balboa gave command to Leoncito to attack. With long leaps, the large hound tore into the first warrior, leaving him lifeless. His fury turned to the next. The warriors turned their surprise and shock and aimed their fury at the animal they had never seen before. Several arrows hung from Leoncito's back, but he never slowed. Warrior after warrior fell to his savage attack.

The large hound was not the only surprise. The blast of arquebuses with spark and smoke, accompanied by the power of the crossbows, turned confident warriors into stupefied statues. They could not conceive where the sound, the smoke, and flames came from. Balboa, with bright sword drawn, charged the petrified warriors. Within minutes, the battle was over.

Alessandro knew conquest was bloody. He just had not been in the middle of it before. He knew of more than twenty tribal chiefs who became allies with Balboa. He visited and traded with them. They were friendly, and they were highly respectful of Balboa. But now he wondered how they came to become so. He just watched his pup kill native warrior after warrior. Was Leoncito no different than the Spanish soldiers, easily killing at will?

When the soldiers re-grouped ready to continue their push up the mountain, Alessandro could not face Balboa, nor Leoncito. Cacica's brother with whom Alessandro served as scout, stood next to the silent Alessandro.

"What is you and Balboa always say? What are you think?" Cacica's brother asked.

Alessandro looked at him. Stared at him. His lips tightened. He felt hot. Hot on the inside. He breathed in. Then out. He looked back to the death laying behind them. For a long time, he said nothing.

"Is this how it always is?" Alessandro finally said.

Cacica's brother nodded, "But not aways for gold. We have gold." He saw the confusion on Alessandro's face. "My people conquer for slaves and power. Your people conquer for gold, slaves, power and say it is for your God and a king great oceans away."

"They are not my people," Alessandro said.

Cacica's brother raised an eyebrow. "Whose people are yours?"

Alessandro said nothing.

The first light of dawn broke through the dense canopy. The air was thick with humidity, earthy and damp. Early morning mist clung to the trees, creating a mystical atmosphere. As the men arose, the inky blue sky transitioned to shades of pink and orange. The vibrant hues of orchids and bromeliads were lost on the men. It was just another miserable day.

Everything was alive. Animals of all sizes foraged for food and contributed to the symphony accented by the buzzing of lively bloodsucking insects.

Alessandro had not slept. In the pre-dawn, he followed Balboa when he left the camp and climbed to the summit. From the most recent massacre, the men cut their way to the base of a giant stone outcropping rising nearly a thousand feet above the canopy, and there made camp for the night.

From this vantage, Balboa hoped to assess what the day's journey might present. Far below, hidden in shadow for as far as they could see, lay an immense sea.

Leoncito, though limping with the wounds of days earlier, followed Alessandro who was so upset, he gave the hound no attention. He had not spoken to anyone.

Balboa looked from the vast ocean to his two companions. "What are you thinking?" he asked.

Alessandro said nothing, his arms folded and staring at the scene before him.

The sun breaking over the mountain top sprinkled the vast ocean with bright blue sparkles. Even from the distance, they saw waves building and crashing on each other. Yet, with a forest between them and the shore, they would not reach it for days.

Balboa asked again, calmly and kindly, "What are you thinking?"

"You killed hundreds of people to find an ocean."

The words did not shock Balboa. He hadn't permitted Alessandro to join other expeditions, feeling he would not understand. He still didn't. He hoped Alessandro recognized it was all for the good. To bring glory and power to Spain, to serve the Holy Roman Emperor Charles V, to serve the Church in purging paganism from the people and bringing them to Christ.

"One day you will understand, this is for the good," Balboa said.

"Will Leoncito understand?"

"By faith, let us get off this mountain," Balboa said. There was no reconciliation, but there was nothing else to be done or said.

The two climbed back to the camp, gathered two dozen men including twice that many porters, and fought their way down the southwestern slopes of the mountain. Balboa knew they would not reach the shore before four days. He hoped for only two.

It took four. Emerging from the thick jungled forest, Balboa stood in full armor, mouth open at the vast expanse of water. He looked from side to side. Where land ended, water claimed the world. He had no knowledge of the timing of these tides. Soon he would know.

He walked out on to the sandy shore and with sword in hand stood ready to claim every foot of this expansive new ocean for the crown. Waves, not so grand as in the Atlantic, began their climb up the shore. The water lapped at his feet. Leoncito did not wait for the tides. He plunged into the water, bounding up and down the shoreline. Alessandro envied his former best friend for his ability to remain unaware of the destruction those days earlier. He waded out into the water. Soon it pounded into Balboa's knees, then the thighs. Balboa several times caught his balance with the aid of his sword serving as a cane.

Adjusting one more time for balance, the water now to his waist, he raised his arms. In one hand was the sword he so valiantly carried to conquer this land. In his other, the banner painted with the arms of Castile and Aragon. In a voice for all along the shore, including the notary who he commanded to record every word, he declared to the creatures of heaven and earth, "Long live the high and mighty sovereigns of Castile! Thus in their names, do I take possession of these seas and regions, and if any other prince, whether Christian or infidel, pretends any right to them, I am ready and resolved to oppose him, and to assert the just claims of my sovereigns. Long live the sovereigns of Spain.

"We will defend these their new possessions even to the death, and against all the potentates of the world. Viva! Viva!"

He stood boldly. The surf pounded against his chest. Slowly, Balboa retreated toward the shore. Climbing from the water, he pulled a dagger and carved a cross into the trunk of a large tree and said, "In this sign we shall conquer the heathen and the blessing of our religion we will give them, in exchange for their barbarous practices."

At the same time on the other side of the world, at the betrayal, jealousy, and false testimony of Balboa's enemies led by former Darién Mayor Martín Fernandez de Enciso, King Charles V appointed Pedriarias Dávila as the new governor of Santa Maria la Antigua del Darién. The new governor would bring order to the new colony.

PART
TWO

CARIBBEAN
SEA
Tubanama
Santa Maria la Antigua del Darién
SOUTHERN SEA
(Pacific Ocean)
TIERRA
FIRME

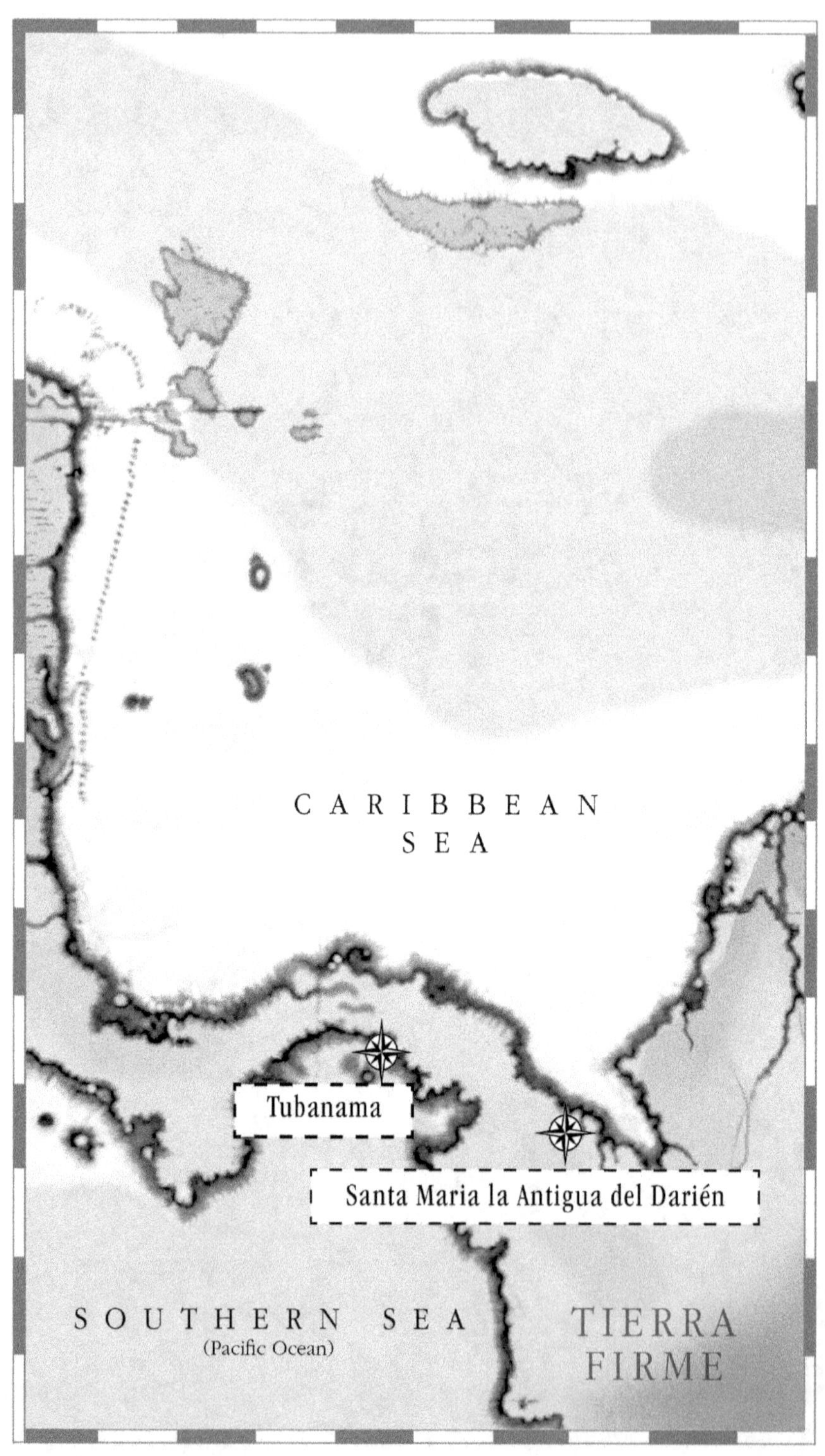

236

Chapter Thirty-Six

(Four years later)
1517 - Tubanama, Western shore of the
Isthmus of Panama

"What are you thinking?" Balboa asked.

"If my father did not marry my mother, would they sell her to the Spanish?" Alessandro asked, as innocently as if he were questioning why the rain stopped.

Balboa looked directly at Alessandro, who seemed to be concentrating on something totally different.

"Why do you ask?"

Alessandro, his eyes following a large orange and yellow butterfly, said, "When the Spanish conquer people, you take some and make them do all your work. You take their gold and their food and then you take some people away and sell them."

Balboa watched the butterfly eventually land on Alessandro's outstretched hand.

"Well?" Alessandro asked.

Balboa loved this boy from the first time they met twelve years earlier. His father was arrested for supposedly helping Captain Bastido and his crew break the law by landing and trekking across Hispaniola without permission from the governor. Balboa could not let little Alessandro and his mother end up like so many Tainos, conquered and dominated by the Spaniards. But why was he asking today? How should I answer truthfully? Of course, she would have been taken. She was too beautiful to leave behind. He focused on an answer.

"I think your father fell in love with your mother so fast, he would not let anything bad happen to her," Balboa said.

"Like you did with Cacica?" Alessandro asked.

"Just like that."

"Do you love her like my father loved my mother?"

"What do you know about love?" Balboa asked.

"I know it feels safe, it feels happy. Did you love my mother?"

Balboa sensed this line of questions was going somewhere, but how could he know the mind of a young man?

"I loved your mother. I love Cacica, and I love you," he said.

"Do you love Leoncito?"

"Yes, I do. Now, why are we talking about love all of a sudden?"

Alessandro pulled a book from behind the rock he was sitting on. Balboa reached for it, examined it quickly, then looked firmly into Alessandro's eyes. "Where did you get this?"

"The monk. He said I could borrow it if you agreed to read it to me."

Balboa opened it to a page marked with a large, folded piece of parchment upon which read, "To my esteemed Alcalde Mayor Vasco Nuñez Balboa. Please read this to young Alessandro and help him understand the words. Starting with the epistle of Paul to the Galatians which starts, "For brethren, ye have been called unto liberty; only use not liberty for occasion to the flesh, but by love serve one another. For all the law is fulfilled in one word, even in this; Thou shalt love thy neighbor as thyself."

"Friar Tomás." Balboa closed his eyes while shaking head. "You have been learning from Friar Tomás?"

"Do you love Friar Tomás?" Alessandro asked.

"By faith, I do," Balboa said. "But by faith, it is not easy. Do you know what this book is?"

"No. I cannot read it."

"Good," Balboa said. "It is nothing but trouble."

"My trouble, or your trouble?"

Balboa taught the young boy to think and to question. He was teaching him to read and write, but not in Latin. Now he held a copy of the Latin New Testament from Friar Tomás, the same friar who refused communion to slave holders in Hispaniola and almost came to blows with fellow landowner

Bartolomé de las Casas over the issue. Balboa chuckled, remembering the sight. A young Dominican friar arguing face to face over the Lord's admonition about freedom and las Casas convinced that since the pope himself endorsed the conquest of these lands, it was no sin to captivate if the natives did not convert. Everyone knew the conquistadors captivated regardless. That was one of the problem areas in the Church's stand on baptism. Balboa offered baptism, but never forced.

"My trouble," Balboa said.

"What do those words mean? The friar said you will explain them to me."

Balboa read through the rest of the Apostle Paul's epistle to the saints in Galatia, his head shaking and lowering with each word. The first few were going to be easy; liberty, service, love, spirit. It was the rest that were going to be challenging; lust, adultery, fornication, lasciviousness, idolatry, seditions, envying, drunkenness, reveling, and witchcraft. He kept reading. Today, he thought, he would start at the bottom of the list; joy, peace, long-suffering, gentleness, goodness, faith, meekness and temperance.

No, I do not love Friar Tomás, and I am glad he went back to Spain, Balboa thought. Balboa promised Alessandro's mother he would teach the boy to be honest above all things. He figured it was not time to break a promise now.

Balboa finished the letter. Alessandro picked it up and began to read. He loved to read. Balboa told him about libraries filled with books. In the earliest days in Darién, there were no books to read. Alessandro saw no use in learning to read and write. When a young monk arrived, and with him the Bible, Alessandro began learning in earnest. The monk enjoyed having somebody interested in the words of God, even if it was a young, energetic mestizo. That monk soon returned to Spain, claiming these men were beyond hope, but he left behind the Latin Bible and made sure Alessandro knew how to find it in the small church. Alessandro did not care so much for the monk who replaced Friar Tomás.

Alessandro learned enough from Cacica about her people and their traditions which were never written, he insisted Balboa teach her to read.

"Alessandro, this might be hard to understand. I do not even understand it. But we will start with this word, maybe the hardest of them all, Libertas. It means…"

Chapter Thirty-Seven

1517 - Granada, Spain

"Ferdinand is dead." Miguel tilted his head in hopes of hearing the two guards. Over the many years, prison guards came and went. Brutal, kind, generous, bitter, and jealous. Miguel's hate had long disappeared. His nights became a time for reflection and prayer. His anticipation of a trial and execution dissipated years ago.

At one point, three guards, curious why he was such a valuable prisoner, engaged in conversation. Miguel's love for the word of God rekindled. Each day, the guards returned with interesting stories from the city and questions concerning their eternal standing with God. Those guards were eventually replaced by other guards with no interest in anything but lust.

But today, all conversation centered around the king's successor. "Julia? Mad Julia?" He heard some ask.

Julia was King Ferdinand and Queen Isabella's daughter and, though married to Philip of Austria, was considered mad. When Isabella died, it was said Julia was put away so as not to threaten Ferdinand's monarchy. He was now gone. And Philip died years earlier, conveniently for Ferdinand. Miguel wondered if he was the only person in Granada or in Spain who would not be surprised if Cisneros had his hand in the deaths, the succession, or the current political state.

Guards were low on political facts of the day, so Miguel knew so little of the world around him. What he did know was Cisneros, with whatever title he might currently be holding or aspiring to, lost all interest in Miguel, if he even knew Miguel was still alive.

"I do not know your name," the young monk, new to the prison, said. He approached Miguel, who leaned over the ledge of a fountain he and two other prisoners were repairing. Cool water up to his elbows softened the hot summer afternoon air.

"Should you?" Miguel asked, "Do I have one?" Miguel did not look up, just grunted as he lifted a large broken tile.

"To God you do," the monk said.

"You think He remembers it?"

"I know He does. He sent me here to remind you of it."

Miguel looked up and recognized the young monk's face. "What happened to you?"

"You…and God."

"If anyone could, God could," Miguel said.

Miguel stood and bowed, then dried his arms on his tunic. The monk motioned for him to sit, then sat next to him.

"You brought me to Christ," the monk said.

The monk pulled several sheets of parchment from under his robe. He handed them to Miguel.

"Can you read these?" he asked.

Miguel scanned the pages. He pointed at the first column. "Latin, from the book of Matthew, Christ heals the leper." The monk pointed to the next column. Miguel said, "Hebrew. It has been a while. I am not so fluent. Same miracle, same leper."

"And this one?" the monk asked.

"Greek? Same leper?" Miguel asked.

The monk shook his head. "Can you teach me?"

"Which one? I do not know Greek." Miguel squinted at the monk. "Am I the leper?"

"Why are you here?" the monk asked.

"I am wondering the same thing about you," Miguel said. He held up the manuscript and turned it over. Nothing on the back.

"How long have you been in Alcazaba?"

Miguel shrugged, "Six, seven, eight summers, maybe. How long since you were one of the guards?"

"Four years," the monk said.

"Then seven," Miguel said. "I was supposed to be dead; I was not counting very well." He thought back to one of the few times a guard or two conversed with prisoners, boredom he guessed. They engaged in deep theological and philosophical discussions. He missed that.

"Teach me," said the monk.

Miguel examined the monk's face. It was softer. Still very young. No facial hair. The tonsure was well groomed. Here Miguel sat with a former royal guard turned monk who wanted a prisoner who was condemned to death to teach him.

"Why me? I have not read much for seven summers."

"Because you teach the truth—as it is written."

"There are much greater scholars and linguists than me. Most of them are not condemned to death for heresy and murder."

"Is that why you are here?"

"I thought so."

"Nobody ever knew."

"You are not afraid to associate with a murderer and a heretic? Let alone be taught by one? What if I teach heretical doctrine?"

"I hope you do. And if I do not learn quick enough, you can murder me and run."

"I could run?" Miguel asked. "Where to?"

"Nobody knows why you are here or for how long. I told the bishop you brought me to Christ, and he believes in redemption."

Miguel raised his eyebrows.

"Actually, he does not know what to do with you, so he said I could have you."

"I cannot teach Greek, I do not know it. You certainly know Latin by now, so I teach you Hebrew?"

"No, you teach me the gospel of Jesus Christ, directly from the written word. Greek, Latin, Hebrew, I do not care which."

"But I teach you and I go free?"

"You can go free now. I just hope you will teach me along the way."

"Along the way, where?"

"Wherever you might be going."

"Where am I going? I lost everything. The Cardinal Cisneros killed my wife and sold my only true friends to the slave markets. And the only real disciple of Christ who I have ever known, was unjustly arrested and wasted away right here. I have nowhere to go."

"Then we will go nowhere together. I am Friar Alejandro Dominguez Tomás. It is an honor to be your student and companion."

"Alejandro Dominguez Tomás. Call me Miguel. I come from the Basque Country, Ziortza-Bolibar."

Friar Tomás waved to a guard, who immediately came and removed Miguel's fetters. The clang when they hit the stone patio echoed throughout the plaza. Miguel, for the first time in seven summers, filled his lungs with free air.

Tomás waited for the jubilation within Miguel to level and said, "Since you have no urgent business up north, we will stay clear of there. Spain is waging war with Navarre. Determined to conquer, our dear regent is away again to impose the church on infidels."

"Our regent? Not King Ferdinand?"

"Ferdinand is dead. Archbishop Francisco Cisneros is regent. Until Charles returns from the Netherlands."

No wonder I am forgotten. Miguel thought. But not for long.

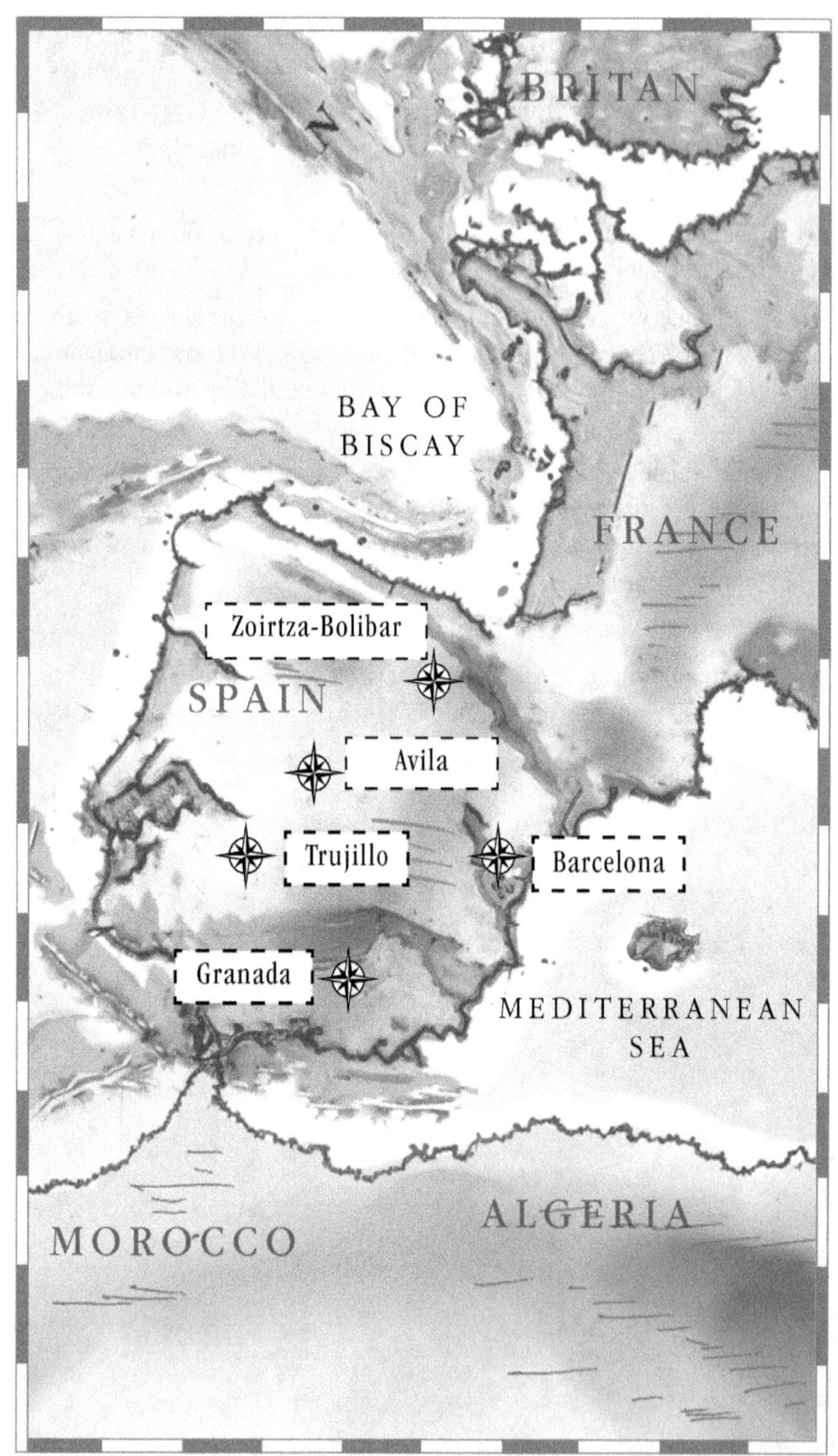

BRITAN
BAY OF
BISCAY
FRANCE
Zoirtza-Bolibar
SPAIN
Avila
Trujillo
Barcelona
Granada
MEDITERRANEAN
SEA
ALGERIA
MOROCCO

Chapter Thirty-Eight

1517 - Ziortza-Bolibar - Basque Country
Navarre, Northern Spain

"You will make new friends."

"What if I do not?"

"You will."

"What if they are mean to me?"

"They will not be," Maria lied. She lived the truth that people are mean. The kind, gentle, meek ones are few. She was grateful she had known a few and knew what was possible with mankind. She also knew an army of the mean ones were about to conquer Navarre. They already sacked Pamplona, just a few days' march away. Since the Pope sanctioned Ferdinand's quest, the English and Spanish squeezed France and soon Navarre would be the prize.

Reports of the conquered being turned into slaves flowed into Ziortza-Bolibar and the adjacent Basque towns lying on the edges. Many fled to Bilbao, but that was not far enough. She knew the reach of Spain's regent, so she was returning home to Trujillo, a friendlier home. A home where she hoped family would welcome her and her son.

"Let me say goodbye."

"Who else do you need to say goodbye to?"

"Edith."

"Edith's family left this morning. She said goodbye to you."

Martín did not know evil yet. He knew bullies, but not evil. But mostly he did not like change. When they left Ziortza and lived in Pamplona, the change so upset him, she felt he lost all the security he ever knew. Which was not much. Without a father, he was the subject of constant unkind teasing.

Both horses were packed, along with Preat, their pack mule. Maria delivered Preat during a violent storm. One evening while working in a vineyard, Maria noticed the commotion in the barn and drew near to see what was happening. Four-year-old Martín, who was at her side, wandered into the barn. Maria followed to be sure he was not troubling the people. A mare was fowling a colt just as lightning struck close by. The mare got frightened and bolted into a wall and fell unconscious. Maria quickly attended to and saved the unconscious mare. The mule colt arrived in such distress, he was left for dead. Since Maria stabilized the mare saving its life, she was rewarded with the colt if she could save it. Martín named the colt Preat, claiming the mule would grow up to be his protector.

Nighttime stories were a favorite of Martín. From the earliest days, Maria shared historical stories about heroes and battles. The most recent stories were about how his daddy was like the Praetorian Guard in Ancient Rome. He was the most elite of them all.

Maria helped Martín up onto his horse. She paused, leaned her head against the horse's neck and breathed in slow measured breaths. Soon the dizziness abated. She mounted Andi and the little family climbed up and over the narrow rock bridge crossing the Oiz River. They passed the cathedral of Ziortza and trotted west out of Cisneros' army's reach.

Fear of the unknown swallowed the excitement of an adventure which would be normal for any other six-year-old boy crossing undiscovered territory. But Martín had Preat. Maria's familiarity with much of northern Iberia made it easy to plan each night's stopping place. She avoided the bigger cities. She saved enough of her wages working for the husbandmen of the vineyards and tending for various caballeros' horses. Yet she was careful not to squander it. She had no idea in what condition she would find her sister's family or the family manor when they arrived in Trujillo. The weeks wore on, and the routine became nothing but work. Water was the challenge that worried Maria the most. Next was highwaymen. The route she chose avoided the most common thoroughfares, but posed a challenge crossing rivers without bridges or ferries.

Each night, Martín cuddled with his mother and she told the stories of great knights battling invaders. She told stories about the Gitanos, a wandering people who sang and danced. She told stories of Jesus.

"Would Jesus heal you?" Martín asked.

"I am sure he would."

"Would you touch his robe to get healed?" he asked.

"Yes, I would."

"Would you know Jesus if you saw him in the garden?"

"I hope I would."

"Is that why your name is Maria?"

"I think my mother and father loved Jesus and His mother so much, they wanted me to be like Jesus' mother," she said.

"Am I like Jesus?" he asked.

"Very much."

"Tell me about all the Maria's. They liked that name, right?"

Maria loved telling the stories about the wonderful women in the Bible. Maybe because she had their same name. Did her parents name her Maria so she would remember how much Jesus loved the Marias in His day?

One night Maria stumbled into the story of the woman brought before Jesus who the crowd wanted to stone. Maria hoped to teach how Jesus is loving and forgiving, only to be sidetracked with a lesson she was not ready to teach.

"What is adultery?" Martín asked.

They neared Avila. Breathing became more difficult. The higher elevation challenged her stamina. Oh, how she wanted to take Martín into the city and show him the grandeur of the cathedrals, and the Roman castle walls. But a woman traveling alone with a young boy would draw attention like a wolf to a lame ewe nursing her lamb. Which was exactly how she felt.

They stopped, ready to retire for the night.

"This will not do." A woman, maybe fifty or sixty years old, a staff in her hand stood aside a tall poplar. Maria had not seen the woman when she entered the small grove and dismounted.

Startled, she said, "We are sorry, we will move on." Maria prepared to remount, but hesitated to catch her breath.

"Indeed, you will," the woman said. "You will move on with me. There will be no sleeping outside while you are on my mountain."

Her mountain? Maria looked about. It was not a real mountain like the Pyrenees up north. It was just a high plateau with clusters of trees which grew along the riverbeds. Did she own it? Maria remounted. The woman led Maria and Martín from the small cluster of trees through a barren ravine covered only in brush. They climbed from the ravine into a tiny meadow that butted against a ragged bluff. Surrounding the meadow, young popular trees stood like sentinels striving to protect what appeared to be a small settlement. Butted up against the bluff sat a small mud and stick home. Leaning from its side, Maria guessed was a makeshift barn, or at least a stable. A roughly built corral finished the right edge of the settlement. Inside the corral stood a fine dappled mare content feeding from a manger filled to overflowing. Did this old woman build this? Maria wondered. Was she alone? Where did she get the feed? Cautiously, Maria dismounted. There was no sign of trouble. There was a peaceful feeling in the secluded area. Only one horse, and maybe this woman was all there was.

"Your mother is ill, but very wise," the woman said to Martín as he dismounted. He nodded but kept Preat between himself and the woman. "She keeps her little lamb away from the wolves."

An interesting observation, Maria thought. Who was this woman? Maybe they should move on.

"You would be more comfortable in Avila, yet you choose my mountain. You are either poor or wise," she said to Maria. "You are safe here tonight."

Martín kept his distance.

"We will eat and you can sleep there," she pointed to the stable between the house and small corral. The stable was only large enough for a handful of animals. It was clean with what looked like fresh straw on the ground.

Within minutes, she had a small fire heating a pot hanging from three steel poles connected at the top.

"Where does a pretty young woman take her son in such dangerous times?" she asked.

"Home," Maria said.

"To his father?"

Maria shook her head. It was enough for the woman. Maria wondered if the woman thought she was a widow or a tramp. Should she clarify? She left it.

"And pardon me, but how does a lone woman survive alone on a mountain?" Maria's curiosity begged the question.

"Come with me." The woman led Maria and Martín past the small meadow and up over the bluff. They stopped twice to let Maria catch her breath. There stood a flock of sheep as large as she had ever seen. "I am their shepherdess."

Maria immediately understood.

"How many?" Martín asked.

"Can you count?" she asked.

"Not that high," he said.

"Me either," she laughed. "I think thousands. But one less today. We will enjoy a mutton stew."

She could not have been more right, Maria thought. She was an injured ewe and wise enough to protect her little lamb, and they did enjoy the mutton stew. They ate quietly. This old woman knew how to cook. The intense scent of the stew was matched by its flavor. It rivaled any they had eaten in the many weeks they traveled. Maria thanked the woman and God for the kindness.

Maria wondered if the true shepherd, leaving his ninety and nine, ever went out looking for the lost sheep only to find it made into stew. She pondered that thought all night.

The next morning, they packed Preat and mounted ready to leave. The woman who had not been as talkative as Maria assumed a lonely woman would have been, again, used what Maria appreciated to be astute observation.

"In Avila, they consider me crazy. They laugh at my visions. But I can see things. I have a son in Avila. Alonzo. He gave me a granddaughter named Teresa, after me. In a vision, I saw Teresa become an important woman in the church. When I prophesied Teresa would become a famous saint, they laugh. But what I saw, I saw. I know it and God knows it."

"Do you see your granddaughter often?" Maria wondered if her alleged rantings were why she was forced outside the society of Avila. And why she was a poor hermit of a woman.

"Oh yes," Teresa said. "Beatriz, her mother, brings her out here and we pretend to be shepherds." She laughed when Maria's confusion turned her empathetic look to shock.

"That flock of sheep?"

Teresa nodded. "My son Alonzo owns them. He is the wealthiest wool grower in Avila. They think I am crazy because I like to escape the corruption in the cities. But when my husband, a Jew, was condemned by the inquisition, I lost faith in the church. But my granddaughter will bless it back."

Maria said nothing. This turn of perception about a crazy old woman could not have been more shocking. From a lonely insane woman to the grandmother of a prophesied saint and mother of the wealthiest man in Avila. Maybe she was crazy. Or maybe not.

The women bid farewell. She took Maria's hand. "God told me a young boy was coming and showed me where to find you. That is why I came here. I saw your boy help bring the words of Christ to common people. Then I saw him teach in foreign tongues, in foreign lands."

Maria looked deeply into Teresa's eyes. Was this true?

She put her wrinkled hand on Martín's leg and said, "You, my dear boy, have a sacred work ahead of you."

Martín just stared.

Chapter Thirty-Nine

1517 - Granada, Spain

The weight of emptiness surprised Miguel. He had not expected to receive the same reception as he did the first time he entered the shop, but this was something he had never felt. Sorrow, regret, and anger battled for prominence. Under a decree from 'the cardinal' as everyone referred to Cardinal Cisneros, and to demonstrate the fate of those who fight against the Holy Church, Sukayna's once popular shop remained closed and locked. It was a silent reminder to all the shop owners and patrons that no one was beyond the reach of the cardinal and his inquisitors.

Miguel looked to Tomás for answers. He did not need to ask. But he waited.

"Rumors only. Sold to the Ottoman slave markets," Tomás said.

"We will give this shop an opportunity to lend one more service," Miguel said. He smashed the chain with a stone. It tore free from the large wooden handles, shackled these many years. Too easily broken, the bonds keeping the shop closed were symbolic only. Fear was the true jailer, Miguel thought.

He and Tomás stepped inside. Dust and spider webs ignored the cardinal's decree. Before being locked, it appeared that a thorough destruction was attempted. A show of power, Miguel thought. Throughout his entire journey to Rome and back, the memory of Sukayna's stunning eyes never faded. He stood where they first met, and that memory dissolved into the nightmare she and Jalaf must now be living. He felt his heart was being crushed. Breathing became heavy. He ached.

Finally, and with less stunning success than his first visit to the shop, Miguel adorned himself as a proud Morisco, and offered Tomás a change from his plain brown robes. Tomás kindly declined. They stepped into the street, where merchants and shoppers stood in surprise.

Miguel served these people at the side of Archbishop Talavera. He realized many would remember Talavera's goodness. Certainly, they knew and loved Sukayna and Jalaf. He picked up the chain and shattered handle.

In perfect Arabic, he said, "You know Archbishop Talavera was chosen by God to teach, in your own language, the gospel of Jesus and to preach deliverance to the captives. When the shackles of ignorance no longer hold you captive, you will truly be free."

"No better way than a bold declaration of truth to a hungry crowd to stir up a revolt. We might want to follow Christ's example and pass through the midst of these and go our way, far away," Tomás said.

Miguel dropped the chains and walked through the crowd.

"If what you said is true and I am free, permit me three stops," Miguel said. He did not wait for approval. Miguel led Tomás from the shop up toward the home of Anna Maria. It, too, was left desolate. The gardens, which once sang praises to God in their beauty, grew wild in need of a husbandman as mentioned by John.

"Do you believe Christ is the true vine?" Miguel asked as he pushed through the overgrowth toward the house.

"I do," Tomás said.

"Are you willing to work in His vineyard?" Miguel asked.

"I thought I was working in His vineyard," Tomás said.

They reached the house. It was empty. Miguel wondered the fate of Anna Maria and her secret husband Bishop Martínez.

"Did you know these people?" Tomás asked.

"Are you willing to be a husbandman in His vineyard, not just a branch?" Miguel asked.

"You may need to share what you are thinking. Did I free you too early?" Tomás asked.

Miguel smiled, and looked around at the mass of vegetation overtaking the once beautiful home. "If I am truly a free man and if you are willing to serve God with me as husbandmen, we may best serve God by cutting out a bad branch and casting it into the fire to be burned."

Tomás did not answer. He squinted and waited.

"Do you have money?" Miguel asked.

"Enough for my needs," Tomás said.

Miguel pushed back through the garden and walked quickly up into the Albayzin neighborhood on San Cristobal Hill. Again, Miguel found the locations he frequented were left desolate. He pushed into the house where he and Maria began their married life together. Determination that sprouted in Sukayna's shop and was nourished in Anna Maria's garden, took strength with roots firmly planted in the soil of indignation. Tomás said nothing.

Miguel quickly crossed the big room and pushed open a panel, revealing a secret cavity. He pulled out a bag and blew the dust from its top. The dust danced in the sliver of sunlight pouring through a crack in the closed window shade.

"Complements of the cardinal," Miguel said. "We may not travel in style, but we will travel." Miguel did not say more. Leaving the door wide open, he marched from San Cristobal Hill back into the city. He hoped his next destination was not abandoned. He stepped into a livery, hoping to find a grumpy Ubayd who could provide two horses. Instead, they faced a young man who looked more a light pole than a horseman. Several inches taller than Miguel and at least fifty pounds lighter, Miguel thought if any kind of wind ever caught his loose pant and shirt, he would sail away.

"Ubayd?" Miguel asked.

The young man shook his head.

"Two stout and fast horses," Miguel said. He pulled several gold coins from the bag. Within an hour, and with a few provisions they bought in the waning hours of the afternoon market, the two men rode out of the city of Granada. Miguel looked back only once, and that was to see if Friar Tomás was still following. So little had been said, Miguel was surprised Friar Tomás put up no resistance. He had freed a very important condemned prisoner, followed him through the city, and now abandoned his work in Granada to travel with a heretic to certain death—his own or that of an unprofitable branch. Or both.

They traveled late into the night. One small lantern lit the front of a tavern. They stopped, begged a cold bite to eat and a bed. Early the next day, they mounted and continued north. Though it was Friar Tomás' eagerness to learn from Miguel, it was Miguel pulling from Tomás everything that had happened politically, theologically, culturally, and even environmentally over the past seven years. In the evenings, as they rested around a fire or in an inn, they studied the New Testament written in three languages. Tomás called it a polyglot. It surprised Miguel when Tomás credited the cardinal for commissioning it. Maybe Miguel could find some good in the man.

Tomás was a great student, but deeply Miguel knew he was not his student. He was a student of the words of Christ. Not all clergy were, Miguel knew. During long days in the saddle, Miguel shared the stories of his time in Africa, Rome, and his early years when Talavera, with great patience, took a young delinquent and taught him of Christ.

Tomás hoped their journey north was only an effort to return to Miguel's roots in Ziortza-Bolibar. He knew better, however. Conversations with residents, fellow travelers, and merchants nearly always focused on the impending conquest of Navarre and where its leadership was located. This night it was no different, as they rested in a tavern enjoying a hot stew.

"Let me know before you march in and sever the branch from the vine. I may not be ready to be that husbandman," Tomás said.

"No, I certainly would not ask that of you," Miguel said. "But you have known our destination since you set me free."

"I hoped I was wrong."

"Am I wrong?" Miguel asked.

"From what I know and what you experienced, I cannot say you are. But I wish I had your courage."

"I have nothing but love for my God. I have yet to love my enemy," Miguel said.

"Ferdinand's death puts young Charles on the throne. When he arrives from the Netherlands, our regent will be powerless. He is old. I fear your soul is not worth risking."

"I need to see him," Miguel said. "His age or position does not prevent him from orchestrating the siege of Navarre."

"And when we find him?" Tomás asked.

"One of us will be free."

"And the other dead?"

The discussion ended when six stout soldiers entered the tavern tired and dusty. They dropped their helmets and swords on a table and sat. Vessels of wine were emptied immediately. The innkeeper brought more, spoke briefly, and returned to the kitchen. When he returned with a large platter of meats and breads, a soldier asked, "How far to Roa de Duero?"

"Three hours, maybe two if your horses are rested," the innkeeper said.

"Royal guards," Miguel whispered to Tomás. "What is in Roa de Duero requiring these attendants?"

"Nothing of importance, I hope," Tomás said.

"Nobody of importance, you mean," Miguel said.

The two men sat silently, trying to overhear the conversation. The guards held no secrets, but they divulged little. Until one asked, "If the cardinal is no longer there?"

Miguel winked at Tomás.

"You gentlemen are unfamiliar with Roa de Duero?" Miguel asked, leaning back over his shoulder to address the men.

"You know it?" a guard asked.

"My monk and I are riding there on the morrow," Miguel said.

"You have business with the cardinal?"

"A debt," Miguel said.

"Take us then," a guard said.

Listening for more stray comments that might confirm which cardinal they meant, they got none.

Miguel and Tomás were saddled and ready when the guards came into the tavern's courtyard the next morning. In the few hours riding with the guards, they heard they were carrying a message from their new king who expected an audience in Valladolid. They also learned the guards had traveled five days already and a few hours' ride in the morning would be a trifle.

Wild grasses bent leisurely in the cool morning breezes. Fields of grass eventually gave way to vineyards now dormant. Only months earlier, these vineyards bustled with workers. Roa boasted great wines made possible from the fertile landscape fed by the Duero River, which wound its way through the valley. The church rose above the vineyards on the horizon.

Would seven years of conquest, seven years of inquisition, seven years of political intrigue, be seven years of forgetting what Cisneros did to the lives of Granadians? Or the North Africans? And the people of Navarre? Within minutes, Miguel might stand face to face with the man who took everything from him. He would also be surrounded by six of King Charles' own guards. Miguel looked at each. Seven years ago, he might have been equal to three or maybe four of them. Was he ready for six? How many did he kill in Granada? Not enough. They murdered his Maria. These six were certainly more skilled than Cisneros' guards. The vision of Maria, still and lifeless, a sword piercing her chest and pinning her to the ground haunted him. It added to his failure to protect Talavera and nearly drove him mad.

He had to meet with Cisneros alone when the guards were away. He did not know if their intentions were to escort the cardinal to Valladolid to meet with the king or just present the letter they mentioned. Would the cardinal even remember him?

Which of these guards looked the fiercest? Which of their horses the fastest? Then he noticed Tomás watching him assess their situation. Tomás stared directly into Miguel's eyes and shook his head. You know what I need to do, why are you following me? Miguel thought. The small market that usually spread throughout the plaza was deserted. Most residents, busy during harvest, were back in their vineyards or farms. The streets were mostly empty.

Miguel knew that only a few days away, the battle for his own homeland raged between Spain and Navarre. From what they gleaned from fellow travelers, Cisneros had laid siege and demolished castles, towns, and cities in his quest to conquer the peoples of Navarre. Would today help bring an end to it?

A guard leapt from his horse and entered the tall stone church. Minutes later, he returned. "The cardinal welcomes us," he said.

The guards dismounted and secured their horses. Miguel and Tomás sat motionless and were soon alone in the plaza. One small tavern sat opposite the church. Several other buildings surrounded it. Miguel motioned with his head and the two men left their horses and entered the church. Voices echoed through the nave. Slowly, Miguel made his way toward what sounded like a pleasant interchange, but the echo blurred the words. There, sitting in a large wooden chair in the north transept, was Cardinal Francisco Jimenez Cisneros surrounded by his own and six of the king's guards, three bishops, a handful of monks, and who Miguel assumed was the captain of his army. What are all of them doing there in the middle of the morning? But what else had Miguel expected? Cisneros was directing a conquest of lands, not of hearts.

Chapter Forty

1517 - Trujillo, Extremadura, Spain

Maria was grateful Martín was too young to consider Teresa's prophecy as anything to ask questions about. She had no answers, and thought about how fifteen hundred years ago an angel visited a young unmarried Maria with news of her soon-to-be-born son. Just as the Maria of old, Maria kept these things and pondered them in her heart. She could not bring herself to compare her circumstance.

"Teach me to count to thousands," Martín said. As mundane a task as that was, Maria cherished the break from the worry, confusion, and pain of her condition.

The climb back down off the plateau into Extremadura made breathing easier, but the land was less inviting. She remembered how harsh it was living here when her mother died. That was when she decided to leave this place and she struck out on her own, a young woman in a dangerous world.

Maria could not decipher between dread or excitement when the impressive silhouette of the city's fortified walls rose high above the landscape. Trujillo's sturdy stone walls were punctuated by battlements and watchtowers, which testified of the city's history of defense and strategic significance.

They passed through the city gates. The sounds of hooves clattering on the uneven stones and the bustling chatter of merchants and townsfolk filled the air. The road was lined with houses of stone and adobe.

So much had changed since Maria left Trujillo. She and Martín entered the crowded town. Having now been to Rome, she recognized how the various buildings reflected the different eras of conquest. She recognized a tangible link to the city's past. Buildings with wooden beams and small windows stood side by side to new structures with ornate facades and intricate carvings. It was a fusion of Moorish, Roman and Gothic influence.

She felt a vibrancy she had not remembered. They reached the heart of the city and the Plaza Mayor. It was teeming with activity. Memories, both good and horrible flooded her mind. She resisted the thought, but this was home. She remembered vividly how she and her mother came here. Traders peddled their wares under colorful awnings. Locals gathered, socialized, bought, and sold. She slowed, letting Martín soak in the feeling of his new home.

They passed through the plaza, narrow alleys, and hidden courtyards. They reached the Church of Santa Maria la Mayor with its towering spires and elaborate entrance. Though Maria had experienced great cathedrals, even in Rome, this was her childhood church. She paused and pondered. Memories of the scent of incense mingled with echoes of prayers filled her.

These many weeks traveling were about to come to an end. She could almost taste the hearty stews, freshly baked bread, and the wine from her sister's vineyard. How her sister would be surprised and welcome her back home. She could almost feel the embrace. Tears of joy began to back up behind her eyes. They stood at attention, ready to pour forth at the instant they were called. What if they were not called? What if they were the wrong tears ready to flow? Which tears would be required? Too often, these past years, disappointment and heartache forced the tears of joy back and replaced them with tears of anguish and sorrow. The tears of joy waited. Would they ever again be called upon?

And Andi, her precious gift from Vano's father, was no longer a young filly. She carried Maria across the continent and back and now deserved a much-needed rest. They left the bustle of the city and wound their way through a quiet alley. It was too quiet. She dismounted and readied to pound on the courtyard's thick wooden door. It was cracked open. She pushed. A creaking whine echoed through the alley. The courtyard was empty. Afternoon sun cast long shadows across the empty yard. Nothing. Nobody. Just a barren courtyard.

Where had they gone? Who would know?

The earlier tears of joy froze in place, then melted into streams of despair. Maria pulled Andi, Preat, and Martín into the yard. Hand in hand, Maria led Martín across the yard and into the empty house. No sign of a hasty exit. No furniture. No remains of untouched food for man or beast. Martín pushed the large door closed. Maria crumbled to the earth and wept. Martín climbed into Maria's arms quivering. Hours passed. The sun set. They crawled to their feet. She unpacked the animals and led them to the well, where she prayed she might find water. If no other prayers were to be answered, she was relieved at least this one was. She pulled water and filled the stone trough.

She made as comfortable a bed as she could, determined that tomorrow might bring hope. Tonight, there was none. Martín fussed and fidgeted until the early morning hours. She knew he felt the despair in her heart. She left him sleeping when she went out to care for the animals and to get a fresh look at her new life, alone in a place she abandoned more than a dozen years earlier. Would the man she fled and his family still be here? Would they remember her? Of course they would. Twelve years was not enough time to forget. She had not.

She would find her sister's family. She would establish some sort of stability for her boy and raise him up to be a credit to his father. Could she? The animals would need some feed, and soon she and Martín would too. First, she needed to find a friend.

Maria could not go far. If Martín woke without her near, this would be anything but a fresh start. She cared for the animals. They seemed content to have a day or two free of their burdens. She put on her happy, hopeful face and welcomed Martín with a smile when he entered the now empty but once modestly appointed dining hall. Maria remembered how the finely crafted tables and chairs built by her father and adorned with well-prepared meals by her mother made this room a sacred place for the family to gather.

The joyful memories of her childhood soon vanished, pushed aside by the nightmare. She was certain that when her parents fell ill and died within a week of each other, her sister and her new husband planned to take over the trade. Maria's father was once a highly respected farrier, caring for the large horse herds bred by the monastics. She grew up loving to work side by side with her father. It was so until a new marshal was hired to manage the large herds. His demands and failure to support Maria's father with necessary feed and medicines compromised the health and safety of the horses. When her father was blamed for the loss of important breeding stock, the prior dismissed him. He fell ill under the stress and died within weeks.

But it was the marshal's son who caused Maria to leave. He forced himself on her. She held him back with a hoof knife, practically turning him into a gelding. The boy was too humiliated to make his failure public, but he became more mean to man and beast. He threatened to kill Maria, or worse, he would say. She knew it was time to leave the manor house to her sister's family. Now, these years later, she realized this was no place her sister wanted to remain either. But where did she go? Was she driven out? There was no sign of hostility. Would she have gone to her husband's home? She could not recall where her brother-in-law called home.

Following a scanty breakfast, she and Martín walked through the alleys hoping to find a face or place that looked friendly and possibly aware of her sister's whereabouts.

In many ways, nothing seemed to have changed. It was the same dirt roads, the same cobblestones, the same mud walls, even the same smells both repulsive and inviting. When they got to the church, she wanted to rush in and seek answers from the priest. The large wooden doors were locked shut. It clearly was not a wealthy church, but it looked neglected, disregarded, abandoned. Why hadn't she noticed last night?

"We are waiting for a new priest." It was a kind voice. A comfortable voice.

Maria turned and faced a full-figured woman. She could not be more than a few years older than Maria. The white blouse was open across the shoulders, leaving them bare several inches down her arms. Her long brown dress was sleeveless and looked sturdy. It was closed with wooden buttons and gathered at the waist, exposing her ample female shape. Her long black hair hung loosely over her right shoulder. She was carrying a large basket of narrow orange squashes.

Maria struggled to put a name to the face. This was a woman she knew, or at least once knew.

"Until a new priest comes, the prior at the monastery receives our confessions," the woman said, "if that is what you need."

Maria shook her head. "No, looking for someone who used to live here."

"I am Señora Lopez." She looked closely at Maria, then to Martín. "Who are you? I guess you are about twelve?"

Martín was shy, but Maria gave him a nod to respond.

"Seven," he said.

She raised her eyebrows and stared at him waiting. Maria nudged him.

"Martín," he said. He kept close to Maria.

"Martín, it is nice to meet you. Does your mother have a name?"

"Maria," he said.

"Maria, it is a pleasure to meet you too. May I ask who you are looking for, or might it be presumptuous of a stranger to ask?"

Maria shook her head. "My sister and her husband, Manuela and Roberto de Leon. Do you know them?"

Señora Lopez smiled. "I know you. It has been a long time. Welcome home. Maria? You do not recognize me?"

"Not as a señora."

Señora Lopez nodded toward Martín. "You are not a señora now?"

Maria's memory-struggles ended.

"Guadalupe?"

"I am married, widowed, and a bit healthier." Guadalupe padded her ample hips and chuckled. "Come with me."

Guadalupe led Maria and Martín away from the church, past the square, and into a pension where several customers were finishing breakfast.

Maria glanced toward heaven and whispered a thank you. Two prayers now answered, she prayed for a third.

Guadalupe dropped the basket on a bench, gave some instructions to some helpers, and ushered Maria and Martín to a table.

"Your kindness is an answer to prayers," Maria said. "We hoped to find Manuela. We found the manor deserted."

"They left after you did. The herds that were once the pride of the monastics dwindled. They released the marshal, who they eventually found dishonest. Your father was vindicated, but too late. Your sister and her family are gone."

"Do you know where they went?" Maria hardly expected Guadalupe to know. She asked anyway.

Shrugged shoulders confirmed a third answered prayer was not eminent.

Guadalupe motioned to a young girl who brought two warm bowls of porridge to her guests. Martín waited for an approval from Maria then dug in. With Martín's attention on a warm breakfast, Guadalupe asked, "Will the boy's father be coming?"

Maria knew it was a kind way to ask if she was married. She shook her head and quietly said, "Killed protecting an old man."

Guadalupe gently shook her head. "Are you staying?"

"I have no place else to go. This is my home. His father's home in Navarre is under siege."

"You have a home here now. Do you have your father's talent with horses?"

It was as if Maria's face resurrected. A smile, long missing, brought with it a feeling of hope. It pulled Martín's attention from the last few spoons full of porridge. He squinted at Maria.

Guadalupe smiled at Martín, "You have more exploring to do. Return this evening for supper. Then we will go see the new marshal."

Maria flinched. Guadalupe saw it and said, "not to worry, the marshal is a monastic…with no son." Guadalupe winked.

The horrifying scene raced back through her mind of the day when the son of the former marshal was left bleeding and screaming. That memory heavily hung on Maria during her entire journey from her home in Navarre to Trujillo. What would she find here? Who might she find here? Her feelings to find her sister outweighed her fear. And she had her knife.

"You know?" Maria said.

"I was a fool. I did not know I was marrying a eunuch."

"I am so sorry."

"So am I. But not to worry, he cheated a highwayman and found himself on the wrong side of an argument. We held a small funeral. His father, the marshal, was already gone. This small tavern provides well enough."

Guadalupe's lack of sorrow for the loss of her husband surprised her. Maria had a husband for a few scant days and knew him only weeks, and she could not move on. The hole in her heart still ached more than the hole in her lung. She unconsciously rubbed the scar.

 Maria and Martín returned for supper. Guadalupe refused Maria's offer to pay. On their way to the new marshal's manor, Guadalupe shared the decade of Trujillo's history. She told how the extreme poverty and harsh environment of the Extremadura drove so many of the men from the area in search of fame and riches in the New World. Those who had not joined the armies joined the expeditions.

Guadalupe was careful when she told how her husband was typical of the kind of men in these lands; hard, coarse, and desperate. She joked that her new, more ample, feminine shape was intentional to help slow the unwanted advances. She suggested the same for Maria who, she said, would likely face another suitor like the former marshal's son.

The current marshal was out in the yard where two Andalusian mares and an Arabian stallion were haltered and secured to a long post. He was dressed in his coarse black robe tied at the waist with the same type of rope securing the horses to their post. He was a handsome and confident man and reminded her of Miguel in size and coloring. Yet his face was clean shaven and sported a ready smile when Señora Lopez introduced Maria and Martín.

"Father, you certainly know of the reputation your herds once proudly wore, a prestige you are expected to regain? This is Maria and her son Martín. Maria's father was the farrier who built and maintained that reputation. She has returned, and having learned the trade from her father and practiced it these many years, is in need of a job. You will be wise to employ her."

Practiced it these many years? Maria's eyes widened at the statement. She wondered if it took more than one confession if the lie was to a priest. She did not correct it. Her eyes tightened again when she assessed the confidence of Guadalupe. She did not ask the marshal to consider Maria; she told him he would be wise. She liked Guadalupe's style.

The marshal's visual assessment of Maria gave her peace. It was pure. There was no guile in his eyes. A third prayer answered?

"Tell me about my three new horses," he said.

No greeting, no conversation, just an immediate test of Señora Lopez's claim. Maria placed her hands on the stallion and slowly walked around him, never losing contact. He was at peace. When she ducked under his head, she wrapped her arms around it and whispered to the animal. It responded with a nod. She then did the same with the two Andalusians. They were a bit taller with longer manes. She ran her fingers through them and laid her head against the neck, seeming to bond.

"These are as fine a horse as you will find."

The marshal glanced toward Guadalupe and said, "The señora thinks you can help. What do you think?"

She tucked a lock of hair over her ear, released her lip, nodded and smiled.

"We start early. I'll see you tomorrow," the marshal said.

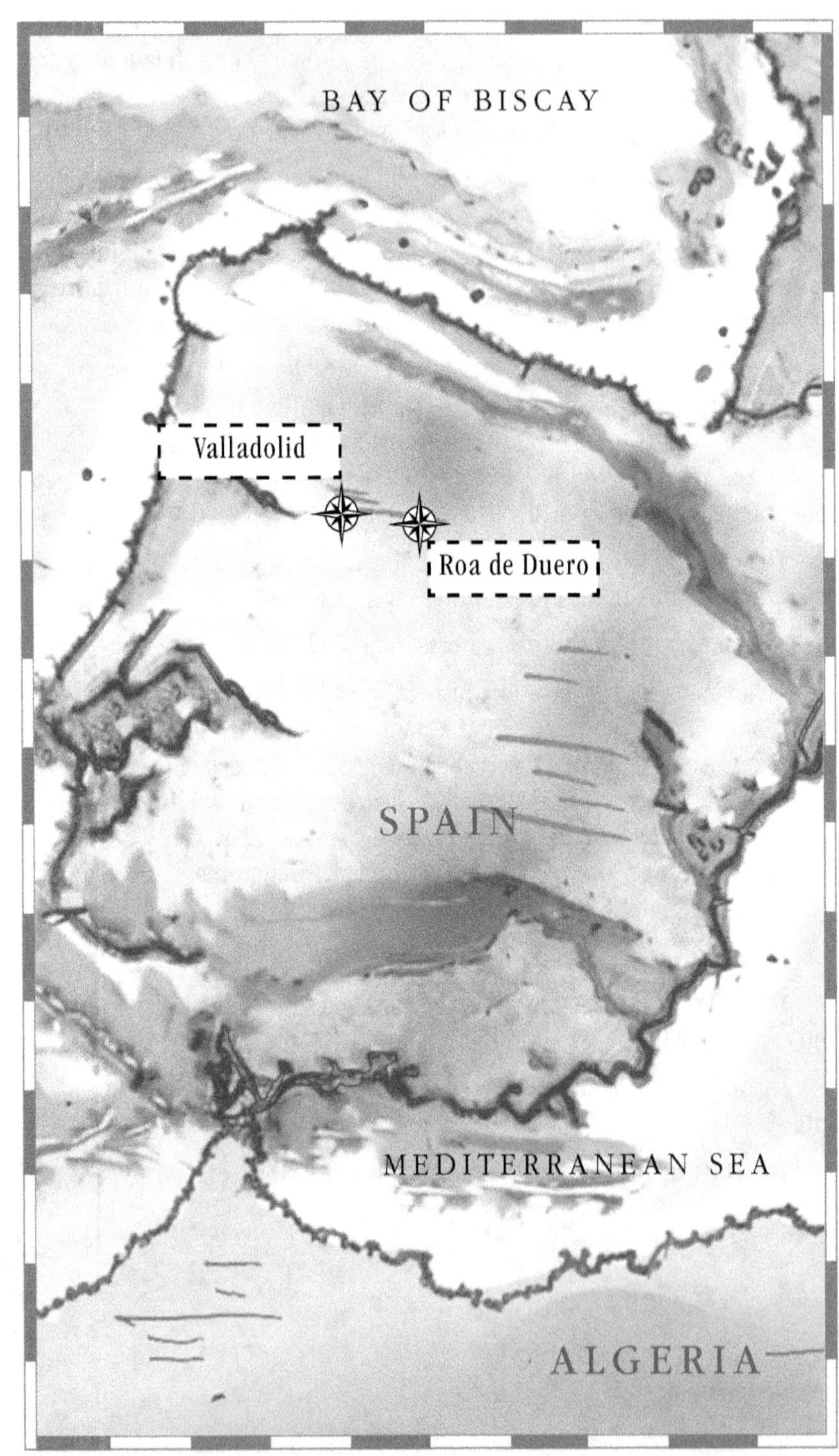

BAY OF BISCAY
Valladolid
Roa de Duero
SPAIN
MEDITERRANEAN SEA
ALGERIA

Chapter Forty-One

1517 - Roa de Duero - Northern Spain

"Valladolid?" Cardinal Cisneros set the letter on his lap and his cap on the table. His breathing was shallow. On each side stood his royal guards. His captain from the Navarre siege in Pamplona waited for an opportunity to report. The king's royal guards interrupted his report when they took priority delivering the letter from King Charles.

Cisneros felt unappreciated and betrayed. After all he had done for the young king, for the king's grandmother Queen Isabella, and serving as Regent of Spain at the death of Ferdinand, holding Aragon, Leon, and Castile together? He conquered Mers-el-Kebir, Oran, and now was sealing the fate of rebellious Navarre. Here in a tiny insignificant chapel in an insignificant village, not large enough to even be a city, Charles, in a letter, says, "Thank you. You are no longer needed, rest in peace."

The young king left the Netherlands and was now in Spain. Of course, a regent was no longer needed. Yet, no other man on earth had done more for Spain, for the unification, the inquisition, the conversion of Jews and Moors and now the conquest of Navarre. He was now dismissed with a seal on a sheet of parchment?

He coughed, wheezed, looked up to his captain and motioned to continue his report about the conquest of Navarre. The report was positive. The siege of the Castle of Xavier was complete. The castle was a symbol of defiance for the Kingdom of Navarre. Its fall signaled a major victory for Cisneros' army.

Miguel stood unobserved among several soldiers and guards in the nave just outside the cathedral's left transept. The words echoed off the tall ceilings. Everyone stood silently, awaiting the cardinal's response.

"Destroy it," Cisneros said. He looked up from his wrinkled hands, which held his gaze during the report. A contorted smile filled his worn face.

"Destroy it. I want them to know you cannot stand against me. Leave no stone standing upon another."

If the large cathedral was not already quiet, the hush that command fostered would have smothered any sound.

Cisneros, surrounded by soldiers, guards, monks, and bishops would be impossible to confront. Miguel led Tomás from the chapel. They crossed the plaza and entered the tavern. This was more like it. At least a dozen soldiers sat at tables, quietly complaining they were not somewhere else.

Miguel and Tomás were silent. Miguel picked at the platter of food.

"The cardinal is available," a guard said. The king's guards entered the tavern and sat near Miguel and Tomás. "We told him we were escorted by a monk and a troubadour here to pay a debt."

"A troubadour?" Miguel said.

"Actually, we do not know what you are," a second guard said.

Another guard spoke up. "You port like a gentleman, dress like a Moor, you are armed like a highwayman, you speak like a Christian, you ride like a caballero, yet you travel with a monk."

"Do you keep the monk for easy confession when you stray into trouble?" The guards burst into laughter.

Tomás joined the laughter. "You underestimate my burden," he said.

"Well, my friends," Miguel said, "I do what I must do, and your kind observance does me justice." Miguel stood, bowed, left the tavern, and crossed the plaza.

"Go to it," Cisneros said. He stood slowly. The captain bowed, turned, and led his men away. Cisneros waved the others away. He turned and, with the help of a white flocked bishop, slowly walked out into the cloister. Winded and tired, he sat to rest. He motioned the bishop away as he sat in the shade. Now alone, he pulled the letter, unfolded it, and read again slowly. He closed his eyes, breathed as deeply as his aged lungs permitted, and read again.

Miguel watched from behind a pillar. The once powerful, domineering and demanding cardinal looked old. He was old, but now he seemed so frail and weak. He had no audience. He had no one to impress or command. It looked to take everything he had to command his own hands to hold the letter as he read it a third time.

Miguel knew the letter was personal and important enough that the new young king, King Charles V, newly arriving from the Netherlands, sent it with six personal royal guards.

It was not good news. Miguel watched Cisneros' eyes tighten, his cheeks flush and flex, and shoulders cringe. This was Miguel's chance. This was a moment he thought about for seven years. But he had not let those years fill with hate as much as he did sorrow. Sorrow for those who suffered at the hands of a man so determined to force Christ upon them. Sorrow for the Jews, the Moors, who were forced from their homes, families, and country in the so-called conquest of the heathen. Sorrow for the church's betrayal of one its finest servants, Archbishop Talavera. And sorrow for the loss of his Maria. Why did Talavera work so quickly to marry them? Why was it so important that he and Maria marry, only to be separated days later? Did he know they were soon to be separated or killed? Did he hope a wife could persuade him to flee? And sorrow for two special friends, who now, if they were alive, were certainly suffering a hellish existence in bondage.

Miguel leaned against the pillar shaded by the portico, his arms folded. Sorrow for this man. Had he ever known joy? Had he ever felt empathy for the thousands he displaced, for the thousands he destroyed? Had he ever felt remorse?

Cisneros leaned his forehead into an open palm, elbow resting on a knee. His head moved so slightly Miguel guessed he was praying, or crying? His shoulders shook. Crying. He wiped his eyes with the hem of his cassock, then took another strained and shallow breath. When he saw the silhouette leaning against the pillar, he said, "Cannot you leave an old man in peace?"

Miguel stepped from the shadow, advancing to within a few feet of his mortal enemy. He was helpless. Even too weak to yell for help. Old, sick. Yet his eyes had not lost their will to hate. Miguel wondered how this moment would be. For seven years, he prayed for it.

Cisneros tried to speak. He opened his mouth. His breathing became so quick and short, Miguel wondered if the surprise might bring the man to an early grave. No, if he died now, it would not be too early.

"You got it all wrong," Miguel said.

Cisneros stared, squinting to assure himself he was looking at a face he had forgotten years ago.

"Yes, it is me. You forgot? Yes you forgot. You shouldn't have."

Cisneros said nothing.

"I am sad for you," Miguel said. "You spent a lifetime forcing men to Christ and you know nothing about Him. You destroyed the one man who actually knew Christ, was like Christ in every way. Just like the leaders of the Jews did to Christ, you betrayed, persecuted, and killed Archbishop Talavera."

Cisneros said nothing. Miguel knelt on one knee. They looked each other eye to eye.

"That letter? From Charles? I can only imagine it says thank you, but I do not need you anymore."

Spite filled Cisneros' face. It burned red hot.

"We are all expendable. You know that. I was expendable. I hope that is not fear in your eyes. I doubt it is. I wanted to kill you. I wanted to hate you. I wanted to see you stopped. I wanted to undo all the evil you imposed on others. I want my Maria back. I want Talavera to rest with God until I may die and be with both him and Maria, my wife!"

Cisneros shifted in his seat. The letter fell to the ground. Miguel gently picked it up and set it back in Cisneros' lap under his hand.

"But I thank you for the good you have done. I now know Greek and Hebrew through your polyglot. I love the people in North Africa who you so viciously conquered."

Cisneros squinted to comprehend that statement.

"Yes, I was there," Miguel said. "Who do you think escorted your personal slaves to freedom? Like I said, you lived your life wrong."

Miguel placed his hands on Cisneros' trembling ones.

He wanted to pull his sword and drive it through the cardinal's heart, as his men did to Maria. He wanted to release all the anger, regret, hate, and sorrow crowding his heart and load it on this man who used the name of Christ not in vain, but as a weapon to destroy. Miguel looked deeply into Cisneros' eyes. They were defiant. Tired. Afraid. They were not sorrowful.

"People will believe you were a great servant of Christ, a great servant of the church, a great regent of Spain, a leader of conquest. Universities will carry your name. You may even be sainted. But I pray that Christ Jesus will forgive you," Miguel said. After many moments, he added, "Because I do."

With those words, which Miguel had never planned to utter, a peace entered his being—a peace he had not felt in a long time. The heaviness of anger and hate fled. A sadness for this lost man filled his heart, pushing a tear down Miguel's cheek.

The bishop entered the cloister from the north transept. "Your eminence," he called, "the captain seeks a moment more with you."

The bishop, accompanied by the captain, one of his soldiers, and one of the king's guards, stopped in mid-stride when they saw Miguel kneeling next to the cardinal with his hands cupping the cardinal's. Cisneros pulled his hands free from Miguel's gentle grasp. The strength of his voice surprised Miguel.

"Traitor," Cisneros yelled, jumping to his feet, "Navarreen spy, sent to assassinate me!" Immediately, the exertion of the accusation and his effort to stand crippled Cisneros. He collapsed. Miguel instinctively caught him before he hit the ground. Cisneros lapsed into a fit of violent coughing, ending nearly as abruptly as it started. Cisneros went limp.

The bishop lurched forward to help steady the cardinal's body whose head flopped forward. Blood ran from his nose and mouth. The captain pulled his sword, as did his soldiers. With one arm still around the cardinal's motionless body, Miguel pulled a sword that deflected the captain's first thrust. With a push of thigh and hip, he released the cardinal's lifeless body onto the support of the bishop. Unprepared for the added weight, the bishop tumbled to the ground, landing on the cardinal. With the two clergy out of the way, the soldier and the royal guardsman engaged, steel crashing against steel.

Miguel did not plan to pull his sword against Cisneros. His swordsmanship sat idle for seven years. How he had underestimated Cisneros' resistance to what Miguel felt should have been guilt and remorse.

Miguel now had three professional swordsmen erasing away any time to reflect on the total ineffectiveness of his deeply sincere words.

A quick sweep with his blade and the soldier backed away, tangling his foot with the guards. The soldier fell over the cardinal's leg, landing on the bishop. Miguel's swipe at the guard caught him on an outstretched arm. He pulled back a step, preventing the swipe from catching his chest.

The captain seized the opening and pierced Miguel's forearm, knocking the sword to the ground. Out came the whip so quickly the soldier, trying to stand, dropped back onto the bishop when the sting of the whip tore into his cheek, drawing immediate blood. Miguel rolled trying to grab his sword, but the gash inflicted by the captain prevented a firm grasp. From a kneeling position, Miguel launched a scorpion like-sting on the guard, lunging toward him. The whip kept his attackers cautious, but against three swords it could not last long. He had to get to his sword.

The captain circled behind Miguel as he climbed to his feet. Any reach for the sword left him open. They surrounded him. Miguel tried to keep the bishop and cardinal inside the circle, making it awkward for at least one of the attackers.

The clanging of the swords echoed through the cloister, drawing an audience of monks and bishops. The clangs reached the tavern and since steel on steel was an uncommon sound coming from the church, the tavern emptied, and men flooded toward the action. Tomás did not follow. He hurried toward the livery and their horses.

The soldier moved closer, reaching over the bishop who tried unsuccessfully to pull the cardinal's body from the fray. Miguel snatched the sword from his hand with a snap of the whip. It slid toward Miguel, who plucked it off the stone. The motion pulled the soldier down again. Miguel had two on their feet but saw others entering the cloister. To run was his only choice. But where? Two quick cracks, one aimed at each man, put them on their heels. He darted back into the north transept. Boots echoed through the great, empty cathedral. He charged down the nave toward the large chapel doors. The surprise registered on the captain, the guard, and the soldier struggling to get back off the bishop and the cardinal. They charged into the cathedral.

The guards entering the cloister turned quickly to try and meet Miguel as he exited the chapel. They knew who they were chasing. He had just led them to Roa de Duero. They knew nothing more. They saw the captain, his soldier, and one of their own, chase this man into the house of God.

They entered the plaza to a stampede of horses chased by a monk hurling rocks in every direction. They ducked and dodged as projectiles crashed into them. The shock of the source of the flying death balls sent all sense of normalcy fleeing as well.

Riding atop his black stallion sat Friar Tomás, screaming, yelling, and throwing stones. He and the horses reached the front entrance of the cathedral just as the doors burst open spewing Miguel out into the plaza. Tomás guided his horse and Miguel's toward the cathedral doors. Unable to slide the soldier's sword in his own sheath, Miguel dropped it and swung up into the saddle. They turned away from the stampede, through a dormant vineyard, and along the Duero River.

Chapter Forty-Two

1517 - Tubanama - Western Coast, South Sea, Isthmus of Panama

"What are you thinking?" Alessandro asked. "I say that not as a question, but as an accusation of ignorance."

Alessandro spent less time in Darién following the arrival of the new governor, Pedro Aririas de Avila, who everyone called Dávila. His disgust of the governor grew more as days went on. Dávila arrived in Darién at the appointment of King Charles V with a personal vendetta based on lies told by Enciso to the king. Power and authority combined with incompetence and jealousy make a bad combination. Alessandro had seen this combination too many times. The governor's wife however, was not only beautiful, she was kind. She helped protect Balboa from the governor. Alessandro knew the governor would eventually find a way to destroy Balboa if she was not here. But her new scheme for Balboa to marry the governor's absent daughter was too much. Alessandro thought what the governor's wife was doing was her design to save Balboa from her husband. But Alessandro objected.

"This is not God's will!" Alessandro demanded. "Years ago, you said you regretted that Friar Tomás taught me to read the Holy Book. Nowhere does this book give the governor power to take away your Cacica and make you marry the governor's daughter! And, the governor's daughter remains in Castile!"

Balboa's firm submission to the will and power of authority given to Dávila by King Charles confused everyone. Alessandro loved Balboa from his earliest childhood. He never knew life without him. But now, injustice after injustice was mixed with betrayal, conspiracy, and total incompetence. Everyone knew it. The men demanded Balboa remove the governor, as he had with Enciso and Nicuesa. Under Balboa, the settlement thrived. Now, it withered in starvation, mistrust, and death.

"This morning, Carlos de Salva, one of your valiant supporters, struggled into the street begging food. He received none. He laid down, unable to continue." Alessandro continued his challenge. "Seven hundred men are dead. Others will be unless you return as governor."

Alessandro, now in his late teens, stood tall and strong. Not a soldier hardened in battle, but a wily warrior sharpened through experiences with conflicting cultures, he fought against any injustice. His father sailed with Columbus, but refused to destroy the native Tiano people. He served the natives, married Alessandro's mother to raise a family, then was betrayed by Governor Bobadilla, also appointed by the king, who in turn executed Alessandro's father. In all his sixteen years, he virtually worshiped Balboa for his justice, his mercy, and his unselfishness. But now, Balboa's stubborn loyalty to men equally wicked as the men who took his father away disgusted Alessandro.

"Who gives a king the right to appoint a demon to conquer and control a people oceans away? You owe him nothing. Is this for the good?" Alessandro was done. He shook his head and left Balboa alone with the servant helping him into his full armor, which he chose to wear at the wedding to his absent bride.

Leoncito followed Alessandro from the deserted town square. With hundreds dead from starvation, disease, and abandonment, Darién was more a cemetery than the bustling town inherited by Governor Dávila. Alessandro disappeared into the forest. Somebody needed to tell Cacica she no longer had a husband. A husband she loved and who loved her in return.

Chapter Forty-Three

1517 - Plains of Duero, Navarre, Northern Spain

The two fugitives on horseback continued along the Duero River for several miles. They left the banks of the river and climbed a rise to see if guards or soldiers pursued. There was no sign in the distance.

"You killed Cardinal Cisneros?" Tomás asked.

Miguel shook his head. He pulled the sleeve of his bloody tunic to reveal a long laceration just below his elbow. The blood was drying. He pushed the sleeve back down.

"You did not kill him?" Tomás asked.

"He was ill."

"So, you did not kill him because he was ill, or you did kill him because he was ill?"

"That was no reason to kill him," Miguel said.

"Why did you kill him?"

"You know I had plenty of reason to do so," Miguel said.

"Yes, and right now I cannot point to just one."

"He was devastated," Miguel said.

Tomás stared at Miguel, his head shaking. What was going on in that head, Tomás wondered.

"Devastated?" Tomás repeated.

"Did any of Charles' guards know what that letter contained?" Miguel asked.

"They wondered."

"I watched him read it three times. Each time it hurt deeper," Miguel said.

"He is no longer regent. His life revolved around power," Tomás said.

"Without power, he would be lost. Is that why you killed him? Seems like a kind thing to do."

"I did not kill the cardinal," Miguel said.

"Why not?"

"I did not need to."

"Is he dead?"

"Yes, I believe so."

"Then who killed him?"

"God was the merciful one. I challenged the purpose of his life. I believe he knew I was right, and that he wasted it destroying others' lives."

"God killed him?"

Miguel starred at Tomás. "Does it matter who killed the cardinal?"

"Did it matter who killed Goliath?" Tomás asked.

"What?"

"I just want to know if I rescued a heretic or a murderer," Tomás said. "Or both."

"What has Goliath got to do with a dead cardinal?"

"Ever since I read that story, I wondered about David. Was he really that good?" Tomás asked.

Miguel slowed his horse and stared at Tomás.

"I mean, the sling was David's. But the rock was God's. So, were you the sling or the rock?" Tomás asked.

"When the bishop and the captain entered the cloister and saw me with the cardinal, Cisneros quickly rose, and vigorously accused me of attempting to assassinate him. His strength gave out. He died in my arms."

"So you did kill him…in a way," Tomás said.

"He who is without sin, let him cast the first stone," Miguel said.

"I did. That is why you are not dead," Tomás said.

Miguel squinted at Tomás. "About that, where did you learn to cast stones so skillfully?"

A grin, like that of a little boy proudly pleasing his mother, filled Tomás' face.

"Darién," Tomás said. His chest lifted and expanded.

"Darién?"

"In Castile de Oro. New Spain."

"You went to the New World?" Miguel's shock pleased Tomás, the smile grew broader.

"You inspired me to find Christ. Said He would set me free. I joined the cloth, got the chance to help bring savages to Christ. I found our Christians more savage than the natives." Tomás seemed to drift from his stone-throwing-pride to disappointment in his own people. "We have it all wrong," he said.

"That is what I told the cardinal. He knew it too," Miguel said.

"Men must choose," Tomás said.

"That is why you came back?"

"Only two men I know teach that we can only come to Christ by our own choice," Tomás said. "One is dead."

"There is a third," Miguel said.

"A third?"

"A monk, just like you, with his eyes open. He, too, understands that without liberty to choose, God's plan does not work."

"He is a heretic like you?"

"Like us."

"Now about those stones," Miguel asked.

"A young mestizo, in Darién. My only convert. I traded the word of God for jungle skills. The little savage could really throw. And now he can read." The smile returned, and with it the pride of a father whose son just became a man.

"A little savage?"

"Maybe not so little anymore. And not as savage as our people. You would love him."

Chapter Forty-Four

1519 - Tubanama - Western Shore, South Sea, Isthmus of Panama

Another year passed. Alessandro spent only brief times with Balboa who was busy establishing a shipyard near the shore where they first entered the south sea. Transporting supplies, tools, and materials across the isthmus required massive man-power.

Both the governor and Pizarro resented the influence Balboa had with men and natives alike. Even as Darién rotted from the inside, Balboa developed relationships with laborers and natives as ships took shape. He had now set one new brigantine to sail. The first ship likely to ever sail the south sea. Balboa claimed it so, regardless that nobody knew what might be on the other side of the vast ocean.

Alessandro took the descent down toward the shore slowly to accommodate the aging hound. The many wounds healed, but over the years they took their toll. There was even gray around his haunches and joules.

When they reached the shipyard, Alessandro's pride returned in Balboa's ability to instill purpose and respect in the men he served. Both soldier and native worked together in partnership. Many of the natives now spoke a spattering of Castilian. Alessandro heard one conversation where the Spaniard was doing his best with the native tongue. He smiled as he walked by. Leoncito spotted Balboa first. In a stiff and painful leap, he put his front paws on Balboa's shoulders. The hound still loved his master, Alessandro thought. Maybe I should do the same.

Balboa embraced Alessandro, now several inches taller than himself.

"I miss you," Balboa said.

Alessandro held on for several minutes.

"Cacica forgives you. I told her everything. Come back to her,"

Alessandro said, "or can I bring her to you? We will be a family."

"I miss her too. But I cannot give the governor reason to mistrust me."

Alessandro stiffened. He hoped his success here in Tubanama might strengthen Balboa's confidence he did not need to remain under the domination of a tyrant. He pulled away and with his arm on Balboa's shoulder, he shook his head.

"You are going to go? You are going to sail?" Alessandro said.

Balboa nodded, his smile bigger and broader than it had been in many years. It seemed to wash away the stress and worry. It warmed Alessandro's heart.

"Come with me," Balboa said. "Not just to the pearl islands, but to Beru."

"How far is Beru?" Alessandro asked. "I hope very far from here. Take us. Take me and Cacica. And…" he paused re-considered his thoughts, "and this." He ran his hands through the graying fur on Leoncito's head.

A messenger arrived on horseback from Darién interrupting them. The trails between Darién and Tubanama were now roads. They were clear and worn enough that travel between the coasts took only days, not weeks or months. The messenger handed a letter to Balboa, who opened and read. His smile disappeared. Alessandro took it from Balboa's limp hand. Alessandro's smile disappeared as well.

"You cannot go back to Darién. They cannot do this. You know I am right!" Alessandro said.

Balboa said nothing. He looked out to sea, his sea, then to the ship, his ship, then to Alessandro, his Alessandro.

"I have to go."

"It is a trap. You know it!"

"I am innocent. I will prove it and I will be back here. Then we will go away. These charges are false."

"You know as well as I do, charges and innocence mean nothing to those men."

"I will appeal to the king. He knows I am loyal."

"He knows nothing!" Alessandro practically yelled. He threw his arms up in exasperation bringing even Lioncito to attention.

"Justice will win out," Balboa said. He reached out to calm Alessandro. Alessandro pushed Balboa's hands away.

"When has justice ever won out?" Alessandro said. He wanted to shake Balboa from his stubborn loyalty to an ideal Balboa alone believed in. "If you go back now, you will never enjoy all you worked for." He bowed his head and shook it in disgust.

Balboa gave instructions to his men, bid farewell, then assured Alessandro that all would be well and, God willing, this was for the good. He mounted a second horse brought by the messenger and accompanied him from Tubanama back toward Darién.

"Come Leoncito. We have nothing more here." Alessandro left the shipyard and set off on a run. Now it was Leoncito struggling to keep up.

Unlike Balboa's many journeys between Tubanama and Darién with the convoys of men and supplies, the blatantly false accusations felt heavier than the tools and provisions which made up the typical cargo. Certainly, his captain and friend Francisco Pizarro would defend him against the false charges by the governor. Governor Dávila's dislike for Balboa's popularity would not deny his rights to appeal to the king. Balboa's wife, the governor's daughter, though they never met, proved Balboa's loyalty and would stand as witness against any accused treason. Balboa was confident this misunderstanding would be cleared up and he would be back to Tubanama to finish preparations to sail south to Beru, the lands of gold.

By the afternoon of the third day, Balboa's mind was exhausted playing out every possible scenario where the governor could justify the accusations made in his warrant for arrest. Maybe Alessandro was right. He would soon know. They would soon be in Darién.

When Balboa considered he was an hour or two from Darién, they were met by Balboa's former lieutenant Francisco Pizarro and three soldiers. When Balboa dismounted to greet his friend, Pizarro locked Balboa in manacles immediately.

"My friend, these are not needed, I came willingly to face these false charges," Balboa said looking directly into Pizarro's eyes. There was no light in those eyes. He remembered the answer many years earlier, when he asked what Alessandro thought of Captain Francisco Pizarro. "I do not think I like him." Those words echoed in Balboa's mind. I do not like him either, he thought.

No words were spoken. Pizarro marched Balboa directly through the shambles of a settlement to the palace, a building Balboa built especially to accommodate the governor's wife. Appointed by the king based on the false accusations of Enciso, Governor Podrarias Dávila proceeded to exercise oppressive dominion. In his six years of tyranny, he destroyed the settlement.

Pompously, he now sat at a wide white table. Next to him was a lawyer and next to the lawyer, a bishop.

The trial began immediately. Dávila told the lawyer to read the charges, each one more preposterous than the previous.

"Vasco Nuñez de Balboa, you are condemned for…"

Condemned for? Balboa thought, not accused of?

"Treason."

"Infidelity to your lawful wife."

"Failure to render to the crown."

"Sedition."

"Lies, they are all lies! You know they are lies!" Balboa realized Alessandro was right; there was to be no justice. How foolish he had been. How foolish he had always been. The lawyer continued reading a long list of charges.

"You construct ships without permits."

"You set men against me, their lawful governor."

"You maintain unlawful friendships with savages."

"You permit natives to worship their pagan gods."

"You send messages to Spain without approval."

The governor stood. "These charges demand the death penalty! You and your accomplices will be beheaded tomorrow!"

"Accomplices! There is no crime. These are lies! The only accomplices are those crafting the lies and you supporting them knowing full well they are lies!" Balboa stood firm, not cowering even an inch.

Pizarro and his soldiers dragged Balboa from the farce of a trial. From the trial room, Dávila yelled, "Secure him to the floor inside the cell. He must not escape!"

Accomplices? The names were never shared. He demanded Pizarro tell him the names of the accomplices. Pizarro said nothing. They shoved him into a cell and anchored his chains to the floor with long steel spikes.

"Francisco! Francisco! What have you done?"

Francisco never looked back. He never uttered a word.

Balboa languished in the prison three days, given relief once each day under the guard of four men. During one of the relief breaks when he was allowed to stand and leave the cell, a guard whispered the names of the other five men condemned. Balboa realized the only reason he had not experienced an immediate execution was because all five accomplices had not been arrested yet. Each of the accomplices were close friends of Balboa. They had not sold their souls to the governor nor to Pizarro, who was now the mayor of Darién. The mayor, he thought. The mayor of what?

It was late afternoon. The small glassless window let the sun peek through, casting a shadow of Balboa's seated figure against the far wall. Balboa watched as it grew the further the sun set. Footsteps preceded the jangle of keys and the creaking door swung open. Balboa turned. This was the second time today. Two guards released the spike holding him to the ground. He stood, stretched his stiff joints. The guards said nothing. This was it he thought, they now arrested, convicted, and jailed any who dared oppose the despots. Balboa thought about Alessandro's question of who gives the king the right to give one man dominion over another.

Dávila had a platform built during the few days Balboa laid on the floor in chains. In the center of the platform was a large block carved perfectly for an execution. He was about to die, yet he found it interesting the inept governor, who could do nothing but complain and destroy, could create such a magnificent monument to execute the only men who could stand in his way. The square, empty days before when Balboa was arrested and taken before the governor, was now crowded with citizens, slaves, and soldiers. How else could an oppressor cling to his power? He never can without threats and fear.

Balboa struggled to climb the stairs with the manacles on both hands and feet. The lawyer read the charges aloud. The priest offered Balboa a sacrament. Balboa addressed the crowd. He could not see Dávila watching from behind a fern, nor Alessandro and Cacica standing in the shadows of Balboa's own house. Pizarro stood on the platform but refused to make eye contact with Balboa when he called his name. "You coward," Balboa said.

Balboa stood tall, proud. He knew Dávila was cowering near, fearful something might stop his triumph. Ever jealous of truly earned power, Dávila had to destroy what he never could have himself.

Balboa looked to the crowd, held up his chains, and shook them for all to see and hear. "God alone will hold Governor Dávila and my lieutenant Pizarro accountable for this lie. These cowards know these accusations are lies.”

“Dávila! Pedrarias Dávila!” Balboa yelled. “Hear me! Your titles are given by a king who takes lands from others with blood he does not own. Justice would demand he live under the tyranny of the men to whom he gives lands and titles.”

Balboa expected the executioner to stop his speech. The executioner stood still.

“One day, this land will be free. You and cowards like you may rule with intimidation, fear, and brutality. Pray God, one day a liberator will throw off these chains. With God given liberty, this people will one day rule themselves. They will choose who to follow.”

“Caesar conquered, ruled, and dominated vast worlds. But he could not stop the influence of a carpenter’s son from Galilee. Two worlds clashed, and both sought to destroy one insignificant carpenter who taught of a world where man was free to think, act, and believe. Together, the two worlds destroyed him. Yet, his teachings led to the spread of Christianity and hope for redemption.

“Now, some fifteen centuries later, we pretend to conquer in the name of that carpenter!” Balboa reached out his hands as far as his manacles permitted and swept them across the crowd.

“We must all become like my Cacica. In her purity, she chose Christ. Something I fear you have never done.”

He lowered his hands. Tears trickled down his cheek and disappeared into the forest of his beard.

“To keep the peace, you made me marry an absent bride. You never could change my love for my Cacica. She is a greater, more noble follower of Christ than you will ever be. By faith, I will one day be reunited with her.”

Balboa stopped his speech, breathed deeply, and scanned the crowd. Many of them stood with bowed heads, including Pizarro who refused to face him. “I now go to Him. I pray for eternal forgiveness for the wrongs I, too, have committed. I leave my fate in the hands of the only true judge.”

He dropped to his knees. The executioner took two chops before the head of the founder of the first successful settlement on the continent and discoverer of the south sea rolled to a stop.

Cacica buried her face into Alessandro’s chest. He held her tight. Leoncito’s deep howl echoed through the square muffling the sound of the confused and crying baby boy held tightly in Cacica’s arms.

PART
THREE

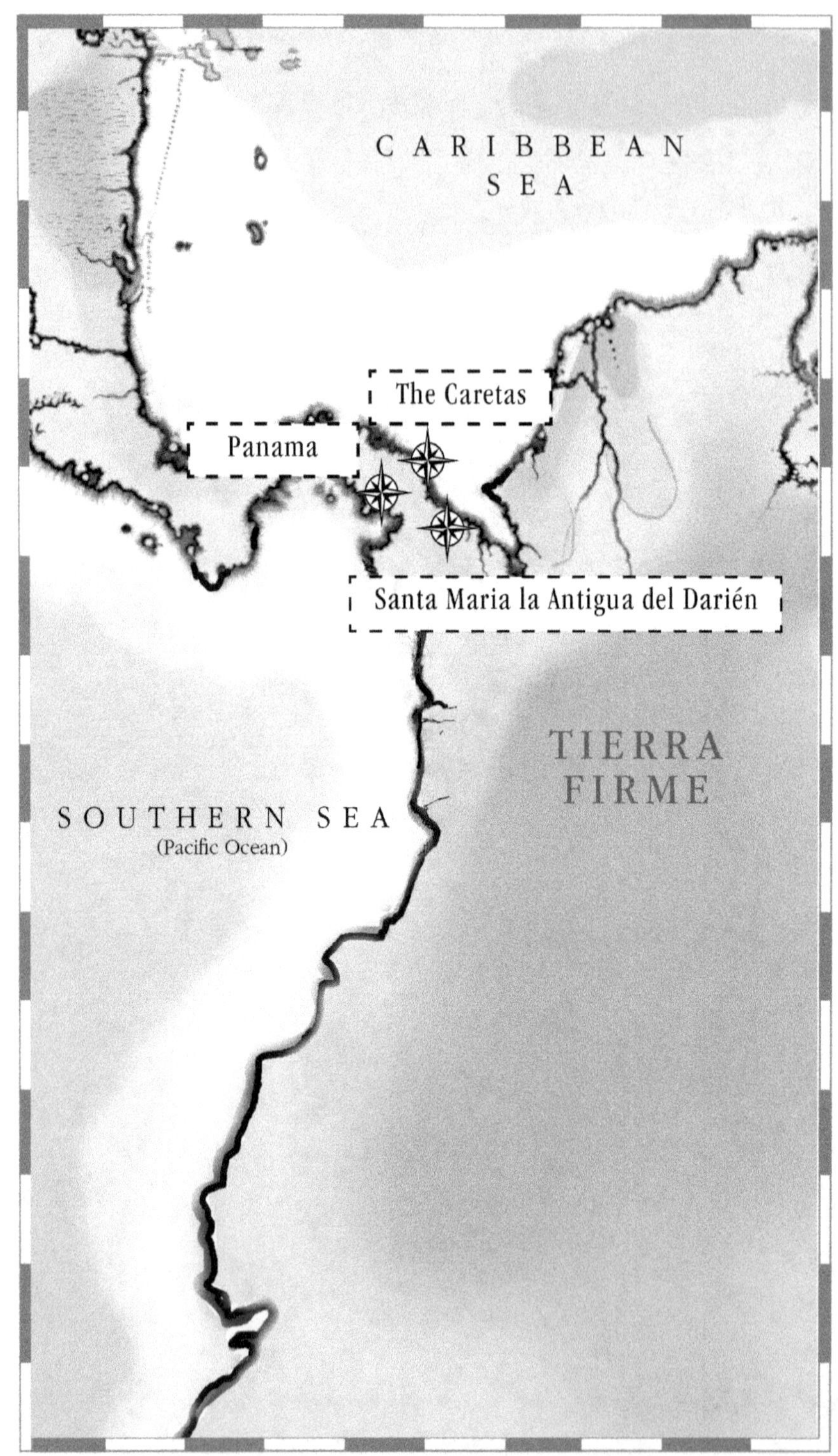

CARIBBEAN SEA
The Caretas
Panama
Santa Maria la Antigua del Darién
TIERRA FIRME
SOUTHERN SEA
(Pacific Ocean)

Chapter Forty-Five

1521 – Three years later- Careta Village

"Alcalde Mayor Espinosa is no better than the governor. Darién will continue to rot," Cacica said. Her long black hair hung braided over her shoulder. She continued weaving a colorful fabric with finely dyed crimson and blue threads.

Alessandro reached out and fingered the soft fabric. " I cannot argue that fact, but with Dávila and Pizarro in Panama now we suffer less."

"Panama?" she asked.

"That is what they call it now."

"So they take even the names of his discoveries from my husband, so they can steal his glory!" Cacica's anger, though infrequent, tickled Alessandro. She showed anger so poorly. Her genuine goodness only let it out when the pot was overflowing.

"But they will never steal this little discovery." An energetic little boy bounded from the jungle. Naked as the day he was born, he charged into Alessandro's arms, who snatched the blow pipe from him before the two crashed into each other.

"What happened to your pants?" Alessandro asked.

The boy acted like he knew nothing about pants. He slipped to the ground and scurried across the meadow and climbed onto an aging Lioncito who seemed to tolerate the expression of love, but age prevented the hound from the games Alessandro cherished when the two grew up together under the watchful eye of Vasco Nuñez de Balboa, little Vasco's namesake.

Cacica watched as her little boy tumbled over the hound. She was lost in thought as she often was over the recent three years following her husband's execution. Cacica refused all contact with the Spanish soldiers. She knew there were many who were loyal to Balboa, some even returned to Spain rather than remain under the governorship of Pedrarias Dávila. Darién collapsed under his rule and as rumor held it, Dávila fled Darién attempting to distance himself from the responsibility of its failure.

Now, the fact the name Tubanama Balboa gave his new settlement,was changed, added to Cacica's distress. Balboa gave the new settlement its name after the local Tubanama tribe with whom Balboa befriended and helped protect. Balboa was proud that the name also reflected its meaning to two different tribes. One said it meant "abundance of butterflies, the other tribe insisted it meant "far distance." Balboa agreed with both tribes' interpretation of the word.

Alessandro stood arms folded as if he were the protector of the tribe, which in many ways he was. Cacica, without looking up at Alessandro said, "If I had let you tell my husband he had a son, Balboa would still be alive."

This was a statement, even an argument Alessandro and Cacica had from the day Alessandro told Cacica about the forced marriage between her husband and the governor's absent daughter. Alessandro insisted Balboa needed to know. Cacica forbade he tell Balboa. She wanted her husband to return to her because of love not duty. Alessandro begged her, telling her it would be love and duty. For nine months, each argument ended the same. Balboa's stubborn duty to God and country would one day cost his life. It would certainly be taken by those whose duty was only to self.

Now in these years since their prophesy had been fulfilled, the argument Cacica kept alive was her personal guilt in the savage death of her little son's father, the love of her life. She insisted it was her fault, yet Alessandro insisted the opposite.

For many minutes the only sound was the occasional low growl when Lioncito scuffled for relief from the little wrestler. Even the birds and monkeys seemed to silence their banter in respect to the never ending struggle in Cacica's heart.

Alessandro knew there was much more to the guilt Cacica carried. He knew of the many soldiers jealous of Balboa having such a wife. Some thought as a scorned native wife, they could take her for themselves. She claimed it was her faithfulness to Balboa, that caused the spurned soldiers to turn their jealousy into hate and then to the destruction of her husband. She carried with her a regret she had not let them have her. If she had, she claimed, "Balboa would still be alive and safe in his kingdom to the south, the land of gold, the land of Beru."

When he later learned it was the maniacal soldier Garabito who was once faithful to Balboa that betrayed him, Alessandro recognized he needed help from the only monk he ever trusted, Friar Tomás. Alessandro learned that because of Cacica's refusal of Garabito, he threatened to have her tortured as was her brother years earlier for refusing the Spanish request for more gold. To save her own life and the life of little Vasco, she consented to say that Balboa wanted to take her to Beru. She hoped that was true. That hope was falsely and treacherously used against her husband.

That guilt ate her alive. Now she only lived for little Vasco. Alessandro knew if it were not for Balboa's only son, Cacica would have ended her own life the day Balboa's life was stolen.

In response to Alessandro's insistence Balboa's death was not her fault, she quoted from the very book used by Balboa to teach her to read, "For whosoever will save his life shall lose it: and whosoever will lose his life for my sake shall find it. What did I give in exchange for my soul?"

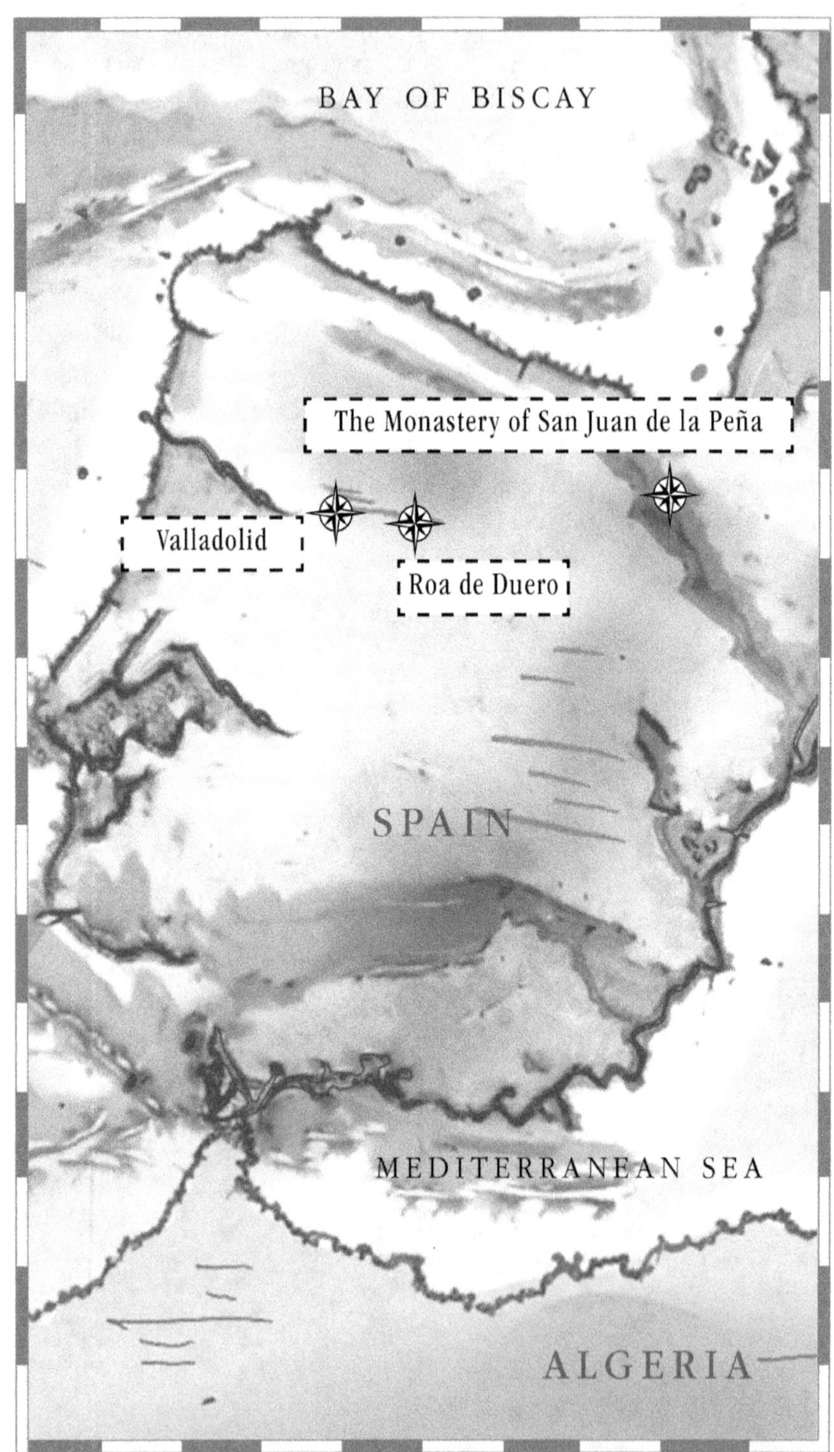

BAY OF BISCAY
The Monastery of San Juan de la Peña
Valladolid
Roa de Duero
SPAIN
MEDITERRANEAN SEA
ALGERIA

Chapter Forty-Six

1521 – The Monastery of San Juan de la Peña

"Is this your monk?" Tomás laid a printed parchment on the table. Miguel pushed his empty plate aside and took the sheet with one hand. He wiped the other on a cloth and held the tall sheet off the table.

"Disputatio pro declaratione virtutis indulgentiarum," Miguel said softly, then repeated the words, looking up at Tomás. "He went and did it. A Disputation on the Power and Efficacy of Indulgences." Miguel shook his head as he read. "And he published this thesis. He is bold."

Tomás stood over his shoulder, reading as well. Miguel pointed to number forty-three. "I said that! I told him we should teach that 'he who gives to the poor or lends to the needy, does a better work than buying pardons.'"

Tomás pointed to number forty-four, "You and I talked about how love grows by works of love, that man becomes better, but by pardons man does not become better. He only feels free from penalty. I think I like your monk," Tomás said.

"And he is a reverend now, Reverend Father, Master of Arts and Sacred Theology. Where did you get this?" Miguel asked.

"The band of Gitanos gave it to the prior. They preach the word better than most of our priests," Tomás said.

Miguel paused, looked up at Tomás, "Gitanos? Did you see them?"

"No, but they are preaching and dancing in the meadow tonight," Tomás said. "You in need of some fresh gospel?"

Miguel smiled, "I think I am."

Miguel could not help but laugh. There he sat, skirts flying all around him, legs kicking, strings and tambourines lightening up the evening. Even a few of the monks escaped the monastery to enjoy the show. Of course, the monks were here to see how the devil stole the local peasant's hearts.

Ten years had not done anything but thicken him up a bit, take some of the rich darkness from the mop on his head and add some character to his face in the form of a wrinkle or two. But it was him. Vano the Gitano.

Miguel worked through the crowd. He did not feel ten years older. Hiding out at the monastery with the good Friar Tomás for a few years, gave him time to recover his health, get back to writing, and from the good polyglot Bible so nicely provided by Cardinal Cisneros, Miguel and Friar Tomás were now translating the Bible from the Greek and Hebrew into Basque for Miguel's homeland.

Vano read a passage from the First Book of Peter, expounding how Peter commanded that clergy should feed the flock of God providing oversight not by constraint but willingly and not for filthy lucre but of a ready mind. Miguel smiled at how that offended the priests listening.

"Yea, all of you be subject one to another," Vano paused, squinted, and leaned forward to refocus his eyes, "be clothed with humility," the words began to stumble as they left his lips, "God resisteth, grace, proud, humble," he tried again, "God giveth grace to the humble." Vano's mouth hung open, then spread into a smile that pushed his cheeks up into his ears.

Miguel's head shook at Vano's realization this was not an apparition of a ghost. Vano shook his head one more time to confirm he was not dreaming. He stood and threw his arms around Miguel. Tears soaked Miguel's shoulder.

Vano pulled back, holding Miguel with hands on each shoulder.

"You died."

"I wanted to."

"Maria?"

"The reason I wanted to." Miguel shook his head.

"There was no news. Rumors. You, Maria, Talavera, dead. Jalaf and Sayyida slaves. Bishop Martínez and his wife burned." Vano wiped his sleeve across his face.

Vano turned to the crowd watching in earnest. "Right here, ladies and gentlemen, is the man who taught me to think. Now, like Lazarus, returned from the dead!"

Miguel turned to see the crowd. In the few minutes Vano was distracted, the crowd's attention turned to the two beautiful women floating their dresses to heaven.

"You preach like you want to join Bishop Martínez," Miguel said.

"I am not afraid. Truth is truth. Years ago, I spent some time with heretics. It changed my life. You read about our monk from Wittenberg?"

Miguel nodded.

"He has done us a great favor," Vano said. "Charles, our dear king, the good Pope Leo, and the inquisitors have their hands full with our friend. These local bishops leave us alone."

The music stopped. The skirts fell loosely. Two youths, a young boy sporting the same vest, bright colorful shirt, and trousers as Vano, and a young girl in a bright orange blouse, beads hanging from her neck, several bracelets on each arm, and beautiful dark hair falling over her shoulders worked the crowd collecting coins from the onlookers. The girl's skirt was just as full as her older counterparts, yet in her youth she could not fill it and the blouse like she would in years to come. Her eyes met Miguel's when she held the pail up to receive a coin from him. He reached down and took the cup and her hand in his.

Miguel knew immediately, these two children had to be Vano's. He knelt. "Do you belong to this knave?" he asked. Vano's smile confirmed it. She shyly nodded.

"Carmelita," Vano said, "Do you remember the stories of the cardinal and the orphans?" She nodded. "This is the orphan boy."

She squinted at him, her small hand still held in his. She turned to her father and with a sweet innocence said, "You said he fought the whole Spanish army to save Maria and her baby. He gave his life for them."

"Baby?" Miguel turned to Vano.

Vano flinched, shrugged his shoulders, "They are children's stories. Babies make children stories better."

Small talk and not small talk filled the evening. Miguel and Tomás spent the rest of the night with Vano and his family. Stories of adventure and sadness, and a bit of exaggeration on Vano's description of his rescue and matchmaking entertained, then moved everyone to tears. A beautiful wife and two young children gave Miguel a sense of reverence for a family, something he never knew, and would never know. Deep joy for Vano settled in his heart. Little Carmelita eventually accepted Miguel as more than a ghost. When he shared the sad but somewhat toned-back story of Maria's death, she climbed up on his lap and cuddled into his arms, where she eventually fell asleep.

The night's discussion ended having circled around "the monk" as they all called the Reverend Martin Luther. Miguel found it interesting how his fame and the trouble he caused the Pope was gaining recognition two countries away.

After a troubled night, Miguel arose with the commitment to do more. "Tomás, I am leaving here. I am going back into the lion's den. I am going to help the monk."

"Inspiration or boredom?" Tomás said.

"Does it matter?"

"Only if I get to accompany you."

"Which one gets you to leave the monastery with me?"

Tomás leaned back against the stone wall and stared at his friend and mentor. "No, it does not matter. When do we leave?"

"Now," Miguel said.

Tomás turned and left Miguel alone in the library, where he'd started early on the translation of the Basque New Testament.

"Both," Miguel yelled. The word echoed down the long stone hallway.

Before the sun even peeked over the eastern horizon, Tomas and Miguel had packed a few provisions, their holy books, and a satchel of writings. They rode down to the Gitano encampment. The smell of hot bogacha drifted up from the camp. Vano was out caring for the horses while his wife was preparing to feed the family. Vano smiled as they approached.

"We have chosen to visit our friend the monk. I would love to have you join us but I think you do not need any more heresy based on what we heard you preach last night."

Vano nodded in agreement. "I thought you might," Vano said. His smile never faltered.

Young Carmelita climbed from her wagon and rubbing her eyes walked over and put her delicate arm around her father's waist. Her hair failed to find a comb this early. It looked more like the mane of a mighty lion. She looked up at Miguel on his horse and gave a tiny smile. The early morning sun peeked over the hill. Carmelita shifted into the shadow cast by Miguel's horse. He became a silhouete but it let her beautiful young eyes open wider. He thought how one day those eyes will captivate some young man. He thought back on the first time he looked into Sukayna's eyes.

"There is an unusual man of God from whom you should seek shelter when you fall into distress and are crossways with the church," Vano said.

"When I fall into distress? Not if? Is it that inevitable?" Miguel said.

Both Vano and Tomás nodded their heads.

"Frederick the Wise, Elector of Saxony," Vano said

"The Elector of Saxony?"

"When you arrive at Wittenberg, you will find Luther, but it will be Frederick who protects you from the church," Vano said.

"I do not need protection."

"You will," Vano insisted.

Miguel and Tomás continued their New Testament translation as they worked their way over the Pyrenees into France and up toward Saxony. Cool nights and hunger drove them to reach Annaburg by nightfall. Wittenberg was only days from there.

The sun set and the warmth of the afternoon disappeared. Annaburg featured only one tavern. With horses secured, they welcomed the warmth and the aroma. Lanterns hung on each timbered wall. Miguel thought this tavern probably started as a hunting lodge. Antlers and skins covered the walls.

Of the dozen rough-hewn tables, only three were occupied with guests. Each looked like Miguel felt; tired, hungry, and grateful to be out of the cold night air. Though it was early in the spring, late winter hung in the air. Tomás led Miguel to a table away from the door. They sat, and a platter of breads and two large tankards of ale plopped on the table before them. A large burly woman looked down over a red dimpled nose and said, "Beef, venison, or turkey?" She smiled and added, "There is no turkey, nor beef."

"I believe venison is just right," Miguel said. She winked and shuffled off. Almost immediately, she was back with piping hot bowls of venison stew and winked at Miguel again.

The door burst open, bringing with it a cold draft and six loud Castilian soldiers. They demanded attention before they even sat. Tomás' eyes widened. He dropped his spoon and pulled his hood over his head. Miguel, whose back was to the door, quickly looked and turned back to his bowl, lowering his head, and putting his hand to the side of his face.

They ate quietly. The soldiers did not. This would be another cold night in the woods. Miguel had no desire to spend the night in the same inn with the royal guards of King Charles. Especially after he humiliated them back in Orn. Would they remember after four years? Would they recognize a monk traveling with a swordsman? Miguel carefully reached to his waist and slipped the whip loose and tucked it under his leg. The captain of the guard would certainly remember the bite the whip took from his cheek. They finished eating, slid a few coins onto the table and, as invisible as they could, slipped back into the night.

Miguel apologized to his horse. Rather than give him a nice night in the sheltered livery, they saddled up and prepared to move on toward Wittenberg and find shelter in the forest again.

"Those guards interrupt your plans?" The words were Latin, the accent English.

Miguel said nothing. Even in the darkness, he knew the man was not weak. The voice was too strong, too confident and it came from a figure his own height. "If you will trust an English highwayman in the dark, you may still lodge in comfort," the man said.

"You admit you are a highwayman," Tomás said.

"Aye, and I do not need your money, but I might need your help. By your reaction to those guards, I take it they are not friends. Nor are they friends of mine."

"And what is an English highwayman doing wandering the forests of Saxony?" Miguel asked, hoping to sound as confident.

"Come with me. You will sleep well and warm. You will also meet an interesting character. Then you can choose to stay or to go."

"And your name, Englishman?" Miguel asked.

"Sir Humphrey Kynaston."

"I have not known an honorable highwayman. This might be interesting," Miguel said. He mounted his horse, and patted the whip now returned to his side. "Lead on."

The horses seemed to be at peace following in the darkness. For the next what seemed like an hour, the three men wound through the trees before stopping in front of a hunting lodge nestled on a hillside surrounded by thick forest. Sir Humphrey led the men past the lodge to a small barn where they dismounted and led their horses into the shelter, out of the cool breeze that had extracted every degree of warmth from the men. Light from the lodge shone through a large window next to the finely carved door. Its beauty became evident when, without knocking, Humphrey opened it and ushered the men inside.

The large, overstuffed throne of a chair, upholstered in finely tanned and dyed red leather, hosted a large overstuffed man. The man turned his attention from the warm fire to the men interrupting his solitude.

"That was fast. You found it so quickly?" At first the man seemed not to notice the two strangers.

"I found better," Humphrey said.

"Those two do not look like relics," he said. The man's face was wide and fleshy. From the ears down around his chin hung a black beard. The cheeks and mouth were cleanly shaven. Where he wore a hat all day, the hair was tight around his head with a clean top. It was evident the top had cleared itself. He did not stand nor did he move quickly.

"Miguel, Tomás," Humphrey nodded to his new friends, "Meet, Frederick the Wise, Elector of Saxony."

"Elector?" Miguel said. He turned to Humphrey. Humphrey shrugged and turned back to Frederick.

"Charles' guards are in Annaburg," Humphrey said.

"For Luther," Frederick said.

"The reverend? Martin Luther?" Migual asked.

Frederick nodded.

"Luther needs the king's guards?" Tomás asked. Despite the warmth of the fire which Miguel and Tomás clung to, chills ran the length of his spine.

"Forgive my rudeness," Frederick said. He still did not rise, but motioned for the men to sit. "Let us get acquainted. You know the monk?"

"We met in Rome," Miguel said.

"You are him… he talked of you."

"Rome was an awakening," Miguel said.

"Was your archbishop freed?" Frederick asked.

Miguel shook his head, "Two hundred ducats bought his forgiveness and deliverance with an indulgence. Too little and too late. He never was freed. He passed soon after," Miguel said.

"I am sorry for that," the elector said.

Miguel felt the sincerity. But why was the Elector alone in a hunting lodge and surprisingly a friend of possibly the most criticized heretic in all of the Holy Roman Empire? Second to King Charles, as the elector of Saxony, this Frederick may be one of the most influential men alive, short of the Pope himself.

Frederick shifted in his seat, then assessed his two new companions.

"You came to see the monk? I do not align with all he teaches, but I also do not align with injustice. I do align with man's right to choose how he serves God." Frederick watched those words set with Miguel and Tomás.

"He is not at Wittenberg," Frederick continued. "He is on his way to trial in Worms. King Charles himself is there. The full power of the church and empire demands he recant his writings. If he will not recant, they will be forced to destroy him before he creates a division in the church."

Miguel realized this was not a simple trial. "And the guards?"

"Charles guaranteed me Luther's safe passage to and from Worms. The only way Luther was willing to go," Frederick said, "to assure his safety."

Miguel looked deeply at the elector, then to Tomás. The tightened muscles on Tomás' face confirmed he was thinking the same thing. Those guards were not sent to protect the monk. He glanced toward Humphrey, who was reading the faces of both Tomás and Miguel.

"You do not believe that?" Humphrey said.

Miguel shook his head slightly.

"What is this?" Frederick asked.

Humphrey paused a moment as he looked at each man intently and turned to face Frederick.

"In the tavern, these two were quick to disappear when the guards entered. There is some unfavorable past experience there," Humphrey said.

Frederick lifted a cup to his lips, and sipped what Miguel assumed was some mixture of ale and medicine because he cringed as it went down. He looked back to Miguel but said nothing.

What to say? It had been years. He was free from the guards as far as he was concerned. As far as he knew, the guards had not seen him. Or if they did, they did not recognize him.

"There was a misunderstanding in Roa. Having a bit of experience with accusations and justice, we chose to leave the issue in the hands of God." Miguel said.

"When?" Frederick said.

Of course an elector would be aware of the wars throughout the empire. He would know about the conquest of Navarre and how the Regent of Spain, in the middle of the conquest, was murdered. On which side of justice would this news fall?

"Four years ago," Miguel said, hating himself the minute the words slipped from his lips.

"You murdered the regent?"

Yes, he knew. He at least knew the accusation of Cisneros' final words. He also likely knew it was by an expert swordsman who brandished a whip and traveled with a monk.

"Not murder. He was sick. God blessed me so that I did not have to kill him. He died in my arms."

"I thought so," Frederick said. He took another unwelcome sip from his cup. He shivered as it went down.

Humphrey stirred the fire. As he stood, he asked, "What are you thinking?"

That question dipped into Miguel's memory of Maria, how she asked that very question. He shook it away.

"I think our monk is not safe in the hands of those guards," Tomás spoke, saving Miguel the risk of sounding bitter.

"Is he safer in your hands?" Frederick asked.

"Not alone," Miguel said.

"You do have me," Humphrey said. "And the monk here. If you and I fail, Tomás can pray our souls into heaven."

"Tomorrow, you will go with my blessing and on my errand. If the king's guards fail to protect Luther, I trust you will. You have my backing." Frederick took another sip. Every muscle in his thick neck quivered. He got up. Each movement was labored and slow. He excused himself and closed a bedroom door behind him as he retired for the night.

"You do not think he will recant?" Humphrey said.

"I know he will not," Miguel said.

"We will get to him before the guards do," Humphrey said. He showed them to separate rooms, comfortable rooms. It would have been a pleasurable night. But all Miguel could do was wonder what God wanted of him.

The next morning, his wonder changed to that about an English highwayman in Saxony at the bidding of the elector. The Englishman spoke very little, but with some cautious questions, Miguel learned King Henry in England wanted him for murder. That seemed appropriate. Two wanted murderers riding into a king's court where if they failed, a triple prize would be handed to the crown. Two murderers and a heretic.

What was Tomás thinking? Was he learning what he wanted to learn when he extracted me from prison?

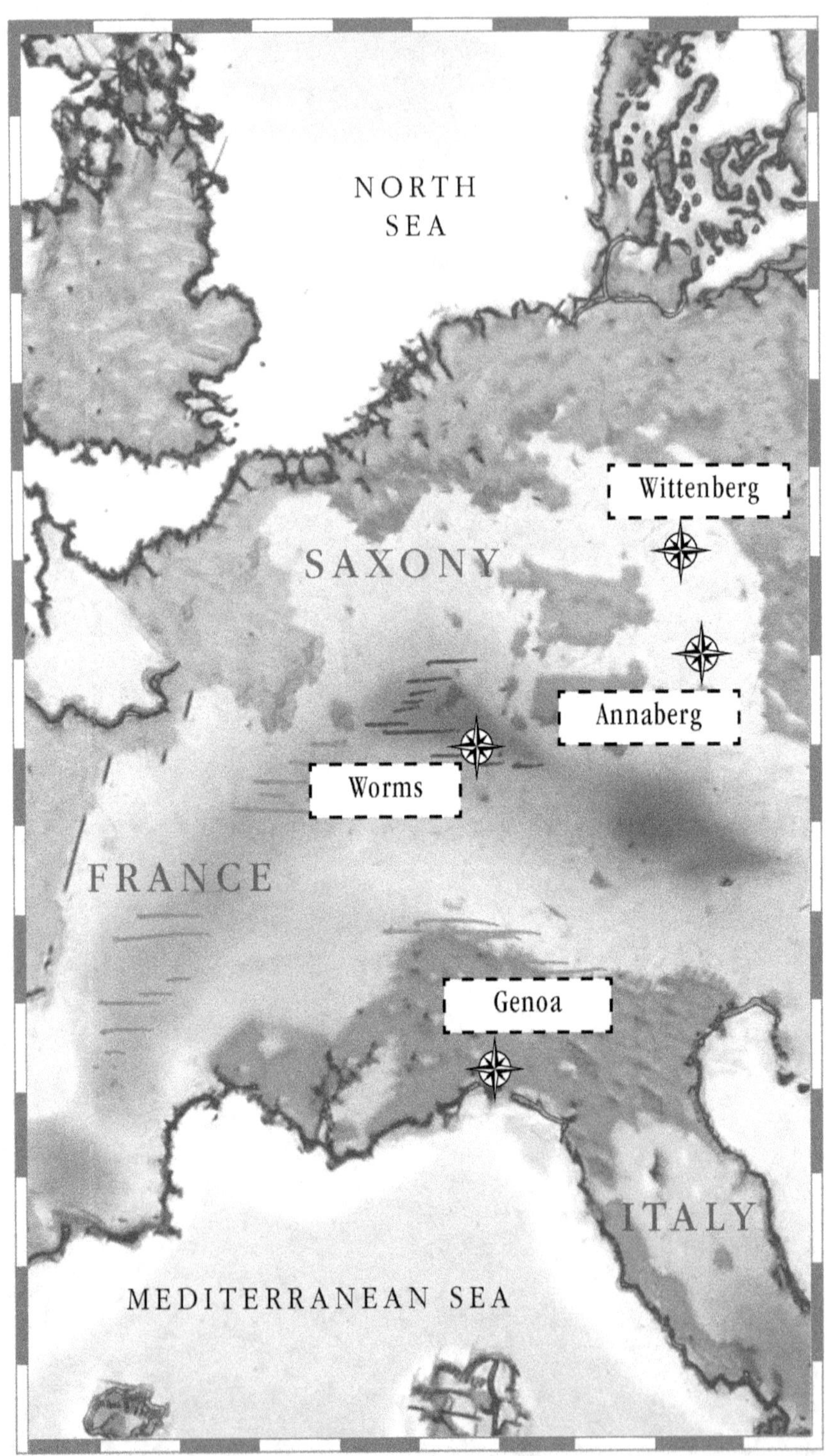

NORTH SEA
Wittenberg
SAXONY
Annaberg
Worms
FRANCE
Genoa
ITALY
MEDITERRANEAN SEA

Chapter Forty-Seven

1521 - Worms, Saxony

Miguel and Tomás arrived in Worms to a circus of people. The Reverend Martin Luther arrived the night before and was on trial at the very moment. Crowds filled the plaza. Royal guards, soldiers, dignitaries from the church, and peasants stood shoulder to shoulder awaiting word. Would the monk recant? That question and disparate answers were on everyone's lips. In such a crowd, Miguel felt safe blending in with the throngs of people. Yet, he remembered those dozen years earlier when Cardinal Cisneros singled him out in the crowd and set him on a life he could never imagine.

The crowds parted. The trial ended. Four imperial guards and four pairs of soldiers pushed through the crowd. In the center was the monk. Miguel recognized that tonsure. Where in Granada he wished to be smaller, now he wanted to stand above them all and catch the monk's eye. He stood on his toes. There was no safe way to get close. Rumors rolled across the crowd like a wave upon the sea.

"He refused to recant."

"He recanted."

"He did not do either."

"He was forgiven."

"He will be burned."

Tomás pushed through the crowd. He joined a contingency of monks following the procession from the great hall to the tall stone fortress where the accused monk was being 'protected.' Tomás, along with the monk and guards disappeared into the fortress.

The crowd did not disperse. A second group left the great hall. Guards and soldiers pushed the crowd aside. Surrounded on all sides, young King Charles V, newly crowned Holy Roman Emperor, exited. The crowd seemed as anxious to see the emperor as they were to see the condemned monk. He was followed by an entourage of bishops, cardinals, and monks. Oh, the arrogance, Miguel thought. They have no concept how their whims elevate or destroy these people. The crowd silenced and many bowed as they passed. Miguel did not care to bow. He stood proudly watching them pass. At one point, the emperor averted his eyes from his steeled stare ahead of him to look over the crowd of subjects. His eyes caught Miguel's. The moment was enough for Miguel to see this young man was no different from other men with power. Yet he looked so young to wear it so proudly. Miguel gave him a nod, more to say "I see you," than to say "I respect you."

The entourage disappeared and the crowd dispersed. Talk of the first day of the trial filled the inns and taverns in Worms and likely the rest of Saxony, Miguel figured.

The Worms Episcopal Palace was called the bishop's castle by local peasants. Two imposing towers stood prominently at the entrance of the grand castle. Other towers and turrets of various sizes surrounded the palace, showcasing the defensive nature of the massive building. Beautiful arched windows featuring intricate stained glass accented the powerful stone and timber structure.

On the second day of the trial, with a certificate handwritten and sealed with Frederick's seal, Tomás, Miguel, and Humphrey were admitted into the gallery of the great hall where onlookers watched the proceedings below. The hall was imposing, with its high ceilings and ornate wooden beams.

Cardinals, bishops, and monks paraded in behind the king and took positions around the hall. Miguel wondered if seniority or if favor dictated their position.

When Martin Luther was summoned to appear at this Imperial Diet by the Holy Roman Emperor, how many of these clergy began their quest to be present and see the great heretic? How many were simply positioning themselves for rank and recognition of their own piety? Miguel looked from face to face. Did any of them even believe what they individually taught?

He learned from Tomás that the night before, when the Church launched the accusations, Luther challenged the court to prove his writings were wrong by means of written scripture. If they could, he would recant each one. The accusers refused to refute his writings, to which Luther afforded them the concession that he would make an official statement the next day.

From the gallery, Humphrey and Miguel spotted three of the men they saw in the tavern at Annaburg. They were part of Charles' contingency no doubt. It took no words between Humphrey, Tomás, and Miguel to confirm the guards were not here to rescue Luther.

A large oak table stood in the center of the hall. Neatly stacked were books, manuscripts, and pamphlets. On a large parchment, in what from the distance looked like handwritten script, laid the "Ninety-five Theses" or "Disputation on the Power and Efficacy of Indulgences" as Luther's early heretical document was called. Miguel learned that when Luther nailed a printed copy of these theses on the door of the All-Saints Church and other churches in Wittenberg, his troubles with the Church began in earnest. Miguel wondered if Humphrey appreciated the magnitude of the writings on display as evidence of Luther's heresy. Miguel had only read the printed copy of the Ninety-five Theses given to the prior by Vano. He realized that one document alone could justify this tribunal. It claimed the repentance for sin that Christ required involved inner spiritual repentance and change, rather than external confession. The thesis argued that the indulgences not only padded the coffers of the church, but led believers to believe they could forgo sorrow for sin by buying an indulgence.

Miguel wanted to reach down and browse through each of the other documents presented as witnesses against his friend.

The room was brought to attention. Everyone stood when Charles entered. He took his place on a throne constructed for the judges appointed for the various diets held in Worms. Miguel learned early from Cardinal Talavera how the diets held here in Worms were more a deliberative body rather than a legislative gathering. Yet it was clear this diet was not designed for deliberation. It was a trial, plain and simple. Pope Leo X's papal bull condemning Luther and his writings forced a showdown between the Pope's power and the popular heretic. Who better to preside than the emperor himself. Miguel recognized how Charles probably did not care about the theology, but he did care about his popularity with his people and the Church.

Miguel counted the pieces of evidence so neatly displayed. Twenty-five. How many of those pretend clerics present actually read all of these? Had Charles?

The room silenced again when they escorted Luther into the great hall. It had been over ten years, but Miguel saw that same determination in his eyes as he did the day they parted in Rome. No, he was not going to recant. Miguel knew it.

The proceedings began immediately. A valiant defender of the Church, Johann Eck acted as spokesman for the emperor and the Pope and with no formalities, approached Luther and confidently demanded of Luther if the collection of books and writings were his. He placed his hand on the table, drawing all attention to the evidence that so damningly sat silent. He requested the titles be read. A bishop stood forth and read each.

"Are these yours?" Eck asked.

"They are," Luther said.

"Are you prepared to revoke their heresies?"

The great hall was silent. Nobody moved. Few breathed. Luther looked around the great hall. He glanced up into the faces of those in the gallery and paused ever so slightly when he saw Miguel. Miguel nodded almost imperceptibly. Luther then looked toward heaven.

"Will you keep your emperor waiting?" Eck demanded.

Miguel began shaking his head. This Johann Eck knew nothing. Charles held no power over Luther's heart. Miguel knew that.

"Your Excellency, I apologize that I lack the etiquette of the court." Luther bowed, then looked at his writings displayed on the table. "These are all mine." He stepped over to the table and reorganized it, placing the books and pamphlets into three different stacks. He pointed to the first stack. "These are well received, even by my enemies. I will not reject them." He pointed to the second stack. "In these I attack the abuses, lies, and the desolation of the Christian world…" he paused and took a deep breath, "… and the papacy." A collective gasp spun through the great hall. "If I now recant these, I will encourage abuses to continue." He stepped to the third stack. "If I recant these, I would be doing nothing but strengthening tyranny."

Murmurs echoed through the great hall. For a few moments, Miguel feared the crowd might light upon Luther and tear him to pieces. But Eck held his hand to the crowd. As if he just conquered all, Johann Eck's face declared a sentence of death on the heretic. But Luther interrupted his moment of triumph.

"Unless I am convinced by the testimony of the scriptures or by clear reason, for I do not trust either in the Pope or in councils alone, since it is well known that they have often erred and contradicted themselves, I am bound by the scriptures I have quoted and my conscience is captive to the word of God. I cannot and will not recant anything, since it is neither safe nor right to go against conscience. Here I stand, I cannot do otherwise. God help me. Amen."

Was this victory? Or defeat? Certainly, without the promised safe passage for Luther that the emperor himself guaranteed to Frederick the Wise, Luther would now be marched to the pyre and bundles of sticks piled below his feet. But this would not stand. King Charles himself made no royal declaration. Miguel knew Charles was in a difficult place. He needed support from Saxony and its neighboring regions for the conquests and power consolidation, yet he needed the Church as well. He stood, gave no weighty public royal decree, and left the great hall followed by many of his own guards, cardinals, bishops and lastly Johann Eck. Miguel still could not sense triumph or defeat in Eck's face.

The same guards and soldiers from the night before escorted Luther from the hall. He requested the escort to accompany him safely back to Wittenberg immediately. He waved, bowed, and reached out to the extended hands as he passed through the throngs gathered. He defied the Church. He would not be silenced. He would not recant. The crowds' cheers offended the Church officials. None understood how this could happen. Before the king himself, Luther stood firm in his criticism of the Pope, the Church, and the clergy who were so anxious to see the great heretic burn. Mostly they hoped he would not recant, and the king's displeasure would demand immediate execution.

Luther climbed up into an open carriage pulled by four horses. They wound through Worms. Well-wishers cheering and throwing flowers, expressing support, crowded every route. Once gone from the main plaza, Miguel prepared to leave, but noticed guards remained behind, those from the tavern and several others huddled in conversation, pointing, and motioning with hand gestures. They were in no hurry.

"How well do you know the road to Wittenberg?" Miguel asked.

"Well enough," Humphrey said.

He motioned toward the guards. "Where will they attack?"

"Darmstadt," Humphrey said.

"Why?"

"Darmstadt is past the protection zone and before Saxony," Humphrey said.

"It is going to be a long night," Miguel said.

They gathered up Tomás, hired another horse, packed supplies, and charged out of Worms toward Darmstadt some three to eight hours away. How fast would Luther's carriage travel? When might they stop for the night? Too many questions.

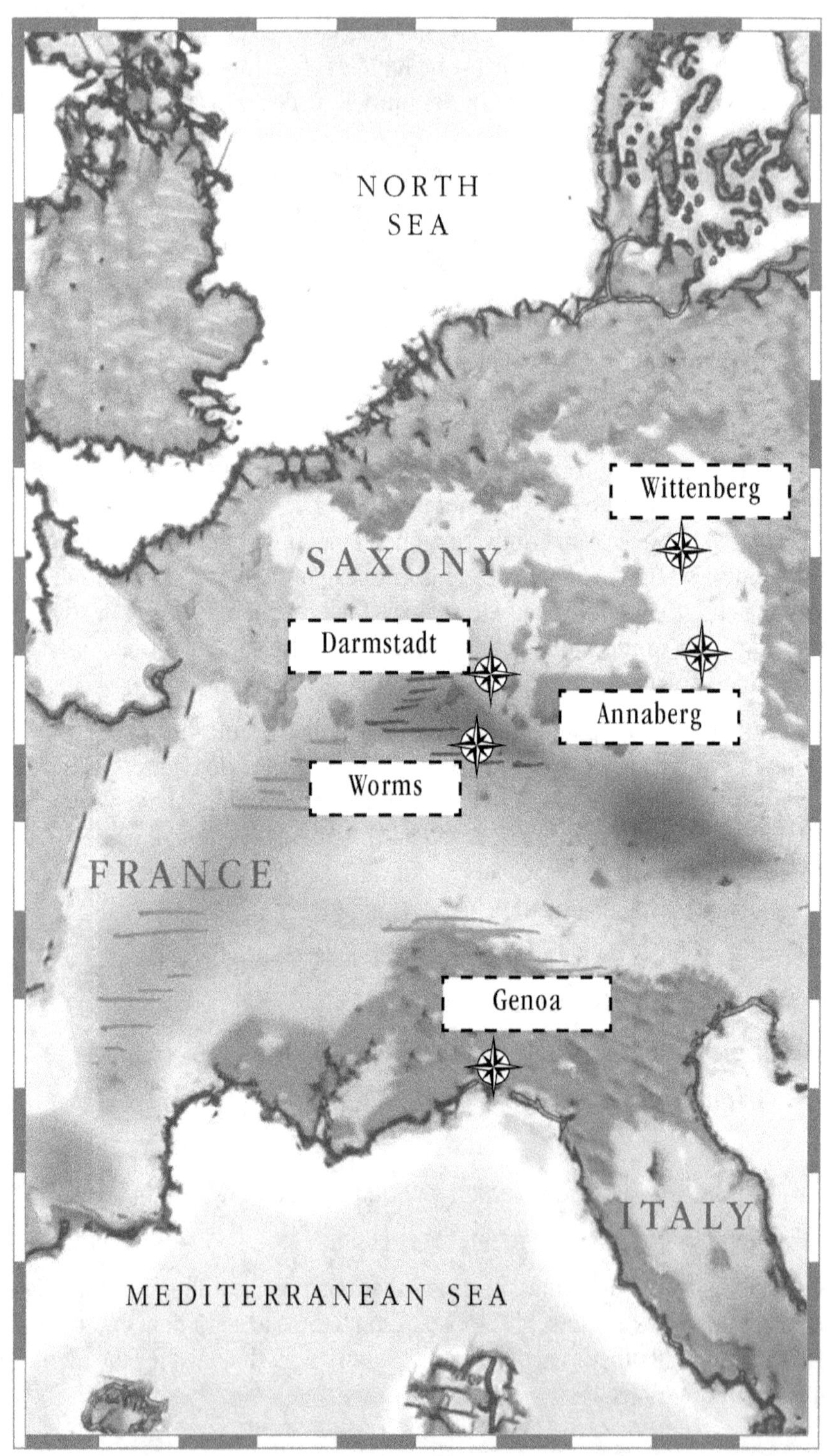

NORTH SEA
SAXONY
Wittenberg
Darmstadt
Annaberg
Worms
FRANCE
Genoa
ITALY
MEDITERRANEAN SEA

Chapter Forty-Eight

1521 - Darmstadt, Saxony

Humphrey insisted they were ahead of Luther's group. They waited in darkness and quiet. Hours passed. Luther's carriage could not be that slow. Had they stopped in one of the small abbeys? Did the guards outsmart them?

Finally, the distant sound of hooves and wheels broke the silence. Humphrey was right. They were headed to Darmstadt. The steady sounds of approaching cart and horse grew. The moon broke over the eastern horizon enough to cast a light on the approaching carriage, accompanied by two men on horseback. Only two men. "This should be easy," Miguel whispered to Tomás. The plan included Tomás riding out to accompany Luther and escort him to the monastery in Darmstadt. Once the group was comfortable with Tomás, Humphrey and Miguel would distract the two riders, then Tomás would encourage the driver to flee with him for protection in the monastery. When they arrived, the driver would be left behind and the three men, with Luther in tow, would charge off into the forest.

Tomás approached the group. His Castilian accent seemed to worry the two riders escorting the carriage. They drew their horses closer to the carriage.

With a swish and pop, the first rider grunted and fell from his horse. The second yelled, "Go, Go, Go!"

The driver put the horses to run. Tomás joined the chase. A second swish and the second rider fell from his horse. It was now just the carriage and Tomás.

Miguel watched the carriage flying by at full speed, pulled by four frantic horses and a monk leaning low in the saddle racing toward where he and Humphrey hid. Where had the archers been? Four horsemen broke from the trees charging toward the carriage, which was now bouncing and pounding directly away.

"New plan," Humphrey said. He dove into the chase. His pitch-black horse charged forward. Moonlight reflected off its shiny coat. It appeared like a ghost upon the hoof. Humphrey removed the first horseman from his saddle with a swing of his long sword. Miguel heard another swoosh. The archer was behind him but aiming at Humphrey. Miguel turned into the woods. He had to neutralize the archer. Was there only one? Another swoosh flew past him. He was now the target. He took the next swoosh in his thigh. It glanced off, but cut a gash, drawing blood.

A reflection from a helmet caught Miguel's eye. He turned and charged directly at the archer. The archer nocked an arrow and drew back. Miguel plowed directly into him, removing him from the attack. A second arrow caught Miguel in the back, nearly throwing him from his horse. He turned so quickly his horse lost its footing and threw Miguel to the ground. He tumbled, but returned to his feet. Protected in the shadow, he tried to locate the second archer before the archer found him.

He heard the release of another arrow, but from the wrong direction. A third bowman. He climbed through the trees but could not see either. Over a small ridge, he saw the carriage was stopped. Several silhouettes of men on horses and two on foot rose above the horizon. Who was on foot? Where was Humphrey? Was Tomás one of the men? The silhouettes moved. Miguel recognized two shapes were men in clergy cloaks. Luther and Tomás? Then he noticed two more figures emerge. The archers. At least they are not behind me, he thought, and breathed a bit easier. He felt the wetness on his thigh. It was not bad enough to stop him. He reached behind him and pulled the arrow from his back. Not quite deep enough to kill, just hurt and bleed.

He could not charge in, wounded and alone. And with two archers ready to finish their work? Unless…could those men be rescuing Luther from supposed highwaymen? Were they fighting the wrong people? At that moment, a man on horse pulled a sword and struck one of the monks. He knew then. These were the guards sent to do the work the king and the Pope were cowards to do in public. Miguel circled back and found the downed archer. He lay motionless. Miguel did not wait to see if he was alive. Miguel scooped up the bow, gathered the quiver, and made his way toward the ridge. Clinging to the edge of the forest, he remained in the shadows. With the rising moon, he saw Luther standing defiantly. On the ground he thought he saw Tomás, but he was sitting, not lying. The relief he was alive washed through Miguel. But where was Humphrey? The archer must have eliminated him.

Miguel counted four on horseback, the two archers who now reached the group and the two captives. No carriage driver or attendants. This was no rescue. It was an attack, an assassination. Or at least an abduction. There were at least six men and he had only five arrows. How fast could he launch an assault? How close did he need to be? He thought he would start with the archers. Without them, the horsemen would have to come to him—clear shots each. One he would have to battle hand-to-hand, but only if each of the five arrows arrived deadly.

Swoosh. The first archer fell. When the next archer turned, an arrow caught him in the throat. He fell next to his partner. Two horsemen turned and stormed toward Miguel. The first one fell to the ground, another arrow through the neck. Abu's archers had taught Miguel how to avoid the armor and chain mail protecting the 'heartless' Spanish conquerors, as Abu called them. But that required exceptional skill for a bowman. It was now three men to his one. The horse closed the distance so quickly, Miguel barely had the arrow nocked when the horse was upon him. Rather than release the arrow, he dove out of the way, the arrow shattered against his chest, snapping the string of the bow. He pulled the whip free and tried to stand. His left leg failed him. The shattered arrow had entered where the other arrow had just glanced off. Searing pain shot up into his back. It was like the two wounds competed to prove which hurt more.

From a knee, he uncoiled the whip and as the guard reeled his horse, Miguel's whip wrapped around his throat and yanked him to the ground. The man tumbled. He got to his feet and drew his sword but kept his distance. This was not the first these two men faced off. Miguel now faced the captain of the king's royal guard. He knew the power of Miguel's whip. Even in the darkness, lit only by a rising moon, these two knew each other.

"You should not have come back," the captain said. "You embarrassed my men by killing the cardinal and escaping. They may have forgotten these many years, but I prayed for God to give me another chance at you. And here you are."

"I pray for God to deliver my soul from hell," Miguel said. "I do not want to spend my eternity with you."

Those were Miguel's last words. All went dark. A wounded and bloody archer dragging a shattered leg, struck Miguel in the head with a rock. The archer tumbled to the ground beside him. Miguel never saw the carriage slip away into the darkness.

Chapter Forty-Nine

1521 - Trujillo, Spain

For the first time in Martín's eleven years, Maria felt hope begin to sprout. Could hope possibly take root? Was it too much? Morning could not come fast enough. Work was a blessing. Prayer number four answered.

Weeks passed. Martín stayed close, despite Maria's efforts to encourage his independence. Yet, her strength was limited. Spring arrived and with it the promise of new life. The marshal's two new mares of a year earlier were among seven in foal. Even in this harsh country, the air filled with the sweet scent of blooming flowers. The rising sun painted the sky with hues of pink and orange.

Martín set out on his daily rounds to check on the animals. When he approached the stables, Maria was already whispering soothing words to a mare in distress. Martín immediately began stroking her mane. Hours passed until the mare foaled, bringing a beautiful, dappled foal into the growing herd. The foal was a chestnut miracle with a white splash on its forehead.

As spring edged into summer, six more foals joined the first one. But as new life invigorated the herd, Maria spent more time resting, struggling for breath. Long days with the animals turned into short spurts. Martín tried to help where he could. The marshal was kind and patient, but he missed Maria's expertise. He regretted the need to begin looking for another horse magician. Maria's title was farrier, but her strength was no longer adequate to muscle the horses' hooves. Still, she was one with their souls. She seemed to communicate with them heart to heart.

The hot summer sun hung low in the western sky. Martín climbed the stone wall and hopped into the pasture and found himself facing three strange men. They had lead ropes on four horses and were attempting to put one on Andi. Martín scrambled back over the wall and with every ounce of energy charged back to the manor. Maria sat on the porch shaded by a cherry tree which had long since lost its blossoms but was yet to ripen its fruit. When Martín blasted into the yard, she rose to his shouts that men were stealing the horses. She got him to slow down. Maria knew some of the horses would be sold, but not yet.

She took a deep breath. "Martín, run to the marshal. I will meet you at the corral." She steadied herself and hurried as much as she could. She hoped Martín and the marshal would already be at the corral. The marshal would know if the men Martín saw belonged with the horses. The corral consisted of two horse-high stone walls and timber-railed fences on the other two sides. Maria approached from the walled direction and could hear an argument in process. She could not scoot over the wall like Martín preferred to do. He seldom ran all the way around it.

When she rounded the wall and saw the source of the conflict, her pounding heart confirmed it was trouble. Three men on horseback held lead ropes on six of the prize horses. The marshal stood defiantly with three monks blocking the gate of the corral. Maria knew thieves like these. Monks on foot, untrained in battle, would never hold these men back. She reached for her knife. She knew she could not stop them either.

The argument, she assumed, was whether the marshal and his monks would move out of the way or be run down. Maria wondered why the horse thieves paused to argue. Why not just run the monks down. Was there some flicker of conscience? To steal horses, which was a hanging offense, but to run down, seriously injure, and possibly kill a monk must require some qualms. Either way, the monastics were losing valuable horses. Then she saw her Andi with the chosen horses. It became personal. Martín stood close to the open gate, certain to be clear of the riders if they chose to charge. Her heart pounded. Her breathing became short and violent.

When she reached the gate and stood alongside the marshal, she knew they never could hold these men back. But they had her Andi! A gift from the Gitanos, a gift from Vano's father. A gift she refused until that gift carried her damaged pregnant body from Granada, all across northern Spain looking for Vano and his group. When she gave up and returned to Bolibar, alone with help from the nuns, she gave birth to a baby boy who would never know his father.

She looked at Martín. At first, she thought he was safe enough. She eyed the men and realized she gave away too much. The man closest to Martín saw the concern in her face. He dropped his rope, reached down, and snatched Martín up onto his horse. Maria did not hesitate. She was not going to let her little boy be a negotiating chip or be taken with the horses. She lunged forward, driving her knife deep into his thigh. She pulled hard, dragging the knife toward her. He dropped Martín, but pulled his sword. He was not quick enough. She drove her knife into the horse's flank and back out again. Nobody heard her apologize to the horse. The horse jumped so hard the man flew into the tall timber post. He never moved again. Maria dropped to her knees. Her lungs begged for breath, while her heart struggled with its might to continue pumping blood. It wanted to burst.

The marshal jumped forward, taking the reins of the next man's horse. With help from a rather large monk, they yanked the rider to the ground. The other two monks tried to do the same with the third rider. He was too quick and charged his horse into the two monks, who tumbled over each other. He maintained control of the two horses he was leading, who trampled the two fallen monks as he charged away. Now alone, the lone thief fought his way to his feet, drew his sword, and ran it through the marshal as the marshal tried to get to his feet. The marshal sank to his knees and dropped face first into the dirt.

Maria's heart and lungs made their last sacrifice. She rose and lunged into the man just as he pulled his sword from the chest of the second monk and readied to kill Martín, who stood frozen throughout the massacre. Her knife caught him just below the neck. Her momentum brought her down on top of him, both tumbling into the dirt. Martín remained frozen. He waited for someone to move. Nobody did.

Now loose, Andi walked over to Maria's still body. He nuzzled into her hair, pushing her motionless body. Martín broke from his shock. He dove down and pulled his mother into his arms. Her hand, once secure on the knife protruding from a dead man's chest, dropped to the ground, limp and lifeless. Martín pressed his face against hers. Tears refused to flow. His young mind could not comprehend what just happened.

The sun was long set before monks came down to the corral to see why four of their fellowship had not returned for supper or evening mass.

No questions were asked. Two dead horse thieves, four dead monks, a young boy, holding his dead mother required no immediate explanation. The brotherhood of monks collected and cared for the dead. The abbot carried Martín up to the manor house where the monks carried Maria. They laid her body on the marshal's bed. They pulled a sheet over her body and head, invited Martín to kneel and together, accompanied by six more monks, prayed for her quick and glorious reunion with the Father, the very God in Heaven.

PART FOUR

ATLANTIC OCEAN
HISPANIOLA
Santo Domingo
CARIBBEAN SEA
The Caretas
Santa Maria la Antigua del Darién
SOUTHERN SEA
(Pacific Ocean)
TIERRA FIRME

Chapter Fifty

1528 - Caribbean Sea - New Castile
(Seven years later)

"Captain, the ship is coming apart. We will not make Darién."

This was not surprising news for the captain. Shipworms ate their way through countless ships in the warm waters of the New World. Captain Gutierrez was careless. His men knew it, but none dared to force the point. Now, their lives in peril, they feared the depths more than Captain Gutierrez' wrath. The ship took on water faster than they could pump it out.

This was Gutierrez' first slave cargo. Taken on consignment from the king, these slaves were convicted criminals sent to work the mines in the New World. Now he would never make the fortune he and his investors hoped. Within hours, the ship will fall victim to the legion of shipworms literally eating it out from under them.

"I want four oarsmen," Gutierrez said.

Three longboats were being loaded with the gold and provisions readied to abandon the sinking ship.

Four men from the slave hold still in ankle shackles arrived on deck.

"Not the preacher!" the captain said. "Anyone else."

The coxswain ignored the captain and quickly had the four slaves in the lead longboat lowered into the sea.

"And the other slaves?" the preacher asked. He held still, not willing to row. He was defiant.

Gutierrez demanded he row and to forget the many men left in chains. With one quick sweep of his oar, the captain flew over the bow of the boat. The oar continued around and took with it two other officers.

"Back to the ship," the preacher said. He stood, still in chains, but his command carried more authority than the sailors dared resist. The preacher picked up the nickname because he consistently praised God and promised delivery from tyranny, either in this life or the next. Surprisingly, for a convicted criminal, he communicated with the many slaves in their own tongue. Most men were of Castile, political dissidents who, for some reason, escaped execution. Other slaves were convicted Jews and Moors, accused of various crimes.

The second boat loaded with sailors was now in the water and the third being lowered. From the water, the captain and his two officers screamed for the sailors to attack the returning boat. But they were too interested in fleeing the sinking ship to be concerned with a captain who brought the failure on himself.

When the remaining four sailors objected, the slaves quickly dispatched them into the water. The second and third boats pushed away from the ship. All the while Gutierrez, his officers, and now four other sailors tried to reach them.

The preacher climbed onto the ship, which was leaning starboard, and hurried below decks as quickly as his shackles allowed. Securing the keys to the shackles, he loosened himself and each of the other captives. They bounded above decks and fought to climb into the remaining boat, where they overwhelmed it. The boat capsized, plunging a dozen former slaves into the water. The speck of land visible from the deck disappeared from view at water level. Remaining on board were only a handful of unshackled convicts. They all turned to the preacher for some kind of direction.

The captain and his two officers made it to the second boat, and it appeared the four sailors plunged from the first boat were climbing aboard the third. The first boat, now surrounded by flailing desperate men, looked like a bobble surrounded by hungry fish fighting for a bite.

"Hoist all sails," the preacher said. "We will sail till we swim!"

The wind was fair, but the movement was marginal. The water-heavy ship seemed to move only at a swimmer's pace. Yet, they left the two boats behind, which rowed off toward a different shore, a shore the preacher could not see.

"Find something to keep you afloat. We are swimming the rest of the way," the preacher said. He went into the captain's cabin and traded his worn and ragged pants. He bundled some of the officer's clothes into a satchel, emptied two casks of wine, filled them with air, and tied them to the satchel.

The land mass ahead looked to be three or four miles away. He estimated when they put the sinking ship to sail it might have been two or maybe three times that. They had made the success of the swim at least hopeful. He wondered where the two long boats might be by now.

The ocean slowly swallowed the ship and it finally ceased inching itself forward. It was an easy step into the water. Men began to swim. Others floated on some beam or door. Hours passed. From water level, it was difficult to see past waves to the shore. One by one, men gave up. Soon, the preacher was accompanied by only five others. These were the determined ones. Those who grew up near water and were strong and confident enough to swim. The sun set in front of them, its reflection blinding them, but confirming they were swimming west toward a distant shore.

One more man was lost before they dragged their pickled bodies onto the sand. In the darkness, all they could do was lie exhausted.

The sun breached the bare eastern horizon. Nothing appeared but wide-open ocean. No sails, no boats, no land, no clouds.

Four men sat up, surprised to be alive. One other, a Moor, died in the night.

"Who are you?" a slave asked the preacher. He spoke Castilian.

"I wonder if even God knows anymore," he said.

"These many months, you preach of Christ. Were you a monk?"

"A heretic," the preacher said.

"How did you avoid the pyre?"

"I murdered a cardinal," the preacher said.

"Why do not all heretics kill a cardinal to escape fire?"

The Castilian stared the preacher down. His grin finally gave way. "Which cardinal?"

"Cisneros."

"The regent?"

The preacher nodded.

"That was ten years ago," the Castilian said. "You have been in prison ten years?"

"Only seven. How do you know about the regent?" the preacher asked.

"At his command, we destroyed the Xavier Castle in Navarre. They commanded me to kill all survivors. I would not. They arrested me and it has been ten long years. We heard somebody murdered the regent. I thanked God. If it was you, I guess I should thank you. Thank you."

The preacher nodded.

"Got a name?" the Castilian asked.

"Used to," the preacher said. "Just a number now."

"What number?"

The preacher stared out across the water. Without looking back to the Castilian, he asked, "You were arrested for rebellion or asking too many questions?"

"Both," the man chuckled.

"Miguel, it is a name I have not heard in years. Say it, I would like to know how it sounds."

"Miguel," the man said.

The preacher nodded. "Thank you. It makes me think I am alive. And you?"

"I think you are alive."

Miguel shook his head. "Do you have a name?"

"Alfonzo Diego Fredrico Rodrigues Domingo de la Vega."

"No wonder they arrested you."

"What now?" It was the Moor. It was the first time the man ever spoke since being herded onto the ship months ago. Miguel turned to him, mouth open and squinted.

"You are Grenadian," Miguel said. The man was older than Miguel by at least a decade. His face was worn. What was likely once a rich black beard was now almost white. But he survived. He was tough.

"I am Gonzalo," the Grenadian said.

"We are free men," Miguel said. "All we need is food and work."

It was not until the men stood and began shaking the sand from their sore bodies they noticed the natives standing at the edges of the jungles watching intently with blow tubes and bows aimed and ready.

Miguel held his open hands away from his body, showing them empty.

"You friends." The words were Castilian. The speaker was native. Miguel nodded, "We are friends," he said.

Three young native children left the cover of the jungle. They approached the men with a basket of fruit and a hot mash wrapped in corn husks. The warriors did not relax their weapons. One of the children offered a leather skin bag from which each man drank. Miguel cringed at its potency. He blew out and took a deep breath to catch his balance. He nodded to the leader of the natives. They followed the natives into the jungle. The heat turned the still air into a heavy blanket. Leaves disturbed by the passersby launched swarms of insects into the air. Streams of light breaking through the canopy illuminated the flying armies.

Bare chested and barefooted, the men were exposed to the onslaught of hungry beaks. The trill of unfamiliar parrots filled the air. It was a sensual overload of sights, sounds, and smells. Miguel wondered if the drink they were offered was meant to dumb the senses, making adaptation to this new climate more likely.

The village they entered had a main square surrounded by buildings of various sizes. The largest looked to be some forty feet by sixty feet. It was made of tightly connected poles and stood several inches off the ground. Miguel guessed it must be the chief's home. Yet, he knew nothing about the New World other than what he read those many years ago between prison terms and the unreliable rumors from the guards on the ship.

A stout brown skinned man with long black hair and a white linen robe approached the men.

"More of you come to my land," the man said. "Where are the rest? I see no ship."

The eloquence of the man was surprising. It should not have been. Spanish linen hung in the windows. Two Toledo steel pikes leaned against a wall. Unless this village had destroyed other Spaniards and learned to speak the language from their dead bodies, this was a settlement friendly to the conquerors.

Miguel was the defacto leader of the four men. He spoke first.

"Our ship is lost. We alone made it to shore. I am Captain Miguel Ziortza de Bolibar. My men tried to save our crew but failed." He chose not to mention details.

"I am Chima, Cajica of the Caretas. Rest and eat. You are welcome here.

There is no gold, so I know you will be leaving soon," Chima said.

"Thank you. We seek no gold," Miguel said. The look on Chima's face and the warriors gave no indication they believed him.

The men ate, their gratitude clearly demonstrated. As they finished, a beautiful woman dressed in a long white linen dress approached. A red Spanish belt gathered at her waist pulled it such that it demonstrated a fine figure. She looked to be nearing thirty years in age based on Miguel's experience with European women. Yet her native skin and jet-black hair might say she was younger. He was confident Maria would still be this pretty. He reached up and rubbed his cheek. He scratched the scraggly beard more than rubbed. What then caught his attention was the tall black man standing next to her. He was muscled as finely as any man he ever knew. His eyes were bright and intelligent.

In the many years Miguel associated with men of every race, he was yet to find one inferior to another. More or less educated, yes. More or less civil, yes, but he was convinced culture played more into that than race. Yet with each and every people, he found goodness, and evil. This Chima and the Careta, were no different. He knew that already.

He watched how the black man was so solicitous to the woman. Were they married? Was he a slave? Several times, their eyes met. Miguel saw this man was assessing the visitors as much as Miguel was assessing their hosts. The black man carried with him a defiance. Not anger, but not defenseless. Miguel felt the man could easily handle anything a Spanish soldier could dish out. Finally, the man smiled and approached Chima with deference and respect. He bowed to the guests. His wide, beautiful smile almost put Miguel to ease.

"So, you swim for your supper?" the black man said.

What kind of greeting is that? Miguel raised his eyebrows. There was no accent. This man was Castilian all the way or at least very well educated. In six words, Miguel knew this was no savage.

"Ship worms destroyed our ship. We alone survived," Miguel said.

"I am familiar with that. Years ago, ship worms changed my life. Hello, they call me Alessandro. Please, reverence the Princess Cacica."

All four men bowed.

"I am Miguel."

Each man introduced himself.

"I am Pedro."

"I am Gonzalo."

And standing next to Miguel, the man last bowed, "Alfonzo Diego Fredrico Rodrigues Domingo de la Vega."

Alessandro smiled broadly, and winked at Miguel, "Don Alfonzo Diego Fredrico Rodrigues Domingo de la Vega, we will call you Al."

At that comment, Cacica's smile nearly melted Miguel. She bit her lip.

Chima invited the men to sit on tightly woven mats. Women, young and old, served the men a variety of fruits and meats. Baskets came and went. The local corn drink Alessandro called chicha took a toll on the men. It tasted too rich for Miguel. He refrained, but did not resist the plentiful coconut water. When Chima and several other tribesmen became too sluggish to move, they succumbed to the draw of sleep. Alessandro, Miguel, and Cacica left the village and climbed to a ridge with a clearing that overlooked the very shoreline where the men dragged themselves from the sea.

"Scouts spotted you this morning. We have many enemies. Four mostly naked men were not frightening, but we worried you might be the first of many. No canoes, no ship, we believe your story," Alessandro said.

Miguel shared the story of the attempt to save the men but chose not to reveal that the four survivors were missing their appointed appearance at the slave auctions in Santa Maria la Antigua de Darién. He asked about the location of Darién and how they might get there to report to the governor. He did not want anything to do with the governor, but to carry the charade he had to appear to need to.

"Stay here with us. You want nothing to do with Rios. He is evil throughout," Cacica said. Her delicate voice warmed him. She spoke confidently in her non-native Castilian.

"The governor is no longer in Darién," Alessandro said. "Gaspar Espinosa is mayor of Darién. Equally evil. The governor Dávila fled from the king. Murdered his way to Panama. He is now murdering in Nicaragua. Rios is our governor now. Still a fool."

"Panama?" Miguel said.

"On the great south sea," Alessandro said.

Alessandro related the story of Enciso's inflammatory lies against Vasco Nuñez de Balboa. How he conspired with a Francisco Pizarro to seize the control and riches of the new Andalusia. He told of the betrayal, the false trial and execution of the only good man in the New World. Then, in fear of the king's displeasure, Dávila ran to the other side of the isthmus and took control of the new land discovered by Balboa.

Miguel never heard of these men or the story of the new ocean. He did see the passion in which Alessandro shared it. When he described the betrayal and execution of his Balboa, tears fought to remain tucked in Cacica's eyes. She bit her lip again.

The New World was not new at all. Fallen man had just found a new land to continue the fall.

"You must decide what to do, Captain," Alessandro said. "But I would do it with a shirt." Alessandro pointed to a scar on Miguel's left shoulder. It was one of many scars his shirtless chest and back displayed. But it was the small royal cross burned into the flesh to which Alessandro referred. Miguel looked down at it. He forgot the brand of a convicted criminal might create some doubt with authorities that he captained the ship.

Miguel looked into Alessandro's eyes, trying to assess his thinking. He could not tell. He asked, "What are you thinking?"

That question brought a sharp jerk to Alessandro. He leaned into Miguel. "What did you say?"

"I simply asked what you are thinking. What you might know about this scar."

Alessandro relaxed. He shook his head and shrugged his shoulders. "Just that you are too valuable to kill for the crimes you committed. Someone wants you gone, but not dead until they realize the profits you might bring."

Miguel breathed out slowly. He squinted, trying to read what Alessandro's intention might be.

"Did you kill the captain and his men when you escaped?" Alessandro asked as if he were asking the temperature of the sea.

Miguel shared the complete story. Complete honesty had not always been to his benefit, but strangely it never condemned him with an honest man. Now he would learn if this tall, strong, intelligent black native was that kind of man.

"Captain, I believe I have the perfect cure for that scar." Alessandro stood and led Miguel and Cacica back to the village where they entered the large main building. The men still resting from the effects of the chicha laid quietly on their mats.

"We can make these fit." Alessandro pulled from a large barrel a worn, but well-made tunic. He removed a breastplate and backplate, then pauldrons and the rerebraces, and laid them next to the breastplate. Each piece of armor could boast experience in battle, but they were polished and well kept. Next, he pulled the cruises and greaves and laid them at Miguel's feet. Vambraces and gauntlets were next. Then, with a smile, Alessandro reached deep into the barrel and pulled the Morion with its wide brim and comb-shaped crest. Miguel wondered if the man would try it on, he held it so reverently. Alessandro tried to help a faded and broken plume stand at attention as he handed the helmet to Miguel. Miguel imagined that in its prime the plume was a beautiful bright red with fluffed rather than matted barbs.

The bright red plume came to life as Alessandro straightened it and fluffed the matted barbs. It almost looked proper again.

Miguel imagined how Balboa must have looked standing in this full armor. He appreciated the offer to arm a stranger in a great man's armor. Miguel knew it would never fit. Sizing up each piece of armor, Miguel felt he might be several inches larger than Balboa, in every direction. He did accept the offer to utilize the tunic, a vest, and other sundry items. Though tight, they rounded off a dignified look.

When the men arose from their slumber, Miguel stood in partial armor. He was able to use a few pieces of it. Chima's wives washed and trimmed his hair and beard. Miguel was not too keen about the armor, he never had the need for it. His skill with blade and whip was all he ever needed. Mastering the bow with Abu was a bonus. Now he had his eye on the blow pipe. He regretted Tomás never taught him the bolas or the sling, which Tomás claimed he learned right here in Darién. Who taught him? He looked at Alessandro. Assessed his age and could not help but ask, "Many years ago, did you ever meet a monk, a Friar Tomás?"

Alessandro's wide-open mouth slowly closed and became a large toothy smile. He turned quickly and dashed into a small building behind the large one. Seconds later, he emerged carrying the Latin Vulgate New Testament. "This Friar Tomás?" He pointed to a note tucked inside the pages. It read, "To my esteemed Alcalde Mayor Vasco Nuñez Balboa. Please read this to young Alessandro and help him understand the words. Starting with the epistle of Paul to the Galatians which starts, "For brethren, ye have been called unto liberty; only use not liberty for occasion to the flesh, but by love serve one another. For all the law is fulfilled in one word, even in this; Thou shalt love thy neighbor as thyself."

A tear fell from Miguel's eye onto the note. He quickly wiped it off.

"You know him," Alessandro said.

"Knew him."

Miguel told how he met Friar Tomás. They talked about the attempted rescue that landed him in prison but cost the friar, a reverend, and an English highwayman their lives.

Cacica shook her head slowly as she grieved the loss of another good man. Gently, she asked, "Why cannot the good men prosper? Why cannot our God in Heaven protect them? Why cannot God wipe evil from the earth?"

Miguel was impressed how Cacica seemed to understand Castilian so well and speak it so clearly. Her gentle native accent was endearing. She told how the Spaniards hated the monk because he insisted they treat the natives like Christ would. Miguel learned that Cacica made her own choice to be baptized once she learned of Jesus. Though Friar Tomás was only in Darién a short time, she loved him for his honesty and goodness.

"By faith, other monks did not like him," she said.

"By faith?" Miguel said.

"Balboa taught her," Alessandro said.

"You taught Tomás to throw stones?"

Another big smile exposed Alessandro's bright white teeth. "And I will teach you."

"And the blow pipe?"

Alessandro smiled and nodded.

The men awoke and were led to a spring where they washed. The same village women shaved and trimmed their hair. They abandoned their razor-sharp obsidian knives for fine Toledo steel blades for which they traded for gold. Each of the men accepted gifts of clothing which had been collected in trades or taken from fallen soldiers. They were a mixed match of uniforms, but better than the worn trousers of convicted slaves.

Alessandro escorted the men from the village to Darién. Where eight years earlier it was a bustling new settlement established by Balboa, it was now a small outpost with a few hundred inhabitants whose Alcalde Mayor Gaspar de Espinoza ruled with rage and fear. Settlers who could leave, did. But where to go? Panama was not much better. Two types of people inhabited the New World, those seeking fame and glory from conquest, and colonizers seeking new opportunities, land, and liberty.

As the heir to Balboa's fame and glory. Most of Darién's residents knew and respected Alessandro. To the Alcalde Mayor Gaspar and other officials, he was a tool, useful to them, nothing more. Known and respected among the various native populations, Alessandro tempered the hostilities.

A large state house stood on a hill overlooking the harbor. Balboa built it for himself shortly after his return from the south sea discovery. It was now the residence of Gaspar de Espinoza. The mayor's secretary welcomed the men and ushered them inside.

"Señor Alcalde," Alessandro bowed, "my friends, recently arrived, wish to meet our esteemed mayor. May I present Captain—"

"Gutierrez de Leon." Miguel interrupted the introduction. He bowed and took the mayor's hand.

Alessandro did not correct the introduction, sensing a need to let the scene play out.

"We wish to be in your service until the first moment we may return to our ship's owners in Spain to relay the unfortunate trouble we experienced." Miguel related the story of the loss of both ship, crew, and cargo. The mayor listened attentively, excused the men, and thanked Alessandro dismissively.

Miguel disliked the man immediately. Once clear of the mayor's house, Alessandro's raised eyebrows asked the question he and the four men had.

"I fought against that man in the conquest of Oran. He served as one of Cardinal Cisneros' captains. If he ever knew…" Miguel touched the shoulder where several layers below the tunic, the royal mark of his conviction for killing the cardinal lay hidden. Alessandro nodded toward the scar. Miguel affirmed.

"Well, Captain Gutierrez de Leon. If you know the man, you know almost all the men in the New World."

They entered a small tavern and sat.

Moments later, a young boy bounded into the tavern

"Govn'a wants a talk a bit."

Miguel smiled, "To me?"

"Falla me," he said and walked back to the door.

"Gentlemen, it looks like I am being called," Miguel said as he stood. He bowed and reached for his helmet.

Alessandro said, "Careful around a man with power. He will use you like he does everyone."

The young boy moved quickly through the streets, requiring Miguel even with his much longer legs to keep a brisk pace. They entered the great hall of the governor's palace and into one of the finished rooms appointed with furnishings that appeared to have been taken from a ship's cabin.

Miguel removed his helmet and bowed. The alcalde motioned for Miguel to be seated.

"Governor Rios in Panama has trouble with one of my investments. I need you to represent my interests there," the mayor said.

"You have known me for less than one hour. How can you trust me?"

"I trust no one. You offered your services. You admitted to losing a ship and want to return to Spain where, if you were dishonest, you would be arrested. A dishonest man would run from responsibility."

"Maybe I am not that smart."

"You are, and that mestizo trusts you. He hates me. But he honors the law. If he trusts you and he is wrong, I will destroy both of you and the Caretas."

Miguel swallowed back a smile. So, it had nothing to do with trust. This was a demand and a threat. That was more what Miguel expected. He accepted the offer to complete a few weeks work in Panama and then return to Spain with the Mayor Alcalde's commendation to the real shipworm-eaten ship's owners. Miguel's men would travel with him and, as Espinoza said, "They could outfit themselves like true Spaniards."

Miguel accepted Espinoza's generous offer, as Miguel described it to his four former galley slave companions.

"We are free men?" Don Alfonzo Diego Fredrico Rodrigues Domingo de la Vega asked.

"Not if you use that name," Miguel said.

"Al," Alessandro said, "there are no free men. Even I, who now live between two civilizations, am not free. As long as men seek to dominate other men, there are no free men."

"You are not a slave?" Al said.

Alessandro looked from Al to Miguel, then to each man's eyes. "Slave may not be the word, but we all have a master we serve. Even my Captain

Balboa, who conquered this land, and brought peace and prosperity to both native and Spaniard, served a king oceans away. When lies told by jealous men influenced that king, he sent greedy wicked men to govern him, the only man who needed no governor. Was he free?"

Miguel's respect for Alessandro grew with each word. He had conversations like this with Archbishop Talavera, the pirate queen Sayyida, the Muslim mercenary Abu, Reverend Luther, Friar Tomás and now with a half Tiano, half Spaniard Mestizo, who seemed to understand the nature of man as well as any.

"When is any man free?" Alessandro continued. "Balboa insisted that I was always serving a master, even if that master was the Christ himself or the very Satan."

The men sat silent, amazed at Alessandro's intensity. These men had little experience with black men who were not fellow slaves. Never had they conversed with one about the nature of God and man.

"Many years ago, a friar came to Darién. He was young. He was unafraid. He saw man's inhumanity to man and considered the savages and the conquerors equal in God's eyes. It is because of him, I read the words of Christ. It was from his Bible that Balboa taught me."

Alessandro pulled a yellowed, torn, and tattered parchment from his pocket. He folded it open and read, "To my esteemed Alcalde Mayor Vasco Nuñez de Balboa. Please read this to young Alessandro and help him understand the words. Starting with the epistle of Paul to the Galatians which starts, "For brethren, ye have been called unto liberty; only use not liberty for occasion to the flesh, but by love serve one another. For all the law is fulfilled in one word, even in this; Thou shalt love thy neighbor as thyself."

Miguel smiled, thinking how Captain Balboa must have reacted to the impertinence of young Friar Tomás calling the Alcalde Mayor to repentance. He looked at the parchment, worn and faded. And Alessandro had kept it these many years. How many? Miguel began calculating. Alessandro interrupted his count.

"Balboa did what the friar said. We started with the word 'Libertas.' Do you know what that means?" Alessandro asked. "Because I do."

No one answered. Miguel waited along with his companions for what appeared to be an upcoming sermon. Alessandro did not disappoint.

"Christ wants our hearts. He wants us to choose to follow Him. If we do, we are serving Him. He is our master. He should be our only master."

Alessandro read from the parchment, "Ye have been called unto liberty; only use not liberty for occasion to the flesh, but by love serve one another." Alessandro looked into each man's eyes.

"We use our liberty, our choices, our freedom to serve one another. That is how we serve the master, Christ. We are called by God to always be a servant."

Miguel's heart wanted to reach into heaven to tell Tomás how in his short time here in the New World, he accomplished more than just learning how to throw bolas to save Miguel from the king's guards.

"You came to my land as slaves. God freed you. You are now free to choose which master to serve. How long you remain free, how long you keep your liberty is your choice. Friar Tomás taught that each choice provides or eliminates future choices."

The men sat in silence for several minutes. Miguel wondered if they understood what Alessandro said. He wondered if Alessandro had this very conversation with other Spaniards or the natives. Finally, the old Granadian Gonzalo asked, "Who do you serve? I mean in the name of Christ your master, who do you serve?"

Miguel realized at least Gonzalo understood. He watched Alessandro's intensity soften, his face relaxed in appreciation of the question.

"I am hated by the Spanish leaders because they cannot own me. I am hated by the natives because I do not hate the Spanish. I serve the Spanish and the Natives as a peacekeeper. I soften the hate between the two."

"Blessed are the peacemakers," Miguel whispered to himself.

"The Careta princess we met, is she your wife?" Gonzalo asked. It was a kind question, full of respect. "I saw the deference you showed her."

Miguel wanted to ask that same question. He thanked Gonzalo in his heart.

"Cacica. She is Balboa's princess. But I loved her from the first time I saw her."

Alessandro's sermon was over. Miguel sensed it. It was time for each of the former slaves to start fresh in a new world, whether they were free or not.

They accepted Alessandro's offer to personally escort Miguel and his men to Panama, the name of the city Balboa established. Originally, Balboa called the new settlement Tubanama after the local tribe's cacique. In common conversation, it became Panama. Alessandro enlisted slaves and several Careta porters to escort Miguel and his men from Darién to Panama. Even the natives had slaves. Miguel marveled how the world could not manage if one people could not dominate another. Oh what he learned since his innocent days with the archbishop in Granada.

Miguel imagined the difficulty traversing this jungle for the first or even the tenth time before the way was cleared for regular passage. Once in Panama, Alessandro bade them farewell and returned toward Darién.

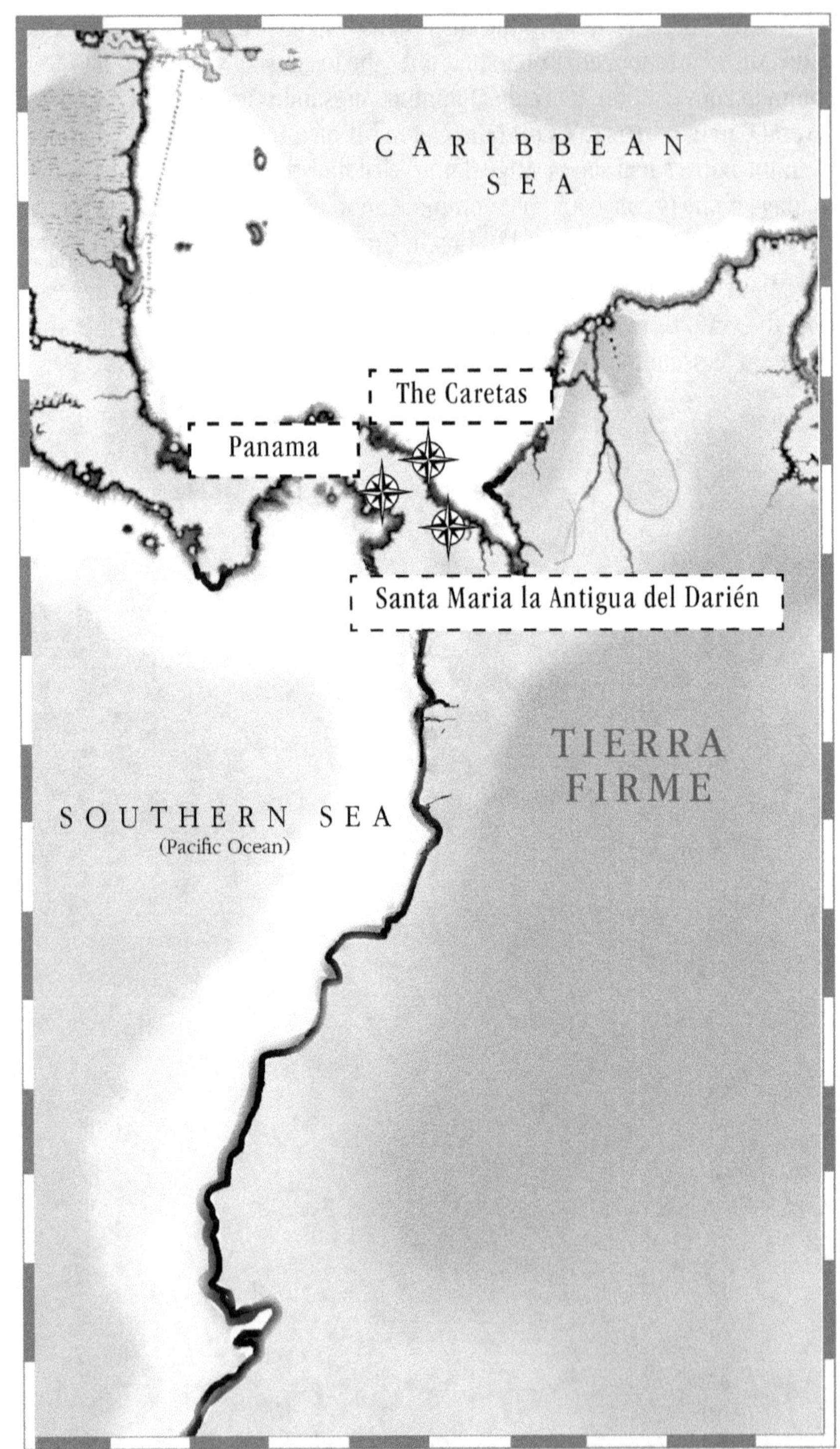

CARIBBEAN SEA
The Caretas
Panama
Santa Maria la Antigua del Darién
TIERRA FIRME
SOUTHERN SEA
(Pacific Ocean)

Chapter Fifty-One

1528 City of Panama - Castilla de Oro
Governor's Residence

Miguel had yet to explore the young town of Panama. Before Alessandro left Miguel and his men, he led him to the governor's mansion and introduced him to the governor. After seven years in prison for heresy, then seven more for murder and heresy with only a few years in between, then being sold to the slave markets, Miguel was curious what more God had in store for him. Before Miguel could make a proper introduction, two soldiers were ushered into the governor's office with a report he had been waiting for.

The two young soldiers stood before the governor. At the bidding of the governor, the first young soldier reported. "Our captain drew a line in the sand and said, 'Gentlemen, this line represents toil, hunger, thirst, weariness, sickness and all the other vicissitudes that our undertaking will involve.'"

The young soldier telling the story, somewhat hunched and fearful, looked from the governor to a fellow soldier who nodded his encouragement to continue. He turned back to the governor and continued.

"Then pointing to one side of the line the captain said, 'There lies Peru with all its riches;' Then the captain pointed to the other side of the line and said, 'Here, is Panama and its poverty. Choose, each man, what best becomes a brave Castilian. For my part, I go to the south.'"

The soldier paused again as if he were practiced in the art of drama. He looked from face to face and continued the narrative, "Then after making the challenge to all of us, the captain stepped over the line."

The governor stood silent as the soldier continued relating how their captain and expedition leader, Francisco Pizarro, defied the governor's command, and refused to return to Panama.

The governor had insisted these two soldiers come to his residence to report on the success of the recent mission to retrieve Pizarro and his men. A light breeze blew through the open windows, disturbing the pale green cotton drapes hanging loosely along the sides of the windows. Governor Don Pedro de los Rios, in his long draping coat, leaned against the large mahogany table brought with him from Spain. When it replaced the previous smaller desk, it became evident this residence was not constructed to the standards of the large haciendas in Spain.

Miguel felt it crowded the space. The room's bright painted white walls welcomed the sunlight. The bold flag of Castile, with its vivid red Burgundian cross extending from corner to corner, was the only other contrast bringing accent to the bland room. Without the flag and the deep mahogany table, the room could masquerade as a hospital room.

"And thirteen men stayed behind with him?" Miguel asked.

Miguel stood next to the governor, nearly a foot taller than the short round governor recently sent from Spain to govern the eight-year-old Spanish city of Panama.

The soldier nodded. He did not address Miguel or even acknowledge his presence when Miguel asked the question.

Miguel was a recent arrival to Panama and recognized he would not know any of the thirteen men who remained with Pizarro, so he did not care to inquire about them. But he was getting to know this determined Captain Francisco Pizarro. Miguel was familiar with the brief history of what was now called Panama established by Balboa as Tubanama and overtaken by its previous governor Pedrarias Dávila. And Miguel did know Dávila.

Dávila was a cruel and unscrupulous soldier who served in the battles of Granada. He carried his vile reputation throughout his governorship. Miguel was surprised that Dávila was still alive. He was old when he fought against the Moors. Miguel guessed Dávila was close to ninety now.

When the governor told Miguel that Dávila was one of Pizarro's first partners, he was not surprised at Dávila's impatience with Pizarro's failure during his first two journeys to explore the coasts of South America looking for the 'Golden Empire'.

Miguel was grateful Dávila retired and sailed north to become a governor in Nicaragua.

The new governor, Rios, however, seemed to struggle with his loyalty to the crown versus his personal attraction to the promises of Pizarro. The mishandling of the administration was evident in the chaos Miguel witnessed in Panama. He fully understood how a headstrong man like Pizarro was no more willing to obey the petty commands of an incompetent governor than he would the power-hungry commands of a greedy governor.

The governor pushed a letter toward Miguel. He picked it up and unfolded it. He was told the letter was secreted into a bale of cotton by some of Pizarro's men. They claimed that when Pizarro's expedition ran out of provisions and the men were left to survive on the Isla de Gallo, they were being held against their will. When the bale of cotton was offloaded from Pizarro's partner Almagro's ship earlier in the year, the note was found, prompting the governor to send two ships back demanding Pizarro's return.

He turned the letter over and showed it to the soldier. "This is your letter?" Miguel asked.

The soldier nodded.

"Tell us. Please," Miguel said.

It did not take prodding. Yet, the soldier directed his story to the governor, ignoring Miguel. The soldier began with the promises made by Francisco Pizarro and his two partners, Diego Almagro and the Friar Hernando Luque, when they recruited the men on their journey to find the great empire of gold.

They were promised unfathomable gold, riches beyond measure. He described the enthusiasm of the men charging off to conquer new lands.

Miguel watched the soldier's countenance change, almost painfully, when he described the battles with the natives on the island of Puna. The loss of many of his fellow soldiers to the battles, the starvation and illness. Yet Pizarro was undaunted; even in his advancing years, he refused to give up.

The soldier told how mutiny was a constant possibility.

It was when the two ships arrived at the Isla to rescue Pizarro's men that Pizarro drew the line in the sand and was able to convince thirteen men to remain on the Isla with him.

"Pizarro and his thirteen remained on the island?" Governor Rios said, more as a confirmation than a question.

Miguel was old enough to be a father to these two young soldiers. He wondered what a son might be like if he had been able to remain in Spain and have a family. His heart felt for the thirteen, but not for Pizarro. Leave him on the island to die, Miguel thought. He knew the greed and passion of these men from the Estremadura. He also saw how easily they switched allegiance when it came to personal profitability and how quickly they could take the lives of the conquered, however innocent those lives might be.

"Excuse me, Governor." The voice came from a tall, slender boy who, without any hesitation, burst through the doorway and came face to face with Miguel. He realized he was not talking to the governor, but he did not pause. He turned directly to the governor and opened his mouth again.

"Governor, Captain Almagro and Friar Luque request an audience at the harbor. They say it is about your lust for gold."

The governor's eyebrows rose nearly as fast as the blood filled his face with anger. Miguel smiled. He thought the young messenger had yet to learn how to temper a message. Certainly, the portion about the lust for gold was not part of the intended message.

Rios excused the young messenger, thanked the two soldiers, and ushered them out.

"May I?" Miguel said, motioning toward the door assuming Rios would exit and make his way down to the harbor. He was anxious to meet Almagro and Luque, even if Pizarro was not with them.

Rios walked surprisingly fast for a man with such short legs and round belly. Miguel was no longer a young man, but though he was pushing forty years, he was fit and strong.

The two men passed a shipyard busy with carpenters building ships that Miguel knew would be sailing both north and south exploring new worlds to conquer and exploit.

The sweet aroma of charbroiled meat reached them before they hurried around a corner entering an open market offering every type of local fruits, vegetables, and meats, from both land and sea. Miguel paused long enough to get his bearing so he could return this way. He took a deep savory breath and hurried to catch Rios.

Almagro and Luque turned just in time to see the two men approach. The young messenger obviously reached the two explorers first, certain to collect the promised payment for delivering the message.

Almagro, the taller of the two men, bowed slightly as Rios and Miguel approached. The broad smile was fake. Miguel had seen smiles like this one from men lacking true confidence and even a modicum of integrity. Yet it seemed to consume his clean-shaven face and nearly shaved head.

"Governor!" Almagro extended a hand which Governor Rios did not take. Almagro stepped back from the snub. "Well," he said, the smile not faltering.

The governor pointed toward Miguel. "Admiral Diego del Almagro," he said, "Gutierrez…" The governor paused, realizing he did not know the full name.

Miguel stepped forward, offered a hand to Almagro. "Gutierrez Miguel de Leon." He said. "I have been anxious to meet you. But please call me Miguel." Miguel was not quite ready to keep up the charade of remembering a false name.

Rios continued the introduction, "Miguel is here in Panama to settle some affairs of your Gaspar de Espinosa."

That raised an eyebrow. Almagro, just a few inches shorter than Miguel, wore the typical shirt and trousers common to the soldiers. Stains of sweat indicated he just removed the full metal Castilian shield. Miguel accepted Almagro's hand.

Rios, done with pleasantries and introduction, jumped directly into the matter at hand.

"Your partner defies my command to return!"

Almagro was slow to release Miguel's hand. His deep brown eye locked on Miguel's. The other eye, lost in a battle with natives, wore a shiny black patch. "You know the man. He is certain a conquest much greater than that of Cortez is at hand. Glory for the king, he says." Almagro's animation grew as he released the grip and turned back to Rios to underscore 'glory for the king.'

Glory for what king? Miguel asked himself.

Luque remained silent as he bowed when Almagro introduced him to Miguel.

"Hernando Luque is responsible for our funding. The perfect partner in our expedition."

A friar? Miguel again asked himself. In the service of who?

"There will be no expedition," Rios said, blood again coloring his face. "Dávila approved one failed expedition. I sent two ships to rescue your second failed expedition. I will no longer bear the expense of your folly."

Miguel knew this was not the first spirited exchange between these two. He sensed it would not be the last.

Almagro was prepared to petition the governor right there on the harbor. Luque, sensing the poor timing, interjected an excuse to continue the discussion at another time. Reluctantly, Almagro excused himself and they returned to the ship.

The governor stormed off, leaving Miguel standing alone watching the two groups part. After several minutes, he turned and made his way back toward the market, following his nose.

A short time later, satisfied with a full stomach, he found his way back to an inn where the wealthy mayor of Darién, Gaspar de Espinosa, made arrangements for lodging.

Over the next number of weeks, Miguel proceeded to carry out the work he was sent to do. It was uncomfortable dealing in slaves. But he was only a few layers of fabric away from becoming one again.

The sun was just waking, letting light creep past the open curtains. Accompanying the soft light, the smell of frying pork was carried softly into the room as if singing a lullaby. Slow intentional breaths invited Miguel's eyes open.

A pound on the door shattered the reverence Miguel hoped might never end. He slid the blanket aside, pulled on a robe and opened the door.

A young slender boy, with almost pitch-black skin, stood ready to pound again. His hand paused in mid-air. A broad smile exposing bright white teeth complimented his two shining eyes.

"From the governor." He handed a letter to Miguel, bowed, and dashed away.

He opened it and read.

"Please prepare to accompany Señor Diego de Almagro and Friar Hernando Luque. You will be my security. With the blessing of the Mayor of Darién, Gaspar de Espinosa, who is financing this recovery, you will see that Señor Almagro and Señor Luque return with Señor Pizarro and his men." The letter was signed "The honorable Pedro de los Rios - Governor of Panama."

"His security?" Miguel muttered to no one. "Me?" Then he chuckled, confirming he finally freed himself of the shackles of heresy and treason which hounded him for nearly twenty years. "What would Archbishop

Talavera, Cardinal Cisneros, and not to mention Queen Isabella think now? Me, the trusted advisor of the rich governors in Castilla de Oro."

A welcome breeze blessed the warm, moist morning air. He was standing on the deck of one of the two ships Governor Rios commissioned, or rather consented to send south to recover Pizarro and his thirteen belligerent men.

As he overlooked the bustling shipyard and beyond it the growing young city, he marveled at how disorganized it felt. Contrasting this young growing city with others in the Holy Roman Empire that grew up over centuries, he wondered why a central plan was seldom ever employed. With a fresh start, he thought a governor might look forward with a confidence of establishing a real organized city.

A gentle voice speaking the local Tubanama dialect interrupted his thoughts, "To celebrate our expedition." Then a hand offered Miguel a large ceramic cup frothing with a thick dark red liquid. The large confident smile surprised him. There stood his newest guardian.

"It is Balboa's Ocean. It is Balboa's Beru. Cacica wants me to go see what his enemies have done with it. And if shipworms leave you swimming."

Miguel lifted the cup to his lips. The rich smell of anise and a delicate rose reached his nose first. He smiled and nodded a 'thank you' to Alessandro, who welcomed the nod with a smile. Xocolati. Despite its somewhat bitter taste, Miguel appreciated the new drink discovered by Cortez in Mexico a decade earlier. It had become a favorite here in Panama.

Over the several weeks Miguel spent in Panama conducting business for Gaspar, he became fond of the people, the climate, and the richness of this new Southern Ocean. But it was as if God gave him a new guardian. Alessandro was like an ambassador. He could not undo all the wrongs, yet it seemed he anointed himself a guardian of the New World.

From Christopher Columbus' first discovery of the New World in 1492, new regions had been discovered, explored, conquered, and exploited. In a short thirty-five years, settlements had been established, destroyed, re-established, and some remained strong and flourished. Yet even among the civilized fellow citizens of this New World, greed, distrust, and envy sowed the seeds of corruption.

Miguel was anxious to meet this Pizarro, who spent most of his adult life here in the New World participating in the greed, distrust, envy, and corruption. He was not afraid of men like that. He spent most of his adult life fighting against them and, so far, had survived. But he now wondered about himself, working for one of the very men deeply immersed in that corruption, a man who he fought against in the conquest of Oran.

Less than ten years earlier, the very explorer of this southern sea, Vasco Nuñez de Balboa, who established the settlement and city of Darién, was arrested by the mayor of Panama, his fellow discoverer, Pizarro himself. Miguel shook his head at the evil twist of it. Francisco Pizarro was one of Balboa's captains when they traversed the isthmus and discovered the South Sea. Pizarro served as mayor of the new city of Panama. Yet, with co-conspirators, Dávila and Gaspar, Pizarro arrested Balboa, who was then tried and executed. Where was any loyalty?

Miguel fully understood the New World was not new at all when it came to the men exploring it. It was the same old world of fallen man, just pushed west.

The ships pulled anchor. As the sails filled with the rich morning air, a foreboding crawled into his chest, telling his heart he would never return to Panama. Miguel sipped his xocolati.

341

ATLANTIC OCEAN
Santo Domingo
CARIBBEAN SEA
Panama
Santa Maria la Antigua del Darién
SOUTHERN SEA
(Pacific Ocean)
TIERRA FIRME
Isla de Puna
INCA - Tumbez
BERU

Chapter Fifty-Two

1528 - Southern Sea - off the coast of modern-day Columbia, Pacific Ocean

Captain Almagro estimated they could reach the Isle of Puna within four weeks. The ships remained clear of the coastline out of the reach of native populations. Twice they saw small craft with large white linen sails. Curiosity was not enough to dissuade the captains from their mission.

Almagro's command to strike sails positioned the ship not more than a hundred feet from shore. With anchor dropped, they began lowering the boats. From the upper deck, Alessandro pointed toward the tall soldier standing in full battle armor leaning on his sword.

"Captain Pizarro," Alessandro said. "He will not be happy to see me. I may remain on deck."

Miguel disembarked with the second boat. When he climbed on shore, he watched the two partners, Almagro and Pizarro embrace and begin a very animated conversation.

Pizarro's thirteen fools, as Pizarro's other soldiers called them, clamored toward the boats anxious to be free of their island prison. Miguel remained at shore's edge. Captain Almagro waved him up to the conversation.

"Francisco, Captain Miguel de Leon is under the employ of our partner Gaspar who funded this rescue. He and Governor Rios insist we return you and your men to Panama." Miguel instinctively knew Almagro said this only to make an official declaration. He knew Pizarro and Almagro discussed this before inviting Miguel to the conversation. He surveyed the old conquistador. He looked too old to have so much sway with these younger, stronger soldiers. He lived up to the hard, stern, determined image Alessandro created for him. Miguel was quick to assess his lack of loyalty to men, the crown, or even humanity.

"Captain Pizarro, I am honored to have been sent to bring you home. Other men's petty descriptions of you do you no justice." Miguel bowed.

"Our captain insists a return to Panama is too risky a chance to take. He insists that with the provisions we carry, we must now sail south. The great golden empire is within reach," Almagro said.

"If we return without proof of the golden empire, Rios, Gaspar, and Charles will never allow our return," Pizarro said.

This was exactly what Gaspar expected. Miguel knew this now. Could he stop this veteran conquistador? Almagro was his partner. He did not seem to even try. He represented one partner and the fourth partner remained on the second ship, Friar Hernando Luque, the accountant. Was Miguel ready to become an instant enemy? Did Alessandro foresee this? Was that why he joined the expedition?

Francisco pulled a golden figure of the sun from a satchel and handed it to Miguel. It was heavy. He scratched it. It was solid. He looked into the captain's eyes. This was the very reason men spent their lives dying in these jungles. No, there was no way to stop Francisco without the sword. He had not enough experience with Balboa's sword which he wore on his side, nor did he know Pizarro's expertise.

"I must forbid with the strongest objection," Miguel said.

"Will you draw Balboa's sword?" Pizarro asked.

Miguel did not want to, nor did he plan to. But his facade was melting. Miguel noted that Francisco recognized his former captain's sword, and likely the pieces of armor. "Do I need to?" Miguel asked.

"If you will not, you are not demonstrating the strongest objection."

"Have you bested Balboa's sword before?" Miguel asked.

"I am the only one that could have," Pizarro said. "We will send one ship back to Panama. You can report to that sniveling Rios and Gaspar you never found us and Almagro's ship is still looking," Pizarro said.

"I will sail with you." Miguel never set hand on the hilt of Balboa's sword.

With the next tide, Pizarro was at the helm of Almagro's ship. They sailed south to the empire of gold, a land the natives called 'Buru,' a land so rich with gold, the people ate off gold platters.

Following the coast, the ship passed countless villages and settlements. On earlier expeditions, Pizarro mistakenly encountered hostile tribes. He felt this time he would sense when he found the right place. Three weeks passed. They continued poking in and out of inlets and harbors. One early morning, they spotted sails on the horizon. All attention focused on those sails. The wind was favorable, and they overtook the other vessel by mid-day. It looked to be a very buoyant wood, for it bobbed in the ocean. Its one tall linen sail was no match against Pizarro's four square and two lateen rigged sails.

Alessandro listened as closely as he could, but could not interpret the language of the native sea faring voyagers. A trade of some sort was taking place. Pizarro insisted that these natives lead Pizarro's ship to their home and commanded Alessandro and Miguel to sail with the natives. Miguel was less enthusiastic than Alessandro. They climbed into the small craft. It was no more than twenty feet square, but the helm consisted of a long rudder secured to a pivot pole secured in the back. Two large oar posts supported the oars which were currently pulled from the water. Miguel immediately touched the wood to assess why it was so buoyant.

"Balsa," Alessandro said. "Soft. Difficult to bury under water."

They sailed for several hours. The sun hung in the western sky. When they cleared a large, forested mountain, a city built on the water's edge glistened in the afternoon sunlight. More than glistened. The reflection was blinding as they approached. Miguel wondered at the jubilation taking place on Pizarro's ship. The empire of gold was real. At least, a city of gold was real.

Warriors stood ready as Alessandro and Miguel stepped on shore. Two old women dropped their baskets and walked up mouths open, saying nothing, then reached up and touched Alessandro's black face. They took his hands in theirs and turned them over and over, touching them to their smooth faces. They then turned to Miguel and repeated the exercise. Gently, they pulled on his short beard with their tiny hands. They began to giggle at their discovery. Soon Alessandro, the more interesting of two men—drew the attention of women and children. Once satisfied he was human, they turned their attention to Miguel. The novelty of the reaction embarrassed the two men. They were relieved when a long boat launched from the ship arrived with a dozen more white, bearded men. Young men in canoes rowed out to meet the ship and the incoming boats. Drums pounded in the square of this glistening city. The reflection from the sun on the rippling ocean, blending with the reflections of the golden buildings, overwhelmed the men. Pizarro's thirteen fools were no longer fools.

Two tall towers stood on each end of a central plaza. In his mind, Miguel compared his first assessment of the new city of Panama, how its paths, roads, and buildings were built in such an unplanned way. Here, these natives designed a city with a central square. Buildings made of intricately carved stones sat perfectly lined up around the central square. Gold glistened everywhere. Beautiful fabrics hung in windows. Doors, some with intricately carved figures of animals and others with inlaid golden depictions of a deity, accented the construction of each building.

Around the central square, were smaller buildings, Miguel assumed were the homes of the residents who lived and worked in the city. He wanted to climb a nearby hill to see what lay beyond. But he could see gardens planted between many of the buildings. Down one street, paved with well-cut stones, he saw what he assumed were large fields, green with vegetation planted in perfect rows and finely cultivated.

The lands, the people, and the buildings decried any reference to this empire being any less civilized than the finest cities in Europe.

Boats from the two ships began arriving. Soldiers poured out into the city. Dressed in full armor, the soldiers appeared as menacing to these native citizens as the warriors did to Miguel.

"This is where we need Balboa, not Pizarro," Alessandro said.

Captain Pizarro showed no fear. Miguel had yet to experience a conquest. He heard and read about them and was thus somewhat cautious. How bloody might this become?

Crew members took native leaders by boat to the ship to see the large floating craft. They returned expressing wonder to others on shore. Natives escorted Miguel, Alessandro, and others into various buildings. These were not primitive people, Miguel thought. Homes had kitchens outside the backs of the homes, living quarters with finely adorned furniture, beds, and even closets.

Miguel sensed a different spirit when he and Alessandro entered a building featuring more gold than the others. The sacred house of ancestry, as Miguel interpreted the unknown words and gestures, housed the carefully preserved bodies of community leaders. It felt more sacred than morbid.

Two young boys stayed close through the entire tour, touching

Alessandro's and Miguel's hands whenever possible. Toward the end of the tour, they returned to the square. A much finer blend of maize found its way into cups decorated with golden figures of tall-necked sheep. The soldiers drank freely. As they did, they became careless. Their rudeness began offending the local leaders.

Noting Miguel's interest in the crops, an older man led Alessandro and Miguel from the square down past the buildings. The large fields, immaculately cultivated, amazed Miguel. He continually looked at Alessandro to interpret. Alessandro insisted he did not understand any more than Miguel did.

The sound of a canon echoed across the fields. Then two blasts from an arquebus musket.

"Trouble," Miguel said. Alessandro had not waited to utter a word, he was already twenty feet ahead of Miguel. When they reached the square, large warriors with blowpipes and long spears ready, halted the two men from leaving the square and rushing to the shore. The last of the boats were some forty yards into the harbor, rowing as hard as they could. Two young native boys in one of the boats struggled to get free. They watched in horror as they lifted the boys into the ship and raised the boats. With anchors pulled, the evening breeze filled the giant white sails. Alessandro's and Miguel's escape, protection, and hope disappeared into the horizon. All eyes watched as the intruder's flying ships vanished. All eyes except those of four muscular warriors with pikes, obsidian clubs, and blowpipes who held the two strangers in place. Miguel held out his hands.

Francisco Pizarro lifted Balboa's sword. It was left behind by Miguel, when, in haste, he obeyed the command to accompany the natives who led the Spaniard's ship to the golden city. There was no danger now. He reflected on the night he narrowly escaped with his life from San Sebastian eighteen years earlier. He was not going back to Rios and Gaspar in Panama, but to Spain, directly to the king. This was his discovery. His conquest alone.

Chapter Fifty-Three

1528 - Trujillo, Extremadura, Spain

Martín ignored the taunts. "They are just bullies," the friar told him time and again. "They are small-minded jealous boys." Martín did not care. Martín had to work with these bullies tending for the swine herds. Before the monastics gave up on breeding horses, Martín worked as a stable boy. It was hard work, but he loved the horses and there was a level of pride for the young orphan to work with the herd. Then the abbot hired a new foolish monk as marshal. He tragically sold off the best breeders. The herd suffered for years before the monastery eventually disbanded the farm. Martín found himself alone with no choice but to tend swine with other boys. Most days, he felt the boys were kindred of the herd.

They were dirty, foul, mean, and brutal. Martín begged the abbot to take him as a novice monk. The abbot liked Martín, so when the church got a new priest, he told the priest to prepare Martín for the vows he so wanted to make. In another year, Martín would be old enough.

The large chapel door closed behind him, shutting out the shouts and jeers. He loved the peace and protection inside the large hall. He crossed it and knocked gently on a simple wooden door.

"Homines dum docent discunt," came the voice inside.

"Men learn when they teach," Martín said.

"Very good," the priest said.

Each session ended with a Latin challenge Martín studied between lessons. Martín stepped into the priest's office, which for the previous two years served as a private school room. He pulled several sheets from a satchel and handed them to the priest. He sat silently as the priest read through each one. The priest glanced up over the pages. He winked.

"I have only known one other person so gifted with languages," he said. "You remind me of him."

The compliment meant nothing to Martín. He was eager to receive the recommendation from the priest to become a postulant and enter the abbey to escape the harsh world. Several priests came and went over the years after Maria's death. Each time, the abbot reassigned Martín's training and preparation to the new local church priest. This priest was different. Martín felt safe. He felt a responsibility to complete his studies. He felt hope that he could soon be accepted into the monastery and make important lifelong vows.

"Martín, you have done well. I plan to make a recommendation to the abbot. Before I do, are you certain it is a commitment you are ready to make? You can serve Christ in many other callings. A monastic monk is a worthy calling. The abbot would be blessed to have you. But you have yet to see the world and other ways you might serve God."

"This is what I want," Martín said. "I have seen what the world is and does. I do not want it." His words were terse. The priest raised his eyebrows, his head pulled back.

"You sound certain," Friar Tomás said.

"I am."

"Very well." Tomás pulled open an envelope, unfolded a letter. "Perhaps it is best. Let me read a letter I received yesterday from our cardinal in Toledo." He adjusted the letter almost to the extent of his arms to focus his eyes. He read.

"Our esteemed Friar Tomás. You have valiantly dedicated your life to Christ. In one more act of selfless service, we request your presence here in Toledo."

Friar Tomás lowered the letter. Martín stared at him, collapsed back into his chair, then covered his face with his hands. He said nothing. There was nothing to say. The cardinal required his presence, just as he had each other priest. Yes, now was the time to enter the brotherhood and escape. He sat quietly, then looked up to Friar Tomás, realizing that once you make the vows, you no longer choose your destiny. You are no longer at liberty to follow your passion. Martín knew he had no passion. Yes, the abbey was for him.

"When do you leave?"

"Tomorrow."

"When will you be back?"

Friar Tomás shrugged. "You will be well without me. You are ready. More ready than any I have ever taught. But I tell you. You have great gifts given you from God. Be sure your heart guides you. Do not let fear and anger push you." Friar Tomás pulled several manuscripts from a drawer Martín had not noticed before. A secret drawer?

"Can you read this?" Tomás asked. He handed the manuscripts to Martín.

Martín shook his head. He looked closely. Ran his fingers across the words. He stumbled through the words, "Stammbaum Jesu Christi, des sohnes nachkommen Davids, des sohnes nachkommen Abrahams." He looked up at Friar Tomás.

"It is the Book of Matthew. I know it, but I cannot read it."

"You will," Tomás said.

Author Kent Merrell

In the mid-1980s, after earning the first of what would become twenty-seven international awards for his innovative and impactful advertising, Kent Merrell was drawn to the allure of Madison Avenue, New York's legendary advertising hub. However, one of the industry's giants offered him advice that would shape his career: "Stay in Utah. We don't need you competing with us, and you don't want to raise your family in New York. You're talented enough; the work will find you."

That advice proved to be priceless.

Over a distinguished forty-five-year career in marketing and advertising, Kent's creativity drew clients from across the globe, including prestigious names like VISA International, Disney, HBO, USPS, Comcast, Wells Fargo, Discover Card, and Buena Vista. His unique approach to creativity has made him a sought-after speaker both in Europe and across the United States.

Kent's work took him to every corner of the world, and on these journeys, he found inspiration for stories waiting to be told. His passion for history and his creative storytelling style eventually led him to the world of historical fiction.

Kent's debut novel, The Blade of Safavid, transports readers through Ancient England, Persia, India, Africa, and the New World. His second novel delves into the global quest for liberty, exploring the Reformation in Europe, the discovery and conquest of the New World, and the fall and eventual liberation of the Inca Empire. Kent's extensive travels and his two-year experience living in the Andes Mountains lend authenticity and vivid detail to his historical narratives.

Kent's own story began with a scholarship to Brigham Young University, where he earned his Marketing Communications degree, married his wife of 46 years, and started a family that has since grown to include five children and twenty-two grandchildren.

Stay connected with Kent and follow his author journey at:

www.kentmerrellauthor.com.

A preview into *The Conquest of Liberty: Book Two*

The Conquest of Liberty

Of Martyrs, Mentors & Masters

Chapter One –

1528 Quito, Northern Capital City
Tawantinsuyu - Inca Empire

Afternoon sun reflected off the intricately molded golden-sun-medallion suspended on a silver chain hanging around the neck of the Sapa Inca, son of the Sun God Inti, Inca Huayna Capac.

Seated on an ornately carved golden chair suspended by a liter carried by eighteen lords, Huayna Capac entered the plaza and halted in front of the royal palace. Only Sarpay, first princess of the empire, dared look the Inca Emperor in the eyes. He returned her smile. As his daughter and only child of the Inca Emperor's first wife, Coya Cusirimay, Sarpay was one of the few in the empire with direct access to the emperor's heart.

A finely woven Vicuña dress dyed deep red hung over her shoulder tufted and held with golden rings matching the long golden loops hanging from her ears. As the fine shimmering fabric hung loosely over her smooth bronze body, a golden rope gathered it at her waist. Long, thin strands of gold woven into her long black hair cascaded loosely over her bare shoulder.

Her regal visage commanded awe from onlookers who stole moments to gape. Yet it was her kindness that endeared her to nearly all who fell under her watchful eye.

As her emperor-father Huayna waited for the porters to lower the litter,

Sarpay recognized the concern in his bold stern face. The smile now gone, he stepped down and strode past her, entering the palace. His soft leather sandals barely made a sound on the marble entryway. Even the gold ornaments hanging around his neck and bouncing on his shoulders seemed to betray what should have been a jubilation for his recent victory over the Cañari.

Sarpay recognized his concern, which was confirmed when he entered the resting place of his mummified mother, Mama Ocllo Coya, upon whose spirit he relied for inspiration.

Days of fasting passed before he reemerged, looking more concerned than when he prepared for battle.

He welcomed Sarpay and his new wife, the Inca Queen Rawa Ocllo, who he took as a principal wife when Sarpay's mother Cusirimay died. Sarpay was yet a young child when her mother died of illness. Huayna invited them both into his private chamber to consort. "A great plague has come," he told them, "a plague with no concern who it kills. The gods take both lord and vassal. Our people are being punished."

How could the mighty Sapa Inca fear something so invisible? She wondered. All she had ever seen was courage from this man. To her, he was God. Never had he shrunk.

"The gods demand a great blood sacrifice. That of the firstborn." Huayna sat, legs crossed on a Vicuña fur covering a golden platform suspended by twelve short silver inlaid posts. "Inti, my father the Sun God, and Quilla, my mother God of the Moon, require an ultimate sacrifice. Only a sacrifice of the firstborn will redeem this people." He took Sarpay's delicate hands in his, forcing himself to look her in the eyes. "My firstborn, the very First Princess of the Empire, daughter of my first wife Cusirimay, only through your blood, will our people be saved."

Great tears flowed down his bronze cheeks. He pulled her close and buried his head in her neck. Never before had Sarpay seen her father weep. Inca Emperors never wept.

She pulled him tight and whispered, "I will go prepare myself." His strong, once solid frame shook. She kissed his cheek and pulled back, lifted his chin to look the mighty Inca in the eyes and repeated, "I will do this for you, for my people, for the gods. For this, I was sent from the gods. For them I will give my life."

"If there was any other way, I would not require this. But the very heavens demand that without the purest, most innocent blood of the firstborn, mercy cannot have claim upon the people," Huayna said, shrinking again into her arms. For many minutes Sarpay held her father as if absorbing his strength, filling her with the courage.

But she did not need his courage. Her mighty father had conquered armies much stronger than his own. He had brought peace throughout the mighty Tiwantansuyu, uniting the people more than any of the former Sapa Incas, his ancestors. Yet, here now, he wept for the sacrifice the Gods demanded of his firstborn daughter. Sarpay realized she must fulfill this responsibility alone and her father was trying to strengthen her with his love. She could not take his strength. She loved him too much to be so selfish. She released her embrace and stood.

She bowed her head toward her father's new principal wife, Mama Ocllo, who quickly took her place and now held the mighty Inca. Though Sarpay had many brothers and sisters from her father's other wives and concubines, she and she only carried the purity of blood that could satisfy the requirements of Inti.

Sarpay was the only living offspring of the Inca Emperor Huayna Capac and his principal wife, his sister Cusirimay, who was also of pure blood. Both Huayna and Cusirimay were born of parents of pure Inca blood, making them literal pure children of Inti the Sun God and his wife Mama Quilla Goddess of the Moon. Though this expectation had never been spoken, Sarpay knew that only her blood could save the people. She had thus been purified and ordained as the high priestess of Tiwantansuyu, the great Inca Empire.

She slipped off the platform and summoned the priests and priestesses to help her, the Inca's First Priestess Princess, prepare for and make the journey to the Temple of the Sun.

For the perfect youth sacrificially offered to the gods, it was a lifelong preparation. Tribes from throughout the empire selected a perfect boy or girl to be dedicated to the gods of the empire. These children sent to the sacred Coricancha in the capital city Cuzco, grew up separated from the major population. They spent lives in service to the gods. Undefiled, they grew up to serve. In times of famine, war or celebration, the most perfect were chosen by the gods and anointed for the honor of giving their life for the empire.

It was now time for the most perfect of them all to seek the divine blessings of the gods.

Sarpay's virtuous life had also been a lifelong preparation. She recognized that now. Where others of her sisters had already been given in marriage to both brothers or other nobles, she had been, "preserved for this very time" she thought. Tradition required a procession to Cuzco from the home of the sacrificial child, then a trek to the chosen Andean peak to be buried alive.

Sarpay knew for her, this would be a sacrifice of blood on the sacred altars at her father's own citadel in the Temple of the Sun. This would not be a personal sacrifice for her. This would be an honor to give her life for her father and for her people. Soon she would join the Gods looking over the people. Only her blood could save the people. She had thus been purified and ordained as the high priestess of Tiwantansuyu, the great Inca Empire.

Huayna dried his tears, regained his composure, and motioned for his chaskis to enter. These native runners arrived breathlessly at court. In a sophisticated system of relays, young runners carried messages across thousands of miles of roads. These two arrived with messages from the coastal town of Tumbez. Kneeling, and with bowed heads, they confirmed the reports that a sickness had appeared in the north. This terrible sickness was devastating the inhabitants. It wiped out complete villages. Those inflicted by this invisible illness first developed a frightful skin irritation all over their bodies. Blisters then turned to open sores, then in painful agony the people died. The chaskis reported the sickness was now spreading toward Quito.

In order to protect himself from the invisible invader, Huayna Capac, the mighty Inca, retreated into seclusion. Following three days of fasting, food carefully prepared and provided to prevent any contact with the outside world, he struggled to keep himself away from the sickness' lethal reach.

Days turned into weeks, and when a month ended, he realized it was too late. Shadows danced on the walls of his secluded palace bed chamber. The air was thick with a mixture of despair and the pungent scent of fever. The mighty emperor's once-powerful form was becoming a fragile shell. The memory of his strength and spirit seemed like a distant dream. It began innocuously, with a fever and a dull ache that settled in his bones. His forehead burned and his muscles screamed with every movement. At first he brushed it off, then prayed it away, but as the days passed, the illness tightened its grip. Fatigue gave way to an agonizing headache and an unrelenting backache that left him bedridden.

His skin, once smooth and bronzed in the sun, now bore the cruel marks of the disease. It started as a rash, small red spots that dotted his face and forearms, then spread with a malevolent persistence to his chest and legs. The spots swelled into blisters, filled with cloudy and thick fluid. Each pustule was a testament to his suffering, bulging and angry against his skin.

As days passed, Huayna realized he would likely die, and he called for his nobles. "I command you to seek the sign of the llama to confirm my choice for my son Ninan Cuyochi to inherit the empire. If he is not the gods' will, then I anoint my son Huascar."

Huayna laid motionless, drifting in and out of delirium when new chaskis arrived from the coast. Huayna rose to his elbow, mustering what strength he had to receive a report.

"Great Inca, a strange floating craft arrived from the north and moored before your conquered Chimu city of Tumbez. Its people have white skin and hair on their faces. And one is black like the night. They carry with them strange tools which make smoke and speak like thunder. These strange men stole two of the Chimu boys and used the wind to carry them across the great waters. Two of this enemy, one black and one white, were captured by the Chimu. They remain as prisoners. The Chimu await your will."

Long silence. The emperor drew a laborious breath. He was teetering on the edge of consciousness. Huayna said nothing.

"We await your will," the second chaskis said, never raising his head. Silence, except for the struggle to breathe. The two young runners backed away from the emperor, leaving him alone with two attending priests.

Huayna lowered his weary head back down upon the royal pillow whispering to himself, "will the gods not wait for one more sacrifice? Will I be in the heavens with my father-god Viracocha, to receive my Nuesta Sarpay?"

The nobles slaughtered a llama, opened it up and removed its lungs. They looked carefully at the animals' veins for an omen. The pattern of the veins unfortunately appeared to foretell a bleak future for the Sapa Inca's two sons, Ninan Cuyochi and for Huascar.

When the nobles returned to the palace with the bad news, the Great Huayna Capac ninth ruler of the vast empire of the Inca, laid motionless on his great royal bed. Receiving word from Coya Mama Ocllo, that the gods had taken the great Inca, the nobles dutifully went in search of the new young emperor, Ninan Cuyochi.

After nearly three weeks following one of the great Inca highways, the small entourage of nobles arrived at the secondary northern capital Tumi-pampa only to find the local priests preparing the body of the young emperor Ninan Cuyochi who was already dead of the pestilence.

Huayna's priest told Sarpay of her father's death as she readied for the trek from the northern capital of Quito to the central capital in Cusco. Soon she would see her father. Would he be pleased that she fulfilled her royal duty, or disappointed she did not proceed more quickly? It did not matter. Tears flowed down her smooth bronze cheeks and disappeared into a rich royal cloak covering her shoulders, which shook as she wept.

It was time to begin her own pilgrimage to the Temple of the Sun. She climbed up onto the golden seat padded with alpaca fur pillows under a finely woven wool canopy dyed a royal red with golden fringe and tassels. Her own select porters raised the liter, and her procession left the palace. She pulled the silken curtains closed so the people could not see her collapse in grief.

Chapter Two

1528 - Trujillo Spain

The squeak echoed through the empty courtyard. Martín wondered if he would ever hear it again. In ten years, why had the gate never been greased? His six-month postulancy sharing the work of the novitiate was now over. At eighteen, he was eager to finally become a novice monk. Monastic life promised him fulfilment and purpose.

The few remnants of his solitary life lay still in the empty manor house. After his mother's murder, it felt as hollow as his heart. Life in the monastery serving Christ would fill that void. He pulled the gate closed and turned his back on the past.

The silence that seemed to haunt the abandoned cobblestone street shattered into panicked screams. He knew that scream. It was louder and more frantic. Martín quickened his pace. One more solitary day was all he wanted. Then he would be safe beyond their reach, inside the monastery.

He rounded the corner to find exactly what he feared. Two of Trujillo's worst, trying to subdue the one young girl they failed to conquer even after multiple attempts. Martín carried many a scar from his entanglements with these two. He couldn't permit this. He just could not. But how? And why now? Why today? He dropped the satchel containing his only earthly possessions worth keeping and readied to earn a few more scars.

Martín stood paralyzed, unable to will his feet to intervene as Juanita fought back, arms flailing as the brutes pushed her against a wall.

Señora Lopez and her two hundred pounds of fury rounded a corner at the sound of Jaunita's screaming. Before she could levy her first blow, the brothers backed off laughing, claiming only to be having a little fun. "No harm was done," they claimed. They both scowled as they passed the frozen Martín. Juan stepped over and slammed Martín against a wall. Martín said nothing.

Señora Lopez, with an arm around Juanita, accompanied her on her way past where Martín stood. Neither of them acknowledging him. Did they see him as the coward he felt he was?

Slowly, he worked his way through the labyrinth of squalid homes and headed toward the monastery. Inside the holy walls, everything would be better. After his mother's violent death when Martín had barely reached his ninth birthday, it was the new Friar Tomás, who became his guardian angel. He was the first and only friend in this inhospitable land.

These years later, once again, since Friar Tomás was given the new role in Toledo, Martín stood alone, without family or friend.

For the third time in three days, he crossed the portico and climbed the stone steps. He stepped into the chapel. It smelled of incense, the same that burned during the services held before each of his lessons. No candles burned. The only light was provided by tall windows cut high in the stone walls. The first image that met visitors to the chapel was that of the Savior Jesus Christ hanging lifeless on the large cross. Martín made a genuflect bow and continued across the empty room, each step echoing against the cold stones. He passed the altar and knocked on the recently-arrived friar's door. With no answer, he pushed it aside. Empty as well. His heart and stomach ached.

"He is not here. He is not coming back. It is time you grow up. The church is not here to care for lazy boys. Be gone!" Juan, the large caretaker, pulled the large wooden door closed so hard, its echo reverberated throughout the chapel, putting an end to Martín's hope of a blessing before entering the monastery.

"I am not lazy," he muttered, leaving the chapel.

As Martín entered the small market, he wondered if they all knew he shrunk when Juanita needed him. Would he shrink when Christ needed him? He felt the imagined disdain.

At the other end of the market, a commotion gathered a crowd. It was near where the only merchant Martín felt was a true Christian sold melons. Martín, just as curious as any young teenager would be, worked his way into the crowd to see the disturbance.

"Away from here, Gitano!" The bullies had just transferred their failed assault on Juanita to a young man Martín did not recognize. But when he heard the word Gitano, his skin bristled. His mother spoke kindly of the Romani groups that often passed through his own homeland up north. He remembered when his mother anxiously took him to one of their camps when he was very young. All he remembered was her disappointment when they did not know some friends of hers from before he was born.

Martín recognized that voice contending with the Gitano. It was like recognizing the squeal of a familiar swine. "Gonzalo," Martín whispered to himself in disgust. Gonzalo had his hands on the tuffs of the young man's shirt, pushing him away from the stand of melons. With a jerking push, the young man hit the dirt, puffs of dust accentuated the fall.

Who Martín only guessed was the young man's girlfriend or sister, struggled to free herself from the grasp of Gonzalo's brother Juan.

With fire in his eyes, the young man on the ground surprised Gonzalo, lurching at his legs bringing him down hard on his back. The young man was on Gonzalo so quickly, Martín caught his breath and found himself imitating the rapid blows the young man made pounding on Gonzalo's face and chest.

Juan released the struggling girl and dove onto the young man, freeing Gonzalo from the shock and surprise. Martín wondered if that may have been the first time anyone ever had the better of Gonzalo. Now two Pizarros against one boy, blow after blow, the young man received the worst of the battle.

Once again, within only minutes, Martín stood frozen as injustice took place before him.

Then, as if out of nowhere, a wild cat joined the fight. The young girl, not even dusting herself off, rose from the ground and ripped into Juan with a fury of claws and screams that shocked the crowd as much as it did the Pizarro brothers. With only Gonzalo on the young man, he reengaged and threw Gonzalo onto his back and leveled a powerful blow to the side of his head, stunning him. The young man pulled back before leveling a final blow to end the fight. As he did, the young woman came flying at him as Juan caught her by the face with his powerful fist. The young man caught her and knelt, holding the unconscious young woman.

Gonzalo struggled to his feet and readied to finish the fight when he found himself facing Señora Lopez again, who seemed to be the only person on earth with power to control these bullies.

"Bastante!" Señora Lopez gave no ground for Gonzalo to object. She also gave him the power to retreat. Now the crowd could perceive him as victor, though for the first time, he had been bested by another man, and worse, a Gitano.

Mustering the posture of a victor, the two men spit at the Gitanos and marched off triumphant.

As the Pizarro brothers walked away, Martín noticed Juanita was helping the young woman.

"Martín!" Juanita woke Martín from his frozen stupor. The quick motion of her hand commanded Martín's help. He quickly knelt and helped lift the young woman to her feet. Señora Lopez took Martín's place, and she and Juanita helped her into the shade of a large umbrella, protecting several carts of vegetables from the sun. Martín turned to the young man and helped him to his feet.

"Thank you," he said. Blood from the large cut on his forehead ran past his swollen eye. It met with a small stream of blood pouring from his nose, only to collect with the blood oozing from his lips. When he opened his mouth to utter the thank you, Martín saw more blood filling the cavity once held by a proud tooth now lying in the dirt.

Martín knew himself well enough to recognize the tensing of hate in his muscles was not aimed at the loathsome Pizarro's, but at his own failure to live up to the almost god-like image of his father carved by his mother as she told him stories how he gave his life to protect the rights of Muslims who rejected being forced to become Christians, and him being a devout follower of Christ. His mother told stories how her being named after the woman called Maria Magdalena who was cured by the Christ. She taught Martín there was a responsibility to live like she too had been cured by His grace.

Now, as a young man, all he became was a weak, frightened sheep. He hated himself for it.

"I am Foustino. Foustino Moreno," the young man said, looking into Martín's sad eyes.

"Martín de Bolibar," Martín repeated back.

"I thank you, my friend Martín," he said, working to form a smile between the blood running down his face.

How could he call me a friend? I stood afraid, like all the other sheep as a wolf tore into an innocent lamb, he thought to himself.

When they reached the spot where Juanita and Señora Lopez attended to the bruises, cuts and torn dress on the young woman, Foustino said as though triumphant, "Martín my friend, this, my valiant protector, is my baby sister Carmelita. As you may have noticed, it is not wise to cross her. Carmelita, this is my new friend Martín."

Señora Lopez stood and turned her attention to Foustino's face. He winced at her not-so-gentle grasp of his chin, turning it side to side to reveal the damage inflicted on both cheeks.

"Sit!" she demanded and pulled him down into the reach of her wet cloth, where she immediately revealed the true damage done to his smooth, sun-baked face.

"And to my liberator, who do I owe the honor?"

How could a man battered and beaten, bloody and bruised be so hearty? Martín never knew anyone like this. Was his father like this?

Señora Lopez took her attention away from the cut above his eye, which was supplying the bulk of the blood, and looked into his eyes, now mostly free of the red river. "You will not be so fortunate next time you tangle with those devils. I would advise you and young Carmelita here to scoot on. Those two will not settle until their hunger for blood is satisfied." She returned her attention to his forehead.

"Is that a welcome, Señora Protectora?" he asked.

"Lopez. Señora Lopez," Juanita said. "She may be the only person on earth who can keep those two from killing all who get in their way."

"We are glad to make your acquaintance," Carmelita said. Martín turned his head sharply toward her in disbelief. The sweet voice surprised all three of them. It was not at all what he expected coming from the jungle cat that sprung to her brother's aid.

"Are they always like that?" Carmelita asked. "We did and said nothing. They pounced on us like dogs after raw meat."

Señora Lopez did not look up. "You are different, thus inferior, thus deserving mistreatment. They pray upon the weak. You stood up to them. You defended yourself. Therefore, in their sick and twisted minds, you must pay. Here with me right now, you are safe. We will get you fed, get you what you came to the market for, and get you as far from here as possible." Señora Lopez could not be more firm or honest.

"We have faced worse than those two," Foustino said, wincing as Señora Lopez dug dirt from the now bleeding-again cut above his eye. She then wrapped a cloth around his brow and pulled his hat over it to hold it tight.

Señora Lopez led them through the cobblestone roads to a small hacienda. She sent Juanita back to gather the supplies they needed in the market.

"Are you traveling alone?" Martín asked, finally joining the conversation.

Foustino turned to Martín, peering at him as if he were reading something into the question. The pause was awkward for Martín, like he was opening himself up to be hurt.

"No, my friend, our people are working their way toward Toledo. We are enough. We do not fear bandits. My sister and I volunteered to stop here at your market for fresh produce and will catch up later."

"Toledo?" Señora Lopez asked, "Why Toledo? They will not welcome your kind."

Foustino's grin wiped away any offense, if any were intended. "Señora, you are a rare exception in the world. Nobody welcomes our kind."

She shrugged off the comment and placed large plates of corn wrapped in their husks, large chunks of bread and cheese blended with peppers in front of the two visitors. She filled stone cups with wine. Then she went back to the kitchen and returned with another plate for Martín. More than once had she saved Martín from starvation, yet Martín's pride kept him from becoming a beggar. He mouthed a silent gracias to her.

"Martín, you will do me a great favor if you accompany these two as far as Madronera by way of Don Diego's Colonia."

"Through the mountains?" Martín asked.

"If they travel past the vineyards, they will never meet their friends. The Pizarro's will be waiting."

Martín knew that was true. He looked from Foustino to Carmelita. Both sets of eyes welcomed Martín's company.

He knew Señora Lopez was aware the abbot expected Martín at the monastery. He stared at her suggestion. How long he had waited and prepared for this very day. Today he would make his sacred vows and escape the world and dedicate his life to God. How could Señora Lopez ask this of him? Now?

"I will tell the abbot you are serving Christ in another way for a few days. He and God can wait," Señora Lopez said.

Is she reading my mind? Does God wait? He looked back at the two Gitanos. Bandages and bruises softened Martín's resistance. The slight tip of his head accepted the request.

Juanita returned from the market, and Señora Lopez busied herself packing bundles. She put Juanita and Martin to work gathering not only the produce Juanita brought from the market, but added from her treasure of baked breads. As the food stuffs grew, Martín wondered if Señora Lopez was sending him not for safety but as a pack mule. She disappeared with Juanita and Carmelita for what seemed like an hour, though it was only minutes.

"You are kind, my new friend, to leave home and escort two strangers into the wilderness," Foustino said.

Kindness? Martín thought. No, it's hate for the Pizarro's. A strange feeling of delight trickled through him as he thought of the brothers' disappointment when they realized the Gitanos got away. A tiny grin pulled at the edge of his mouth. He said nothing. He did not know what to say. He was just called a friend. Martín did not have friends. He did not know how to have friends. Could he be a friend?

The three women returned, and Señora Lopez gave Martín an additional bundle she claimed would sustain him on his return voyage. He wanted to look inside. It was heavy. She shooed them on their way.

The three said their goodbyes and, with Martín leading the way, slipped through the cobblestone streets and empty alleys, and headed toward the hills, leaving Trujillo behind.